G000140007

THE MAN BEHIND THE WHEEL

Also by the author:

Non-Fiction

Cold Steel (Lakshmi Mittal and the Multi-Billion-Dollar
Battle for a Global Empire)
617: Going to War with Today's Dambusters

Fiction

Cut and Run

THE MAN BEHIND THE WHEEL

HOW ONKAR S. KANWAR CREATED
A GLOBAL GIANT

TIM BOUQUET

MAVEN
RUPA

Published in Maven by
Rupa Publications India Pvt. Ltd 2016
7/16, Ansari Road, Daryaganj
New Delhi 110002

Sales centres:
Allahabad Bengaluru Chennai
Hyderabad Jaipur Kathmandu
Kolkata Mumbai

ISBN: 978-81-291-4500-0

10 9 8 7 6 5 4 3 2 1

Printed and bound in India by Replika Press Pvt. Ltd.

Contents

Foreword

When most people near their seventy-fifth birthday they tend to look back on their lives and their achievements and take a well-deserved rest. My father, as you will discover in this book, is not like most people. In the pages that follow, you will read of a life that has been lived to the full. It has had great triumphs, numerous disappointments and a great many challenges, all against the backdrop of an India that emerged out of an empire during my father's lifetime. It is the story of a family, a company and a country.

In spite of all that, Onkar Singh Kanwar only knows one direction and that is forward. Whatever life throws in your path, you carry on, you stand on your own two feet and you follow your dream. It is a trait and a value that he and my mother have instilled in their children and grandchildren. These have guided me every day as we have worked together to create a global company.

My father has a number of favourite phrases, including 'listening is learning' and 'analysis leads to paralysis.' Both of them are intrinsically linked. My father is a great listener. This is something I am still learning. He takes things in; he instinctively knows whom he can trust and then he cuts to the chase and lets them get on with things. He is not a fan of focus group analysis and meetings for the sake of meetings, which he feels is the route to stagnation and a lack of adventure. Apollo has been described by some as audacious and unorthodox. That it does not behave like other companies in our industry. That sense of adventure and a core belief that anything is possible, which stems directly from my father, is what has driven this company to where it is today. My father is and will always remain my guru, my mentor and the true inspiration of my life. You mean the world to me, Dad!

Neeraj Kanwar,
Vice Chairman and Managing Director, Apollo Tyres
London, September 2016

◆

My grandfather has always been there for me. When I was little if I did anything naughty, everybody would be angry with me except him! He loves me the most. He encourages me and would do anything for me. Whenever he is in London, I see a lot of him. I think he comes mostly because he misses me! He takes me shopping and out to dinner and tells me stories about his past. He tells all his grandchildren where the family came from… He says it is important to remember. He is the kindest, nicest and most loving person and he makes me laugh. He is the best grandfather one could have! I love him the most in the whole world.

Syra Taru Kanwar, aged ten
London, September 2016

◆

The word journey is much overused, but in nearly fifty years of being married to Onkar, I can say that the life we have shared has been an epic and eventful journey in every sense, as you will see in these pages. We stood together in the face of many challenges and shared our successes with family and friends. Through everything, Onkar, as a man, a husband, a father, a colleague and an employer has remained constant to his beliefs and values. Never once have I seen him waver in his love, his loyalty or his sense of duty. He knows how important it is for our children and grandchildren to never forget our humble roots and to keep any successes we have had in perspective. Both of us believe that giving back is the most important thing of all. Onkar is serious when necessary, but he can still make me laugh. He has great fondness for fun and adventure and a deep dislike of pessimism and negativity. In a cynical world, Onkar is driven by hope and the art of the possible. Beyond anything I can say about Onkar, I thank him for asking me to be his life's companion and for this wonderful and precious journey, where each day is an adventure in itself.

Taru Kanwar
New Delhi, September 2016

'You work, you put in your best efforts and you believe in God.
Without that faith I do not believe you can achieve anything.'
Onkar S. Kanwar

one

Crossing borders

Karachi, 25 May 2005

As soon as he emerged into the international arrivals hall at Jinnah International Airport, Onkar Singh Kanwar was showered with flowers and petals and greeted by a phalanx of photographers and their cameras. He felt like a cross between a bridegroom and a movie star. Most of the welcoming crowds were like him—Punjabis—and some of those casting flowers were women, highly unusual in a strictly Muslim country. But Kanwar's arrival in Pakistan had become a big box-office event. As the President of the Federation of Indian Chambers of Commerce and Industry (FICCI), Kanwar was leading India's largest trade delegation comprising 105 leading businessmen and industrialists on FICCI's first-ever visit to Pakistan to improve trade links between the two most populous and largest economies of the South Asian region.

Known to friends and colleagues as OSK, Kanwar was a good choice to lead. As Chairman of Apollo Tyres he had transformed his company from virtual bankruptcy and a single plant in Kerala, which was hobbled by strikes and lockouts, to being a premier producer in India with 6,500 employees and an annual turnover of $600 million in 2005. With ambitions to take Apollo global, Kanwar is like his equally entrepreneurial and irrepressible father Raunaq Singh, a champion of the free market and unfettered trade. By 2011, he would transform Apollo into a company with an annual turnover of $2 billion.

India had liberalized its centrally controlled and restrictive red-tape economy from 1991 under the New Economic Policy of former Prime Minister P.V. Narasimha Rao, perhaps one of the country's most underrated prime ministers and the architect of modern India's economic success. In 1996, India had granted Pakistan 'Most Favoured Nation' trading status to increase bilateral trade but Pakistan, forever suspicious of its larger neighbour, was yet to reciprocate. Ever since Independence, the relationship between the two countries had been one of ups and downs, steps forward and steps backwards—a relationship described with precision by former Indian Prime Minister Inder Kumar Gujral as 'tormented'. With a history of three wars between the countries, plus one undeclared war in 1999, then being on the verge of nuclear conflict in 2001, and simmering enmity over Kashmir—were things beginning to change with the FICCI visit?

'Now, we all felt that things were opening up,' says fellow industrialist Dr A.C. Muthiah, Chairman Emeritus of Southern Petrochemical Industries Corporation Limited (SPIC). 'Onkar is a very positive and dynamic person and as somebody who has taken a small Indian company to multinational status, he knows how to make positive things happen.' Dr Muthiah is an old and close friend of Kanwar's and preceded him as President of FICCI in 2003—the organization's platinum jubilee year. Dr Muthiah was also President of the Board of Control for Cricket in India in 1999, when Atal Bihari Vajpayee asked him to set up a landmark tour of India by the Pakistani cricket team. 'Onkar played a very important role in business relationships and policy,' says Muthiah.

This thaw between the two countries had begun in September 2004 at the United Nations in New York when the then Indian Prime Minister Manmohan Singh and Pakistan President General Pervez Musharraf had held their 'historic' first face-to-face talks to try and diffuse tensions and restore normalcy and cooperation and also to propose a gas pipeline between the two countries. In April 2005, the two leaders met again, for the first time on Indian soil at a summit in New Delhi. Again, Kashmir and the Line of Control (LoC) ceasefire were high on the agenda but Musharraf was equally desperate to encourage foreign investment into his country's stuttering economy. After a 40-minute summit side-meeting Commerce and Industry Minister Kamal Nath and his Pakistani counterpart Humayun Akhtar Khan agreed to create a Joint Economic Commission and revive the Joint Business Council to, as Nath put it, 'facilitate interaction amongst business and to strengthen economic ties and promote trade'.

Just a few weeks later, Onkar Singh Kanwar had now come to Pakistan armed with a seven-point FICCI agenda to increase bilateral trade from its then $400 million to $5 billion. He would call for dismantling of trade and tariff barriers, enhancing road and rail links, liberalizing visa regulations and de-freezing the restrictive list of items that could be imported into Pakistan from India.

His delegation included representatives across the spectrum of Indian industry including pharmaceuticals, chemicals and paints, hospitality, tourism, processed food products, paper and textiles, electrical equipment and steel and even amusement park equipment.

'Augmenting business-to-business cooperation between the two countries is uppermost…a priority that we feel will pave the way for the policymakers in India and Pakistan to remove infrastructural bottlenecks and improve the business and economic environment,' Kanwar told journalists.

In response Abdul Waheed Jan, chief of the Islamabad Stock Exchange, told the Pakistan News Service, 'The visit will open new avenues for promotion of bilateral trade and accelerate the process of building economic relations between the two countries.'

During the six-day visit organized by the chambers of commerce and industry in Karachi, Lahore and Islamabad, Kanwar's delegation would meet the prime minister, the foreign minister, the commerce minister and the governors and chief ministers of Sindh and Punjab. There was no doubt that this was a high-profile, high-visibility visit, but as he boarded a motorcade Kanwar wondered how much could be achieved. Sweeping policy gestures were for politicians. He was more concerned that he and his fellow industrialists would have the chance to get into the nitty-gritty of forging lasting and practical business links that would bring two countries with a shared and intimate history of antagonism and misunderstanding closer together.

After two days of meetings and official dinners in Lahore—one of which catered for a thousand guests on the manicured lawns of a wealthy auto parts manufacturer—Kanwar was due to fly on to Islamabad with a smaller FICCI group for a meeting with President Musharraf. The presidential bureaucracy began to kick in. How small was smaller?

'We were told that no more than eight could go to meet Musharraf,' says Dr Amit Mitra, who is now the Minister for Finance and Excise, Commerce and Industries of West Bengal and was for many years the Secretary General of FICCI. He was a key member of Kanwar's core team. 'We argued that all facets of the delegation should be represented. Eventually they relented and twenty-five of us were allowed to go.'

Kanwar's party flew on to Islamabad. Checking into his hotel he noticed three suited men close by, watching him carefully.

'Can I help you?' he asked them.

'No, no...' they replied. 'We are your personal security.'

Later that day, refreshed and prepared, Kanwar and his new-found protection detail were driven up the wide vista of Constitution Avenue in the city's high-security Red Zone to Aiwan-e-Sadr, the vast and imposing modern step-pyramid structure which is the official residence of the President and stands between Parliament House and the Prime Minister's Secretariat.

The FICCI motorcade was halted at the outer gates. 'We were told to get out of our cars and we were transferred to other vehicles for the final yards inside,' Dr Mitra recalls. It was no wonder security was so tight. In a country where governments are often changed at gunpoint, Musharraf had already survived four assassination attempts in five years.

Immaculately dressed as always, sporting a grey pinstripe suit, crisp white shirt, silk tie and his maroon turban, Kanwar was ushered into the opulent interior of the presidential palace to be greeted under twinkling chandeliers in a huge room big enough for a hundred people by the similarly besuited President Musharraf. Like Kanwar, Musharraf was also a visitor to the palace. Even though Musharraf was the President as well as Army Chief, he preferred living within the safer confines of the Army House in Rawalpindi.

'We had been told that the visit would last no more than fifteen minutes,' Kanwar recalls. In addition only official government photographers would be allowed to record the occasion. It looked like those from the Press Trust of India had made a wasted trip, until Musharraf's security weakened.

'They were allowed to take pictures and then they were immediately ushered out,' Amit Mitra says.

The allotted fifteen minutes with the President came and went. 'In the end we talked for nearly two hours,' Kanwar says. 'He seemed in the mood to listen. We tried to convince him that more trade barriers should come down to benefit both countries. For example, removing the ban on importing cheap, freely available medicines from India into Pakistan where people, especially children, were dying of preventable diseases.'

'In Pakistan you see so many poor people,' Musharraf said.

'In India too,' Kanwar replied, 'but unlike Pakistan we have had a middle class come up. Things are improving.'

While Musharraf's tone was warm Dr Mitra sensed that the General 'was also extremely strategic. Whenever we raised issues to do with trade, power supply or water purification, he would respond, "Your Minister will have to discuss with our relevant Minister." He was happy to talk but would not shift an inch when we came within a mile of issues of policy.'

Kanwar thought that if Pakistan spent less on the military it might have more to spend on alleviating poverty; but diplomatic politeness and good manners ensured that he kept his opinions to himself.

Indian businessmen, including Kanwar, had seen a few encouraging signs in the past. In the 1970s, when Kanwar visited Pakistan, he had invited staff from a Pakistani tyre company to Apollo's inaugural plant in Perambra, Kerala, to receive skills training.

5

As the President seemed in no hurry to end the conversation, Kanwar ventured, 'Sir, I can tell you that when I studied and worked in the United States as a young man, I knew many Pakistanis and I have never felt that we were two different nations. We eat the same food and share much of the same culture and yet we are not together. The Berlin Wall has fallen; what can we do to tear down the barriers between our countries?'

Musharraf's tone changed. 'Mr Kanwar, economic ties depend on political will and sincerity. First, we have to sort out the problem of Kashmir. Economic development can only happen if there is peace.'

'Sir, I am a businessman, I cannot comment.' FICCI is resolutely non-political with a guiding philosophy that trade benefits all.

Suddenly Kanwar realized that the President was no longer looking at him and his colleagues but instead talking over their shoulders, addressing his remarks firmly to the TV cameras that had assembled to record the farewell handshakes. The General's earlier visit to Delhi had also been marred by his fondness for the camera.

'I knew that he was getting Kashmir on the record for his own people,' Kanwar says. Only a few weeks ago, at a banquet in Delhi, Musharraf had said, 'I think the [peace] process is irreversible.' His home constituency was harder to please and was increasingly critical of his leadership.

By the end of the meeting, FICCI had won agreement on setting up an Indo-Pakistan Chamber of Commerce and Industry, which Kanwar would head.

As he headed home to the capital and to the more achievable challenges of running India's leading tyre company, even the ever-optimistic Kanwar reflected that in spite of the open-arms reception and respect that he and his delegation had received during their six-day visit, smoothing the economic roadmap between India and Pakistan remained a long-term project.

Even so, perhaps the most poignant and symbolic achievement in that climate of guarded optimism and reconciliation with Pakistan was the landmark Kashmir bus service that had opened on 7 April 2005 to allow travel across the LoC between India and Pakistan. Twenty-four

Indian passengers had been waved off in Srinagar in Jammu and Kashmir by the then Prime Minister Manmohan Singh while thirty headed out from Muzaffarabad in Pakistan Occupied Kashmir for Srinagar. For the first time since the creation of the two countries, following Britain's exit from the subcontinent fifty-eight years ago, Kashmiris stepped off the buses and walked across the 'Peace Bridge' on the LoC to be reunited with their families.

◆

Lahore Junction Railway Station, 1947

With its twin towers, bastions and turrets, Lahore Railway Station looked more like a fort than a major railhead. Fort was exactly the intention of its British architects, who built it in the aftermath of the First War of Indian Independence; it was a defiant Imperial architecture built to last forever. However, Imperial British India was then in its final throes.

By 1947, no single word had greater significance or greater fear in 'British India' than 'Partition'. Nearly two hundred years after it took power, Britain's newest and last Viceroy Lord Louis Mountbatten swept into India in March 1947. A cousin of George VI, a former Supreme Allied Commander of Southeast Asia and a man of high self-regard, Mountbatten was on a rapid-exit mission. A Britain bankrupted by World War II could no longer afford to maintain its empire and an army of occupation. Having moved his family into the Viceroy's House in Delhi with its 5,000 staff, Mountbatten shocked the Indian National Congress and the Muslim League leaders in June by announcing that the transfer of power would happen on 15 August 1947, ten months ahead of schedule.

With the leaders of the Indian independence movement unable or unwilling to agree on the future of the subcontinent, British barrister Cyril Radcliffe, who had never been east of Paris, was summoned by the Viceroy and given just five weeks to divide one of the most ethnically and

7

religiously diverse nations on earth, where Hindus, Sikhs and Muslims had lived in harmony, into two new states of India and Pakistan. They were to be divided on religious grounds. When asked why Britain would not adhere to its original 1948 exit date, Mountbatten said: 'Why should we wait? Waiting would mean that I should be responsible ultimately for law and order.'

A largely peaceful country, albeit with ancient prejudices and customs between castes and religions—for example, in Lahore's old city Muslims were forbidden from drinking from the same taps as Hindus—imploded into communal violence and religious cleansing. Towns and villages burned. People were uprooted from communities where their families had lived for generations and joined a desperate migration to be on the right side of the border.

One of Radcliffe's borderlines on the new map of South Asia slashed the Punjab, one of India's wealthiest states and home to six million Sikhs, into two. West Punjab went to Pakistan including the cosmopolitan 2,000-year-old city of Lahore—once the capital of the Sikh Empire forged by Ranjit Singh, the Maharaja of Punjab. The sites of some of the most holy places in Sikhism, including Gurudwara Panja Sahib, were now stranded in an Islamic state.

There were huge migrations of Muslims from India to Pakistan, and Sikhs and Hindus to secular India. Born in Lahore, the six-year-old Onkar Singh Kanwar was one of them.

There is a saying in Punjabi *'Jis Lahore nai dekhya, o janmeya nai'*, meaning, 'He who has not seen or visited Lahore is not born yet.' In August 1947, people were more worried about dying in Lahore. Parts of the city were on fire. Most British troops had gone home and local military and police could not keep order. The liberal, tolerant, cosmopolitan Lahore was gone.

Communal disturbances had broken out in Punjab in March 1947 whipped up by local politicians, religious extremists and hoodlums. Official figures showed that about 150,000 people had died in West Punjab and East Punjab alone by September. Muslims blamed Sikh and Hindu gangs for starting the violence. Sikhs and Hindus accused Muslim fanatics as terrifying sectarian attacks spiralled out of control.

The Military Evacuation Organisation, India's advanced headquarters in Lahore, was wilting under the pressure of those desperate to leave. The city's old railway station was bursting at its seams as Onkar and his family pushed their way through the crowds. Cast into the abyss as refugees, most people looked agitated, bewildered or just plain scared. Every time a train came in, waves of them clambered on to the roofs of the carriages or struggled for pitches on the coal wagons of the steam engines.

'We had been at a wedding in Kasur town when we were told suddenly that we could catch a train to Delhi,' Kanwar remembers. His mother Satwant Kaur and his uncle, Swaran Singh Kanwar (S.S.), guided Onkar and his younger siblings—sister Rani and brother Aravinder Pal (A.P.) who was just two years old—through the rush. 'It was chaotic at the station. We finally managed to struggle aboard a goods train. There were no carriages. We were crammed into wagons open to the elements. For part of the journey it rained. There were hundreds probably thousands of Sikhs and Hindus on board. I don't think we expected anything beyond just getting out. I do remember they gave us free food—vegetable, dal and roti. People talked about all the fighting that was going on, of trains being attacked and passengers being killed and our train kept stopping. There was the sound of gunfire. But I don't remember being frightened. When you are six, you are not fully aware of what is going on and my mother and my uncle gave us great confidence that we would be okay.'

It was the greatest mass migration the world had ever known and it took the authorities by surprise. Between 17 August and 7 September 1947 alone about 838,000 non-Muslims had crossed over principal frontier posts between Pakistan and India. Some 325,000 Muslims had passed the other way on special refugee trains, trucks and in barefoot convoys more than 50 miles long, that were sustained by intermittent airdrops of food. These were the easiest targets for armed bands. Four-hour train journeys took four days. Some trains pulled into New Delhi carrying nothing but dead bodies. Equally gruesome cargoes arrived in Lahore.

By the end of November, millions of non-Muslims and Muslims had been evacuated. They carried what they could.

One of the Muslims heading for Pakistan—as he was to tell Onkar Singh Kanwar fifty-eight years later when they met in Islamabad—was a four-year-old Pervez Musharraf. His family had left their large home, 'Neharwali Haveli', in Delhi's Chandni Chowk in August 1947 and caught one of the last trains to the new nation he would one day rule as a four-star army general.

The United Nations High Commissioner for Refugees (UNHCR) estimates that about fourteen million Hindus, Sikhs and Muslims were displaced during the Partition. By the time Pakistan and India declared independence on 14 and 15 August, respectively, more than a million had died in communal riots, revenge attacks and unbelievable atrocities. Some put the figure at double. To this day nobody knows for sure. Nearly seventy years later, some families are still trying to find out what became of their lost relatives.

Independent India's first Prime Minister Jawaharlal Nehru, who had argued for a united secular India, announced that nearly a quarter of Delhi's population now consisted of refugees. About 75 per cent of Lahore's wealth and business was owned by Sikhs and Hindus, which over subsequent decades proved to be a major economic gain to India and a significant entrepreneurial loss to Pakistan.

After a train ride punctuated by frequent unexpected stops that spooked the passengers, the Kanwar family arrived in the capital. The Government of India provided temporary accommodation for as many refugees as it could. Those who had documents to prove the worth of their properties abandoned in Pakistan were eligible for compensation but the vast majority had left with little more than the clothes they were wearing.

Many were housed in the Gole Market neighbourhood, less than a kilometre from Connaught Place in the heart of New Delhi. The white octagonal market building was designed by New Delhi's imperial architect Edwin Lutyens in 1921 and stands on a roundabout which is the hub of four radial roads—Ramakrishna Ashram Road, Shaheed Bhagat Singh

Road, Bhai Veer Singh Road and Peshwa Road.

Today, it stands boarded up, neglected and declared unsafe; its shops, restaurants and confectioners consigned to history. Back then it was buzzing with refugee families, just thankful to be alive. The chatter on the neighbouring streets of two-storey apartment houses was in Punjabi and Bengali rather than Hindi, for there were also refugees from the eastern state of Bengal, which too had been split between India and the then East Pakistan.

The Kanwars were among those whose first footfall in India was Gole Market. 'There were thirteen of us in this one small room, including my father and his two brothers, my mother and us children,' says Onkar Kanwar. 'I do not remember the living conditions. To be safe was what counted the most.'

Onkar's father Raunaq Singh had joined the family after they had arrived. He had stayed behind in Lahore trying to salvage what he could. 'The fighting in the city was getting worse. Mobs were burning houses. My father was taking a shower when soldiers came and told him he had to get out. They brought him by an army truck to India.'

◆

Raunaq Singh was born in 1922 in Daska, an industrial town in Sialkot District, Punjab, now part of Pakistan but within touching distance of the Indian border. Raunaq's father, S. Nihal Singh, had died when Raunaq was just ten years old. Educated at a village high school, at sixteen he and his friends were busy selling second-hand steel water pipes, visiting their clients on their bicycles. Later, he worked as a salesman for a steel pipe merchant in Lahore at just ₹8 per month. This was where his entrepreneurial skills were refined and his appetite for business grew further. And even more when his boss asked Raunaq to dispose of his pipes. As Subhrangshu Roy of *The Economic Times* puts it: 'That was when the villages around Lahore were faced with an acute shortage of water pipes. Singh found a customer, sought ₹1,000 from him as an advance, bought out the old man's stocks, before [selling them on] at twice the price his employer had demanded.' Now, aged twenty-five, he would use the profit to start his own steel pipe business.

As a result of Partition, Raunaq Singh like a lot of other budding entrepreneurs lost it all. When he joined his family crammed into that small room in New Delhi's Gole Market, he had no money, no contacts, no higher education and nothing to fall back on but his energy and ingenuity. He was also blessed with a larger-than-life charisma, which was to prove a launch pad to success.

He started working in a small local spice shop called Munilal Bajaj & Co., earning just 1 paisa a day. It just about kept the family fed but it did nothing to satisfy his entrepreneurial appetite. In November 1947, he went to the bustling old market in Chandni Chowk, close to Old Delhi Railway Station and Red Fort, where he sold his wife's jewellery for ₹8,000. He decided to try his luck in Calcutta (now Kolkata), where he opened his own spice trade shop at 85 Netaji Subhash Road. N.S. Road, as it is best known, was also the city's main market for agricultural machinery, pumps, diesel engines, hardware and paints. Raunaq Singh's spice shop was soon trading successfully, but it was not in spices that his future lay. It lay in a chance encounter on a train from Delhi to Kolkata where he was headed to close a major spice deal.

Unable to buy a sleeper class ticket, he had to go first class, where, as luck would have it, he found himself sitting next to a German. They fell into conversation. The German, who was also on his way to Kolkata on business, was the CEO of a steel tube manufacturing company. As the journey progressed, he asked Raunaq if he would be interested in starting a pipe-making plant in Kolkata. The German would invest the money; Raunaq could invest his expertise and knowledge of local markets. In those days it was impossible for a foreigner to set up a company in India without a local partner. Raunaq Singh jumped at the chance and Bharat Steel Pipes was born in Kolkata.

Back in Delhi, Onkar had started lower elementary school and Raunaq Singh opened up a store on Garstin Bastion Road selling pipes and hardware. Better known as G.B. Road and running from Ajmeri Gate to Lahore Gate parallel to the railway lines, it is famous for two reasons. By day, at ground level, it is the largest market for machinery, automobile parts, hardware and tools, pumps and pipes. If it was shopkeepers by day, it was prostitutes by night. When the shops closed, hundreds of multi-storey brothels or kothas on the floors above opened for business, making G.B. Road Delhi's largest red light district.

'My father did well from day one because there was a shortage of everything in those days,' Onkar recalls. 'To start with, he imported pipes but there were also a few local producers like the Tatas and Kalinga Tubes. Kalinga was founded by Biju Patnaik, who was a few years older than my father and a prominent leader of the independence struggle. Post-Independence, Patnaik was building an industrial empire that included textile mills, mining, steel mills and factories making domestic appliances.'

It dawned quickly on Raunaq Singh that he wanted to follow the path of Patnaik and other entrepreneurs rather than be at their beck and call, but for now 'they were dictating trading terms to him', Onkar continues. 'He established himself quickly as a good name in his business and he had a lot of repeat customers.'

So much so that the shop on G.B. Road was no longer big enough. His next showroom was as far removed from G.B. Road as it is possible to be. 'In the late Fifties, he found an empty church in Hauz Qazi. The priest liked him and let him run his business from there.' Deep in the heart of Old Delhi close by the Jama Masjid mosque, Hauz Qazi was, as it remains today, a teeming bazaar area of congested lanes and shoulder-width alleys, its tenements strewn with spaghetti-like power cables and rattling air-conditioning units. It is home to dealers in stainless steel, pipes, fasteners, taps, machine parts, cables and pumps and even artificial limbs. A natural salesman, Raunaq Singh stayed there till 1964 earning a good living.

As the rupees rolled in, Raunaq Singh moved the extended family to a rented house in Dev Nagar in New Delhi. Then he built a bungalow on Pusa Road near Ganga Ram Hospital. 'I did not see much of my father because he was always working,' Onkar recalls. 'We led a simple life. There was no concept of leisure time back then and my father was not fond of going to movies and all those things but on Sundays the family would always have lunch together.'

Onkar spent his teens as a pupil at West Delhi Public School and then college at Delhi University. At that time he did not have any ambitions to go into business like his father. 'My ambition was to go abroad. Very few Indians went overseas in those days but I wanted to see what was outside India and my big dream was to get to the US. I must have talked about it so much that one day my father said, "I have a friend whose son went to California State University. Why don't you study in America?" I applied for college and I got admission. I had never been so excited.' Today, at least 130,000 Indian students enrol in American universities but back then the US seemed a very long way away.

In September 1960, Raunaq Singh gave his nineteen-year-old son $1,000 and Onkar boarded a plane for California to study for a BSc in business administration and industrial engineering. His father, siblings, cousins, uncles and aunts were all at Delhi airport to wish him well and place garlands around his neck. Onkar now had two more brothers, twins Narinder Jeet Singh and Surinder P. Kanwar.

'I was the first member of my family to have ever taken a plane and left India. I had no real idea of where I was heading.'

After several refuelling stops, Onkar's flight put down in Hawaii. 'This pretty girl came up to me, she put a garland around my neck and a photograph was taken. I thought this must be the way they greeted you in every country, just like in India. Then she asked me for $10. I asked why. She said it was for the photograph.' Onkar retorted that he had not asked for the photograph to be taken. The warm Hawaiian welcome then turned a little frosty and he paid $10. 'That's how I spent the first of my father's money.'

America was as alien as it was exciting and youth was on the march. John F. Kennedy was on the cusp of becoming America's 35th and youngest President. The month Onkar arrived Chubby Checker's 'The

Twist' topped the Billboard charts kicking off a whole new teen dance craze. Jack Nicholson had opened his third film, *The Wild Ride*, playing a rebellious punk, and Onkar Singh Kanwar found himself in a hall of residence dwarfed by college football players. 'The guys were all so big, the diet was bland and strange, and living in a hostel was so different from living with the extended family at home. When I arrived I looked around and thought, "Where am I?"'

Most Americans he met had never seen a Sikh before. 'They were fascinated by my turban and asked why it was worn and how it was tied, but there was never any hostility.' Unlike his brother A.P., who was to cut his hair when he studied in the US subsequently, 'Onkar never minded being the odd one out,' says his sister Rani. 'He was always very religious and believed that as a Sikh he should wear the turban. It was part of his identity.'

To boost his funds, Onkar took a job in the college kitchen preparing vegetables. 'Then, I got a better-paid job in the administration office. I had a traditional Sikh upbringing that meant that while family would always support each other, you were expected to make your own way and learn to stand on your own feet.'

Communication with home was limited and Onkar soon got used to the American lifestyle. As his course drew to a close, he began to think of his next steps. Until now he had little desire to go into business but things were beginning to change. 'I knew that I wanted to return to India but first I wanted to establish myself, do something in my own right. Punjabis are very positive and enterprising people. It's our exclusive trait that we want to do everything in a different way.'

Instead of returning to family life in Delhi and being in the shadow of a father who was quickly making a name for himself as a formidable salesman, Onkar got himself a job in Riverside, California, working as an estimator for a company that laid concrete pipes underground for the local municipalities, where he spent six months drawing up the tenders for government contracts.

'It was a good learning experience but now I was keen to get out of California.' He applied and won a junior job with a company called Abbey Etna Machine Company and boarded a Greyhound bus for the two-day trip to Toledo, Ohio. As he headed to the Midwest, Onkar did not realize that Ohio was famous for something other than machine manufacturing and engineering: tyres. Goodyear, Firestone, the Goodrich Corporation and General Tire—which would play a role in the early days of Apollo—were all headquartered in Akron, Ohio, popularly known as 'Rubber City'. Findlay, Ohio, was the base of Cooper Tire, which would feature prominently in Apollo's recent history.

Kanwar's destination was Perrysburg, Ohio, 12 miles south of Toledo on the Maumee River and home to the Abbey Etna Machine Company. Edward F. Abbey had founded the Etna Machine Company in Toledo in 1901, which quickly won a reputation for its pipe-making machinery. His thirty-six-year-old grandson Nelson D. 'Dan' Abbey, Jr. was now the President of the company where he had started driving a truck hauling castings when he was just fourteen years old. He also attended the Culver Military Academy in Indiana where he was captain of the polo team. 'When I met him he still had twelve polo ponies,' Kanwar remembers. 'He was larger than life, drove a Cadillac and a Lincoln Continental and he showed a lot of warmth to me.'

Kanwar started work on the shop floor and lodged with the factory supervisor. He then migrated to the sales shop, picking up a good grounding in every aspect of the business.

Dan Abbey took an interest in this young Sikh because he had a taste for travel and culture. His father, Nelson, Sr., had given him the responsibility for expanding Abbey's international sales of tube and pipe mills. He had visited Japan, but his overriding interest was India.

Onkar told him about how well his father was doing trading in pipes and tubes, building a business from nothing. 'Dan Abbey's view was typically American: if you have a home market you should manufacture there and not be reliant on the vagaries of imports. It was the right philosophy, of course, but setting up manufacturing businesses in India in those days was incredibly difficult.' Since the country was only a decade and a-half into independence, it was a shortage economy, and cash investment was a principal shortage unless you were of those established industrial houses headed by business maharajas like the Birlas or the Tatas that had grown gigantically during the British Raj.

Conversations like this obviously got Dan Abbey thinking. 'One day he told me that he and his wife wanted to go to India and asked, "Can I meet your father?"

'"You must go. My father will look after you," I told him.'

In those days long-distance calls from America to India were very difficult to make and expensive. 'You would barely say hello and the line would go dead. To keep in touch with family, I would record messages on a reel-to-reel tape recorder and send them back home. They would take weeks to reach. This time I wrote to my father and told him that Mr Abbey was coming.'

Nelson D. Abbey was sociable, gregarious and loved to tell stories. He had worked his way up through the engineering side of the business and was a natural salesman. He also had a good nose for sniffing out a project. He and Raunaq Singh were cut from exactly the same cloth.

'He was totally charmed by my father. He understood my father's frustration as a salesman having to rely on inconsistent monopolistic pipe suppliers.' Abbey said to Raunaq, 'Why don't you set up your own factory?' He had also seen with his own eyes how the Government of India was heavily reliant on imports of basic products and hardware when these were exactly the sorts of products Indian companies should have been producing.

'When he got home Mr Abbey told me, "I am ready to give your father the money to build a factory."' He agreed to invest $2 million via a 'turnkey' arrangement—his investment would build the factory and equip it to the point of operation. 'Bringing money into India in those days was very difficult, there were so many restrictions and restraints, but because we were in a partnership where we had over 60 per cent [of the stake] the government gave permission.' It was also the first time that the government came into contact with Raunaq Singh's persuasive powers. He was not a man to take 'No' for an answer.

Next Onkar's father went in search of a site. He found it at Ganaur, a bustling town in the Sonepat District of Haryana, 62 kilometres north of Delhi, just three kilometres off National Highway No. 1. Traditionally, Ganaur was a grain market and warehousing centre. 'Somebody else had acquired a government paper licence, which you had to have in those days, to build a factory there, but they had no resources so he sold that to my father.'

It was now that Raunaq Singh contacted his son. Onkar recalls, 'He said, "It's time for you to come home and build the factory."'

two

Tubes, frog legs and gears

Onkar Kanwar Singh was just twenty-three years old when he returned to India in 1964. His extended family of at least twenty people greeted him at Delhi airport and placed garlands around his neck. His sister Rani, four years younger, was especially thrilled to see her elder brother. 'I had special clothes made to wear when we picked him up from the airport—black salwar kameez with pink embroidery, I'll never forget. It was such an exciting time. As the only sister all my brothers are very fond of me but especially Onkar who has always protected me and almost treated me like a daughter. For him when he came back I was the most important person around. I don't think it is possible for anybody to have a better brother.'

Rani had noticed a change in Onkar. 'He had absorbed the American attitude that if you worked hard you would succeed and if you were knocked back you picked yourself up and pressed on.'

If Onkar was daunted by the task that now lay ahead he tried not to show it. 'I knew nothing about civil engineering. I had no experience of building anything, let alone a factory.'

By now Raunaq Singh had bought a large house in New Delhi. Grey in colour, it was in Friends Colony West secluded by mature trees, a high perimeter fence and a chowkidar manning the gates. Although there were seven rooms, there were a lot of occupants. Onkar, his mother, Satwant Kaur, his three brothers and sister, his uncle S.S. Kanwar, his wife and four children, a widowed aunt and her family and his grandmother all lived there.

So too did Raunaq Singh's second wife, Gurmeet Kaur, and her son Satinder Pal Singh, Onkar's half-brother, who was born in 1965. 'The arrangement was unusual, although not unique, but it is what my father wanted,' Onkar says. It is not surprising that Satwant and Gurmeet did not get along. Onkar's mother Satwant, a small fair-skinned woman with only a basic education—Rani describes her as 'sweet and very kind'—lived on the ground floor while Raunaq Singh and his second wife had rooms on the first. When Raunaq Singh went out socializing it was Gurmeet he took with him.

'When we were children we did not realize that she was my father's second wife,' Rani says. 'There were so many family members living in the house that we just thought she was another aunt who had come. As we grew up, we did understand. My stepmother was very mean to my mother and saw herself as the leading wife. My mother never responded. She never had arguments with anybody.'

Any discord expressed or harboured by the two wives (Satwant died in 2005 and Gurmeet in 2016) did not seem to worry Raunaq Singh. He was buoyed by the excitement of transforming himself from market trader to manufacturer—especially the day he had been able to tell his son, 'I now have official permission to acquire the land and build the factory.'

◆

Every morning at 6 a.m., Onkar drove nearly 100 kilometres from Friends Colony to Ganaur to supervise the building. He would not return until midnight. The site his father had found was 129 acres on the edge of town. Dan Abbey had sent two engineers to assist him but the bulk of the electrical, mechanical and civil engineers and cost accountants working on the project were recently qualified young Indians. 'I went to all the technical institutes and recruited about four dozen. They were keen and worked very hard.'

As the 200-metre-long black-clad plant went up Onkar Kanwar understood a principle that has guided him ever since. Do not micro-manage. If you set clear goals and allow people to do the job then the results will come. And young people were more flexible and less set in their ways. They were also cheaper!

With the building complete, the equipment started to arrive, most of it from the United States from Abbey Etna and some from Germany. Because there was a rail siding next to the plant it could be delivered to the door. 'There were three processes: electric seam welding to bend and seal steel sheet into pipe, galvanizing to prevent rust and corrosion, and threading machines so pipes could be joined together with a tight fit.'

The Ganaur plant opened in November 1965 and the name on the gate said Bharat Steel Tubes Limited (BST). Building and equipping the BST plant had taken just eleven months. The timing could not have been better. India was on the verge of launching its 'Green Revolution'. It would transform a country that had historically been at the receiving end of food shortages and famine—notably the Bengal Famine of 1943 when an estimated four million people had perished—to agricultural self-sufficiency, create jobs and improve the quality of life in rural communities. This would be achieved through expanding acreage under cultivation, double cropping of existing farmland, and the use of new high-yield-value (HYV) seeds from the Indian Council for Agricultural Research. The revolution led to record grain output and allowed India to repay its loans to the World Bank, which had financed such projects in the country.

Significantly, for BST, none of the above would have been achieved without improved irrigation. 'We had farmers standing in queues to buy pipes as soon as they came out of the plant,' Onkar remembers. 'They all wanted a tube well and because we were making pipes to US standards they came for ours because they were better. They all turned up with cash. "So much money," I said to my father. "Please send some people to put up a bank branch so we can manage the cash well."'

Meanwhile, BST was also exporting. During 1966–68, exports rose from ₹3.85 million to ₹20 million. As Raunaq Singh's stature grew, it was

21

no surprise that he was soon dubbed 'Mr Exporter'. In March 1970, the then Prime Minister Indira Gandhi presented him with the FICCI Award for outstanding performance in exports at a ceremony at Vigyan Bhavan, the government's premier convention centre in New Delhi.

Onkar had ideas to expand BST. 'I said to my father, "Why don't we set up a steel plant next to the pipe factory? We have a rail siding there, so we have the infrastructure to bring in the raw materials."' It would have saved them money. 'He was ambitious and all for it.'

Raunaq Singh applied for permission from the government. It was refused. He had come up against a nonsensical barrier that was to blight entrepreneurship in India for more than forty years: the Licence Raj.

After Independence, India decided to adopt a centrally planned economy, which was largely controlled by the state, especially infrastructure, power and utilities, radio and TV, airlines, education and healthcare. Nobody could operate a private business without a licence.

The architect of the Licence Raj was Jawaharlal Nehru and such was the suffocation of red tape that up to eighty government agencies had to be satisfied before private companies got permission to operate small-to medium-sized businesses. Under Nehruvian socialism, expanding a company in the same sector in the same location was frowned upon. The Monopolies and Restrictive Trade Practices [MRTP] Act prevented any company from becoming too large in its field and all it did was push entrepreneurs with a desire for growth and access to capital to create the Indian conglomerate model, which was a consortium of companies involved in a seemingly random and, from today's standpoint, an economically illogical spread of activities. So the existing business maharajas, including the Birlas and the Tatas, were measured as much by the variety of their activities as with their economic success.

Five-year plans along the lines of the then Soviet Union, an inconvertible currency, high tariffs and import licensing produced growth and jobs at first, but by the mid-Sixties the new wave of first-generation entrepreneurs like Raunaq Singh were increasingly frustrated as the nation's economic needle began to swing in the opposite direction.

'Under the government's economic model, steel prices were fixed, whether it came from next door or from a thousand miles away,' says Onkar. 'They were not interested in listening to the economic logic of building a steel mill next to BST. It was the government, and not the market demand, that regulated production and the quality of goods that were permitted to be produced. It caused inefficiency, corruption and shortages. It set India back many years.'

As Patrick French says in his book *India A Portrait*, by the time of Nehru's death in 1964, 'His devotion to insular socialist planning had not brought prosperity and the country's share of world trade had halved.'

After Nehru's death, the Licence Raj and the permit culture still held sway and the only way to get ahead in business was to cultivate contacts in the government and ministries to win licences. The waiting rooms of ministerial offices at the central and state levels were crammed with hopefuls eager to grab the ministerial ear and a nod of approval. Many slipped cash under a first secretary's table to win that all-important piece of paper. Others employed a tactic that is commonplace today—networking—to gain influence. And perhaps the greatest networker of his generation was Raunaq Singh.

'He had taken office space in the Allahabad Bank Building at 17 Parliament Street in New Delhi,' Onkar says. 'His office was on the first floor and mine was on the fourth, although I also had a cabin next to his. Every day there was a constant stream of influential visitors and he would call me down to sit with him to listen and to learn. I think he also wanted to show me off to them—the son who had built BST with him.' Politicians, bankers, bureaucrats all beat a path to the rising star.

Father and son were extremely close. Every day, they had lunch together and dinner at least three times a week. They even dressed the same—always smart—a shirt and tie, trousers neatly pressed, shoes polished and turbans of similar maroon silk, although Onkar wore his at a more rakish angle. They even walked the same with military straight backs. At the office there was formality, Onkar says. 'There [at the office], I would always call him "Sir". At home, it was "Papaji".'

For Raunaq Singh business, networking and socializing were intertwined. 'Every night at home he would have a dinner or a party. If he met an ambassador or a minister, he would invite them for dinner,' says Onkar. 'My father was an inspirational man and a visionary man but he was not an operations man, which is why we worked so well together.'

There is no doubt that Raunaq Singh was great to be with. A raconteur, he loved the company of women and a glass or two of whisky. He was a man to whom people would gravitate without a second thought. It is no coincidence that one meaning of the name Raunaq is 'celebration'.

Raunaq Singh was also displaying his networking skills as he rose through the ranks of three apex associations: FICCI, the Associated Chambers of Commerce and Industry of India (ASSOCHAM) and the Federation of Indian Export Organisations (FIEO). Through them he was making yet more contacts. He would eventually become the President of all three, the only man ever to do so, as well as being Chairman of the Engineering Export Promotion Council (EEPC).

Apollo Tyres' first employee, Harish Bahadur, who joined as a management trainee in 1975 and is currently head of corporate investments at Apollo Tyres, remembers Raunaq Singh as 'a grand personality', 'dynamic' and 'very well connected in government circles'. Bahadur recalls, 'One morning, he [Raunaq Singh] came into the office with an air of triumph. "I have just had breakfast with Madam," he announced.'

'Does he mean his wife? And why is he telling me?' Bahadur mused. It was only later he discovered that 'Madam' was India's Prime Minister Indira Gandhi.

Raunaq Singh, who was riding around town in a large black Buick, had indeed arrived.

◆

Meanwhile, a significant woman had also come into Onkar's life. On 7 May 1967, he married Taru, whom he describes as his 'dear strength'. Her family came from Sialkot in Pakistan, but they had moved to Indonesia before Partition, where Taru was born. Her father had started a textile business in Jakarta and Sumatra. After Partition, he decided to move to Delhi, where Taru grew up with her six brothers.

'Onkar's aunt spotted me at an Indian wedding, liked me and told his father. So we met,' says Taru.

A long and happy marriage might never have happened, as Taru's eldest brother Jot Kapoor explains. 'My brother and I went to the BST factory at Ganaur and presented our card in the hope that we could arrange a first meeting with Taru; but nobody told Onkar that we were coming and when he saw the card he thought it was just another business card, and took no notice. We had got off to a bad start, to say the least! However, Raunaq Singh was very interested and luckily things progressed.'

In the days when arranged marriages were the absolute norm 'we were not allowed to date', Onkar says. 'We met in nice restaurants or hotels and we were always chaperoned. Taru was accompanied by her brother, Jot, and I by my sister, Rani.'

'And, no late nights,' Taru adds. 'I had to be home by 11 p.m. My brother [as head of the family] was very strict!'

In those days, life for a young woman was circumscribed by tradition. 'It was also very difficult being the daughter of someone as famous a Raunaq Singh,' says Rani. 'I never went out on my own and was always accompanied to parties by my brothers. One had to be very careful not to say or do anything that might harm his reputation.'

When Onkar and Taru got engaged, their friends and both families held a series of parties, including one at Raunaq Singh's house, where the guests included government ministers and the then Vice President Zakir Husain, who would go on to become India's third President.

They were married one month later at Raunaq Singh's house. Marquees were set up on the lawn and 2,000 guests attended the ceremony. In keeping with Sikh tradition, the bridegroom, dressed in ceremonial finery, rode a horse and led a procession to his bride-to-be's house the previous day for the meeting of the families. Onkar is not a natural horseman, 'but it was only for a few hundred metres', he says. As the two families met, they said *ardas*, the common Sikh prayer.

The wedding was solemnized by a priest and Onkar led by his new wife, in her bridal clothes and veil walked four times around the Sikh holy book, the Guru Granth Sahib, which is considered the final guru of Sikhism. Containing devotional hymns and prayers, it is the supreme spiritual authority and head of the Sikh religion. Most Sikhs, and Onkar and Taru Kanwar are no exception, have a copy in their prayer rooms at home and read from it every day. Every year, many devout Sikhs and their families will devote a period of seven days to prayer and readings from the Guru Granth Sahib.

The wedding was followed by a solid month of parties once the couple had moved into Raunaq Singh's Friends Colony house.

'Too many parties!' the new bride commented. The relentless socializing was in stark contrast to her quiet and more conservative upbringing. 'My family was a very simple family and I was quite shy to begin with but I soon got to know his [Onkar's] friends and became more comfortable with meeting them all. Mr Raunaq Singh was also very warm and kind to me and he loved me very much. Most mornings he would say to me, "About twenty or thirty people are coming to dinner tonight and you should be ready to greet them at 7 p.m."'

Her husband advised: 'My father is a stickler for time, so be ready by 6.30 p.m.!' Onkar is equally wedded to punctuality. To him turning up late shows lack of respect and lack of intent.

He and Taru spent their honeymoon at Dr A.C. Muthiah's house near the hill station resort of Ooty in Tamil Nadu where the British government would relocate for six months every year to escape the heat.

Returning to Raunaq Singh's house in Delhi, Taru's calming influence was soon at work, easing the tension between Onkar and his stepmother. Friends and relations all remark on her innate ability to diffuse tension in a room just by being there.

Onkar and Taru's first child, Shalini, was born a year after their marriage. With BST running well and profitably, Raunaq Singh was eyeing a new challenge. He asked Onkar to go to Bombay (now Mumbai), as it was known then, to set up a general export import business under the banner of Raunaq International, a company that had been incorporated in 1965. Onkar was on the board as was his brother, A.P. Kanwar, and his uncle, S.S. Kanwar.

'My father decreed that because I would be living in the Taj Mahal Hotel, it would be more suitable if my wife stayed back in Delhi in his house with our daughter. My wife and daughter could come to see me once a month. That was the way we went on for six months,' Onkar recalls.

'And, of course, no mobiles in those days and telephone connections were not that reliable, so we had very little contact when Onkar was in Mumbai,' Mrs Kanwar says.

Not that she had any time to be on her own! Not only was Raunaq Singh's Friends Colony house full to bursting with extended family, other relatives also came to call. 'Because Onkar was the first one of Raunaq Singh's children to not only get married, but also have a child, the family was all very excited,' says Taru Kanwar. 'His aunts would come to visit every day and the cousins also came frequently and they would discuss which movies to go and see and where we should go for lunch.'

Being tired of living in a hotel and missing his wife and daughter, Onkar found a place for them to live in Mumbai. There is an interesting story behind this too. 'I had made a friend in the textile business, who invited me to a beach house party on Juhu Beach. Used to Delhi parties, my driver took me out to Juhu at 8.30 p.m., but there was nobody there. I didn't know what to do but wait. I did not want my friend to think I had not bothered to turn up. My host came at 11.30 p.m.! The guests arrived at 12.30 a.m. There was lots of dancing and singing and drinking but nothing to eat. I was not used to these kinds of evenings. That's the difference between Mumbai and Delhi. By 3 a.m., I was tired and hungry and wanted to get back to the Taj. My driver was also drunk, so I caught a taxi back. Next day my friend called me and said, "I can offer you a flat on Napean Sea Road, near Malabar Hill." Napean Sea Road, named after a former British Governor of Mumbai Sir Evan Napean, is one of the most upmarket parts of the city. He told me, "I like you so much that I will not charge a deposit, just a simple rent on condition that when you leave town you hand the flat back."'

After staying apart for six months, Taru and Shalini joined him and they lived there for two years. It would not be the last time in Onkar's life that chance encounters or a strange turn of events would work to his advantage.

◆

For Onkar Singh Kanwar, a whole new world was opening up. 'I went into exporting almonds, spices and walnuts. Then at a trade fair in Cochin (now Kochi), I met Bob Sessler, an American importer. He was a very successful Jewish businessman, who had a big house on Long Island, which I visited. He said, "Why don't we go into exporting frozen fresh fish from Kerala to the United States?" I told him I knew nothing about it and I didn't have any trawlers. He said, "I know exactly how we will do it."'

Onkar went to the smaller Keralite fishermen who found it difficult to compete on price with the larger operators, and bought lobster, fish and prawns direct from their boats, which he then had frozen and shipped into America's eastern seaboard. He discovered that he was a natural negotiator. 'Then, we started exporting frog legs.' Next, he got a licence to import and bought galvanized sheets from Japan that were used for movie poster hoardings.

Onkar was not only making Raunaq International 500 per cent profit, he was also establishing himself in his own right, geographically removed from his father as well as his father's growing profile.

By the end of the 1960s, Onkar was also a frequent visitor to markets in the Middle East, filling his passport with stamps for Saudi Arabia, Dubai, Muscat and Abu Dhabi. 'There were a lot of young men of my age working in those countries, setting up import/export deals. But there were very few hotels in those days. In one hotel in Dubai, there were four of us in one room: myself, a German, an Iranian and a Britisher. They insisted on charging all of us the full room rate. There was no other hotel so we had no choice.'

Just like the hotel plumbing, things did not always run smoothly. 'In Dubai I engaged a Pakistani driver for a whole day and went to the market. I visited a huge wholesale warehouse, where you could buy and sell steel rods, building materials—literally anything. I was hoping to sell BST steel pipes. I told my driver to wait and that I would pay him when I came out and that he should then take me to the post office as I had to send a fax to my father to report on progress.'

Onkar took so long talking to a dealer over endless cups of tea that he lost track of time. 'When I came out it was early evening and my driver had gone. I managed to get a taxi to the post office. When I got there I was greeted by my driver, who was very angry with me. With him were some police officers. They said they were going to arrest me for not paying the man. The driver demanded to know why I had not shown up. I told him, "I should be getting upset with you for disappearing; please take the money and go."'

Avoiding the handcuffs, Onkar Kanwar moved on to Iraq. Meanwhile, Raunaq Singh was proposing the creation of a consortium of Indian contractors to take on construction and agricultural projects in the country. In Baghdad one of Onkar's fellow exporters was bemoaning the fact that he had lost his local sales contact and fixer.

'"Where's he gone?" I asked innocently. He was going to be publicly executed and the execution was live on television,' Onkar recalls.

Back in India, Bharat Steel Tubes was doing so well that Raunaq Singh decided to explore other business options. He opened the Raunaq Public School, a few hundred metres from the factory, and a township, Raunaq Nagar, comprising 480 flats for senior factory managers.

Soon, he summoned his son back to Delhi. Taru Kanwar was relieved. 'Onkar had been travelling too much.' The family set up home in a rented house in Anand Niketan in the southwest of the city. Shortly after moving to Delhi, Onkar and Taru became parents three times over. While their elder son, Raaja, was born in Mumbai in 1970, Neeraj was born a year later after they moved to Delhi.

Onkar, however, had some misgivings about returning home. Though he respected his father immensely, he felt he was back under Raunaq Singh's considerable shadow in a way he had not been for two years.

Raunaq Singh's empire was about to grow further, funded in part by the continued success of BST. He tasked Onkar to set up another company called Bharat Gears in Mumbra, Maharashtra. Incorporated in December 1971, its foundation stone was laid in 1972 and it would open for business in 1974 producing a wide range of gears for HCVs (heavy commercial vehicles), MCVs (medium commercial vehicles), LCVs (light commercial vehicles), utility and off-road vehicles.

For the first fifteen years of its life, Bharat Gears was run by Raunaq Singh's son-in-law, Surinder Kapur. Kapur's family had a jewellery shop—Kapur di Hatti in Connaught Place—but Surinder had studied engineering and also completed a doctorate from the University of Michigan in the US. The Douglas Aircraft Company had sponsored his PhD in aerospace and fluid dynamics. That he married Rani Kanwar was majorly due to the efforts of Onkar. 'My father had met him and thought he was the right one for me, even though he was not a Sikh, but I could not make up my mind,' Rani explains. 'I had barely met him. Then, at a party Onkar met him, for the first time, and came rushing over to me and asked me what my problem was in not agreeing to marry Surinder; what was I thinking of? "He's such a nice guy," he said.' Rani bowed to her elder brother's better judgement. 'I took the decision and I never regretted it for a single moment.'

In Surinder Kapur, Onkar Kanwar had found a lifelong friend, ally and confidante. 'It was love at first sight for me!' he says. They were two men cut very much from the same cloth—unflashy, resolutely hard-working and with a desire to one day build their own businesses.

three

Maruti and Menon

With Bharat Gears in the capable hands of Surinder Kapur, Raunaq Singh was now preoccupied with a vehicle of a very different kind and one that would quickly become highly controversial. He was by now a particular favourite of Mrs Gandhi, always visiting her official prime ministerial residence at 1 Safdarjung Road, where she had moved in 1964, shortly after the death of her father. Coming from north India, Mrs Gandhi definitely had a preference for the entrepreneurs and industrialists from there rather than those from Mumbai. 'She would meet people every morning at Safdarjung Road between 8 a.m. and 10 a.m.,' says Rajinder Kumar Dhawan, who was Mrs Gandhi's private secretary and closest confidante, who had worked with her since 1962.

'Mrs Gandhi had an "open door policy", there was no security like today and people could just turn up.' However, nobody got access to the white prime ministerial bungalow without going through R.K. Dhawan first. Sitting in Mrs Gandhi's house rather than in her office across the garden at 1 Akbar Road, some called R.K. Dhawan 'the gatekeeper'. Others said that he was so influential that he was really the 'deputy prime minister'.

'Raunaq Singh came weekly to see Mrs Gandhi and they would talk either in her study or sitting room,' says Dhawan. Both the rooms, painted white like the rest of the house, were furnished modestly, almost austerely, with rugs on polished stone floors and much space given to books that were shelved from floor to ceiling. There were many pictures on the walls and framed family photographs of Sanjay, Rajiv and Pandit Nehru, but significantly none of her husband in name only, Feroze Gandhi.

'Raunaq Singh took a great interest in politics and was pro the Congress Party but he never discussed politics with Mrs Gandhi. It was always a social call,' Dhawan says. 'I think she liked to hear about his plans and activities and listen to his view of what was going on in Delhi and in India. They became extremely close.'

While Mrs Gandhi was charmed by him, there is no doubt that Raunaq Singh would do anything to help 'Madam'. And now the Prime Minister needed help to guide her wayward, headstrong son and groomed successor, Sanjay.

Sanjay Gandhi had nurtured an ambition to make cars since boyhood. As journalist and author Vinod Mehta writes in his book *The Sanjay Story*, 'On his sixth birthday Panditji (Nehru) presented Sanjay with a pedal car, and this instantly became the boy's proudest possession. On the lawns of Teen Murti Bhavan [the first prime minister's residence where he (Nehru) lived for sixteen years until his death in 1964, and which is now a museum and library], grandfather would push the car and the grandson would take off at what he thought was great speed.'

Speed would prove Sanjay's Achilles heel. He ignored the advice of his mother and grandfather that he should study mechanical engineering at university. He said he could learn all he needed to know on the job. Instead he began a highly sought-after three-year apprenticeship with Rolls-Royce in England. However, he quit after two years, announcing that there was no more that he needed to learn about making cars. He left the UK without qualifications but an arrest against his name for speeding and driving without a licence, potentially a serious offence. Once more the Indian High Commission in London had to step in to prevent Sanjay's motoring misdemeanours from going further.

Back in India, Sanjay was determined to launch an affordable small car. The 'people's car' was an idea that had been on the agenda for several years. He was determined to make it a reality. Maruti Motors Limited was floated in 1971 on the back of a government letter of intent, which allowed Sanjay to make up to 50,000 cars a year. Mrs Gandhi was soon having doubts that her do-it-yesterday, short-fuse son had the patience or enough experience to deliver the project. A high-profile failure would have political consequences.

The 'gatekeeper' had a word. 'I thought that Maruti needed some wise heads as directors,' says R.K. Dhawan. 'In September 1971, I suggested to Mrs Gandhi that Mr Raunaq Singh should be one of them. She agreed and when I put it to him he accepted the offer readily. He thought it was a great idea.'

Raunaq Singh's good friend M.A. Chidambaram was the Chairman of Maruti. Chidambaram was the Mayor of Madras (now Chennai) and also the third son of the Raja of Chettinad. He had begun his business life with a scooter factory in Mumbai and founded SPIC, which was run after his death by his son Dr A.C. Muthiah, Onkar's close friend.

As Chairman of the expanding Raunaq Group—with Onkar Singh Kanwar as the Managing Director of BST and creator of Bharat Steel Gears—which also included Raunaq International and a small steel and alloys factory (Universal Steel and Alloys Limited) in Chennai, Raunaq Singh had created the platform for a new industrial conglomerate. He liked to joke with Mrs Gandhi and others about the Birlas and the Tatas being dinosaurs.

Meanwhile, there had been frustrations in the rising industrialist's progress. In 1965, while running BST, Onkar had been in discussions with Bechtel, a US-based engineering, construction and project management company, on a pioneering scheme to alleviate severe droughts and floods. 'The idea was to connect rivers with dams, pipes and pumps to create a necklace around the country so that water could be moved to where it was needed most. I went to the government for the licence. They threw me out!'

The government also blocked Bechtel's ambition to build power stations at pitheads and use new technology to clean up the coal, a technology they were already employing in the United States to great effect.

'The ministries were run by babus [bureaucrats], who were only

33

interested in taking rents (bribes),' Onkar explains. 'One of them said to me, in 1968, when I went to apply for a licence for a factory at the industry ministry, "Young man, I know you are the son of Mr Raunaq Singh and that he knows Mrs Gandhi. However, you know my power? I can make your file lost. It will take one year to get it reconstructed." He suggested I might like to give him 10 per cent, then, he said, "₹50,000". I never gave him anything. That system along with production quotas and fines is where we went so wrong as a country.'

Raunaq Singh was undeterred. A promoter on the rise, there was no doubt that one day he wanted to match and outstrip the Birlas and the Tatas. By now, he was Chairman of the EEPC and President of FIEO through which he had become close to A.C. George, who was the Union Minister for State for Industry and Civil Supply.

'Raunaq Singh was a shoot-from-the-hip entrepreneur,' says Vinayak Chatterjee, Founder and Chairman of Feedback Infra, an international infrastructure design and consultancy business. It is one of the largest in India employing 8,000 people and specializes in national highways and power plants in more than twenty countries. Early in his career, Chatterjee was an executive assistant to both Raunaq Singh and then Onkar Singh Kanwar. 'In those days of shortages and the Licence Raj, if Raunaq Singh smelt an opportunity he would go for it. The fact that he could network and get finance for himself meant he would chase every business opportunity.'

Singh was at a cocktail party and dinner at Kerala House on Jantar Mantar Road in New Delhi, when Achutha Menon the development-minded Chief Minister of the state took him to one side.

'So, Raunaq, you don't have anything in Kerala, do you?'

'No, it's too far away.'

'We've got a company down there called Ruby Rubber sitting on a 400,000 tyre/tube licence since 1972, but they haven't implemented it.' Menon, often described as a 'no-nonsense' Chief Minister, was desperate for industrial development in his state. Kerala had very little industry and Menon, a lawyer-turned-politician who had been active in the Quit

India movement, needed to create jobs in the state. He had written a personal letter to Indira Gandhi lobbying for the licence and now he was frustrated. 'Raunaq, I can transfer that licence to you,' he said.

Until then, the Indian tyre industry had been run by an international oligopoly of Goodyear, Firestone, Ceat and Dunlop—which had opened its first tyre factory in India in Kolkata in 1936. The group had enjoyed a sellers' market since 1968 and did not face any problem in marketing whatever they produced. So the quality of the product and introducing the technological innovations happening in the rest of the world, such as nylon or cross-ply tyres, did not rank high.

'There was no competition, just a distribution of the cake,' says Onkar Singh Kanwar. 'In an economy driven by shortages, companies rather than the markets predetermined profits. Goodyear, Dunlop, Firestone and Ceat brought in equipment from the 1940s; they didn't bother to modernize and anyway it was very difficult to import. When you are managing shortages and the government controls the licences, it is not a case of economic viability, it is a question of who has the pull.'

Now the government had decided to decontrol prices and open the market to encourage Indian business houses to compete. Modi Tyre Company, part of the Modi Group, had signed a technological agreement with German tyre manufacturer Continental Corporation and became the first local firm to enter the Indian tyre industry. JK Tyre, founded in West Bengal, also had a licence and was pressing on with building a factory in Rajasthan.

Raunaq Singh, buoyed by three whiskies and hip-shooting confidence, replied without a second thought to Chief Minister Menon: 'That's a good idea. I'll take the Kerala licence!'

With project costs rising as a result of the oil crisis in the early Seventies, Ruby Rubber Company had run out of cash to build a plant. So far all it had managed to do was tie up with General Tire as a technical collaborator and register the name of a new company.

It was called Apollo Tyres Limited.

four

Red flags in the rubber state

Perambra, Thrissur District, Kerala, Sunday, 13 April 1975

Raunaq Singh smiled at the assembled guests and took out his speech. 'I cannot express adequately my feeling of happiness and gratitude at the presence of such a large number of distinguished guests and friends at the launching of our tyre project today.'

The distinguished guests comprised then Kerala Chief Minister Achutha Menon, Union Minister A.C. George and from Akron, Ohio, America, Clarence Carpenter and John Porosky, senior executives of General Tire—one of the world's largest tyre companies and Apollo's technical collaborator on the Perambra plant.

'General Tire has developed sophisticated technology and acquired vast experience in the manufacture of a wide variety of automobile tyres and tubes,' Raunaq Singh explained. 'It is operating more than forty plants in thirty countries. Our collaborators will supply technical know-how, engineering data, specifications and standards, and systems and procedures.' Not only would General Tire help build the plant, it would also equip and commission it and train Indian personnel in all aspects of tyre technology and engineering.

The General Tire & Rubber Company had been founded in Akron in 1915 by William F. O.'Neil known as 'W.O.', and his partner Winfred

E. Fouse. Throughout its history, it had been known as an innovation leader introducing new styles and technology, particularly for truck tyres in its early years, although it had also been making passenger car tyres since 1955, first as General Motors' supplier and later for other major auto producers. In 1973, the company's sixth American plant equipped for full radial tyre production came on stream.

'General Tire scientists enlarged the state of the art in the rubber industry,' its website proclaims proudly. 'They solved at least a forty-year-old industry problem with the discovery of the carbon black latex-mixing masterbatch principle in 1943, and the invention of oil-extended rubber in 1949.' Adhesives, fabrics, radial tyre building machines and a method and machine for improving the performance characteristics of pneumatic tyres; the list went on.

Apart from having General Tire and its technical know-how on board, Raunaq Singh's decision to build a ₹255 million tyre plant on the 90-acre Perambra site that was capable of producing 500,000 tyres a year, 70 per cent of them truck tyres, was based on two factors: cash and opportunity. About ₹65 million would come in the form of foreign exchange, with the Government of India, the Industrial Finance Corporation of India and the Industrial Credit and Investment Corporation of India together financing foreign exchange loans to the tune of ₹40 million with a further ₹25 million arranged through commercial borrowings abroad. 'As for the rupee finance, we received commitments from term lending institutions and a number of banks,' Raunaq Singh explained.

There was backing from the Industrial Development Bank of India (IDBI) of ₹40 million and an initial public offer of equity capital of ₹54 million.

The confidence from the banks and the institutions rested on the fact that BST was one of the promoters of the project and had exports exceeding ₹100 million in 1974–75.

The opportunity was the rapid development and expansion of road transport in India. 'At the time of Independence, India had only 3.38

lakh (338,000) kilometres of roads,' Raunaq Singh told his audience. 'The Indian road network is now one of the largest in the world having crossed 12 lakh (1.2 million) kilometres.' In 1961, India's trucking industry carried only 16 per cent of railroad traffic. Now, it was nearly double at 31 per cent and was growing. With the increased use of tractors and the need for bus tyres, the future looked rosy. A government task force estimated that the demand for tyres would be eleven million by 1978–79 against current production of about six million.

And then, of course, Kerala produced 90 per cent of India's natural rubber, much of it grown on plantations right by the Perambra plant. The southern state also had a surplus of power on a scale that is lifeblood to a tyre factory to power its machinery and the boilers producing the steam essential to tyre making.

Raunaq Singh moved to his conclusion. 'Through Apollo Tyres, we will have the opportunity to serve the people of this state by generating employment [and] to strengthen the economy of Kerala. I seek the good wishes and blessings of all our friends who are present here today for the success of our project and I request Shri Achutha Menon kindly to lay the foundation stone.'

For Menon—who served two terms as Chief Minister from 1969 until 1977—the Apollo project had a personal dimension. The factory was to be built in Thrissur District, where he was born in 1913 and where he still had his residence.

'Today is a significant day for all of us and our Nation,' proclaimed a newspaper advertisement that had been issued by the Government of Kerala and Apollo Tyres Limited, which was billed as 'A Raunaq Enterprise'. It was headed: 'The Beginning of a Bright Future'. 'This plant will be a forerunner producing superior quality steel radial belted tyres that are in high demand. Today is a significant day for all of us and for our nation.'

'People welcomed us with open arms and flowers,' Onkar recalls. 'There were lots of fireworks in true Kerala style. It was a great day.'

With everything set fair in terms of cash, technological support, political goodwill and a ready supply of raw materials, what could possibly go wrong?

◆

In April 1957, Kerala had made history when it became the first state in the world to democratically elect a Communist government headed by then Chief Minister E.M.S. Namboodiripad. At the height of the Cold War heading fast to the Cuban Missile Crisis, this news generated huge interest around the world as well as in India. According to the authors of *A Journey Through Time 1857–2007,* which charts Kerala's economic history and cultural heritage, 'Globally this was viewed as a triumph of mature democracy. Internally, it was seen as the beginning of a fascinating experiment in building a free, fair and open society.'

Early optimism soon gave way when the communist government brought in an education bill, which advocated improved wages and better working conditions for teachers in private schools and colleges. The Catholic Church and other faith groups, which ran many of these schools, objected. The Congress Party, which had narrowly lost the election to the Communist Party of India (Marxist), saw this as the chance to foment unrest and Kerala dissolved into strikes and protest. About 150,000 demonstrators were jailed and many were killed in police lathi charges. The Nehru government brought in President's Rule, in July 1959, to restore order.

After seven months, a Second Assembly was elected, headed first by the Praja Socialist Party and then the Indian National Congress. CPI(M) and Congress then swapped power back and forth in the subsequent elections with Achutha Menon of CPI(M) taking over as Chief Minister in 1969. Still regarded by many as the best Chief Minister the state ever had, Menon wanted to see Kerala's economy diversify from its reliance on spices and money sent home by plumbers, labourers and carpenters working in the Middle East. This is why he had wooed Raunaq Singh to take on Apollo Tyres and was delighted to perform the foundation stone laying ceremony.

However, the flowers and the fireworks were soon forgotten and Menon would have been concerned to see construction on the Perambra plant grinding to a halt in the face of unofficial strikes and walkouts that were all too common in Kerala. He introduced a policy of 'No Work, No Pay' to tackle strikes by trade unions and government employees, but the Apollo project looked doomed.

A young subdivisional magistrate in Thrissur District, Vinod Rai, who went on to become one of India's finest administrators, was called in virtually every week to intervene during the construction phase of the plant. Originally from the northern state of Uttar Pradesh (UP), Rai rose to become the Finance Secretary of Kerala and spent twenty-two years in the state before being appointed the Comptroller and Auditor General of India and a scourge on corruption. 'In those days, Kerala was known for having a very active trade union movement at the unskilled labour level,' Rai explains. In many ways, it was the communist influence that made workers so militant. There were red flags and anti-business demonstrations on the streets most days. Now that Apollo was building the plant it was coming face-to-face with worker unrest.

Familiar intimidation tactics included *gherao*—forcibly confining management to their offices until they gave in to union demands—and *bandh*—totally paralyzing activities of the state for political ends including closing down production and blocking roads.

While Rai's valiant and diplomatic attempts to get the construction workers back on site usually bore fruit, the Central Government was to ride to Apollo's side on the night of 25 June 1975 in the most unlikely guise.

At the behest of the increasingly unpopular Prime Minister Indira Gandhi—on whose watch the rupee had been devalued by over a third, making it worth just 7.50 to the dollar, and who had nationalized fourteen leading banks in 1969—President Fakhruddin Ali Ahmed proclaimed a state of national emergency. The reason was 'internal disturbance' under Article 352(1) of the Constitution. Other destabilizing factors cited were the 1971 war with Pakistan, drought and the 1973 oil crisis, which had left the economy in bad shape. But what really sparked it was a case in the Allahabad High Court, which had found Mrs Gandhi guilty of electoral malpractices in the 1971 election and banned her from holding elected office for six years. Strikes and protests against her spread across the nation.

Within hours of suspending the Constitution, and beginning her rule by decree, Mrs Gandhi had her political opponents arrested and the power supply to all newspapers was cut. Urged on by her increasingly powerful son Sanjay and a small coterie of advisers, she suspended elections and curbed civil liberties. In the twenty-one months the Emergency lasted, nearly a thousand opposition leaders and political opponents were arrested and detained under the Maintenance of Internal Security Act, including premiers-to-be Chandrashekhar and Atal Bihari Vajpayee and other prominent political leaders, including Lal Krishna Advani. Compulsory birth control was introduced and Sanjay Gandhi embarked on a highly controversial programme of mass sterilization.

The Emergency, which remains highly sensitive to this day, did ironically bring one advantage to Raunaq Singh. It banned all strikes. 'The Construction of the Apollo Perambra plant was then completed very rapidly in a record time of thirteen months,' says Vinod Rai.

As the Perambra factory was finished and the equipment supplied by General Tire was installed and tested, life did not change much for Raunaq Singh in spite of the Emergency and increasing signs that Sanjay Gandhi's Maruti project was mired in technical difficulties and financial irregularities, was unlikely to produce a commercially viable vehicle from its factory on the Gurgaon–Palam road.

Sanjay was certainly in no mood to heed the advice of Raunaq Singh or anybody else just as he had believed that Rolls-Royce had nothing much to teach him about making cars. As Vinod Mehta puts it: 'The eve of the Emergency saw the affairs of Maruti in a state of Byzantine complexity; a public scandal whose hydra-headed ramifications subverted banking, civil, criminal and company law, import licensing, marketing, state politics.'

Sanjay Gandhi was a frequent visitor to Raunaq Singh's office in the Allahabad Bank Building. 'He was a very ambitious, aggressive man,'

Onkar recalls. Raunaq Singh had no personal investment in Maruti, although BST had bought shares worth ₹500,000. When R.K. Dhawan asked him to invest five times more than that in the project, Raunaq Singh refused, arguing that he was not a promoter of the firm and maybe sensing that it was doomed. Even so, Onkar worried that Sanjay was using his father.

One day, a purchase order for a plane arrived on Onkar's desk. 'I questioned my father; he said "We have to buy a plane." It was a Cessna type aircraft. "But why? It's not relevant to our needs."'

Before he got a satisfactory answer, Onkar got a call from the chairman of the bank: 'Your letter of credit is ready.'

'Then, I got a call from the chief controller of import and export. He said that the licence for the plane was ready.

'I went back to my father and questioned his priorities. I said, "The Apollo factory is in trouble; why do you need a plane? We don't need it. For years, flying has affected your balance and made you ill and you have to take medicines every time you board a plane so why own something that makes you sick?"'

'Sanjay wants it,' Raunaq Singh replied.

Perhaps with political ambitions of his own, Raunaq Singh wanted to impress the Gandhi family. Sanjay Gandhi had a passion for flying—a passion that was to kill him—but for him to be seen buying a plane when Maruti was leaching money would have not gone down well with 'Mummyji' and been grist to her political enemies.

'Sir, it will just be a white elephant. Don't buy the damn plane.'

Onkar won that argument.

Plane or no plane, Raunaq Singh, 'Mr Exporter', was still a regular and welcome visitor to the prime ministerial bungalow at 1 Safdarjung Road. Maybe the fact that he did not discuss politics with 'Madam' was a welcome distraction from the international accusations of human rights abuses being heaped on India.

That Raunaq Singh was still very much inner circle is emphasized by the fact that he was chosen to be among a group of eminent industrialists and others to meet the President of the World Bank, Robert McNamara, who led a World Bank delegation to India on 18 October 1976.

It was to focus on imports and exports and McNamara's briefing notes highlighted the fact that Raunaq Singh had been awarded the first prize by FICCI in 1969 for the highest export performance by any individual manufacturing unit in the country. '[He is] chief spokesman for the community of exporters,' the notes explained. 'Educated in a village high school in West Punjab…Raunaq Singh is one of India's most brilliant rising entrepreneurs. He is never embarrassed about his relatively unsophisticated background. On the contrary, he is rather proud of it.'

◆

Raunaq Singh was especially proud when on 15 November 1976 he arrived at Apollo's Perambra plant to witness the first tyre coming off the line. It was a truck tyre called 'Rajdhani'. Ensign Photos of Kochi was there to 'register the birth sequence when the steam gushed through the utility lines [and] Rajdhani, made its birth inside the bag-o-matic press'.

A Hindu priest blessed the new plant and its workers. Inside was an elaborate endlessly moving sculpture of clicking, clanking, hissing, muscular machines floor to roof and wall to wall. At the beginning of the process natural rubber, synthetic rubber, carbon black and rubber chemicals delivered to one end of the factory had gone into the mixers to produce the different compounds needed to make the tyre's many components including the side walls, the carcass—the internal cord layer of the tyre that sustains load and absorbs shock—the bead—the edge of the tyre that sits on the wheel—and the tread—the rubber on a tyre's circumference that comes in contact with the road.

A lava flow of hot rubber resembling thick black treacle emerged from the mixers and was then extruded and flattened before being passed through a series of pressure rollers and cutters required by the different components. These arrived on the building equipment where Rajdhani was assembled into what is called a green tyre without any tread patterns or markings. From here, it was put into a curing press and sealed and exposed to 200 degrees centigrade of steam heat and pressure for a dozen minutes and more to vulcanize or fuse the tyre's various components together and mould the traction patterns and markings to produce the tyre as we know it. It was hot, back-breaking work, much of it manual, decades before the days of mechanization and robotics.

In a photo album entitled 'The Raunaq dream comes true!' workers posed with their first tyre. Some were serious-faced, standing to attention. Others wore the smiles of celebration and relief. As he strode through this new world of steam, humidity and the sweet slightly clawing smell of cured rubber, Raunaq Singh, with the sleeves of his open-necked white shirt rolled up, looked like a man who was ready for business.

Three months later Apollo Tyres went into full commercial production.

five

Dreams and reality

Apollo Tyres Registered Office, 6th Floor, Cherupushpam Building, Shanmugham Road, Kochi, September 1978

Harish Bahadur was sitting at his desk wondering how to meet that month's wage bill for the Perambra plant. 'It was a very cash-crunched company, there was no liquidity at all. It was a constant struggle to pay vendors too.' Sales were poor. Apollo's tyres were not winning over the market.

It was galling for Raunaq Singh to see Modi Tyre, which had also started commercial operation in late 1974, achieving a significant market share in just two years. Unlike Apollo, Modi was already a force to be reckoned, with thanks to its enthusiasm for technologically superior products and an independent and competitive sales network.

Raunaq Singh had relocated Bahadur from Delhi to Kerala, eight months after appointing him, to sort out Apollo's accounts and look after relationships with the company's banks, which were based in Kochi. He was to spend four years on a never-ending struggle but he is proud to this day that he never missed a payment.

His task was not made easier by endless strikes and stoppages at the plant. If the raita (flavoured yogurt) in the canteen was sour, it could trigger a walkout. 'There were times when accounts could not be prepared for months,' Harish says. 'In those days financial reporting rules were not as stringent as they are today.'

The fact he was based this day in the company's registered office and not at his usual office in the admin block at Perambra was due to more industrial unrest in the factory.

With production halted again, Harish Bahadur's problems were about to get a whole lot worse. 'A gentleman walked in with a letter and told me he had been appointed by the Government of India to take over the company.' Completely nonplussed, Bahadur read the letter. 'In exercise of the powers conferred by Section 15 of the Industries (Development and Regulations) Act, 1951, the Central Government passed an Order dated 17 September 1978, authorizing the taking over of the management of the company.' It was signed by George Fernandes, the Union Minister for Industries in the newly elected Janata government. The new government was a 'big tent' coalition of forces, led by the Janata Party, which had opposed the Emergency.

With international criticism of the Emergency mounting, Mrs Gandhi had suddenly gone to the polls in March 1977, reckoning to win, only to lose 200 seats to a sweeping Janata majority. She lost her seat, as did Sanjay Gandhi. Congress seats in the Lok Sabha were slashed from 350 to 153 and Morarji Desai became India's first non-Congress Prime Minister. It was a spectacular gambling failure that forced Mrs Gandhi to move out from the official prime ministerial residence at 1 Safdarjung Road and relocate across the garden to 1 Akbar Road, taking R.K. Dhawan with her. He refers to those days as 'the turmoil'. Dhawan recalls, 'Mr Raunaq Singh stood by Mrs Gandhi during those difficult days.'

It was a loyalty that did him no favours as far as the Janata government was concerned. The new government set up the Shah Commission to investigate crimes, cronyism and corruption during the Emergency and it would result in indicting many Congress leaders.

Now in power, Industries Minister George Fernandes was a force to be reckoned with. A veteran strike leader and union organizer, his most notable agitation was the Railway Strike of 1974, which had brought the entire network to a standstill. Although he was imprisoned during of the Emergency in 1976, convicted in the infamous Vadodara Dynamite Case—a plot to blow up government establishments and railway tracks in protest of the Emergency—he won his seat in Bihar from behind prison bars with a 300,000 majority. Now, he was free and on a mission. He was to force American multinationals IBM and Coca-Cola to leave India for violating the Foreign Exchange Regulation Act, which stipulated that foreign investors could not own more than 40 per cent of the share capital in their Indian businesses.

Maruti Motors Limited had been liquidated in 1977 and now Fernandes was after Apollo Tyres, accusing the company of financial mismanagement and corruption. It was true that accumulated losses suffered by Apollo amounted to ₹280 million against a share capital of ₹80 million—more than three times the capital. An interim board appointed by the Supreme Court of India would take over the management of the company.

'The company was in chaos,' admits Onkar, who was devoting most of his time to Raunaq Singh's other businesses, which at this stage were performing well under his guidance. 'Nobody was paying attention.' Apollo had loans from eight banks and four investment institutions. 'In its first year, Apollo alone had racked up a loss of ₹15.1 million. What had begun as a ₹250 million project had spiralled to more than ₹350 million.' On the verge of sickness, it threatened to become the Raunaq Group's millstone.

To put Apollo's performance in context, profits right across the Indian tyre industry were at an all-time low, amounting to barely 2 per cent of total sales. 'Hit by a demand recession and plagued by low profitability, the tyre industry is in a tailspin,' *India Today* reported. 'The industry is producing tyres at about 75 per cent of its total capacity. Only Dunlop, Ceat and Modi Continental have kept their heads above water; all others are in the red.'

So why pick on Apollo? Onkar Singh Kanwar was never in doubt. 'The decision to nationalize was 100 per cent political. My father was too close to the Gandhis.'

The gentleman now standing in Harish Bahadur's office turned out to be the Chairman of Inchek Tyres from Kolkata—which ironically was then itself a sick company and today is part of the Tyre Corporation of India. "'I have been nominated by the government to take over the factory," he said. He would not even let me use the phone or talk to anyone,' Bahadur recalls. 'He told me, "You are the senior man here. Come with us to the factory." In those days, it took about two hours to reach Perambra by road. On the way there, he asked, "Which is the nearest police station to the factory?"

"'Why? I asked.

"'Because we would like to have police protection," he said. "They might attack us."

'When we got to the police station, he showed them the letter. We then set off again with two van loads of police officers. At the factory, the security guards at the gate did not know what was going on but when they saw me sitting in the car they allowed us to go in. I took him to the manager of the plant and told him the whole thing. He was completely taken aback.'

Surrounded by confused and suspicious workers, Bahadur had one piece of advice for the Chairman of Inchek: 'If you don't make the wage payment on the due date, they will kill you.'

The same day at 11 a.m., Onkar Singh Kanwar's phone rang in his fourth floor office in the Allahabad Bank Building on Parliament Street. It was his father. 'You come down, now!'

When Onkar reached the first floor, Raunaq Singh was far from his jovial self. His mood was dark, not to say bleak.

'Sir, what happened?' Raunaq Singh gave the George Fernandes letter to Onkar. 'This is a blatant political decision,' Onkar told his father. 'It is because of your closeness to Mrs Gandhi.'

Raunaq Singh's involvement in Sanjay Gandhi's Maruti project did not help either. It was not so much that the people's affordable car, had it ever been produced commercially by Gandhi, had incurred such development costs that it would have been beyond the economic means of 80 per cent of the population. It was the fact that the compulsory sterilization programme and his bulldozing of slums in Delhi, both delivered with a combination of arrogance and brute force, had made Sanjay the most hated and feared man in India.

'Cleaning up Delhi improved the city,' Onkar Singh Kanwar reflects. 'But Sanjay Gandhi went about it in completely the wrong way and the sterilization programme was a disaster.'

Mrs Gandhi's close associates, including Raunaq Singh and fellow industrialist Rama Prasad Goenka (Founder of the RPG conglomerate), were now tarred with the same scandal.

'My father was always making pro-Congress statements that were politically ill advised,' Kanwar says. 'My view is that a businessman should never get involved in politics in any way. Apollo was not doing well partly because he was not taking enough of an interest in it, only visiting Kerala twice a year, and now, politically he was on the wrong side.'

◆

Facing the nationalization of Apollo, Raunaq Singh knew he had to move fast. 'The first thing we must do is show that this office is a BST office and has nothing to do with Apollo,' he told Onkar. Straightaway, the five Apollo staff shifted operations out of the Allahabad Bank Building to a small marketing and sales office that Apollo had in Old Delhi.

'Next, we sent staff to the Gazette of India office in Nirman Bhawan in New Delhi, which publishes all official government legal notices, to get a copy of the nationalization order so we could study the detail,' Onkar says. 'It had still not been printed so we told them to grab one as soon as it came off the press.

'While we waited for them to come, we appointed Fali Sam Nariman to file an appeal in the High Court of Delhi to overturn the nationalization order. Nariman is a brilliant lawyer, one of the most distinguished in India. We felt we were in the very best hands. If he could not help us, then no one could.'

Nariman was born in 1929 in Rangoon, Burma, to Parsi parents and began his law practice in Mumbai where he worked in the city's High

Court for over twenty years. He was appointed a Senior Advocate in the Supreme Court of India in 1971, a position he holds to this day. Aged 88, he is at the court every day, while his office at his house in New Delhi is knee deep in legal documents. Back in 1972, he and his wife Bapsi had moved to Delhi when he was appointed the Additional Solicitor General of India. The day after the Emergency was declared, Nariman resigned in protest and returned to private practice.

'As opponents of the Emergency were rounded up, I was so damn scared that I sat down and wrote my will,' says Nariman, who was also an architect of the laws enshrined in the Indian Constitution. He believed that the Gandhis were behaving entirely unconstitutionally. Nariman was not rounded up. 'In fact Mrs Gandhi sent me a very nice letter, reassuring me that I would not be. She did have her lucid moments!'

In the city where Fali Sam Nariman made his name, 'Apollo staff have been forced to quit their plush office in Hoechst House on Nariman Point,' *India Today* reported, 'and shifted to a little godown on Lamington Road known as the "tyre street" of Mumbai'.

Accused by the new government of mismanagement, the Apollo Tyres board, which included Onkar Kanwar's brother-in-law Surinder Kapur, was dissolved and replaced by an Interim Board by order of the Supreme Court of India dated 26 September 1977. Raunaq Singh was still there but as a titular Chairman only. The Interim Board comprised of nominees of the banks, Kerala state government officials and bureaucrats. Raunaq Singh was not going to give up the company without a struggle. He would fight all the way to the Supreme Court if necessary. And nor—as many others were now doing—was he going to shun Mrs Gandhi, who along with Sanjay had been arrested briefly and charged with corruption.

Fali Nariman immediately applied for an interim order restraining the government from taking over Apollo. 'It was not successful. We would have a long fight ahead of us.'

The Janata government was not going to give way. It had already passed orders impounding the passports of Raunaq Singh and twenty-three others, including Sanjay Gandhi and R.K. Dhawan, 'in the interest of the general public'.

six

Man on a mission

In January 1980, Mrs Gandhi was swept back to power on a landslide at the head of a Congress (I) government. The Janata alliance had rapidly become brittle and dysfunctional and state assembly elections held soon after also returned Congress majorities. Sanjay set about appointing loyalists as chief ministers.

The old order seemed to have returned. 'As soon as Mrs Gandhi came back my father, my wife and I went to see her at Safdarjung Road and we had a photograph taken of us with her,' Onkar says. 'Mrs Gandhi was a very savvy and intelligent woman and it was good to see her back; but I thought that increasingly she was being badly advised on a lot of issues.'

Raunaq Singh was again pre-eminent in Delhi and would remain so for another two decades, as Neeraj Kanwar's wife Simran recalls. 'I came out of The Oberoi hotel one day and all the staff were lined up either side, as though a President was coming. No cars were being allowed in or out. I asked why my driver could not be allowed in to pick me and was told: "Mr Raunaq Singh is coming."'

Once on an Air India flight there was the following announcement: 'We have Mr Raunaq Singh on board and today is his birthday and we invite everybody to celebrate.'

As the new decade dawned, Raunaq Singh had got his passport back and traffic cops would always wave his car through the Delhi jams, but he was no closer to recovering Apollo. As the case wound its way up the hierarchy of courts towards the Supreme Court, Onkar Singh Kanwar would go to lobby Mrs Gandhi most days for its return.

Raunaq Singh was so fed up with the interference by government appointees on the Apollo board that he told Onkar: 'Sell the company for 1 rupee. It's losing too much money. Let's wash our hands of it.' The Janata government had not nationalized any of his other enterprises so he would just put Apollo down to a bad deal in a far-off state. He had lost interest. Delhi and northern India was his natural base.

Onkar begged to differ. 'We did not always agree but he would listen to me in those days. I convinced him that I be given one last attempt to turn Apollo around.' After all, he reasoned, his track record in setting up companies was good so he must have the skills to turn one around, even if it was on the verge of being sick.

Raunaq Singh agreed. His son made one stipulation: he wanted to run Apollo on his own with no sibling involvement. Let his brothers run the other Raunaq Group companies. Raunaq Singh agreed willingly. After all, he could not see why his other sons would want to be involved in Apollo. In fact, Narinder Jeet Singh Kanwar had flatly rejected the idea after paying a visit to Perambra. Raunaq Singh was mystified as to why his eldest seemed so keen.

And so in 1980, Onkar Singh Kanwar joined the Apollo board and took over the running of Apollo Tyres, although Raunaq Singh remained its Chairman.

'I told my wife that now I was going to be married to tyres, [and] that I would have to give it a great deal of my time.' Leaving his wife to bring up three small children in Delhi, Onkar Singh Kanwar headed to India's southernmost state and his greatest challenge. 'I had this burning ambition to achieve something on my own, separate from my father, and to be recognized in my own right.'

Taru Kanwar smiles at the recollection knowingly with a shrug. 'In those days, it could take twelve hours to get to Kerala by plane; first an Indian Airlines flight to Mumbai and then transfer to an Avro Turboprop, which would often be grounded due to bad weather, especially during the monsoon.'

For Onkar, nipping home for weekends was not going to be an option. 'He would not come home more than once a month,' Taru says, 'but when he did come, he was very loving to the children.'

'I must give all credit to my wife for bringing up the children so well and supporting me,' Onkar says. 'Without that, I would have worried about her and the children.'

'It helped that the children were in good Delhi schools,' Taru says. Shalini was at Loreto Convent and then the Convent of Jesus and Mary and Raaja and Neeraj were at St Columba's School in Ashok Place. Founded by the Congregation of Christian Brothers in 1941, it stands next to the Sacred Heart Cathedral in the heart of Lutyens New Delhi. Famous alumni who have passed through its red brick cloisters include Nitin Nohria, Dean of Harvard Business School, Shah Rukh Khan (dubbed 'the world's biggest movie star' by the *Los Angeles Times*) and Sanjay Gandhi.

◆

On the evening of 25 June 1980, one million people arrived in Delhi to witness a funeral that shocked the nation. Two days before, Sanjay Gandhi—who had survived an assassination attempt in 1977—had been killed while performing aerobatic stunts over his mother's official residence. Piloting a new Pitts S-2A aircraft belonging to the Delhi Flying Club, he lost control and crashed, dying instantly, as did his passenger, Captain Subhash Saxena. The heir-apparent to the Nehru–Gandhi political dynasty was thirty-three years old. Some speculated that his death was more than an accident. After all, Gandhi had survived three assassination attempts.

The world's press was there for his cremation. 'An estimated million people stood in the sweltering 43-degree celsius heat as Gandhi's body was carried on a flower-bedecked Army truck through the centre of New Delhi to the site where his grandfather, Jawaharlal Nehru, was cremated sixteen years ago,' *The Washington Post* reported. 'It took the cortege two hours to cover the seven miles from the prime minister's house, where the body had lain in state for twenty-four hours, to the cremation site.'

Onkar and his father were not among the 150,000 other guests, VIPs and diplomats who crammed into the Shanti Van cremation site on the west bank of the Yamuna River where Nehru had been cremated. 'It was just too many people,' Onkar says. As for his father, maybe Raunaq Singh just wanted to draw a quiet line under his involvement with the deceased. As Sanjay's brother Rajiv lit the pyre, army helicopters flew in formation overhead and the crowds shouted 'Sanjay Gandhi *amar rahey*! (Sanjay Gandhi is immortal!)'.

Onkar Singh Kanwar's thoughts, however, were preoccupied with a tyre factory in Kerala.

◆

With hindsight, taking on Apollo might be considered foolhardy given the problems Onkar was going to face. 'You can't succeed in business on hindsight,' he says. 'You have to follow your own beliefs and I believed that if I gave Apollo my full attention, then I could transform it.'

When he arrived in Perambra, the plant had a workforce of 650, five trade unions, mostly sponsored by political parties, and was producing thirty-two metric tonnes of tyres per day, way below what it should have been. 'I thought the workers were welcoming me in their own language, which I didn't understand, because they were smiling. The plant manager took me to one side and said, "I apologize for the bad language." They were swearing at me, telling me to go home. They wanted the factory to be nationalized.'

Onkar called together the senior management. 'I told them, I have come here to save this business but I need you to help me do it. I see great potential. We could be doing ten billion rupees. At that time we were doing nothing. I implored them. Let's work as a team. Believe in me and give me a chance.'

Three of them thought he had no chance and asked to be paid off immediately, before the little money Apollo did have ran out completely. 'I did not stand in their way. I needed people who were with me, not passengers.'

The factory was producing 20,000 truck tyres a year under four initial brand names: Rajdhani, a ribbed tyre, Sardar, in a lug pattern, Balwant, which was semi-lug, and Bahadura, a nylon casing, steel-belted truck radial tyre. Apollo had invested in truck radialization, about 25 per cent of its initial budget.

Michelin had invented revolutionary steel-belted radial tyres with their increased life and longer mileage for vehicles in 1948, introducing them to the American market in the 1960s. A decade later, it was still a technological leap too far for Apollo.

'The problem was that tyres were being returned to the plant faster than they were going out,' Kanwar explains. 'The technology General Tire had given us was designed to produce cold compound lighter truck tyres that worked well on smooth American roads in reasonable temperatures and at high speeds. Indian roads were rough; temperatures were high and speeds were low.' Tyre reliability was also compromised by the heavy overloading of Indian trucks—something not permitted in the US or Europe. Indian six-wheelers designed to carry six tonnes routinely carried sixteen and more at low-gear speeds up the mountains, across deserts, down pitted highways and through monsoon storms. The compounds and technical architecture Apollo was employing to make tyres were just not up to the grind and attritional wear of India's roads. They had an unacceptable failure rate and to truckers, 70 per cent of whom were solo driver-operators, time was money. They could not afford to have a truck off the road so they would not buy Apollo's unreliable tyres from the dealers. Instead they were opting in increasing numbers for the Modi N416, a much tougher, heavier rear lug tyre—52 kg compared to Apollo's 49 kg—which had won a 60 per cent share of India's heavy load market.

With a number of key staff deserting Apollo for surer pastures and morale low, Onkar Singh Kanwar was forced to replace most of his senior management. From BST, he brought in K.V. Ramaseshan as Vice President-Operations. Another of his hires, D.V. Kohli, a close friend of Raunaq Singh's, came in as Vice President-Marketing, to which Kanwar quickly added responsibility for manufacturing. With General Tire—which was also giving technology to JK and several other Indian tyre companies—refusing to increase its support for Apollo, it was Kohli who convinced Kanwar that Apollo must develop its own heavier truck tyre with a lug and rib pattern that could match the performance of the Modi N416 and the Ceat Fleet Master, a front rib tyre.

'The technology General Tire had given us was outdated, and I knew from talking to their people that they were going to give us nothing more suited to Indian roads. They were not bothered about tyre function. It was not their job,' Kanwar says.

Some would say and many more would have thought it that a man who knew nothing about tyres was not a good bet for turning around a tyre business. 'Knowing nothing was a big advantage because it meant that I had an uncluttered mind. I was open to doing things a different way.'

As he had done while building BST, Kanwar looked to younger people to help him out in his quest. One of those was thirty-six-year-old Keralite P.K. Mohamed, who lived in Thrissur and had recently married. His wife was a bank manager and they both had strong ties to the area. 'PK' had joined Premier Tyres, also in Kerala, in 1962 as a laboratory chemist and had come to Apollo in 1976. He had gone to General Tire in Akron, Ohio, where he had received extensive training in rubber compounding, fabric dipping, calendering and heat engineering. At that time, there had been no course in tyre and rubber technology in India.

Mohamed, a slightly-built man, has a sense of science and a keen sense of humour. Everything is punctuated with a deep-rooted laugh. 'I liked PK's enthusiasm,' says Kanwar, 'so I promoted him from being manager of compounding to take charge of the technology department.' PK says: 'Apollo had reached the position where the raw material suppliers were refusing to supply, General Tire was refusing to provide any more technology and the dealers had stopped stocking our tyres. And now

Mr Kanwar was asking me as Manager Technology, to identify the weaknesses of Modi's N416 and develop a tyre with a new design concept!'

Kanwar told him, 'Either we sink together or we rise together. The heavy load market is very brand conscious. If we can establish quality, then demand for our tyres will be consistent. It is also a cash-rich market which means Apollo could turn around the money faster than other markets, which is why I have also decided to concentrate solely on truck tyres and cease production of all others.'

Until then Apollo had been producing a range of tyres, for two-wheelers, bullock carts, tractors and trucks.

Mohamed had spotted a major difference between Raunaq Singh and his son. 'Mr Raunaq Singh was very much liked, loved even,' he says, 'but he was not a driver of people. Mr Kanwar can always see what a person is capable of achieving, often before they can see it themselves.'

Kanwar brought in BTech graduates from the new Polymer Science and Rubber Technology course at Kochi University to work with Mohamed. 'What they lacked in experience they more than made up for in enthusiasm.'

While the new team got busy in the lab, P.K. Mohamed headed for the heavy load markets in Kanpur, Udaipur, Indore and Bhilwara to talk to the truckers and study the performance characteristics of the Modi N416. Truckers told him that the Modi tyre was number one. 'It can carry the heaviest load.' By contrast, Apollo's tyres were the butt of jokes among the trucking community and tyre dealers. 'When I asked them what was their second favourite tyre, they replied, Modi N416!'

P.K. Mohamed returned to Perambra from his fact-finding mission. He had identified one major weakness in the N416. 'It was the best, but the lugs (the rubber blocks on the outside of the tyre) would wear off. The N416 had 48 lugs, but when the tyre ran five lugs would chip and wear off, weakening the casing of the tyre and causing tears.'

The race was on—to produce a tyre that would not suffer lug chipping but with the same load capacity or better than the N416.

♦

Meanwhile, several new people were appointed in the marketing department, notably U.S. Oberoi who joined Apollo as General Manager Marketing under D.V. Kohli. He had worked for Premier Tyres, also based in Kerala, and for JK. U.S. Oberoi was not a typical marketing man. 'He was different from the rest,' says Baljeet Ravinder Singh, who is Apollo Tyres' Head of Corporate Affairs and Administration, but was previously Divisional Sales Manager of Premier Tyres. 'A bachelor all his life, he was wedded to his work, and his relationship with dealers was very, very good. In fact, his relationship with most people was very good. He knew how to get the best out of them and to be there for them,' says Baljeet.

Oberoi, whose family had settled in old Gurgaon after Partition, was a thickset man with a physical presence and a frequent smile from behind his full dark beard. He also had a certain style, says Baljeet Ravinder Singh. 'When he was in Lucknow, heading sales in UP for Premier, he would often come to work in a small horse carriage wearing a black turban and, as always, sporting a long black coat so he looked just like the old nawabs, who used to like that kind of carriage.' On other days, he would arrive on a racing bicycle, somewhat differently attired. However, he was most famous in Lucknow and in Delhi for driving a red sports car with the personalized number plate 'USO 1'.

'His energy levels and abilities were commendable,' says A.S. Girish, who is Apollo's Head of Human Resources (HR) but who joined Perambra as Deputy General Manager (HR). 'Oberoi was a multi-tasker for whom no detail was too small.'

He was also immensely loyal. It was not long before Onkar Singh Kanwar realized that Oberoi's talents for getting on with people and getting things done could be put to wider use. Before long, he made him Technical Service Head.

◆

Another pressing item on Onkar Kanwar's lengthy agenda of problems were the rubber merchants of Kerala. 'The whole rubber market was controlled by 15–20 Kochi-based families,' says Salman Mahdi, who today is Managing Director of Deutsche Asset and Wealth Management in London and has advised both Raunaq Singh and Onkar Singh Kanwar over the years. Then, he was a young banker with the American Express International Banking Corporation and had been sent to Kerala to help Onkar's cash flow, by Raunaq Singh, whom he had advised on BST and other projects.

'It was a struggle because these guys wanted cash up front. Apollo, like all the tyre companies, had a very long cycle in terms of working capital.' Profit margins in the tyre business are notoriously small, no more than 4 per cent. 'They needed to buy the rubber, process it, make the tyres, sell them, give credit to dealers, and then recover the money, so it was hugely working capital intensive. Onkar and some other tyre companies asked me if there was a way that we could change this around and have some kind of a financing arrangement where he did not have to pay the cash up front.'

Mahdi took up the challenge. 'I spent a fair amount of time down in Kerala with the rubber merchants and we set up a financing scheme where we said to them you sell the rubber to the tyre company, you draw a 90-or a 100-or a 180-days bill, we as a bank will pay you up front so we discount the bill and we will recover the money from the tyre company. We were comfortable doing that because the tyre companies were large, had big balance sheets and we weren't taking any risk on the actual rubber dealers themselves.'

To achieve this, the rubber dealers became American Express clients. 'I went to them all with account opening forms. They were all either individuals or single-proprietary-type companies, and we asked them on opening their accounts to put in a nominal deposit which is, I guess in today's money about ₹10,000. I remember, one of the rubber merchants—a very humble, sweet guy in his traditional lungi—signing the forms and producing a cheque to open his account. I looked at it and blinked. It was for ₹5 million! He said, "I hope this is enough." You would never know that these people were so wealthy.'

Salman Mahdi noticed the contrasting styles of Raunaq Singh and Onkar Kanwar. 'I first met Mr Raunaq Singh, when I attended one of his big parties, when I was barely out of university, just starting out in banking. The Friends Colony house was lit up so it must have been a birthday party or a wedding anniversary. There were a lot of guests and an amazing atmosphere, good food and drinks, dancing and singing. My father was head of the fertilizer division at the Ministry of Agriculture and was rolling out the entire biogas programme in India, which was a very big project. He had first met Raunaq's younger brother S.S. Kanwar who was equally flamboyant and outgoing and we had all become good family friends.

'Mr Singh welcomed us with that big warm smile, which he wore most of the time. He was very, very effusive and warm, and always put you at your ease. He made you feel special very quickly, whether you were a college student or a minister. He was quite loud, always talking, but equally a good listener with expansive gestures. You certainly knew when Mr Raunaq Singh was in the room!

'Onkar was less flamboyant and much lower key but he was incredibly focused. I loved working with him because he was on a mission. Unlike some Indian entrepreneurs, who talk the talk, he listened to advice. He really wanted to build his business, he was extremely conscious of building a brand and a quality operation. He was very ambitious. Even then, with all the problems he faced, he wanted to grow Apollo into a very big business.'

Another major obstacle that stood in Kanwar's way before he could achieve that was the workforce. On 19 June 1981, Onkar Singh Kanwar faced his first clash. Productivity had dipped again and now the workers wanted more money and to work fewer hours. 'I had reached an agreement with the unions on quality and norms for the output of each machine. I told them that I did not expect them to produce more than what was agreed but I did expect them to meet what we had agreed.'

E.C. Warrier, a thorough, line-by-line accountant, who joined Apollo in December 1975 as Deputy Manager for Accounts and would rise to become General Manager of the accounts department in a thirty-two-year career with the company, remembers Onkar Kanwar being 'very tough but very fair and always calm. He had honoured his side of the bargain when it came to pay; why were they not honouring theirs regarding productivity?'

'I don't negotiate anything without productivity,' Kanwar told the workers. When he would not agree to their demands, they went on strike, in defiance of their unions. Kanwar shut down the plant and locked them out. He knew he had to take a stand. The lockout would last six months.

Raunaq Singh was threatening the workers by offering to donate the Perambra plant to the local gurudwara (Sikh temple). Onkar took a different tack. 'I talked to the workers and emphasized that I was trying to turn around the factory for them. "We are doing this for you; this is *your* company and whatever money we make will be distributed to you before it goes to any shareholder. But first, we have to make money and we can do that by working hard together." I hoped they would see reason.'

To make sure, Kanwar visited the workers' homes and talked to their families. 'I went with my general manager and factory works manager. The wives knew that if their husbands were always on strike they would not be paid and they and their families would not eat.'

To improve the skill levels of the workforce, he sent his HR people to technical colleges. 'Find me guys whose parents have stable jobs such as librarians, stationmasters or educationists because it is likely they will be stable and ambitious too. We began to pick up young people with skills in engineering, and in electronics and industrial costing, or those training to be chartered accountants. For the long-term health of Apollo, it was vital to build a better blend of skills and a different mentality.'

That mentality, to move Apollo away from a them-and-us company to being one company belonging to all those involved in it, was to become increasingly a signature guiding principle for everything Onkar Singh Kanwar would go on to achieve. After six months of inactivity and unfulfilled orders, the Perambra plant finally reopened. 'I was able to make a good agreement with the workers to ensure that from now on everything would be linked to productivity.'

◆

When he was at the Perambra plant, Onkar Singh Kanwar always stayed at the guest house his father had built in the grounds next to the factory's admin block. 'I stayed there because it was cheaper than staying in a hotel and being right by the plant meant that I could make the best use of my time. I convinced visitors from General Tire to stay there too rather than in Kochi, which was two hours away. I didn't see why I should be paying them for four hours a day to sit in the back of a car!'

The guest house, set in pretty landscaped gardens, has fourteen rooms on the first floor that open on to a balcony walkway that skirts the entire building. From the moment he checked into the Chairman's Suite, Onkar Kanwar was looked after by T.V. Poly, who had joined Apollo as the guest house cook in June 1980. Poly soon discovered that Mr Kanwar is a man of habit, who likes everything done just so and is very particular about his diet.

'He would wake at 6.30 a.m. and I would give him a glass of lukewarm water with a little salt alongside for gargling and also a glass of chilled water for drinking,' Poly says. 'I would take away his shoes for polishing and lay out his clothes for the day. At 8.30 a.m., he would take a breakfast of fresh orange juice, fresh papaya and pineapple cut into small pieces to be eaten with a fork and one idli and one glass of sweet lassi. Lunch would be light Kerala dishes of dal, salad, ginger pickle, all made in the kitchen, and fish steaks, which he very much enjoys. He likes very fresh, healthy food and small amounts.' Dinner would be similarly light. 'Maybe lobster prepared with masala, tamarind, onion and garlic, spicy.' This would be followed by one peg of Johnny Walker Black Label, or Chivas Regal—'lots of ice and no water'—and into bed by 9.30 p.m. After Mr Kanwar had gone to bed, Poly would prepare the 8-metre-long turban fabric, for tying the next day.

Poly was promoted to guest house supervisor and worked there until he took an early retirement in 1999 to set up a small business dealing in spices. Even though he is no longer with Apollo, whenever Mr Kanwar visits Perambra a call is put through to T.V. Poly to come back and cook lunch and dinner and look after him. 'Over the years, I could tell what Mr Kanwar would like to eat just by looking at him.'

In return Mr Kanwar knows that when he visits, everything in the guest house will be just so.

◆

By 1982, P.K. Mohamed and his small team of six chemists and engineers had perfected a new recipe of their own. It had numerous ingredients which when put together created a new heavy load-bearing rear truck tyre. Its name was Hercules.

'We had studied the N416 in detail, and we believed that with Hercules we had achieved Modi-fication,' Mohamed joked.

Success was not instant. 'On the first 3,000 Hercules tyres produced there was a 20 per cent failure rate,' P.K. Mohamed says. 'Within three years, we had perfected the tyre and it had a failure rate of just 3 per cent, which meant it was seen by the trucking community as a very reliable tyre.'

Hercules was hauling Apollo out of the mire. In 1977, Apollo's total sales had been languishing at ₹32.5 million. By financial year 1982–83, they had grown to ₹576 million based on Onkar Singh Kanwar's decision to focus on truck tyres alone and the ability of P.K. Mohamed's team to perfect a product that found increasing favour in the market.

The workforce too was hitting its production targets. However, when Kanwar presented the workers with a specially commissioned commemorative silver plaque to mark their achievement, he did not get the response he had expected. 'We had five unions then, and when we handed it out they refused to accept it.' Kanwar called a meeting and took a firm line. 'If you invited me to your daughter's wedding and I brought a gift would you not accept it and would you throw me out?' The workers shuffled uneasily. 'This is not part of a wage agreement. I am giving this on my own in recognition of your great efforts.' They apologized and accepted it.

Cynics might suggest that people in Kerala generally prefer gold to silver.

◆

Apollo Tyres was on the up. 'When I came in, the company was losing ₹40 million. In my second year, we made a profit of ₹60 million,' says Onkar Kanwar. Although some went into the Raunaq Group kitty, 'I tried to put as much money as I could back into Apollo, so I could develop more production and increase the returns. Profits went up to ₹150 million.'

Apollo had indeed turned a corner but the losses prior to his taking the reins were still dragging at the company like a millstone. 'We were dealing with eight banks, of which the Punjab National Bank was the lead, and four investment institutions.' Kanwar was desperate to reschedule some of the loans and win breathing space so Apollo could really move on to challenge Modi, JK and the rest with more than one type of tyre.

The lead institution backing Apollo was the government–owned IDBI, India's principal financial institution for providing credit and other facilities for developing industries. In terms of development funding, IDBI is the tenth largest bank in the world.

In 1982, Kanwar submitted a rehabilitation proposal. Raunaq Singh, who was on good terms with the IDBI Chairman, started lobbying him to have the proposal ratified, and hopefully approved, at the very next monthly board meeting. Without it Apollo was facing another crisis. It was still hobbled by early losses of ₹280 million against an initial share capital of ₹80 million.

They failed to take into account IDBI's Deputy Chairman, M.R.B. Punja. Punja was an old-style banker. Tall, thin and with a hawkish eye, he was thorough and steadfast and willing to back companies only if they showed significant evidence of understanding their strengths and their weaknesses.

'I asked my general manager to take an initial look at the Apollo plan and to get it back to me as soon as possible with his comments and suggestions,' Punja recalls. 'My Chairman had told me that time was of the essence. The general manager kept postponing and I did not get it back until two days before the next board meeting.'

As he was busy with daytime meetings with banks and businesses, Punja took the Apollo financial rehabilitation plan home to read. 'As I went through the cash flows, I was astonished to see that my general manager had made no comments in the margins at all, which is what he usually did. He had not even shifted a full stop or a comma.'

Punja was suspicious. 'When I went through it I found it was not good. A good paper should identify and analyse problems and suggest solutions. This was way below standard. I had no choice but to put the plan aside and send it up to the next board meeting the following month, by which time I would have improved it.'

The next thing Punja knew was he was summoned to the IDBI Chairman's office. 'He told me that Mr Raunaq Singh had come to see him [the Chairman] and formally complained about my professional competence. Mr Raunaq Singh was extremely angry. My Chairman demanded to know what was going on,' recalls Punja.

Punja remembers telling the Chairman, 'My general manager has not even understood what is going wrong in Apollo because he has not applied his mind to it; he has not found a solution. A month's delay will help us decide how best to help Mr Raunaq Singh.'

That diplomatic answer bought Punja some time. After all, he liked to be able to help turn companies around to grow and succeed, it was in India's interest, but he was not in the habit of gambling on blank cheques.

After the next IDBI board meeting, Punja invited Raunaq Singh and Onkar Singh Kanwar to his office in IDBI Tower, which stands in the World Trade Centre on Cuffe Parade in Mumbai.

'We are prepared to give you a long holiday for repayment, interest concessions and to put in additional funds on condition that Apollo sets up a proper board with technical and financial competence,' Punja told them.

All accusations of incompetence were forgotten as far as Raunaq Singh was concerned. The beaming smile was back in full evidence. Punja had revised their rehabilitation plan so it was logical, achievable and economically viable.

He had also spotted another weakness. 'Apollo is making money now and could make a great deal more but you are setting up other projects at a high cost, all financed by Apollo and high borrowing. You must clean up your balance sheet.' As Apollo went into profit some of Raunaq Singh's other enterprises were beginning to show signs of wobble and were heading the other way. Punja did not want to see Apollo milked like a cash cow.

Singh was not listening to Punja, but his son was. 'I was seeing the future and that was to focus solely on doing one thing not just well, but to be the best. Increasingly the traditional Indian conglomerate model put in place by promoter-led companies was out of step with the rest of the world.'

Obviously M.R.B. Punja was of the same opinion. He had seen potential in Apollo and a spark and determination in Onkar Singh Kanwar. 'In fact, Mr Punja was giving us more than we had asked for,' says Kanwar.

'However,' added Punja in his measured tones, 'you should not have gone above my head to my Chairman and questioned my competence. It was disrespectful and it was unprofessional.' He stared at them through his trademark black spectacles and then he cleared his throat. The meeting was at an end.

◆

On 5 March 1982 came the news that Onkar Singh Kanwar had craved. The Delhi High Court had ruled that in the case of *Apollo Tyres Ltd and others* vs. *Union of India and others*, after a painstaking battle up every rung of the legal ladder led by Fali Sam Nariman, the 'board of directors of Apollo be reconstituted in accordance with the Articles of Association of the Company and the management of Apollo restored in favour of Apollo management'.

Fali Nariman says: 'It was R.K. Dhawan who played the winning hand in getting the company back from government control.' Dhawan insists that it was Nariman's legal skills alone that won the day, although he does admit, 'one of Mrs Gandhi's priorities when she returned to power was to ensure that Mr Raunaq Singh regained the rightful ownership of his company'.

'Mr Dhawan is very kind to credit me,' says Nariman with a smile, 'but I do remember that Raunaq Singh, whom I had got to know well during this episode, was fond of me, telling me, "You know, Fali, if I had to ditch you for R.K. Dhawan, I would willingly ditch you!" He was only half joking.'

◆

'When the company was handed back to the family, it was a basket case,' says Vinayak Chatterjee. 'It had unionized labour, it had been run by government non-entities, there was no cash flow, equity written off five times, and no management. I am sure that in Delhi the advice that industrialist friends gave Raunaq Singh and Onkar was not to pick it up again. There was a huge degree of scepticism as to whether Apollo could be turned around. Here was a north Indian family based in Delhi with its political networks there, and here was this plant in the backwaters of Kerala, which was far, far away. People said to me that Onkar's decision to try and save Apollo was foolhardy.'

Onkar Singh Kanwar was not going to throw in the towel. With meddlesome government appointees gone, he was now in a position to fulfil Punja's condition and improve the competence of the Apollo board. He set about finding those with broader experience of industry and commerce. One of them was in fact a returning director, his brother-in-law and by now a very close friend, Surinder Kapur.

Every month Kanwar travelled to Mumbai to meet and give presentations on Apollo's progress to the eight banks and the four institutional lenders. Things were improving but not as fast as he would have liked. In April 1983, there had been a second lockout at Perambra following an unlawful strike by finished goods staff and a stoppage in the dispatch department. It had lasted only five days compared to the six-month lockout of 1981, but it did nothing for Apollo's cash flow or its reputation with dealers as a reliable supplier.

Once more Kanwar sought help from Punja, who by now was the Chairman of IDBI.

'As Chairman, I did not have to be so diplomatic, so I decided to give Onkar a little piece of my mind. I told him, "I have given you a package and you are to work to the last word of it and follow the spirit behind it. You cannot take it easy!"' says Punja.

'And with that,' Kanwar adds, 'Mr Punja threw me out of his office!'

seven

Faith, family and fear on the streets

Onkar Singh Kanwar is a religious man; a man of such strong faith, he has visited all the most important Sikh gurudwaras, or houses of worship, many of which are now in the Punjab of Pakistan. When he had worked in his father's office in Parliament Street, he would attend Gurudwara Bangla Sahib on Ashoka Road near Connaught Place, every day. Mrs Kanwar's faith is equally strong.

Pristine white and set across several acres, it is famous for its golden domes, a tall saffron flagpole and its association with Guru Har Krishan, the eighth of the ten Sikh gurus, who died there aged just eight. Gurudwara Bangla Sahib is Delhi's most prominent gurudwara and was opened in 1783. Like all gurudwaras, it is built around a large courtyard, which leads to the main hall where musicians perform all day and visitors approach the holy book, the Guru Granth Sahib, to kneel and offer prayers. The Guru Granth Sahib is given exactly the same respect as a living Guru. During the day, the Guru Granth Sahib is read and the Granthi (the appointed reader of the scripture) waves a special fan, called a chauri, over the pages. At night the Guru Granth Sahib is put to bed. Adjacent is a large holy lake, another feature common to all gurudwaras, and a place of outdoor contemplation.

Gurudwara Bangla Sahib, as much a peaceful sanctuary as a place of prayer and service, was where Onkar Kanwar could sit quietly and gather his thoughts. It offered the opportunity in a busy business life to reflect on the tenets of Sikhism: to live honestly and to work hard, to serve others, to treat everyone equally and to be generous to the less fortunate. Sikhism, which does not accept pessimism, but advocates an ideology of optimism and hope, stresses the importance of performing good actions rather than merely carrying out rituals. In Sikhism, there are religious ceremonies and the path to spiritual wisdom is taught but Sikhs worship a God that has no physical form so you will not find in a gurudwara any statues, religious pictures, idols, incense, candles or bells.

All functions in a gurudwara, from cleaning and manning the counter for the visitors' shoes to cooking and serving food, are performed by volunteers, which is why every inch of the place is spotless and cared for.

Every day in every gurudwara around the world, three meals of rice, vegetable, dal and roti are served free to all visitors, Sikh or non-Sikh, from a communal kitchen known as a *langar*. Only vegetarian food is served so those of all dietary persuasions can eat together as equals.

At the Sikhs' most sacred gurudwara, the Golden Temple in Amritsar, in the state of Punjab some 100,000 people sit down to eat every day and not one of them needs to pay.

But on 6 June 1984, the Golden Temple became synonymous around the world with destruction and death. As Sir Mark Tully and Satish Jacob describe in their book *Mrs Gandhi's Last Battle*, 'at about 7.30 a.m. in the morning, one of the most extraordinary battles in military history came to a head when Indian Army tanks pounded the temporal head of the Sikh religion, the Akal Takht, with 105 mm high-explosive squash head shells'.

The Akal Takht is a five-storey structure that stands opposite the Golden Temple and had been occupied by a militant fundamentalist group calling for the creation of a Sikh homeland, Khalistan. Its leader was a rabid but charismatic thirty-seven-year-old preacher called Sant Jarnail Singh Bhindranwale. Ironically, Bhindranwale owed his early rise to prominence in part to the active encouragement of Sanjay Gandhi, who had set out to destroy political opponents in the Punjabi Akali Dal party, which had been campaigning peaceably for more state autonomy.

Bhindranwale and his followers, who had carried out a spree of murders and threatened to disrupt food supply in Punjab, had dug in behind heavy fortifications at the Golden Temple complex until they had their demands met. They were militarily well advised and heavily armed with machine guns. Besieged by five infantry battalions, six tanks and paramilitary police, the stand-off continued. 'Mrs Gandhi was assured by the chief of the army that they would flush out the extremists and that the Akal Takht would not be damaged,' says R.K. Dhawan. Mrs Gandhi seemed wracked with indecision. Raunaq Singh and other prominent Sikhs in Delhi urged her not to put the troops into the Golden Temple complex.

'Every other initiative had failed and she was left with no other option,' R.K. Dhawan insists. Mrs Gandhi went on national radio. Operation Blue Star began. After nine hours it was over. The Akal Takht was blown apart and caught fire. Forty-two bodies were brought out including that of Bhindranwale and the Indian Army suffered more than 300 casualties in fierce fighting.

More than three decades later, Operation Blue Star remains highly controversial. 'It is the gravest mistake when any government puts troops into a place of worship,' Onkar Singh Kanwar reflects. 'After Operation Blue Star, we Sikhs all feared what would happen next.'

The destruction at the Golden Temple had caused outrage among Sikhs around the world, but especially in India. Even for her Sikh supporters and admirers, like Raunaq Singh, Mrs Gandhi seemed to have lost the ability to govern.

Equally etched into the recent history of India and the history of the Kanwar family are the events of 31 October 1984. Five months after Operation Blue Star, Mrs Gandhi was walking with R.K. Dhawan across the gardens from 1 Safdarjung Road on her way to her office on Akbar Road to be interviewed by the British actor Peter Ustinov for a documentary he was filming for Irish television. It was 9.20 a.m. Two Sikh bodyguards Satwant Singh and Beant Singh stepped into her path. Beant Singh fired three rounds into the Prime Minister with his sidearm. Once she had fallen, Satwant Singh unleashed thirty rounds from his sten gun into her.

Today, a crystal pathway marks the route she took across the garden with a glass-covered gap indicating the spot where she died. It is a popular and sobering tourist attraction where visitors are greeted with words from her very last, and prophetic, speech given the day before she died in Bhubaneswar, Orissa (now Odisha). 'I am here today, I may not be here tomorrow. But the responsibility to look after national interest is on the shoulders of every citizen of India. Nobody knows how many attempts have been made to shoot me; lathis have been used to beat me. I do not care whether I live or die. I have lived a long life and I am proud that I spent the whole of my life in the service of my people. I am only proud of this and nothing else.'

Thirteen-year-old Neeraj Kanwar was a student at St Columba's as was his elder brother Raaja. 'We had a public address system and the headmaster came on and said the school is closed because the Prime Minister has been assassinated,' Neeraj says. 'It was as blunt as that and deeply shocking. Before that announcement security personnel had come to collect fourteen-year-old Rahul Gandhi, who was a student there, and visited our neighbouring school the Convent of Jesus and Mary where his sister, Priyanka, then twelve years old, was a student. Once they had been taken to safety we were all allowed to go home. Next morning the riots started.'

Hindu mobs were roaming the streets of the capital attacking and killing Sikhs. 'We had rented a house in Anand Niketan while my current house in Shanti Niketan was being built,' Onkar explains. 'The morning the riots began we were having breakfast when the phone rang. The caller said, "We know where you live and we are going to burn down both your houses."'

Onkar called one of his closest friends, Gyan Chand Burman, who was Vice Chairman and Managing Director of Dabur, India's largest manufacturer of Ayurvedic medicines and related products, and lived close to the Kanwars. He set out immediately in his car. The family packed up and minutes later Onkar, Mrs Kanwar and Shalini, carrying not more than a change of clothes, were scooped up by Burman and driven away.

'There was not enough room for all of us in the car, so Raaja and I started walking, until the car returned to pick us up,' Neeraj says. 'Because we did not wear turbans, we were not as vulnerable as our father. Everywhere you looked you could see smoke. It was as though Delhi was on fire. It was incredibly scary. The rioters did come to our house but the staff told them that it belonged to the American Embassy and they went away.'

Mrs Kanwar could not breathe easily until all her children were safely at the Burmans' guest house. 'That night we went up on to the terrace and all you could see was fires.'

'I had never seen Onkar looking so depressed and scared,' says G.C. Burman's wife Ashi. The Burmans and the Kanwars had known each other since 1975, after the Burmans had moved from Kolkata to Delhi to open a new Dabur factory. 'My husband and Onkar connected immediately. They were both starting out and came from family businesses so they had a lot in common and faced very similar problems as they tried to professionalize their companies.' Dabur had been started in 1884 by Gyan Burman's great-grandfather S.K. Burman, a doctor from West Bengal. 'Our two children were also very close to Onkar and Taru's children,' says Ashi Burman. 'Our son, Amit, who owns the Lite Bite restaurant chain, is still one of Neeraj's best friends.' Today, the two of them together own a famous Italian restaurant in London called Scalini.

As the Kanwars took shelter in the Burmans' guest house, violent anti-Sikh riots broke out and spread across the country. But Delhi was the epicentre and more than 2,000 Sikhs were slaughtered by marauding gangs. Many Sikhs removed their turbans, cut their hair and shaved off their beards so they would not be targeted.

Fali Nariman and a small group of senior lawyers, wearing their white barristers' neckbands and black coats, went out on the streets of Delhi led by Vithal Mahadeo Tarkunde, the prominent Indian Supreme Court lawyer. A former Mumbai High Court judge, Tarkunde was known as the father of the civil liberties movement. 'We went all over the city and what we saw then remains horrific to this day,' Nariman says. 'There were

Sikhs with their beards cut, others with their throats cut, just lying there and the police were looking the other way.'

The violence took Onkar back to the bloody atrocities surrounding Partition but this time it was Hindus attacking Sikhs.

Onkar and his family were relatively safe being sheltered in a Hindu household but after two days with the Burmans, Onkar called another good friend, Y.C. 'Yogi' Deveshwar. Today, Deveshwar is Chairman of ITC Limited but in 1984, he had just been appointed as a director on the board. ITC owned the Maurya Sheraton Hotel on Sardar Patel Marg in the Diplomatic Enclave and Deveshwar instructed that a Sheraton air flight catering van be sent to collect the Kanwars and to bring them to the hotel. 'We helped rescue a lot of Sikhs that way,' he explains. 'Hotel catering vans were a regular fixture on the streets of Delhi and so were less likely to attract attention.'

'Normally the journey would take ten minutes, but there were still mobs on the streets killing people and we had to take the route carefully,' Neeraj remembers. Although Onkar was hidden from view in the back of the van, it did not stop it being the most perilous journey he had made since leaving Lahore for India, as a child. And now, the city that had given sanctuary to thousands of Sikhs had turned its wrath on them.

'When I was studying in the US, wearing a turban was an advantage; it made you stand out for the right reasons. Now, after the assassination of Mrs Gandhi, it was like wearing a death sentence. The mobs were going though all the areas of Delhi and marking Sikh houses, which they burned to the ground or dragged out the occupants and killed them.'

'It took us an hour to reach the Sheraton,' Neeraj says. 'We drove straight into the hotel without stopping at security and down into the basement where we were met and guided through the areas of the hotel that guests never see and went up to the room. We were to stay for ten days. Nobody would have known we were there.'

Onkar Kanwar was very concerned for his father's safety. 'The railway line passed right behind his house and gangs were jumping off the trains as they passed through Friends Colony to start more riots.' Everybody knew where Mr Raunaq Singh lived. 'I called the manager of The Oberoi hotel, which was closer to my father's house, and asked him to send a catering van to rescue him.' Once he knew that Raunaq Singh was safe in the Oberoi, Onkar could set up his office in a suite at the Maurya Sheraton Hotel and started to conduct meetings from there.

After the assassination, Taru Kanwar took her three children to Teen Murti House, once Nehru's residence and now a museum, where Mrs Gandhi was lying in state. It would have been too dangerous for Onkar to venture out, even though the capital was crawling with troops and police.

'We wanted to pay our respects,' Neeraj says. 'Seeing Mrs Gandhi lying there was shocking and depressing. I have never forgotten her face. We were all in tears because it was so emotional.'

Raunaq Singh led a delegation of leading Sikhs to meet the new Prime Minister Rajiv Gandhi, who had been sworn in immediately after his mother's death. 'They implored him to do all he could to protect the Sikh community from greater bloodshed,' says R.K. Dhawan, who even now 'shudders to think of the day that Mrs Gandhi died. That scene comes to my eyes every day of my life.'

Mrs Gandhi was cremated on 3 November at the Shakti Sthal memorial ground near Raj Ghat, the memorial to Mahatma Gandhi, her pyre lit by her only surviving son, Rajiv. Troops restored order to Delhi and after a 15-day shutdown, the city returned slowly to normality. It was now school holidays and Taru Kanwar took her three children to Hong Kong for three weeks where they stayed with her brother Jot Kapoor, who was running the family textile trading business there, and his wife Pamela.

'They were so thankful for a bit of normality,' Pamela says. 'Our children, Rajnish, Tarun and Taniya had grown up with Shalini, Raaja and Neeraj, spending vacations together and so they played together, went shopping and did all the things they had always done. It was very important to Onkar and Taru that their children did not suffer from such traumatic events.'

Back in Delhi Onkar returned to the more humdrum challenges facing Apollo Tyres. In fact he had only missed a couple of days' work in spite of the violence on the capital's streets, but he could not help but reflect. 'What had happened at the Golden Temple, the assassination of Mrs Gandhi, and the killings that followed was a tragedy because historically Sikhs and Hindus had been so intertwined that it was not unusual in a Punjabi Hindu family to find the first son being brought up as a turbaned fellow.

'It took months for things to return to normal. It had been terrifying but our Sikh beliefs got us through. As religious people, we had to forgive and to forget and move on, otherwise it could have become a very big issue. Tolerance returned in place of madness.'

eight

Tyre industry in transition

T he 1980s was the decade when the tyre industry went global in response to technological advances and market changes. When it came to technological innovation, French tyre maker Michelin, based in Clermont-Ferrand in central France, led the way. To Onkar Singh Kanwar, they were the gold standard, the Rolls-Royce of tyres.

Back in the late Sixties, Michelin had introduced radial tyres to the American market. The major US manufacturers had not responded well and it lost a significant market share. So much so that Firestone, once judged the best managed and most innovative of the US companies, which also operated plants in Spain, France, Italy, Portugal, Argentina, Brazil and Venezuela, had been swallowed up by Japanese company Bridgestone on 17 March 1988. Tokyo-based Bridgestone was by now the world's third largest tyre company after Goodyear and Michelin.

As reported by the *New York Times-Business Day*: 'In a stunning move intended to shut out the unsolicited intentions of Pirelli S.P.A., [then the world's seventh biggest player] the Firestone Tire and Rubber Company agreed last night to be acquired by the Bridgestone Corporation of Japan for $80 a share, or $2.6 billion. The new agreement was expanded to also give Bridgestone control of Firestone's domestic network of 1,500 automobile service centres, where its tires are sold.'

That Bridgestone had agreed to pay 38 per cent more than Pirelli for Firestone emphasized just how eager the two rivals were to win a significant presence in the United States, which accounted for 45 per cent of the world tyre market. Now, only Goodyear of the five biggest American tyre companies remained independent.

In a research paper, Professor Donald N. Sull of the Harvard Business School summed up this major tremor in the tyre industry. 'Firestone's historical excellence and disastrous response to global competition and technological innovation posed a paradox for industry observers: Why had the industry's best managed company turned in the worst performance in a weak field? Close analysis reveals that Firestone failed not despite, but because of its historical success. Firestone's reliance on managers' existing strategic frames and values and the company's processes proved counterproductive in a changing competitive environment.' Firestone had become mired in 'business as usual' and paid the price of standing still.

The demise of Firestone as a proud independent company had shown how easy it was to slip from innovation to inertia. It was a lesson not lost on Onkar Singh Kanwar.

Apollo felt the force of change in October 1987, when Germany's Hanover-based Continental AG, the second largest European tyre producer, acquired General Tire. Explaining Continental's strategy, its then Chairman Helmut Werner said, 'The acquisition will provide us with a sound and strong presence in the world's largest tyre market. This step is of vital strategic importance to us and will provide Continental with an opportunity to expand worldwide.'

Onkar was not so sure and had already sounded out alternative collaborators to General Tire prior to Continental's acquisition. 'I had become very interested in Cooper Tire in America.'

The Cooper Tire & Rubber Company, founded in Akron in 1914, and now headquartered in Findlay, Ohio, was among the top ten tyre companies of the world. In 1983, it had joined the Fortune 500 as one of America's largest industrial companies. Producing replacement tyres for most markets, Cooper had been listed on the New York Stock Exchange since 1960.

'It had an excellent technical design department and a very healthy balance sheet,' Kanwar says. 'We were just ₹3 billion but I sought an appointment with the Cooper Chairman. He agreed to see me. I told him, "I want to buy your collaboration because I am not happy with General."

'I explained my vision for Apollo. He looked at me and said, "Who are you?"'

'Onkar Kanwar—Apollo Tyres.

'"Apollo Tyres? Big company! Never heard of it," he said.'

That was the end of that.

◆

In India, Apollo was making strides. By 1986, Hercules had replaced the Modi N416 as market leader. It was refined, improved and relaunched as the Hercules Loadstar in 1991.

In 1986, Raunaq Singh had moved out of the old grey house in Friends Colony, where his first wife remained, and moved himself and his second wife into a superior house in the grounds, which Onkar had built for him. Gleaming white and Lutyensesque, its front door opened on to a big lobby on the ground floor with an impressive central spiral staircase going up to the first floor. On one side of the lobby was a drawing room and on the other a waiting area and Raunaq Singh's office, where he would greet his many visitors. Baljeet Ravinder Singh remembers having a meeting in Raunaq Singh's office when he was the Divisional Sales Manager of Premier Tyres. 'His office was very nicely done. Raunaq Singh was a man of taste.' It was the first time that Baljeet met Onkar Kanwar, who was to become his boss one day. 'Mr Kanwar came out with a tray of cold drinks.'

However, Onkar was showing increasing independence from his father. He had opened an office for Apollo at Nehru Place, a large new commercial, financial and business hub in south Delhi next to the Outer Ring Road, which had been developed in the early 1980s to rival Connaught Place. It comprised high-rise towers, four-storey blocks, large pedestrian courtyards and underground parking.

But as always with Apollo in those days, it was a case of two steps forward and one back. The Perambra plant was once again plagued by strikes. In 1985, a third lockout lasting two months from 14 October to 10 December was imposed following an illegal strike. Minimum production levels had not been achieved and so Kanwar had cut salaries. The unions had gheraoed and assaulted senior management. In December 1989, there was a further lockout following low productivity, indiscipline and wilful damage to machinery. It lasted until 15 January 1990.

Onkar Singh Kanwar refused to see Apollo hobbled by strikes and lockouts. 'I decided that I would open a second factory in another state. Being able to manufacture in a second plant would give me the scope to carry on production and might concentrate minds in Perambra. Apollo could not be held to ransom by unions.'

Prevented from building a new plant in Kerala by the MRTP Act, he went looking for possibilities in Bengal, Maharashtra, Rajasthan, Haryana and UP. However, every state in India already had a tyre factory operated by Apollo's rivals. Except one! That state was Gujarat.

'There was already a licence issued fourteen years previously by the Government of India to the Government of Gujarat to set up a factory in a joint sector (state-private) venture. This licence had been given to Nirlon, which had become sick in 1988. They were making tyre cord, which had always been in short supply. Nirlon was now under the Board for Industrial and Financial Reconstruction [BIFR], which was responsible for trying to rehabilitate sick companies. So I went and met some of its bureaucrats.

'I suggested to them that if I paid Nirlon's outstanding income tax, could I take over the licence?' BIFR agreed but Kanwar would have to strike a deal with the Income Tax Department. 'I sent my Chief Financial Officer [CFO] to talk to the tax department and not to come back until he had done a deal. I told him to pay the money and get the licence transferred into our name. No under-the-table payments, only a straight cheque.

'He called me and said that the outstanding tax was ₹40 million, but the tax department wanted fifty. I said, "Pay it." It was a major decision.'

Although Kanwar thought the way ahead was now clear, another problem reared its head. 'The Government of Gujarat told me they didn't have the money to create a joint venture with Apollo and that I must create another company through which I would build a factory and that they would reimburse by way of dividends. I told them that this was nonsense, not economically viable. On top of that my technology agreement with General Tire and now Continental allowed me to put up as many factories as I liked for a 3 per cent royalty. If I set up a new company I would have to pay a higher royalty for a whole new set of technology agreements.'

Kanwar went back to Delhi and lobbied the Joint Secretary for industrial development at the industry department. 'Madam, this licence has been issued and has been languishing for the last fourteen years,' he told her. 'All I want is the licence, nothing else. I want no government money. I just want to build a factory.'

'Young man, it can't be done. Don't you understand that the stated policy of the Government of India is that it has to be a joint sector project?'

'But the Government of Gujarat doesn't have any money. So what do you want me to do?'

Onkar Kanwar's next port of call was the office of Jalagam Vengala Rao, who was Union Minister of Industry under Rajiv Gandhi and who had earlier been Chief Minister of Andhra Pradesh. Tall and simply dressed in a white dhoti, he heard Kanwar out.

'Everyone tells me it can't be done. That I have to do a joint venture with a state that does not have any money.'

Vengala Rao replied, 'Who is the Minister?'

Kanwar was perplexed. 'Sir, you are the Minister.'

'Well, have you brought any letter of representation with you?'

Kanwar has always been quick on his feet. 'Yes, sir.' He gave Vengala Rao the recommendation that stated Apollo should get a sole licence because it had the resources and technology to build a tyre factory in Gujarat.

The Minister, who also ruled on monopoly issues, reviewed the document and said, 'Okay, fine.'

'Sir, when should I check with you?'

'You will not check with me.'

Vengala Rao looked at his diary. 'A licence will be delivered to your office in three days. You don't have to see anyone else.'

Sure enough, a licence for Apollo to build a plant in Gujarat arrived at Kanwar's office at Nehru Place office three days later. 'I was shocked. I had never met anybody as decisive as that in the government before. In those days people like Vengala Rao were not appreciated, but he was a brilliant fellow.'

Kanwar returned to the Minister to thank him.

'Sir, can I do anything to help you?'

Vengala Rao smiled and said, 'Can you get me elected? What do you think?'

'Sorry, Sir, I cannot do that.'

Vengala Rao looked at him, amused.

Kanwar chanced his arm with another question. 'Can you give me a date for laying the foundation stone for the new factory?'

Vengala Rao glanced once more at his diary and pointed out to him. 'This is the date that I can give you.'

A jubilant Onkar Kanwar called U.S. Oberoi and asked him to go to Gujarat and find some land to build Apollo's new plant. 'It should not be in some remote area but close to a city, where officers and employees would want to live.'

◆

In 1988, Onkar Singh Kanwar became sole Managing Director as well as Deputy Chairman of Apollo Tyres. The turnover of the company, which had been a meagre ₹800 million in 1984–85, was beginning to rise and Kanwar was also improving the professionalism of his board, which now had a new member, M.R.B. Punja, who had left IDBI after his stint as Chairman. He had gracefully accepted Apollo's offer to serve, while adding, 'I cannot have been so incompetent after all!' The board was also assisted ably by its secretary P.N. Wahal. He was a brilliant chartered accountant, a 'topper' of his university, and had been hired by Raunaq Singh to work at Bharat Steel Tubes in 1973.

Raunaq Singh remained the Chairman of Apollo but he seemed to be losing interest in tyres. His burgeoning multifarious Raunaq Group empire now included Raunaq Aker Drilling Ltd, a technical collaboration with Aker Drilling A/S Norway, which would undertake onshore and offshore drilling and related activities in India. Other joint ventures and Memorandums of Understanding (MoUs) he initiated included a silicon project, cotton yarn project, pig iron and coke project, ceramic tiles project and a Gujarat Power Corporation Ltd. project. He announced that he was exploring a joint sector project with the Punjab Agro Industries Corporation to build a ₹4.5 billion printing-and-writing-paper-cum-sugar mill in Amritsar District. He even contemplated going into brewing. When somebody questioned the wisdom of that, the irrepressible Singh replied, 'With my name on it, Raunaq Beer will be a big seller.'

The problem was that most of Raunaq Singh's enterprises were not performing well at all and in 1988, Bharat Steel Tubes, the flagship of his empire, and once only second to Tata in its field, was declared 'sick' under the Sick Industrial Companies (Special Provisions) Act (SICA), which had been brought in three years earlier to deal with the issue of rampant industrial bankruptcy in India.

India's domestic steel industry was running short of supply and a large quantity of steel was being imported by industries against credit. As a result, the entire Indian steel industry was forced to offload finished goods at low margins in order to reduce raw material inventories. Moreover, as domestic demand was also low, the industry as a whole suffered in terms of profitability and operations. The BST management was forced to stop operations due to acute liquidity problems.

Raunaq Singh remained defiant, as Salman Mahdi recalls. 'When I visited him at his office he tore off his jacket and started pulling at his shirt, saying, "I will lose the shirt off my back before I lose BST."'

These were brave words, but only words. In March 2000, the BIFR would issue a winding-up order for BST, concluding: 'The promoters were not serious in rehabilitating the company nor were they resourceful enough to mobilize the funds required for this purpose.'

Apollo on the other hand was on an upward curve. Mr Oberoi had identified a site in Gujarat at Limda, a village 20 kilometres from Baroda (now Vadodara). The state government was now onside, providing incentives to acquire the land and towards the estimated ₹1.6 billion construction costs for Apollo's second factory that would produce 675,000 tyres a year. Union Industry Minister Jalagam Vengala Rao was as good as his word and performed the foundation stone laying and ground breaking ceremony.

U.S. Oberoi was in charge of the building project working alongside Kannan Prabhakar, who would equip it. Prabhakar, always known as KP, qualified as a chemical engineer at the Regional Engineering College in Trichy in Tamil Nadu and studied industrial engineering at the postgraduate level. He joined Apollo in 1989, having worked for a company in Chennai that made nylon tyre cord fabric.

'I was interviewed by Mr Kanwar who gave me the offer letter the same day,' Prabhakar says. 'That is the speed at which he moves. He asked me to take care of equipment procurement and planning and handling the loans for equipment at the new plant. I was one of the first five persons he hired for the project.'

Prabhakar worked closely with the engineering consultant, who produced the drawings for the new plant, the technology and equipment needed to produce truck and bus tyres, and the detailed engineering specifications. After that was finalized and budgeted, the construction of the plant was put out to tender with the successful building contractors hiring the labour.

'The new plant would be totally unlike Perambra,' Kanwar says. 'It would be modern, clean and highly efficient.' With the help of Continental, who were now Apollo's technical collaborators having subsumed General Tire, KP and a small team visited every tyre plant in India to see how they were equipped and configured. 'Then in 1990, we went to the US to look for equipment,' Kanwar says. 'I remember sitting in the office of an equipment supplier in New Jersey and it was snowing and we were discussing buying mixers for the new plant with their head of sales. I liked this guy. He was a tough Colombian. He listened to our plans and said, "All these Indians coming over here; all they do is talk big and do nothing."'

'I said to him: "You are meeting a different kind of Indian today."'

◆

To finance the new plant Onkar Singh Kanwar decided to launch a 'mega issue' share offering in 1989 to raise ₹1.2 billion. To mastermind it, he hired one of India's top investment bankers and renowned dealmaker Nimesh Kampani, Founder and Chairman of the JM Financial Group. Hailing from Mumbai, the fit and fair-skinned Kampani, known to his friends as Nimeshbhai, had ambitions to become a cricketer when he left school. A contemporary of the legendary cricketer Sunil Gavaskar, Kampani's true talent lay in making big financial numbers rather than runs and wickets. Name any major merger and acquisition (M&A) deal in the last forty years and Kampani's hand would have been there somewhere. JM Financial, created by Kampani in 1973, with a capital of ₹5,000, had advised the Tatas on around forty-five transactions and the Birlas on more than twenty big deals, giving the firm a market value of about ₹50 billion. Kampani, Hemendra Kothari of DSP Merrill Lynch, whose great-grandfather had founded the Mumbai Stock Exchange, and Uday Kotak of Kotak Mahindra Bank are known as the 'Three Ks' who between them had shaken up investment banking in India's liberalized economy.

Kampani had worked on smaller public issues for Raunaq Singh's BST and Bharat Gears in the Seventies, but now a cult of equity owning was gaining ground in India, pioneered by Dhirubhai Ambani, the Founder of Reliance Industries, which he had taken public in 1977, bringing in first-time investors with an IPO of 2.8 million equity shares at ₹10 each.

'When I started in 1972, the size of share issues to build a factory or new business was laughable by today's standards,' says Kampani. '$100,000, worth about $1 million in today's value, was typical although it was much cheaper to build a plant back then. The real challenge was getting the licence to build the plant in the first place. Once Raunaq Singh had got that, he would go to the capital markets because he was a classic risk-taker, a very confident man who just wanted to do more and more to achieve a great height. Very few industrialists raised money from the market.'

Kampani had helped Raunaq Singh to raise in the region of ₹30 million to create BST, which is where he first met Onkar Singh Kanwar, who was then running the company. Now, Onkar invited Kampani to Delhi to meet and advise his Apollo team once a month, usually in a room at The Oberoi hotel. 'It was at one of those [meetings] that I urged Onkar to build a second plant because the labour problem in Kerala was killing him and that coincidentally I had a client called Nirlon that was sitting on an unfulfilled licence in Gujarat.'

Now, Kampani was going to help Onkar raise money on an altogether different scale from any other Raunaq Singh company. 'I said to Onkar that he should not go to the banks and run up debt to pay for the new plant but go instead to the capital markets. "You dilute a little bit and make a rights issue and a public issue and take up whatever you can take up. That way your net worth will be very strong compared to the competition. Rather than paying the banks upwards of 20 per cent interest and giving them a slice of Apollo, a public issue will give you a much broader-based company and the publicity generated will mean that people get to know Apollo Tyres better." I advised him that he could take a working capital loan but not a term loan, where conversion clauses apply.'

Kampani and his core team of six drew up and filed the prospectus for a partly convertible bond issue, something he had already done with Tata Motors, which did not want to go to public financial institutions owned by the government. It had attracted half a million shareholders. 'If you increase your shareholder base you are also insulating yourself from government interference or nationalization. If the government tries to harm a company the shareholders will not like it and the government will lose votes.'

The mega issue was called Swarn Ganga (literally 'river of gold'). Kampani and Kanwar and their teams had one month to market the issue before it opened. They went out on the road to meet stockbrokers, sub-brokers and analysts, and to address press conferences in seven cities across India.

Kampani took about two hundred stockbrokers from Mumbai, Delhi, Kolkata, Chennai, Goa, Jaipur and Kochi—in those days there were thirteen stock exchanges in India as opposed to two today—to Apollo's Perambra plant where there was a question answer session.

'I have trained a lot of entrepreneurs the first time they go public but Onkar was different because he already had some experience through the issues we had done with BST and others,' Kampani says. 'Onkar did not need training. He could communicate very naturally and talk to them very well. I organized a formal meeting and then an informal hotel dinner so everybody could meet him and the Apollo management team.'

A communication strategy to engage the press at the local and national levels went hand in hand. 'We needed journalists to spread the word that Apollo was not just some company in Kerala,' Kampani says. 'It was a company on the rise and opening in Vadodara with better technology that would enable it to produce radial tyres compared to bias tyres. We also made sure that the press had every opportunity to discuss all those advantages the share issue would bring with Mr Kanwar and his management team.'

A precisely targeted newspaper strategy helped reinforce the campaign. Start to finish, the whole thing took six months. Under the rules in play then, the government had set the price of the Swarn Ganga issue, based on Apollo's previous performance, unlike today when the market determines it, based on future potential.

'It was a great success; a tremendous response; people liked it,' Nimesh Kampani says. Swarn Ganga, which was underwritten in advance, was one of the first initial mega issues by an Indian company to raise in excess of ₹1 billion. In fact, it was oversubscribed by 50 per cent.

It had also massively increased the profile and prestige of Apollo. With construction of the Limda plant under way in 1990, Apollo's turnover had increased to ₹2.85 billion the previous year.

The problem was that Raunaq Singh was using Apollo's money to invest in or prop up businesses, which had not done well. Onkar's brothers were running some of them. Narinder was running BST and A.P. Kanwar, Apollo Tubes. Bharat Gears on the other hand was a sound company. Onkar's brother Surinder P. Kanwar had taken over the reins from his brother-in-law Surinder Kapur, who had left to set up his own autocomponents business in Delhi, Sona Group, which specialized in making steering systems. 'It was clear to me that Bharat Gears was not where I'd be in the long run,' Kapur explained in an interview. 'I had no equity in the company, my brother-in-law would soon take over and I had to look out.' Kapur, however, still remained on the Apollo board.

Onkar faced two major challenges. Firstly, he was determined to keep reinvesting Apollo profits back into the company to grow it while resisting Raunaq Singh's attempts to divert funds. Secondly, the term loans of Bharat Steel Tubes from Punjab National Bank were personally guaranteed by him, his father and his uncle S.S. Kanwar. 'If he did not attempt to settle his part of those guarantee obligations long before the defaulted loans multiplied it would pose a real threat to Apollo,' says P.N. Wahal.

Nimesh Kampani saw that Raunaq Singh and Onkar Singh Kanwar were heading for different horizons. 'Mr Raunaq Singh had asked me, "Nimesh, why can't we start a pharmaceutical company in Apollo?" I counselled him: "It is a completely separate business. You should become the number one in tyres. After all, even if motor cars fly one day they will still need tyres to land on. Just focus on tyres. Your son is good and he's doing it."'

Raunaq Singh diverted his eyes away from a single focus on Apollo and opted instead for scattergun entrepreneurship. He set up Raunaq Automotive Components (RACL) to make components for motorcycles and scooters, passenger and cargo vehicles, tractors and commercial vehicles. In 1990, he entered into an agreement with Perstorp AB, Sweden, with corporate guarantees from Apollo, for the promotion of a joint venture company named Gujarat Perstorp Electronics Ltd to manufacture electronic-grade copper-clad laminates in Gandhinagar, the state capital of Gujarat. He put Onkar Singh Kanwar's stepbrother Satinder Pal Singh there to gain experience.

nine

A second plant and the threat of Mehta

For India and Onkar Singh Kanwar, 1991 was a landmark year. In May 1990, a Liberation Tigers of Tamil Eelam (LTTE) suicide bomber assassinated Rajiv Gandhi at Sriperumbudur, near Chennai. This was a direct result of his decision to send Indian peacekeeping troops into Sri Lanka in 1987, when he was Prime Minister, to liberate Jaffna from the LTTE. The Indian Peace Keeping Force (IPKF) had been withdrawn in 1990, having achieved very little.

Most significantly for the Indian economy, 1991 was the year that P.V. Narasimha Rao became Prime Minister and ushered in liberal reforms, which put an end to the Licence Raj and other restrictive practices and closed-door economic policies. The old ways could not go on. The country was in a mess, crippled by growing inflation, unemployment and poverty. India's major trading partner the Soviet Union, from which it imported low-cost oil, had collapsed, forcing it to buy on the free market. The first Gulf War had raised oil prices and sent thousands of foreign-exchange-earning Indian workers back from the Middle East.

Running a fiscal deficit close to 8.5 per cent of GDP, India's foreign exchange reserve fell to a low of $240 million, just enough to support two weeks of imports. The International Monetary Fund and the World Bank offered help—but only in exchange for major reform.

In spite of opposition from Congress politicians, Finance Minister Manmohan Singh—a friend of Raunaq Singh's—and P.V. Narasimha

90

Rao eliminated the licences, reduced state control of industry, reformed exchange rate controls and cut tariff levels and import taxes. They opened the doors for foreign companies to invest more heavily in India and for Indian companies to operate overseas.

All this was music to Onkar Singh Kanwar's ears. 'The old ways had held India back. There had been too many obstacles and risk-taking and innovation were frowned upon. Now the brakes were off.'

Not all entrepreneurs welcomed India's brave new world. The Mumbai Club, a protectionist lobby of old-style business maharajas, was set up to oppose the reforms. They had done well by the protectionist Licence Raj and now they warned of floodgates being opened. They claimed that Indian companies would be wiped out by the financial firepower, production efficiencies and technologies of the incoming multinationals. Economic liberalization would unleash a second wave of colonization on India.

Competing with the multinationals was exactly where Onkar Singh Kanwar wanted Apollo Tyres to be and he could see the future taking shape before his eyes on 120 acres of barren Gujarati land as the Limda plant was completed in 1990 and KP moved from Delhi to the plant where he would spend two years. It went into full production in 1992 having completed successful trials at the end of the previous year. 'It is due to the drive of Mr Kanwar and his personal involvement that the first tyre came out within fifteen months from the start of construction,' says Kannan Prabhakar. 'By any standards that is quick.'

Kanwar is heavily involved in all Apollo projects, but he is not a micro-manager. He employs the people he knows can deliver on the detail. He is not big on poring over the minutiae—one of his favourite maxims is: 'overanalysis leads to paralysis.'

He says, 'I have always been very decisive and quick in my actions. Once I have all the facts, I act. Too many companies get bogged down in too much paper analysis and by the time they reach a decision the train of progress has already left the station. That was the difference between me and some of my industry friends.'

With the Limda plant up and running, Apollo Tyres achieved a major milestone in financial year 1991–92, when the turnover crossed ₹5 billion. Onkar Singh Kanwar called P.N. Wahal and said, 'I want to pay off all my personal guarantees in regard to BST.' He also sought to buy Apollo out of guarantees to other Raunaq Singh companies, especially Gujarat Perstorp Electronics Ltd, which was already haemorrhaging cash. It would involve lengthy legal and financial discussions with relevant government departments.

'I told him that it was not a straightforward process,' Wahal says, 'but his was a very judicious call to settle his liabilities at a time when things had not gone so bad with BST as they later would.' Litigation in relation to BST and its creditors is dragging through the Indian courts to this day.

'The total liability with interest was ₹400 million,' Kanwar says. 'I told the bankers I was willing to pay my share, one quarter, and absolve myself from my responsibility. That allowed me to concentrate on running Apollo. I knew that if I was tied to a company [BST] that kept defaulting, then Apollo would get no future loans from banks.'

The process would be completed in 1993, protecting Apollo from being dragged into the mire by Bharat Steel Tubes or any other of his father's companies. Onkar Singh Kanwar could rest easier. 'You see, my father wanted to be like the Birlas and put up factories everywhere and borrow lots of money from banks to do it, but to my mind that was just not sustainable.'

◆

Thanks to Nimesh Kampani's Swarn Ganga, Apollo now had a much broader shareholder base and was not in hock to banks. Raunaq Singh and Onkar Singh Kanwar held only a 9 per cent shareholding each but this relatively small holding was not unusual in promoter-led public companies of the time and neither man had cause to be concerned that they did not own more.

However, unknown to them, 25 per cent of Apollo had been acquired by and on behalf of a man known as 'The Big Bull' of the Indian stock market following his starting a bull run in 1991. His name was Harshad Mehta.

The West has never been short of corporate fraudsters. Junk bond trader Michael Milken, who revolutionized leveraged takeovers in the 1970s and 1980s, Bernie Madoff, the architects of the Enron Scandal, insider trading fraudster Ivan Boesky, and the granddaddy of them all, Charles Ponzi, were now joined in the late Eighties and early Nineties by Harshad Mehta and his Mumbai-based Growmore Research and Assets Management Limited.

With his 15,000 square foot house overlooking Worli Sea Face complete with huge garden, billiard room, mini theatre and a nine-hole putting green, plus a squadron of expensive cars, Mehta, who was constantly pursued by hordes of autograph hunters, was described by *India Today* in a May 1992 cover story as 'the Amitabh Bachchan of the trading ring [and] a stock-broker who became a millionaire by manipulating markets in a way no one had ever done before. It is becoming clear that the flamboyant thirty-seven-year-old Mehta, a fast-talking, fast dealing high-roller is at the centre of the biggest financial and insider trading scam ever in the country's history. The money involved in the past one year alone could be as much as ₹6 billion or more, taken from banks in various ways to play the booming stock-markets.'

The trouble was that the 'various ways' were illegal. He was playing with the banks' money and ignoring any rules of disclosure. Mehta was arrested in November 1992 on twenty-seven criminal charges after the award-winning business journalist and author Sucheta Dalal exposed him in *The Times of India* for misappropriating money from the banking system to buy 2.8 million shares in ninety companies. One of those was Apollo Tyres. Mehta had started by acquiring a 5 per cent stake in Apollo.

'Mehta was a great speculator and investor, a high risk-taker,' says Nimesh Kampani who knew him. 'There was a rule at that time that you could not acquire more than 24 per cent of a company without making a public offer. He acquired shares in seven or eight companies like the Associated Cement Company (ACC) and Apollo Tyres and he had a lot of stockbrokers working directly and indirectly for him who would acquire shares in their name and hold them in trust for him.' It is a process known as 'parking'. 'Mehta liked Apollo,' says Kampani. 'He saw it was a growing company and that Onkar was a great leader but I do not believe those who say he wanted to take over Apollo. Harshad was only ever interested in making money, not running companies. A lot of promoters saw their stock price going up, not knowing that Harshad Mehta was acquiring the shares! But he chose Apollo well after researching its results.'

By May 1992, Mehta's holdings in ACC and Apollo were reported to be worth ₹1.8 billion and his total estimated assets a staggering ₹40 billion. 'Mehta created this gambling frenzy,' says Kanwar. 'Shares he had bought in ACC for ₹100 were suddenly selling for ₹10,000. People were going crazy taking up positions.'

Harshad Mehta by fair means and foul had acquired 25 per cent of Apollo's shares against the 18 per cent owned by Onkar Kanwar and Raunaq Singh.

'We had no idea of his true holding in Apollo,' Onkar says, 'and I would not know the extent of it until 1995, when a rights issue would force Mehta to disclose it, by which time we would be dragged into prolonged litigation as legions of creditors and duped investors fought to get their money back.

'I remember Mehta coming to my father's house once and saying that he was going to be the Merrill Lynch of India. But it was all a scam, based on misappropriating money from the banks and investors and dealing in shares, many of which were duplicate or fake.'

Harshad Mehta's fall was as rapid as his rise. Sentenced to five years, he died in 2002, aged forty-seven, from a heart attack while in judicial custody in Thane Central Jail, Mumbai.

◆

Meanwhile, something was niggling at Onkar Singh Kanwar. At an Apollo board meeting in 1991, he said to his fellow directors, 'You guys have given me so much freedom, I have raised the money, set up a factory and none of you have been to see it. This is not fair. I request you as the supervisory board to make a visit.' Onkar recalls, 'In those days my father appointed all the supervisory board members. I knew very few of them.'

When they visited Limda, they were very appreciative and they complimented Kanwar. After the tour he made a presentation where he was asked how he saw Apollo's way forward.

'This is just the beginning of our journey,' he told them and spelt out his long-term vision to build an institution in the tyre industry. 'But we have many miles to cover. I believe if anyone can do it we can and we may invest another ₹10 billion [to grow Apollo further] either from resources within the company or by raising money in the markets.'

After a presentation by Prabhakar and a factory visit the board had dinner in a private room at the five-star ITC Welcom Hotel in Vadodara. Normally alcohol is not allowed in Gujarat, which is a dry state, but in hotels it was possible to get a special government permit to serve it, so a good evening was had by all. Onkar went to bed relieved and happy.

The next morning, he went to his father's room before breakfast as he always did. 'I said, "How was your night? Was everything okay?" He started shouting at me. "Are you mad? Is something wrong with you?" I could not understand it.'

On the flight back from Delhi, Raunaq Singh was increasingly angry with his son. 'The board is very unhappy at the money you are spending. I am going to take everything away from you. I want to run Apollo myself. All you are thinking is tyre, tyre, tyre. Look at Goenka, look at Modi, look at the Birlas. They diversify.'

'But Apollo is starting to be successful,' Onkar responded. 'Why dilute it by going off in other directions?'

'All my board members are criticizing you and saying that my son has gone mad.' One of those cited by Raunaq Singh was M.R.B. Punja.

Kanwar was shocked. 'My father and I had had our disagreements in the past, but nothing like this.'

As soon as he landed, Onkar rushed to his office and called M.R.B.

Punja. 'Sir, did you say anything to my father that was different to what you said to me at the board meeting.'

'Certainly not,' said Punja. 'We were all very impressed by what we saw and heard in Vadodara. If Mr Raunaq Singh tells you that, it's his problem. We complimented you because that is the way we felt. We are very happy with the way you are going.'

It was the same story with all the other directors Kanwar telephoned.

Onkar was bruised and baffled by the turn of events, as was his wife when he came home and told her. 'Mr Raunaq Singh had always loved Onkar,' Taru Kanwar says. 'They had been so very close...not just as father and son, they had always been the very best of friends.'

'Looking back, the Vadodara trip was where things started to unravel with my father,' says Onkar, who still finds it difficult to comprehend.

Mrs Kanwar adds: 'We had no idea what was coming.'

ten

Falling out

Early in the morning of 16 December 1992, the tax authorities and police carried out a series of search and seizure raids on Onkar Singh Kanwar's house in Shanti Niketan and the homes of some of Apollo's senior executives and directors. The plants at Perambra and Vadodara, the company offices in Delhi and thirty marketing offices all over the country were also raided under Section 132 of the Income Tax Act. Even though Raunaq Singh's house was searched too, some detected his hand behind the operation.

Company Secretary P.N. Wahal was in his house in Delhi and remembers it only too well. 'They marched in and began searching, taking away sacks of paper and possessions which would take us months to get back. They put my wife and me in separate rooms, interrogated us, and correlated our replies for inconsistencies. Then they demanded that I hand over the company books. I told them I was legally not allowed to do that. They had to stay in Apollo's registered office. They left around 4 p.m., saying that I was lucky; at other houses they would not leave until nightfall.' Somewhat ironically, given that this was an alleged tax fraud investigation, some of the raiders suggested to Mr Wahal that he might like to 'sweeten their mouths' to leave earlier!

'It was just one of a string of things that happened—houses raided, offices raided, accounts examined, but they found nothing because we are a clean company,' says Onkar.

But the raids ushered in a year in Onkar Singh Kanwar's life that he would rather forget. With most of his businesses failing, Raunaq Singh wanted to install his other four sons in Apollo, the only profitable company in the group. Onkar had refused. Hadn't his father agreed when Onkar took over Apollo on the verge of bankruptcy that it would be his project alone? Now, it was successful and there was absolutely no business logic in having one company run by five brothers. It would be a recipe for disaster. He also resented the fact that Apollo was having to shell out ₹350 million in guarantees in respect of loans raised by Gujarat Perstop Electronics from the banks and financial institutions. When Raunaq Singh suggested that Apollo pay to set up a fertilizer factory, Onkar told his father, 'Nothing doing. We have a responsibility to Apollo shareholders.'

Company Secretary P.N. Wahal puts Raunaq Singh's change of attitude towards his son down to Raunaq's group of advisers. 'Two of them would accompany Raunaq Singh to board meetings even though they were not members and they were forever putting silly ideas in his head for starting new companies so every few months there would be a new MoU for a textile mill or an iron ore works with no consideration of the financial consequences. In contrast, Onkar Kanwar believed in sticking to what worked best and that as the trustee of a listed company, he was accountable to shareholders and had no reason to divert funds from Apollo into non-tyre-related businesses.'

What Onkar now had on his hands was a toxic recipe for a family fallout to rival any of India's great family business feuds, but with an extra twist. Family business ructions had traditionally involved brothers or cousins—such as the Ambanis, the Modis, and the breakup of the Bajaj family. This one, like 1993's other seismic parting of ways of Bhai Mohan Singh and Parvinder Singh of pharmaceutical giant Ranbaxy Laboratories, was the first to pit father against son.

In a desperate attempt to stave it off and heal wounds, Onkar had got his father to agree to sign an MoU on the way Apollo would be run in future and the division of their shareholdings. Raunaq would be

Chairman and Onkar would continue with the day-to-day running of the business. But it was not enough to paper over the cracks. Raunaq Singh was adamant; his eldest son would not defy him.

In February 1993, at Raunaq Singh's instigation, IDBI launched an investigation into alleged financial irregularities involving Onkar. Next, he filed a 200-page dossier of accusations with the Department of Company Affairs, which ordered an investigation into Apollo.

In 1992–93, Apollo posted a gross profit of ₹405 million. Every other member of the board had approved the accounts. Raunaq Singh refused to sign them off, alleging 'financial irregularities and questionable accounting practices' and 'huge inter-corporate loans where interest payments are not forthcoming.' In a hard-hitting press statement issued on 18 August 1993, he also argued that profits were just ₹13 million 'if other income is excluded'.

Onkar fired back next day in *The Times of India*. 'Apollo has repaid all institutional loans, has disbursed ongoing interest payments and an enhanced dividend. Substantial investments made have been under the authorization of Mr Raunaq Singh himself.'

'The battle royale between the father and son [has] gathered tempo,' the paper reported.

Such was the tension leading up to Apollo's 1993 Annual General Meeting (AGM) that Onkar and his wife had visited Gurudwara Bangla Sahib daily to find solace and the strength to carry on. Taru Kanwar also prayed for them both at Hindu temples. 'Throughout, my wife was a great support and strength for me,' Onkar says. But the feud was also taking its physical toll on Onkar. One day he suddenly lost vision in his left eye. He was understandably frightened but instead of visiting the doctor, he went to Gurudwara Bangla Sahib where he prayed and bathed his eye with the waters from its lake. By the time he got back to his car, perfect twenty-twenty vision had returned.

♦

Apollo's AGM would be held at its usual venue, the Kerala Fine Arts Society in Kochi, where Apollo's registered office is, on 10 September. Raunaq Singh now embarked on a round of what he called Dinner Diplomacy to woo Apollo's eight institutional nominee board members—who formed a majority of the fifteen-member board—to his cause and back a motion of no confidence in Onkar Singh Kanwar at the AGM and have him thrown out of Apollo. Dinner Diplomacy was traditionally how Raunaq Singh managed the strategy of board and other meetings.

On 28 June, he had also succeeded in his campaign of pressure to force Onkar's closest ally, Surinder Kapur, to resign from the board. It put Rani Kapur in an unenviable position. 'Onkar was very upset that Surinder resigned; but my husband felt he had no choice. Going against my father was not easy. Things were soon mended between Onkar and Surinder, but I felt caught in the middle between my elder brother and my father, both of whom I loved.'

There is no doubt that Onkar received huge support through this family crisis from his closest friends. 'My husband and Onkar would confide in each other frequently about business problems,' says Ashi Burman. 'Gyan knew everything that was going on between Onkar and Raunaq Singh and he did his best to advise. Above all he listened and Onkar knew that shared confidences would never go further.'

In addition, the Kanwars and the Burmans would meet socially as a foursome at least twice a month, usually going out to dinner. 'A favourite was the Orient Express at the Taj Palace Hotel,' says Ashi Burman. The restaurant is a Delhi landmark and is an exact replica of an Orient Express dining car serving a menu inspired by the countries that the famous train passes through. 'I think that those dinners also helped support Onkar and Taru,' Ashi Burman says. 'They knew that we were always there for them.'

Shortly before the Apollo AGM, Onkar was having a meeting at The Oberoi hotel in Delhi with the then Chairman of Continental Dr Hubertus von Grünberg. 'He was a good friend and he was very keen that Continental and its three Indian collaborators—JK, Modi and Apollo—put up a large radial factory. We would all produce our own brands and market them but share the expense of building a new factory. I was very excited at the prospect.'

Then, he was called to the telephone. When he returned to the meeting, his son, Neeraj could see that his father's mood had changed. 'The call was from a cousin,' Onkar explained. 'There is a rumour of a plan to kidnap me so I cannot get to the AGM, and even to eliminate me, maybe with a bomb on the flight to Kochi.'

When he got home, Taru said, 'You are not going to the AGM.'

'I have to, for the sake of the company,' Onkar replied, 'and anyway, you cannot choose when you are going to die.'

Today, Taru Kanwar smiles, but she did not then. 'He's a very stubborn man. He is a Sagittarius. Whatever he thinks, he does.'

U.S. Oberoi booked fresh flights to Kochi, paying in cash. Rather than taking the usual flights, Oberoi, Onkar Kanwar and Neeraj took an international midnight flight out of Delhi, which stopped in Mumbai. There they slept in the transit lounge before taking an early morning flight to Kochi.

Kochi airport in those days was very close to the Taj Malabar Hotel, which sits on the extreme tip of Willingdon Island, 900 man-made acres constructed from the sandbank, which once prevented ships entering Kochi's natural harbour. Looking out over backwaters and to the Arabian Sea beyond, the five-star Malabar is a long, low two-storey colonial hotel with red roof tiles dating back to 1935. The U-shaped building was originally a port hotel for seafarers and naval officers, who could relax on the waterside lawns, shaded by palm trees with a drink in hand and watch a continual procession of fishing boats, local ferries, sailboats and passenger ships as guests can do to this day. Inside, it was a calming concoction of teak-panelled rooms and corridors, polished wood and marble floors, several restaurants, a convivial bar and cream walls on which hung pictures of old Kochi and its spice and rubber traders.

An adjoining eight-floor extension had been added in the Seventies, along with an infinity pool but they did not detract from the essential colonial tranquillity of the place.

However, things were far from tranquil on 9 September in Room 111, the two-bedroom suite Raunaq Singh had checked into at the far end of the old building. Today, it is the suite that Onkar Kanwar always stays in when he comes for the Apollo AGM. Prime Minister Narendra Modi has also rested his head in Room 111.

U.S. Oberoi had booked rooms for Onkar, Neeraj, the board members and legal advisers in the modern block. 'After checking in, Dad and I went up to that famous suite to see if my grandfather had everything he needed.' Neeraj recalls. At that time he was not working for Apollo, although he had worked vacations at the Perambra plant and already had a good knowledge of the tyre business through accompanying his father to various meetings. Now, he was here to give him his support.

'The door was shut and we rang the bell. No answer. We could hear shouting and debating. There were many voices all talking over one another. I thought, "What the hell is going on?" Eventually, the door opened and we walked in. All Dad's brothers were there with my grandfather and also his advisers, a group that seemed to grow by the week! As soon as we walked in and they saw my father they all fell silent. It went from 100 decibels to zero instantly. It was partly because they all had such huge respect for my father but mostly because they were feeling ashamed.'

They had obviously walked in on a strategy meeting.

'Hello, Sir,' Onkar said. 'I just came to see if you are comfortable. Is there anything I can get you?'

Raunaq Singh declined, equally politely.

Given that the next morning Raunaq Singh would attempt to get the AGM to pass a vote of no confidence against his son and have him thrown out of Apollo, it was beyond surreal.

'It sounds strange given the circumstances, but we were still very courteous to each other,' Onkar says. 'I still respected him. When all is said and done, he was my father.'

Even more bizarrely, there was a rumour that there would be an attempt to poison Onkar Singh Kanwar before he could get to the AGM, which is why Mr Oberoi was down in the kitchen tasting his food. U.S.

Oberoi had also had a discreet word with the hotel manager to ensure that security was of the highest order.

Next morning after breakfast, the board—which was to reconvene for a meeting back at the Malabar after the AGM—would travel by boat to the Kerala Fine Arts Society which stands on Shore Road, Pallimukku, Kochi. It was the same routine every year to avoid the traffic snarling up the local roads.

As they assembled to board the hotel's boat, it was clear that Raunaq Singh would not be joining them this year.

'I shall take the car,' he insisted.

'But by boat it is ten minutes,' Onkar said, 'By car, it is fifty.'

'I don't trust people,' he replied. 'They might try to drown me.'

The worn-out seats of the Kerala Fine Arts Society were packed with 1,200 shareholders as at 10 a.m., Raunaq Singh, Onkar Singh Kanwar and the board took their seats on the stage. The ceiling fans in the late Sixties concrete auditorium lazily stirred the humid air. The side doors had been left open to tempt the breeze to come and offer some assistance. It also allowed the audience to see the food and refreshments being set up outside which was the most effective way of ensuring that people kept their speeches short and to the point. AGMs lasted thirty minutes at most. Raunaq Singh would round up the company's results, announce the dividend, take a few questions and that would be it.

This year, instead of his usual speech he explained why he had refused to sign the annual accounts for the year ended 31 March and he asked the meeting to reject them.

Company Secretary P.N. Wahal presented the audited accounts and directors' reports and the AGM moved to vote. Raunaq Singh refused to take part. The resolution to adopt the accounts and report was passed unanimously.

After announcing a dividend of ₹3.50 per equity share, an agitated Raunaq Singh moved the meeting swiftly to the motion of no confidence, outlining briefly all the reasons they should vote to remove his son from Apollo.

For the rest of the year, the stage of the Kerala Fine Arts Society features Carnatic music, Kathakali dance, and theatre but none could match the drama of that moment. The ceiling fans seemed to be in slow motion.

Onkar replied briefly, explaining why his father's accusations were just that and emphasizing that Apollo was a transparent company. Its accounts were not fudged as his father had alleged. He spoke calmly, taking to heart the advice of family and friends not to rise to the bait.

The vote was taken. It seemed to take an age. The air was heavy and damp, pressing down on Onkar as he awaited his fate. 'It was almost unanimous in my favour.' Raunaq Singh's Dinner Diplomacy had not yielded enough votes.

The AGM had lasted just eighteen minutes. However, there was still the board meeting to come back at the Malabar Hotel.

◆

Onkar and Neeraj had an early lunch in their room, unaware of the events in the hotel coffee shop where U.S. Oberoi was entertaining his companions, speaking loudly and animatedly as usual. He was always at the centre of things. Raunaq Singh walked in, eyes blazing, and strode straight up to him. 'Traitor!' he shouted and slapped Oberoi in the face.

This did not bode well for the board meeting. As soon as it began, Raunaq Singh and Onkar were at loggerheads over all the same issues. M.R.B. Punja had had enough.

'I proposed a motion that Mr Raunaq Singh and Onkar should leave the meeting because their fight was compromising the board and the running of the company.' It was passed unanimously. Punja had tried previously to get Surinder Kapur to be the peacemaker between father and son but that had come to nothing and now Kapur had been pressured to leave the board by Raunaq Singh.

Onkar returned to his room, where he joined Neeraj and a lawyer and waited for the board to deliberate. Raunaq Singh stormed out of the hotel and headed back to Delhi.

The board now elected Punja to take the chair and turned its full attention to an item under any other business, the 'Formalisation of Management Functions'. 'For the good of Apollo, we had to define very clearly the roles and responsibilities of Raunaq Singh and Onkar Singh Kanwar,' Punja explains. 'I told the board that we should stay in that room until we had reached a unanimous decision.'

Far into the evening, they debated. Finally towards midnight they had a resolution. Raunaq Singh, 'subject to the general supervision and control of the board', would stay as Apollo's Chairman but would 'look after the diversification and development plans of the company and liaison with financial institutions and banks'. Onkar Singh Kanwar 'will continue to look after the day-to-day management and operation of the company in all aspects including dealings with banks and financial institutions'.

In addition, a new Management Committee of the Board would oversee the operation of the company for six months and the board itself would meet at least once a month to monitor closely how the new arrangements were working and to protect shareholders' interests.

The minutes were written up immediately and were signed there and then. 'I did not want any wavering afterwards,' Punja says. He knew that Raunaq Singh would attempt to get them to change their minds.

'Carrying the entire board with me helped me a lot,' Punja says, 'but Raunaq Singh still wouldn't give up. He still tried to get board members to change their minds and back him ahead of Onkar. He tried with me also. I was still very close to Raunaq Singh and I had meetings with him lasting late into the night over drinks and dinner. I tried to convince him that he should retire and Apollo would make him Chairman Emeritus, which would give him honorary status. At night, he would be sympathetic and say: "Mr Punja, give me some time." The next morning, he would ring me up and say "No". He offered to make my son-in-law a director and give him an office. I refused.'

On 28 October 1993, in the Delhi High Court the Honourable Justice

J.K. Mehra passed order 9243/93 in connection with Suit No. 2400/93, *Shri Raunaq Singh v/s M/s Apollo Tyres Limited* and another...in respect of item 'Formalisation of Management Functions'. The new arrangements were confirmed. To all intents and purposes, the feud was over.

Raunaq Singh was not for giving up. The legal action dragged on but came to nothing. The tax and regulatory authorities gave Apollo, Onkar Singh Kanwar and his senior management a clean bill of health and the board put the brakes on any further hostilities.

Raunaq Singh was still the Chairman of Apollo Tyres but it was Onkar who was now running the show and from now on would with the backing of the board steer the company away from the Raunaq Group stable and head towards his dream of building a modern institution in an India that was emerging from the bad old days of red tape and restrictions.

The feud, often fought via leaks, lapped up by an eager press—something else Punja and the board had now put a stop to—had divided Onkar's family, brother from brother as well as father from son. For a while, Apollo was divided into two camps, but as Onkar told *Forbes India* magazine, 'For the sake of the wider Apollo family, I had to take on my father but it left a deep scar in my life [...] it was a defining moment which even today gives me the strength and wisdom and encourages perseverance when I feel weak. My cause was the right one for our stakeholders [and] guided me in the way forward.'

With Onkar Singh Kanwar now firmly at the helm, Apollo's sales turnover by 1994 had increased 36 per cent to ₹5 billion and exports were up 25 per cent.

eleven

Son arises

Neeraj Kanwar was concerned at the pressure his father had been under and decided to stand beside him and so he joined the marketing department of Apollo in 1995. Onkar Singh Kanwar had neither asked Neeraj to join, nor did he expect it, but he was thrilled at his son's decision. Neeraj had often spent summer vacations when a student at Apollo's Perambra plant, where staff were impressed by him turning up at work at 9 a.m. sharp every day, and so he already had a good grasp of tyre manufacturing and marketing.

Like his father, Neeraj had also finished his education in the United States. He left St Columba's in Delhi, where he had excelled at sports, especially tennis, cricket and hockey, and did his final high school year at Northfield Mount Hermon School, a private boarding and day school on the banks of the Connecticut River in Massachusetts. 'It was a hell of an experience for me. It was located in a very small village so there were no distractions and every opportunity to work hard. It also helped me to be independent.'

Onkar Singh Kanwar was keen that his children learn to stand on their own two feet from an early age. When Neeraj was nine, he and his elder brother Raaja, aged ten, were sent by Onkar for a six-week summer camp at Culver Military Academy outside Toledo in Ohio, where Dan Abbey had studied and been captain of the polo team. 'I was keen that they learned to be independent and resourceful,' Onkar says.

'I was totally against it, I thought they were too young,' says Taru Kanwar, 'but he was very determined that they should do it.'

'Going to America never did me any harm,' Onkar says.

'But he went when he was nineteen with $1,000 in his pocket,' Neeraj says, laughing about it now. 'I think I probably cried for the first three weeks. I still have bad memories of it. We spent much of the time on hurricane watch and we had to make our beds so that they were as flat as a table tennis table and if you did not they gave you penalty points.' Aside from these character-building pursuits, 'they did teach me canoeing, which I really liked. I think Raaja enjoyed our time at Culver a lot more than I did and the day I left, I was in seventh heaven.'

As a child, Raaja suffered from asthma but Taru was insistent that daily exercise and yoga rather than steroids and other medicines were the way to cure his condition. She also took Raaja once a year to a family of traditional practitioners in Hyderabad, who claimed they could cure asthma by having sufferers swallow a live fish whose mouth was stuffed with a herbal paste. As a treatment, it might be considered odd by some, but as Raaja says, 'the asthma stopped!'

After Northfield Mount Hermon School, Neeraj enrolled on a four-year industrial engineering degree at Lehigh University in Bethlehem, Pennsylvania. The university's Iacocca Institute 'providing innovative leadership, applied management and cross-cultural learning experiences'— had been founded by Lee Iacocca (class of 1945), the automotive icon, who had been President of Chrysler. Neeraj and his fellow students as part of their studies carried out small-scale time and motion studies for the car company and projects that focused on increasing productivity. Having worked at Apollo's Perambra plant, Neeraj already had, first-hand, real-world experience of productivity problems.

Once Neeraj had his degree, Onkar thought his son should get some experience of the financial world. Neeraj took a back-office trainee job at American Express Bank in New York next to the World Trade Center.

'Then my father suggested that I should set up a finance business in Delhi. He felt that if I had experience of finance and engineering, it would set me up well for the future.'

Neeraj set up Global Finance Ltd. 'It specialized in capital markets, debt and equity. After a year, I had invested ₹30 million and was negative ₹5 million!'

When Neeraj joined Apollo's sales team in Delhi, he insisted that his business card should simply read 'Neeraj Singh'. 'I did not want anybody to know I was my father's son. I wanted to be judged on my own merits. My mother suggested that I should have a driver take me to work because it would be more convenient, comfortable and safer, but I said "no". It would immediately arouse suspicion.'

Equally, Onkar Singh Kanwar did not want his son going straight into the higher echelons of Apollo. 'It was important that he got to know the company from the ground up.'

Although Neeraj would call his father every morning for guidance, he would have little contact with him at work. Neeraj worked in a marketing office at Piragarhi on the edge of Delhi and rarely visited the head office at Nehru Place. It was important to keep the pretence going, so Neeraj would see Apollo as it really was and learn, rather than have people making allowances for him because he was the boss's boy.

So Neeraj Singh spent his early days visiting and getting to know tyre dealers and finding his way around the trucking centres and not be home before nine in the evening.

Apollo was still focusing mainly on truck and bus tyres but had ventured into the two-wheeler market with a tyre called Black Cat for Bajaj scooters. Neeraj was tasked to make the brand better known to customers. 'Neeraj was up to the task,' *Forbes India* magazine reported. 'Every time the traffic signal at Piragarhi turned red, Neeraj would run out and change covers on the scooters' spare tyres. The new cover would have the black cat visual on it, of a scooter driver about to skid but saved by two "black cat commandos". The initiative did not take off.'

In spite of Neeraj's efforts, Black Cat was not a success and Apollo withdrew from the two-wheeler market.

Six months after joining Apollo, he was visiting the company's godown and dispatch centre at Sanjay Gandhi Transport Nagar in New Delhi. More than five thousand trucks leave and arrive at this major transport hub every single day. In churning hot dust it is a hive of activity. Mechanics bash out bent metal, service and repair engines and replace ruptured suspensions. Painters prime, paint and primp cabs and carpenters replenish and replace battered bodies.

All the tyre companies have a presence at Sanjay Gandhi Transport Nagar and Neeraj noticed that compared to the others Apollo's godown was shabby and dirty and the tyres were not looking their best. No dealer would want to buy tyres that looked worn out before they even met an axle.

'I reported this to my father and he told the head of marketing that he wanted to make a visit. When we went there everything had been freshly painted. It was spotless. The floors were scrubbed and the tyres were stacked cleanly and neatly. One of the managers who worked there was talking to my father when he broke off, pointed at me and asked, "Who's that guy?"'

Onkar Singh Kanwar replied simply, 'That guy is my son.'

Not only did Neeraj join Apollo in 1995, he also got married to Simran Marwah, who had been a finalist in the Miss India contest in 1994, the year that both the Miss Universe and Miss World crowns were worn by Indian beauty queens.

Returning from a hard day selling tyres, on 6 January 1995, the last thing Neeraj felt like doing that evening was going to a dinner party, but he ended up going.

'That's where we first met,' Simran says. 'He proposed twenty days later!' In fact they had met many years before but had neither realized nor remembered. Family photographs revealed that Neeraj and Simran had attended the same children's parties. Their families had been intertwined in a way for years although they did not know it. Simran's father had been a close friend of Raunaq Singh's. Simran was born in Delhi but her family came originally from the Indian side of Punjab and her grandfather was the Coal Commissioner in the British days. Simran was a pupil at the Convent of Jesus and Mary. It is separated only by the

Sacred Heart Cathedral from St Columba's where Neeraj was a student, although, as she says, 'When you are growing up you do not really mix with those who are two years older. Then when I was sixteen, I did meet Neeraj's parents at my uncle's house and they said, "We have a son we would love you to meet," but it did not happen and I did not connect that with the man sitting at the dinner table.' Much later, Onkar Singh Kanwar was at a wedding when he came rushing up to Neeraj, saying, 'I have spotted a girl I want you to meet,' but when they went to find her, Simran had vanished.

Neeraj and Simran were married in what is now the Lalit Hotel in Connaught Place. Neeraj waited patiently for Simran to arrive and exchange garlands. She was late as a bride should be. Raunaq Singh said very loudly in Punjabi, 'If your bride is not coming, I will get up on stage and marry her mother!' Simran's mother Raj Gill was Miss India 1971. Laughter erupted and nerves were calmed.

As soon as Simran arrived, Raunaq Singh and Onkar Kanwar burst into tears. 'I was trying to control mine but they were crying buckets,' Simran says. 'I just hoped that they were tears of joy!'

'Dad is very emotional, especially at weddings,' Neeraj says. 'As soon as the father gives his daughter away, the tears start to come.'

Simran refers to Mr and Mrs Kanwar as Mum and Dad. 'She is very sweet, soft and kind. My first impression of him was that he was very formidable and can be intense but I soon realized that he is very easy to get along with and he too has a humility and softness. He is not one of those people who need to be larger than life. Today, Neeraj and I are best friends with them both.'

◆

Now Neeraj's cover was blown he moved to head office, but the time he had spent incognito had allowed him to spot a faultline in Apollo's organization. 'There was no bridge, no communication between manufacturing and marketing. We had many silos of excellence but this was still a 1970s' organization and we were not as responsive as we should be to market needs in the kind of tyres we were producing.'

With his father's backing, Neeraj set up a group within Apollo called Strategic Planning and Coordination (SPC) to build that bridge to achieve much more lateral organization where tyre technologists would talk to marketing and sales staff, who would talk to colleagues in production and distribution. Like a lot of Indian companies in those days, Apollo was held back by and hung up on hierarchy.

When Neeraj made a first presentation to the board, Raunaq Singh complimented him openly and after the meeting was heard telling board members how proud he was of his grandson.

As head of the SPC, Neeraj regularly visited markets and factories ensuring that Apollo's technologists headed by P.K. Mohamed continued producing tyres the market wanted which included the developing XT-7 family of tyres, which proved that long-distance mileage was possible with heavy loads, and the Amar family of tyres, which raised the bar for speed and mileage performance.

◆

During the second half of the Nineties while Neeraj got to know Apollo and its customers intimately, Onkar Singh Kanwar had had other battles to fight, notably back in Kerala where Premier Tyres, which had opened for production at its plant on a 29 acre site in Kalamassery, a suburb of Kochi, in 1962 had become sick in 1992.

Chief Minister Kannoth Karunakaran showed every intention of handing it over to Ceat Tyres run by Harsh Goenka, who had become the Managing Director in 1983 at the tender age of twenty-four. Today, he is the Chairman of RPG Enterprise, one of India's largest business groups.

Kanwar had a showdown with Karunakaran, Kerala's longest-serving Chief Minister. 'How can you give this company to Ceat without giving Apollo first refusal as the leading tyre company in Kerala?'

'Who are you to tell me what to do?' the Chief Minister replied. 'I have decided in favour of Goenka, a big name.'

Kanwar was not taking that for an answer. He went to Delhi to lobby central government officials, notably the Vice Chairman of the Planning Commission.

'All I want is a chance for Apollo to put its case for taking over Premier.'

The Vice Chairman put a call through to the Chief Minister's office.

After a three-year-long fight and constant lobbying, Apollo—thanks to Kanwar's persistence and powers of persuasion—got the chance to put its case and in 1995, Premier became part of Apollo, its third factory, when the BIFR approved its rehabilitation scheme. This involved Premier's plant producing Apollo brands under a lease arrangement before becoming a full subsidiary.

In 1996, Apollo signed a technical collaboration agreement with Continental General Tire International for upgraded technology and in 1997, it signed a joint venture with Continental AG, Germany, to manufacture passenger car radials in Pune, Maharashtra. However, this was ultimately shelved due to a slowdown in the Indian economy and reduced demand in the tyre industry.

Onkar Singh Kanwar was still trying to make peace with his father. He asked the Apollo Board to approve his suggested ₹440 million bailout to save Bharat Steel Tubes. 'By now, Mr Kanwar had earned the complete confidence of the board and we backed him,' says M.R.B. Punja. Equally, Punja had earned the complete respect of Onkar Singh Kanwar. As one board member noted, 'Mr Kanwar always insisted that Mr Punja sat directly opposite him at the boardroom table and would always seek his advice and counsel.'

BST's bankers and the BIFR also backed Kanwar's rescue plan but on one condition: that Apollo management went in to run BST and to supervise how the money was spent.

Raunaq Singh's answer was not long in coming. He told the regulators that he refused all help from Apollo. He alleged that it was just another ruse by his son to gain control of all Raunaq Group companies. He would save Bharat Steel Tubes on his own. After all, he was the only industrialist included on a list of the '80 Most Prominent Sikhs of the Century'.

◆

It is perhaps not surprising that after years of tension Onkar Singh Kanwar's health became an issue. In September 1996, he was diagnosed with an aortic aneurysm—a swelling of the main blood vessel that leads away from the heart, down through the abdomen to the rest of the body. In March 1997, while in Pune, where Apollo had opened a tyre tube plant, he suffered a heart attack. He was rushed to a hospital in Delhi and then flown to the US, where he had a heart bypass at the Cleveland Clinic in Ohio, voted a 'top-five' hospital in America.

It was not 'top five' as far as Kanwar was concerned. 'They did a lousy job. My blood pressure went dangerously low and they had to do it again. They also damaged my lung, which meant I had trouble breathing. Even now, walking at an altitude is a problem.'

Onkar Singh Kanwar is not given to self-doubt but it crossed his mind more than once that his father had also had a heart attack followed by a bypass.

'I have been very lucky,' he says, 'my wife's prayers are strong.'

Taru Kanwar demurs, 'You have your own stars!'

Fifteen days in hospital were followed by ten days of recuperation on the beautiful island of Martha's Vineyard in Massachusetts just south of Cape Cod. It was the longest time Kanwar had ever been away from the business. Even on family holidays, business would have a habit of bumping into him. Typical was the time they were staying at the Hilton on London's Park Lane where he ran into fellow guest Dan Abbey, who had financed BST. Onkar went off for breakfast with him to a chorus of 'Dad!' from his children.

Today, Onkar watches his diet and eats carefully, exercises every morning and walks for an hour most days. He has no doubt that the fall-out with his father was a contributory factor to his heart attack. 'A 101 per cent for sure!'

Taru Kanwar agrees. 'We were all very worried for him but I always held on to the fact that he had the determination to pull through.'

'In spite of the health scare and the operations, I never missed a single board meeting,' Onkar says.

◆

Unlike his father, who traded increasingly on past glories, Onkar Singh Kanwar was always looking to the twenty-first century and he decided that Apollo's office at Nehru Place was no longer big enough or suitable for his growing staff. Instead of looking in central Delhi, where there was a shortage of suitable office accommodation and rents were high, he looked beyond Indira Gandhi International Airport to Gurgaon, 32 kilometres southwest of the capital in the neighbouring state of Haryana. Today, it is a vast new city and business hub with a population of nearly 1,700,000. India's premier companies and the Indian headquarter offices of 250 Fortune 500 companies occupy mile upon mile of corporate towers. With its banks, tech companies, five-star hotels, private hospitals, and multi-storey shopping malls and the burgeoning Delhi Metro and City Metro, Gurgaon has the third highest per capita income in the whole of India. If there is a single symbol of an India on the move as a confident global manufacturing and commercial economic power, it is Gurgaon.

And yet in the late 1990s, there was nothing there beyond the old town of Gurgaon, historically known as Gurugram, and thousands of acres of marginal farming land, which was earmarked for commercial development. Displaying typical pioneering spirit, Onkar Singh Kanwar bought Plot No 7. Institutional Area, Sector 32, and commissioned young architects to design a signature building.

Apollo was one of the first companies to move to Gurgaon, in 2000, when some 120 staff moved out of Nehru Place and into a brand new energy-saving building, which covers 94,000 square metres on two acres of landscaped manicured gardens. The large expanse of glass topped with terrace gardens for insulation allows the outside in and the inside out, adding to the sense of light and space.

The project was seen through on the Apollo side by U.S. Oberoi, who had the vision for the gardens and the planting, but it was typical that Onkar Singh Kanwar should choose young relatively unknown architects to design a sustainable and highly individual building which has been written about on numerous occasions in architectural magazines in India and abroad. For Onkar Kanwar and Apollo, it was all part of the onward march into the future.

◆

Like a successful soccer manager, Onkar Singh Kanwar was constantly replenishing and bolstering his squad as Apollo jostled for supremacy in the Indian market. In 1997, he hired Satish Sharma from rival JK Tyre to join the truck marketing team. Having qualified as a chemical engineer, Satish had added technical engineering and product marketing to his skill set, especially in relation to radial truck tyres, which Apollo was going to produce in Gujarat. Based in Gurgaon, he is now Apollo's President of the Asia-Pacific, Middle East and Africa (APMEA) region, and a member of the management board. He is also Vice Chairman of the Automotive Tyre Manufacturers Association (ATMA).

'When I was at JK, the word Apollo was taboo, not to be discussed at meetings,' says Satish. 'I met former colleagues from JK, who were now technical people at Apollo, and they were very positive, how it was doing things in a different way with a sense of belonging, recognition and rewards. I didn't need much persuasion!'

Another significant hire in 1999 was Sunam Sarkar. He was heading a business unit of Xerox Corps' Indian joint venture (JV) in Delhi, when a head-hunter approached him to see if he would like to join a family-owned company and set up its non-truck tyre business. At that time, over 90 per cent of Apollo's revenues came from truck tyres. From business machines to tyres seemed to be a big jump, especially as Sarkar knew next to nothing about the industry. But he was intrigued enough to go for the interview. It was the first time he met Onkar Singh Kanwar.

'Why do you want to leave?' Kanwar asked him.

Sarkar, whose father Bidyut Sarkar was a respected journalist with *The Economic Times* and Editorial Advisor to the Times Group, is hugely knowledgeable about the business world and eminently lucid and perceptive. He told Kanwar that he was tempted by Apollo because he felt stifled by an American multinational that had a business model that was not suited to Indian commercial needs. It just wanted to sell bigger and more expensive machines to companies, as it did in the United States, but the Indian market, which did not produce the same tonnage of paper, had no need of investing ₹1 million to buy in-house machines, nor could many companies afford them. 'Fifteen minutes into the interview, Mr Kanwar looked at me and at the head-hunter and said, "We would like to proceed." That was it! I had the job, Head of Marketing–Non-Truck tyres. What I liked was his dynamism and decision-making. I was soon to learn that one major reason for his success is his ability to take a decision very quickly and go with his instinct.'

'I take pride in that,' Kanwar says. 'If someone feels right, I am willing to back them.' As he says, too much analysis leads to paralysis.

Early on in his career, Sunam discovered that Apollo had turned its back on silo thinking and had embraced cross-departmental functionality and communication. One day, he gave Kanwar a paper with some HR suggestions on what the company should do to retain and incentivize staff and how it could reduce exposure to fixed costs by adding in variable salaries.

'He went through the paper and said, "What are you waiting for? Do it." I told him that I was not in HR. He said, "That's no excuse, just go and do it."'

Kanwar's instinct with regard to Sunam Sarkar proved to be 100 per cent correct. Sunam rose rapidly in rank and across functions—Chief-Strategy, Business Operations, Chief-Corporate Strategy, Marketing, Chief

Financial Officer—and today is Apollo's President and Chief Business Officer, based in Singapore. In 2004, he was co-opted on to the board of directors and is a member of the executive board as well. While keeping a low profile, he remains a trusted adviser to both Onkar Singh Kanwar and Neeraj Kanwar.

◆

Neeraj Kanwar had been co-opted as a whole-time director of Apollo in May 1999 and Onkar asked him to head manufacturing in Kerala and Vadodara, in addition to being chief of the SPC. The three plants between them had an installed capacity of 150,000 truck tyres per month while radial car tyres were due to come on stream at Vadodara the following year. 'For a twenty-seven-year-old, it would be a big challenge winning over those with a lot more experience of the tyre industry.'

His biggest challenge arrived in May 2001 at the Limda plant. 'A lot of political activists had infiltrated the plant and radicalized the workers to go on strike,' Neeraj explains. The action was in contravention of a four-year agreement on wages and productivity signed in 1999, which had followed a lockout over shop floor discipline and other issues.

He decided to lead a convoy of four coaches of management staff to try and force a way into the blockaded plant. Joining him on the second coach were U.S. Oberoi and Kannan Prabhakar, who having set up the plant had moved back to Gurgaon as head of HR.

There was a police presence as the convoy reached the gates but it was ineffectual and a mob of some six hundred surrounded the buses. Windows started to be smashed and gangs boarded and ordered the occupants to get down. Once outside, several of them were set upon and beaten with sticks and clubs. Neeraj and U.S. Oberoi were escorted to meet the union leaders, but Prabhakar spotted some colleagues from the plant in the third coach being set upon and went to help them.

'I tried to reason with them but there were some outside elements there, who were goading them. Mob mentality was taking over.'

'You, get out of here!' one of the agitators shouted.

Prabhakar refused.

'Remove your shoes and walk!'

'Ordering me to remove my shoes and walk barefoot was their way of telling me I was finished, humiliated. But I did what I was told. They pushed me down into a water drain, which luckily was dry. I skirted the plant wall and took refuge by a rock in a field about 100 metres away, while the altercation continued. Eventually order was restored and two workers I recognized came by and took me back on a scooter.'

It gave Neeraj and Oberoi a story to dine out on for years afterwards but at that time, it was scary. 'Looking back,' Prabhakar says, 'I don't think we planned it very well and certainly the police could have handled the security more effectively.'

The convoy turned around and went back to Delhi and Apollo declared a lockout, which was to last nineteen days and would contribute to a 48 per cent decline in Apollo's profits in the third quarter of 2001 to ₹32.2 million.

At the time Onkar Singh Kanwar was in Washington, leading a FICCI delegation, but through intermediaries he was able to put a call through to Gujarat Chief Minister Narendra Modi and asked if Neeraj could go and see him to try and resolve the dispute.

Neeraj arrived at Modi's office in Gandhinagar, the state capital. 'It was the first time I had met him. He was polite but very intense and asked me how he could help. I explained the situation—that we were being held to ransom by extremists at the plant. He instantly picked up his phone and started issuing instructions. "I don't want this happening again in my state," he said.

Then Modi turned to Neeraj and said, 'Please look internally as to why this has happened and let's try and resolve it in an amicable and proper way. Are there things that your HR people could do to stop it from happening ever again?'

Onkar Singh Kanwar said to Prabhakar, "KP, let's run the radial plant differently.' They decided to only hire diploma holders, who were better qualified and more motivated, to decrease radically the layers of management to achieve a flatter organization and to have fewer supervisory staff.

The results were dramatic. 'At the time of the lockout the radial plant was producing 2,000 tyres a day,' Prabhakar says. 'By 2005, the number was up to 8,000.'

However, strikes and lockouts were still too common at Apollo. Between 1997 and 1999, 147 days of production were lost at Perambra. Since his meeting with Narendra Modi, Neeraj Kanwar had been forming an image in his mind of a different kind of factory where confrontation could be replaced by teamwork. A factory where there would be no white collar, no blue collar, just one management team.

twelve

Restless dealers

Towards the end of the last millennium, India's tyre dealers had become disenchanted with Apollo. This was partly as a result of the infighting and the Harshad Mehta affair which had caused the company to take its eye off the ball while its competitors were focusing hard on the quality of products and service and the inducements that they provided to the nation's 5,000 dealers.

Back in 1992, Apollo's then sales director, concerned at selling production from the Limda plant, became extremely aggressive and announced that he was introducing a policy of exclusivity. Dealers would get a 3 per cent exclusive incentive if they only sold Apollo tyres. About 20 per cent of dealers, mostly in the south of the country, closed immediately. They could not afford to just stock Apollo's tyres, nor was it viable for them to carry on as multi-brand dealers, if Apollo exclusives were undercutting them.

Not put off by this calamity, in the following year the sales director brought in equalized pricing across the country. The policy might have been designed to shift Vadodara production at a time when Apollo Tyres needed to gain and cement market share, but it ignored the fact that India is not one market but many with every state having different trade policies and sales taxes. A blanket approach of equalized pricing was always likely to be doomed.

The sales director then left the company but rejoined in 1995, when he gave away ₹5 billion in unsecured credit to dealers, who said thank you very much and invested it not in their dealerships but in real estate, jewellery and weddings.

Everything Apollo had gained in terms of size and profitability—by 1995, it had become one of the top five tyre companies in India—was under threat. When alarm bells started ringing in the finance department, Onkar Kanwar moved very quickly and fired the sales director. He also chastised himself for not having sensed the danger sooner. He was determined that he and Neeraj would be fully involved from now on in the detail of operations as well.

'It had become a polarized world,' says Satish Sharma. 'Either you were an Apollo exclusive or you were not an Apollo exclusive. The multi-brand boys said, "Apollo is getting ahead of itself; we don't want to stock them any more."'

'The discounts given to exclusives changed hands between dealers to consummate onward deals, which raised a lot of integrity issues. On top of that, those favoured dealers who had been given unsecured credit started asking for more and more and created fictitious accounts.'

Arrogance had hurt Apollo Tyres very badly, particularly in the south where there was great resistance to exclusivity and where the dealers felt that the company was gearing its sales policies to favour the north. They had come to characterize Onkar Singh Kanwar as an aggressive and ambitious businessman from the north with which the transportation sector was perceptually associated, particularly in his home state of Punjab. Equally Apollo's tyres were more suited to cope with overloaded trucks, a phenomenon in India's northern states, whereas truckers in the south are more disciplined and do not believe in overloading their vehicles. In addition, Apollo's trade policies and product portfolio in the past had favoured the north over the south. Apollo had a major challenge to win back the south.

One of the many south Indian dealers closing his doors to Apollo was Mahendra Chowdhari of Anand Tyres in Chennai. Chowdhari is one of the biggest dealers in India, selling over 1,000 tyres a month as well operating service centres. Traditionally a loyal supporter of Apollo, even Chowdhari's patience had worn thin and he is the most mild-mannered of men. A great deal of hard-won trust had now been lost.

'I complained to Apollo and told them that exclusivity will just not work here.'

Onkar Singh Kanwar took the challenge as an opportunity and he along with his management team called a meeting of all south India dealers at the Taj Coromandel Hotel in Chennai. The opulent five-star had played host to Presidents Jimmy Carter and Bill Clinton.

'At the lunch, beforehand, I told the Kanwars that a dealer had to have confidence in a company and that a good product would always sell at a premium,' Mahendra Chowdhari says. They needed Chowdhari on their side if they were going to successfully rebuild bridges. 'They had to be more friendly towards their dealer network and treat us as business partners,' Chowdhari says. 'If you are giving a good product and assured profit then confidence builds.' The carrot of discounts and the stick of exclusivity was not the way to win respect and loyalty among those who were at the interface with customers.

Now aware of the true strength of feeling conveyed by Mahendra Chowdhari, the Kanwars opened the meeting with an apology and then listened to this vital group of stakeholders. The dealers told them that Apollo had a great product and a market-leading product, but the way it was going about selling was all wrong.

Scores of similar meetings followed across the country until Apollo had talked to virtually every tyre dealer in India. At every venue the message was as uniform as it was simple.

'Sanity had to return,' says Satish Sharma. 'We had to go multi-brand. Exclusivity is a flawed concept. Today, about 30 per cent of dealers are exclusive Apollo dealers but the difference is that this is the route they have chosen to take rather than having it foisted on them.'

The change in attitude was instant. 'I noticed it the very next day,' says Chowdhari. After the sales director was fired, Neeraj started taking a more active interest in operations, as did Kanwar. 'Some of the points we had raised they addressed immediately; others very soon after,' Chowdhari says. 'They changed the focus to product and marketing. They brought in young blood and groomed them to go to the market, talk to the dealers and bring back feedback and then take decisions. We felt we were once again part of the process.'

'Looking back, that experience was a good thing,' says Sharma. 'It really taught us what *not* to do.' It was time to make changes. Apollo became a dealer-friendly company bringing in simplified policies and transparency. It stopped giving discounts and focused instead on product quality and dealer support.

Today, Apollo's product managers, product development managers and R&D centres pick up every nuance in the market and adjust the product pipeline accordingly, always listening to the customer to keep on improving the product. 'Truck tyre dealers will not only ask about the initial price,' says Satish Sharma, 'but which product gives them the highest casing value in a tyre because that is what his customer will ask for. If it is retread, he will calculate the cost per kilometre and if he doesn't calculate it, we will and give it to him so he knows that even if he is paying more for our product the cost per kilometre is lower.'

Cheaper tyres are less reliable and are a false economy with minuscule profit margins. Investment in quality wins the day every time in terms of reliability, greater profitability on investment for Apollo and vital repeat business for dealers.

After five pretty bleak years, the sales tide began to turn back in Apollo's favour. Car tyres came on stream and now Apollo has the largest capacity of car tyres in the country. 'We also have zero debt in the dealer market,' says Satish Sharma.

Not long after the Chennai tyre dealer summit Onkar Singh Kanwar asked for a follow-up meeting with Mahendra Chowdhari. Satish Sharma would be coming with him. 'I thought that as the head of a major tyre company, Mr Kanwar would expect me to come to his hotel or ask me to meet him at the airport,' says Chowdhari. 'That is what I was used to from his competitors. But he insisted on coming to my head office where he and Mr Sharma spent an hour talking to my staff and discussing in detail the intricacies of our trade and asking me about the progress and the plans I had for my business and how Apollo could help me achieve them. He had suggestions on how best to respond to market dynamics and how I could widen my objectives further. From Mr Kanwar down people at Apollo are very good listeners. You have to join hands in order to grow together.'

thirteen

The end of an era

On 19 September 2002, at Apollo's twenty-ninth AGM held as usual at the Kerala Fine Arts Society in Kochi, Raunaq Singh signed off as Chairman of Apollo Tyres. Raunaq Singh's departure was low key—he had not attended an AGM since 1997. The meeting passed a sincere vote of thanks for his contribution and that was that. He was talking of writing his memoirs and publishers were jockeying to bring out the story of a big well-lived life. Raunaq Singh had entered into discussions with several possible authors, but nothing had yet been finalized.

Onkar took his father's place as Chairman and Neeraj Kanwar became Apollo's Chief Operating Officer (COO).

A new member of the Apollo Board was Onkar's eldest son Raaja Kanwar. Tall, athletic and with a ready humour like his younger brother, Raaja was making a name for himself as an entrepreneur in his own right. In 1995, he had set up Apollo International to export women's leatherwear and accessories, and subsequently moved into real estate, information technology, pharmaceuticals, tea and rice. As a young man, having studied for a management degree at Drexel University in Philadelphia, he had worked as a fashion photographer for *Vogue*. Raaja, whose business is headquartered in Gurgaon, is married to the model and singer Kamayani Singh with whom he has two sons, Aryaan and Zefaan.

In a 1997 interview with *Business Standard*, which described him as 'an astute and somewhat flamboyant businessman', Raaja said: 'Don't tell me just because I was born into this family that I have to make tyres.'

Raaja served just two years on the Apollo board. However, one of his divisions of Apollo International, Tyre Tech Global, very successfully exports tyres made in China and Thailand to seventy countries and has teams of technicians advising on design and production. 'Dad was always urging me to compete with Apollo as much as possible; he thought it would be good for both of us.'

Raaja's current passion is logistics. His Apollo LogiSolutions, in which the Abu Dhabi royal family has a 10 per cent stake, provides freight management, contract logistics, dry port and customs brokerage in India and worldwide.

'Dad, who sits on the boards of all my companies, has always backed me but he does say "concentrate on fewer ideas"! When I set up UFO Moviez in 2005, I don't think initially he got the concept of movies being digitized, beamed up to a satellite and then on to cinemas around the world. However, he still invested $75,000 to get things going.' Unlike tyres, it was not a production process you could see. Today, UFO Moviez is the world's largest ever networked digital cinema chain and it has revolutionized film distribution. UFO Moviez spans 6,672 screens worldwide. In 2007, 3i, the multinational private equity group headquartered in London, invested $22 million to fund expansion plans.

Standing in the plush private cinema in the basement of Neeraj Kanwar's house in Shanti Niketan, Onkar Kanwar says: 'Isn't it fantastic that within days we can be sitting here watching the latest movies thanks to UFO Moviez.' Onkar loves James Bond films and action movies. Even better is watching the financial returns with revenue currently of ₹5.7 billion.

'I am not a mono-business guy,' says Raaja. 'I am always thinking of new things I want to do. I guess I must have some of my grandfather's spirit in me! I remember him as this hugely generous man, as is my father, but he did not throw his cash around. Some businessmen liked to show off their expensive Rolexes to him but grandfather would tap his trusty

Seiko that he had worn for years. I think like a lot of self-made men, he was careful with money.'

Back in 2002, life was about to make one of its major generational shifts for Raaja, Neeraj, Shalini and their parents.

◆

On the night of 29 September, Onkar took a call from his father's Friends Colony house. It was from his stepbrother, S.P. Singh, who was still living there. 'My father had recently had a change of heart valve and my stepbrother told me that he was having an attack.' Raunaq Singh was eighty-one years old and had been in failing health. 'I rushed to his house, taking a doctor with me but by the time we reached there he had gone. We tried to revive him but it was not possible. His passing away, on 30 September 2002, was a terrible shock.'

Neeraj and his family with also rushed to Friends Colony. 'It was a very bad time for my father because he was so very, very close to my grandfather, in spite of what had happened. He still respected and loved him. When we got back I saw how devastated Dad was. A part of his life was finished. Remember, when he came back from studying in the United States every day he would have lunch and dinner with his father. It was a given.'

When Raunaq Singh was involved in a bad car smash in Germany it was Onkar who rushed to be with him. 'I think his driver had been drinking. I arrived at the hospital in Düsseldorf, where he had been given a new hip and was being treated for a bad wound on his arm. I was astonished and a little alarmed to find he was already having physiotherapy. I said to the physiotherapist how could she do this when my father had only had surgery so recently. She looked at me and asked me if I was a doctor! I had no idea that physio started so soon. When we came back to Delhi I spent five weeks solid looking after my father.' Because of his injured arm Raunaq Singh was never again able to tie his own turban.

Neeraj recalls 'When grandfather died, my father said to me, "I wish

I could rewrite the Nineties. What went wrong I don't know." Grandfather had wonderful positive qualities and so does Dad. Grandfather was a great entrepreneur, full of ideas as is my father; but he is also an implementer who can see ideas through and run an organization. My grandfather could not run an organization. He was not into the day-to-day. He was not a one-plus-one guy. If they could have combined their talents and qualities, then who knows what they might have achieved.'

Ultimately, Onkar Singh Kanwar had probably paid the price of being far more commercially astute and successful than his father who somehow felt belittled by his son's successes when set against his own business failures in later life. For some sons walking in a father's footsteps can be like negotiating an emotional minefield, however much they love and respect them.

On Monday, 30 September, about 3,000 people assembled at New Delhi's Lodhi Road Crematorium for Raunaq Singh's funeral. The car park was soon jam-packed and mourners had to leave their cars both sides of the road outside and walk the rest of the way. Harish Bahadur describes it vividly as 'an ocean of people dressed in mourning white. There were even more at his prayer meeting three days later. He was a very dynamic and charismatic person.'

'Raunaq Singh's last rites were performed in the presence of a galaxy of dignitaries,' *The Times of India* reported. They included Congress leaders Manmohan Singh and R.K. Dhawan, eminent industrialists and representatives of all the chambers of commerce.

Raunaq Singh's funeral lasted ninety minutes. It began with a prayer ceremony around the body and Onkar as the eldest son had to perform most of the rituals, including the use of water from the Ganges to purify his father's journey into the ever after. After forty-five minutes the body was taken to the pyre, which Onkar lit. His eyes were red-rimmed; clearly he had been crying. U.S. Oberoi was nearby at all times, making sure that everything ran smoothly. A Sikh priest recited the final prayer of the day, *kirtan sohila*, and then led the *ardas* or prayer of supplication.

Once the flames had taken hold Raunaq Singh's children and their immediate families lined up by the exit gate and the mourners filed past them with folded hands to pay their respects. All bowed their heads but those who were especially close to the family paused to place their hands on their shoulder to console.

'The next day we went back to collect the ashes,' Neeraj says. 'They gave us the urn and his hip joint which was still boiling hot.'

Onkar Singh Kanwar and ten members of his family, including his children and grandchildren, then drove 225 kilometres in four cars to Haridwar, in the state of Uttarakhand, which has a special significance for both Sikhs and Hindus. There, Onkar and the men in the party immersed Raunaq Singh's ashes in Ganga River and said prayers. Back in Delhi, there were prayers for seven days at Raunaq Singh's house for family and friends and then a large prayer service at the Pahariwala Gurudwara in Greater Kailash in the south of the city to mark the ascension of his soul to heaven. There were also recitations from the Guru Granth Sahib, the Sikh holy book. The prayer service attracted even more people than Raunaq Singh's cremation. 'I think about 5,000 must have been there in a big air-conditioned hall,' Onkar says. The prayer service was one last chance for friends and colleagues to mark the passing of the great man. 'My father certainly knew a lot of people.' Onkar smiles fondly. 'He was a people's man.'

The tributes continued to roll in. The IT entrepreneur Ashok Soota, President of the Confederation of Indian Industry (CII), said the country had lost 'an eminent and charismatic first-generation entrepreneur'. Business journalists knew that they had lost a source of good quotes in the blunt and entertaining Raunaq Singh.

'In his life he had made very many connections, because he was so enterprising,' says R.K. Dhawan, 'and in the days of the Licence Raj he liked to have connections with the powers that be, but I can tell you that Raunaq Singh never messed with the power or went against the rules and regulations. That was one of the great things about him.'

It was the end of an era, but in truth Raunaq Singh's era as an entrepreneur had ended some time before. It had ebbed following the liberalization of India's economy in the early 1990s that consigned the Licence Raj to history. In spite of all his many achievements as a game changer, the ultimate rags-to-riches icon who had built an empire, *The Economic Times* probably was correct when it said, 'Raunaq Singh remained a prisoner of his past.'

As Rajan Nanda, a friend and contemporary of Onkar Kanwar's and who took over Escorts, the agri-machinery company founded by his father, Har Prasad Nanda, puts it, 'Raunaq Singh and my father were of the "know-who" generation. Onkar and our contemporaries are of the "know-how" generation.'

The Bharat Steel Tubes plant where Raunaq Singh's empire began is now a large dark shell lying forlorn and derelict on 129 acres of weeds, creepers and wind-blown litter. The windows of the guardhouse are broken and the entrance gates are chained and padlocked. A peeling legal notice bears the words 'Physical Possession'. The BST plant is in the hands of an asset reconstruction company while the courts decide its fate. Two bored security guards appear with outstretched hands shaking their heads. 'No admittance!' they say. 'After so many years, who knows when it will be resolved,' says P.N. Wahal.

Today, when Onkar Singh Kanwar is driven in his Bentley Mulsanne past Mrs Gandhi's prime ministerial bungalow at 1 Safdarjung Road, now a museum and a visitors' leading attraction, and sees the tourist buses and souvenir hawkers massed outside, he reflects at how much the world has changed since the days when his father, and he too, would call in to see 'Madam'.

Today, the official prime ministerial residence, Panchavati, at 7 Race Course Road, which is no more than a couple of kilometres away from Safdarjung Road, is set in twelve of the highest security acres imaginable. Across the way at the luxury Samrat Hotel all the rooms that overlook the Prime Minister's residence are occupied permanently by members of the Intelligence Bureau.

However, even fourteen years after his death, the name Raunaq Singh still resonates in the twisting, frenetic lanes of Old Delhi, where he laid the foundations of that empire. A close-knit, wall-to-wall world of noise, haze and smoke, screeching tuk-tuks, hawkers and chancers working the crowds, it remains a rickety cheek-by-jowl geography of currency dealers, language schools and business offices, all claiming to be 'international'.

And then pushing in deeper past the teashops and the police post, come the dealers in pipes and gears and pumps. Little has changed since the early days of India's independence but finding the site of one of Raunaq Singh's early shops in Hauz Qazi is like trying to find a needle in a haystack even when armed with an address.

Until one mentions his name, 'Ah, Mr Raunaq Singh's place!' And a boy is deputed to take us straight there. 'This is where Mr Raunaq Singh sat.'

fourteen

French connection

In 2003, U.S. Oberoi had become friends with a Frenchman called Dominique Galopin. Oberoi had helped Galopin find a house in Delhi. Galopin was normally based in Singapore but he had been sent to India to scout the ground for building a tyre factory. Dominique Galopin worked for Michelin.

Through Oberoi, Galopin got to know more about Apollo and it was not long before he asked Oberoi if Apollo might be interested in exploring the possibility of working together with Michelin.

Oberoi passed on the request to Onkar Singh Kanwar. He wasted no time. In May 2003, he took a Saturday evening flight from Delhi to Singapore for an initial informal meeting with Jean-Marc François, Michelin's Asia-Pacific boss.

◆

Landing on Sunday morning meant that Onkar could spend some time with his daughter Shalini, who lives there with her husband Vikram Chand, and their two sons Zubin and Aditya, who were then aged twelve and ten, respectively.

Vikram Chand is CEO of Vega Foods, based in Singapore, which exports food and beverages to Africa and parts of Asia. He also has a passion for stamp collecting. He and Shalini married in 1989 in Delhi, where Shalini studied for a psychology degree at Delhi University. They spent the first four years of their married life in Kobe, Japan. Vikram Chand, whose mother is novelist Meira Chand—'the most wonderful mother-in-law', as Shalini says—was born in Japan.

'To start with, I found living in Japan culturally difficult and challenging but every week my father wrote me a motivational letter, telling me that if I worked hard, I would make a success of it. Encouraged by him and my mother-in-law, I spent three years in colleges in Japan and learned to speak and write Japanese.' Both of Shalini's sons were born in Japan before the family moved to Singapore, where she did a postgraduate course in psychology and went on to work in hospitals and with the Leukemia Foundation of Singapore.

On a Sunday evening, after Onkar had spent time with his daughter and her family, Dominique Galopin arrived to take him to dinner with Jean-Marc François when a call came through to his hotel that Mrs Kanwar had been taken unwell and might have to be rushed to hospital. She had been suffering from dizziness and breathlessness and doctors were worried she might have heart problems.

Galopin drove Kanwar and Shalini to the airport immediately but they did not get there on time for the last direct Singapore Airlines flight to Delhi. Even though Onkar had a cell phone, international roaming was not widespread back then so it was impossible to find out any more about his wife's condition. Given his own experience of heart problems, he was extremely worried. He managed to get tickets for Singapore Airlines flight 422 to Mumbai a couple of hours later. There were only two seats left on the plane. Kanwar gave Shalini the one in first class while he sat in economy for the five-hour trip. In Mumbai, they had a three-hour wait before catching a connecting flight to Delhi—another two hours. They arrived exhausted having not slept, but were relieved to discover that Mrs Kanwar was now okay. She had not had a heart attack but the doctors were right to have been cautious.

Although Onkar Kanwar did not meet Jean-Marc François at that point, discussions soon got under way. 'It soon became clear that Michelin wanted to work with us to manufacture, market and sell truck and bus radial tyres in India,' Sunam Sarkar says. 'Michelin, which had invented radial tyres, had set the benchmark across the world in terms of technology and prices. They had already made two or three attempts to establish joint ventures in India but without success.' In return Michelin would share its passenger radial technology with Apollo.

The CEO of Michelin was Édouard Michelin, the great-grandson of one of the company's co-founders, after whom he was named. In 1999, at the age of thirty-nine, he had taken over the world's largest tyre company from his father. An engineering graduate from the elite École Centrale de Paris, Édouard was the fourth consecutive member of the Michelin family to run the company, which had started in 1889 and now employed 130,000 workers worldwide and produced nearly 200 million tyres.

Édouard Michelin was an intensely shy and private man yet he was ambitious to establish the business in Asia just as his father François, who ran the company for forty years, had established Michelin in North America. He was a young man in search of a legacy.

About 87 per cent of Michelin's revenues came from mature markets in Europe and North America. 'The Indian truck market was the last big prize for Michelin,' says Sunam Sarkar. 'They had already established themselves reasonably well in China and a manufacturing venture in Thailand was also proving to be very successful. India was the next big thing. They had identified Pune as the location for a joint venture radial truck tyre factory.'

To tyre makers of Onkar Singh Kanwar's generation Michelin was the pinnacle, the absolute gold standard. Neeraj was wary. He was concerned that Apollo could end up being swallowed up by Michelin, which had a 20 per cent global market share. 'Do you want me to run a gas station, selling the company business bit by bit?' he asked.

'With all the businesses my father had set up, there had always been an international collaborator but I thought the world was changing and that we should be investing in our own R&D,' Neeraj says. 'Technical collaborators will always give you second-tier technology; they will never give you the best. Why should they? Instead of paying a collaborator I would rather invest that money myself and develop our own tier-one technology.'

However, Neeraj agreed to go along with his father, feeling that there was nothing to be lost by taking discussions with the French giant further and exploring where they might lead.

Truck tyre radialization in India was an untapped market. Even though there were over two million trucks operating on India's roads moving up to 70 per cent of total cargo across the country, truck radial tyres still only accounted for 2 per cent of the market while car radials had captured 75 per cent. In the US, truck radials commanded over 90 per cent of the market and a similar number in Western Europe. Even in China and Thailand truck and bus radialization had cornered 25 per cent of the market.

For Michelin the advantages were obvious. In a highly consolidated market where the top three players accounted for nearly 61 per cent of sales, Michelin with its concentration in mature markets had experienced modest rates of growth over the past five years. Apollo on the other hand had seen a surge in sales in a burgeoning market.

Over the next few months meetings between Apollo and Michelin intensified. Heading Michelin's negotiators was Hervé Richert. Based in Singapore, Richert was Vice President of business development for Michelin Asia-Pacific and was responsible for legal affairs as well. He managed a team of fifty across the region.

Akshay Chudasama, a leading M&A lawyer from the firm of AZB Partners, had been called in by Onkar Singh Kanwar to act for Apollo, under the guidance of Managing Partner Zia Mody, who was lead counsel. Chudasama had a first meeting with Onkar Kanwar in the basement at Kanwar's house. Nimesh Kampani was also there. 'Shortly afterwards, we had a meeting with Michelin in Singapore and Neeraj was there, which was the first time I had met him although socially we had lots and lots of friends in common.'

As Apollo and Michelin embarked on the steps to setting up a joint venture—a complex set of legal agreements covering technology, distribution, shareholdings in the new company, and relationships between the promoters and leading shareholders—Chudasama, who has acted for several Indian family businesses, noticed a difference between them and the relationship that existed between Kanwar and Neeraj. 'They are from different generations—Kanwar is more old school, Neeraj's perspective is more contemporary—but they are both very clear on what they want to achieve and how they want to achieve it. They also complement and understand each other very well. Sometimes Kanwar can be a little trigger-happy and you find Neeraj balancing that out—and vice versa. In my experience of working with Indian promoter families, generational differences often lead to friction. I think there is a huge amount of admiration and respect that Neeraj has for Mr Kanwar and a huge amount of pride that Mr Kanwar has for Neeraj.'

Most of the meetings took place in Singapore or at Michelin's offices in Thailand and Malaysia. Apollo's negotiating team was spending most weeks away from India.

In July, Édouard Michelin was in Bangkok for a conference and asked if Onkar Kanwar and Neeraj could fly in to meet him. He wanted to get to know his potential joint venture partners first hand, particularly Neeraj. He needed to hear Neeraj's vision and gauge him as a person, because it would be they who, given their ages, would be taking this joint venture into the future together.

The three of them met over dinner at the Dusit Thani Hotel along with Jean-Marc François, Michelin's Asia-Pacific boss.

'Aside from the business aspects, I think what also attracted Édouard was that we were both family firms with very similar values, even though Michelin was much older and much bigger than Apollo,' Onkar says. 'We shook hands at the end of the dinner. I came away thinking that he was very genuine in wanting to join hands with us.'

As the deal between the two companies got ever closer to finalization, it became obvious that Apollo would have to end its collaboration deal with Continental or at least radically change their relationship. Onkar and Neeraj flew to Hannover for a meeting with Manfred Wennemer, Chairman of the executive board of Continental AG. They tried to convince Wennemer of the need for Continental to become an investor in Apollo and not just continue as a technical partner. Wennemer, described 'as one of the most down-to-earth CEOs on the planet', made it clear that that was not on his agenda.

The way forward with Michelin was clear as they were committing resources to India and Apollo. Apollo started negotiating a technical assistance fee with Michelin Research Asia along with the royalty and licence agreement to make it possible.

Onkar Singh Kanwar was not involved in the day-to-day discussions 'but whenever there was a roadblock, he would call me', says Jean-Marc François. 'We would meet over breakfast and talk through fears on both sides. Obviously, Michelin guarded its technology closely and Onkar was adamant that he would continue running Apollo the way he wanted. Our discussions were always frank but cordial. He places great emphasis on one-to-one meetings to build trust.'

Even though both sides had agreed on an announcement date for the joint venture of 17 November 2003, negotiations with Michelin were now not going as fast as Apollo would have liked. They looked to be heading down to the wire.

Meanwhile, Onkar Kanwar had sent out invitations to the great and the good of New Delhi to attend a 'special occasion and dinner' on 17 November at The Oberoi hotel but he could not reveal what the event was actually celebrating for reasons of confidentiality. The deal was not yet signed. Speculation was rife. Onkar was not normally so coy. Maybe The Oberoi hotel event was to celebrate a significant wedding anniversary.

With just days to go, the agreement was nowhere near close, and Hervé Richert, Édouard Michelin's right-hand man, was playing hardball. 'In the last two weeks we had felt that he was purposely dragging things out so we would have little negotiating room,' Neeraj Kanwar says.

When the Michelin team went into a huddle, speaking furtively in French, Neeraj Kanwar was pleased to tell them that Akshay Chudasama was a fluent French speaker and was able to understand every word that they said!

On the evening of Thursday, 13 November, Neeraj and the Apollo team had been sitting in Michelin's lawyer's office in Delhi for four full days trying to finalize all the legal agreements. Progress was pitifully slow and the air conditioning wasn't working. 'It was more like a house than a regular office,' Neeraj says. 'We were all spread out, the various negotiating teams working in different rooms.'

One major sticking point involved invoicing. All along the discussions had centred around the joint venture being the manufacturing entity and Apollo the sales entity, the face to the customer. At the very last minute, Richert suddenly announced that the joint venture needed to be a complete entity in its own right and so invoicing would have to be done in its name, rather than Apollo's. Invoices would be handed over by Apollo's sales teams, in effect reducing Apollo to the role of postman.

'Richert took me to one side,' Neeraj says. 'He told me, "If I sign the agreement as it is, Mr Michelin is going to look into my eyes and say what the hell have you signed?"'

Neeraj responded, 'If I sign the agreement the way you want it, Mr Kanwar is going to look into my eyes and ask me the same thing.'

They had reached an impasse. 'Richert said to me, "To hell with this, I am going to tell Édouard Michelin not to come into Delhi on Monday. There is no deal. And now I am off to Singapore." And with that he and his team literally got up, walked out and left for Singapore.'

Neeraj reported to his father, 'The guy is asking for everything; there is no agreement.'

Onkar advised him to be patient. The Kanwars have not found this virtue always easy to embrace, but Neeraj took the advice.

He later discovered that Richert was not really storming out. It was just meant to look that way. It was a ploy. In fact, Richert was attending the annual dinner on Friday for the Michelin business in Singapore, which had been arranged months before. Dinner over, he flew his team back to Delhi the same night, landed Saturday morning and called Neeraj. 'Let's get down to the lawyer's office,' he said with gusto. 'Let's thrash out the legal agreements.'

Neeraj and the Apollo team with their lawyers Zia Mody—one of India's top corporate lawyers and Founder of AZB & Partners in Mumbai—and Akshay Chudasama returned to Michelin's stuffy legal office. There were fourteen agreements to sign.

Neeraj and Sunam Sarkar worked on the main agreements, the share purchase and joint venture agreements. Satish Sharma was negotiating on a sales agreement. There was the all-important technology agreement, which Prabhakar was handling. 'When we were negotiating the technology agreement it was very frustrating because they were so cagey with whatever they were giving,' says Akshay Chudasama who is a quietly spoken lawyer with pinpoint focus. 'They kept trying to introduce things at the last minute.'

At 10 p.m., Neeraj parched, tired and running out of patience decided he needed a beer. 'I was sick of haggling, haggling, haggling.' The drivers were dispatched to the nearest liquor store and everybody went outside for a breather when the beers arrived.

Negotiations dragged on all through Sunday evening and into the early hours of Monday morning. 'Hervé Richert had played a blinder,' Neeraj says. 'What a lawyer, what a negotiator! First, he tried to make us desperate by disappearing to Singapore. Then, he came back and tried to exhaust us, reminding us that Édouard Michelin was now on his way to Delhi.'

Onkar agrees with Neeraj's assessment. 'Hervé Richert was a hard-core lawyer, very tough, and a favourite of the Michelins. He definitely had the boss's ear.'

Kanwar admits now that 'signing that agreement was my biggest blunder; but Édouard Michelin was on his way, I had called a board meeting so I could explain the rationale of the joint venture, along with a press conference that Michelin was due to address and I had invited about three hundred people to The Oberoi hotel. In spite of that, we should have held firm and not signed until we had the deal we wanted.'

◆

At 6.30 a.m. on 17 November 2003, Onkar Singh Kanwar and U.S. Oberoi were at Delhi airport to greet Édouard Michelin and his wife, Cécile, when they flew in from Clermont-Ferrand in central France on his private jet. 'I got permission from the customs authorities to meet them at the steps of their aircraft, which they were not expecting,' says Kanwar. We took the Michelins to The Oberoi where they were met by Neeraj and Simran, who would spend the day looking after Cécile Michelin.'

'An hour after Édouard had checked in, I went up to his room and he was going through the documents with Hervé Richert,' Neeraj says. 'Michelin said, "I am not only signing, I am giving you my family name. It is the first time Michelin has done this, so please respect it." Never before, had Michelin shared the sidewall of a tyre with the logo of another manufacturer. I assured him that I would always respect it. And that was it.'

At 10 a.m. the Apollo Supervisory Board met at The Oberoi to ratify the deal. Once they had done this, Édouard Michelin and Jean-Marc François came in to meet the board to a round of applause. They signed; there was a photograph and more applause.

'The rest of the industry was shocked that we had managed to do such a complex deal in just eight months,' says Jean-Marc François. Some commentators suggested that it was an unlikely marriage between a world-beating company of many years standing and a young dynamic family business coming out of India. 'A lot of that was due to the ability of Onkar and Édouard Michelin to think outside the box to make things happen,' says François.

At noon, the two sides transferred to the Imperial Hotel on Janpath where the press and TV cameras were beginning to arrive. After lunch, the press conference got under way. There was much expectation in the room. The new joint venture was to be called Michelin Apollo Tyres Pvt Ltd (MATPL).

Apollo and Michelin's $167-million joint venture would start commercial operations in September 2005 at a new plant to be built at Ranjangaon in Pune. Truck and bus radials would be priced at about 50 per cent more than the price of a bias truck tyre and the marketing effort would be focused on the southern and western parts of the country along with select markets in the north.

Michelin would have 51 per cent holding in the new joint venture company and Apollo, 49 per cent. The new company's seven-member board of directors comprised three from Apollo—Onkar Singh Kanwar, Neeraj Kanwar and Satish Sharma—and four from Michelin: Hervé Dub, who would be CEO of Michelin Apollo Tyres, Jean-Marc François, Dominique Galopin and Hervé Richert.

Apollo's board of directors also approved Michelin's purchase of 14.9 per cent of equity share capital in Apollo Tyres for around $28 million by means of a preferential allotment. This was the price Apollo, along with a dilution in the Kanwars' shareholding, would pay for Michelin's car radial technology support and which would replace the collaboration deal Apollo had had with Continental. Under takeover rules a 15 per cent stake would have forced Michelin to make an open offer for Apollo. Michelin also had two members on the Apollo Board including Jean-Marc François.

At 12.47 p.m. precisely, Édouard Michelin and Onkar Singh Kanwar symbolically exchanged agreement folders and posed for photographs and then went to the podium to address the media.

'The new factory,' said Onkar Singh Kanwar, 'would drive change in the transport industry,' and with an installed capacity of 3.5 million truck tyres per year 'increase the Indian truck radial market to 5 per cent in the next three years.'

'We want to become Indian in India, French in France and Chinese in China,' said Édouard Michelin. 'We believe that we have just the right tyres to match Indian conditions. With this agreement, Michelin fully intends to establish its presence and to grow in India with Michelin technology products, together with a partner with whom we share mutual ambitions, respect and trust.'

Investor website equitymaster.com described the alliance as 'a win–win situation for both companies.' There was no market overlap between the two. 'It gives Michelin an opportunity to gain a foothold in the Indian tyre market, which is showing a lot of potential and it also does away with the need to set up a marketing network of its own as Apollo has one of the best distribution networks in the country. Apollo Tyres, on the other hand, will benefit from the technical expertise of Michelin and help it come out with better variants in bus and truck radial tyres and thus help it maintain its leadership in this segment. It will also help Apollo make inroads into the car tyre market.'

Until the factory opened, the new joint venture company would import truck and bus radials from Michelin's factory in China.

That evening at 7 p.m. around three hundred A-list guests arrived at the Oberoi for cocktails and a celebratory dinner. There was music and more speeches from Onkar Singh Kanwar and Édouard Michelin. As the two men parted later that evening, Michelin returning to his private jet, Onkar Singh Kanwar reflected that although the marriage between the two companies had been far from straightforward, Michelin Apollo had a very satisfying ring to it.

'Like my father, Édouard Michelin was very down to earth and friendly,' says Neeraj Kanwar. 'The chemistry between them was there from day one.'

◆

The Michelin deal done, there was now the significant challenge of ending Apollo's relationship with Continental. As soon as the deal with Michelin had been agreed Onkar Singh Kanwar had sent a letter by fax to Manfred Wennemer at Continental, explaining the decision to take technical collaboration from Michelin along with the investment deal.

A few weeks later, on a cold early December day, Onkar Kanwar accompanied by Neeraj, Sunam Sarkar and lawyer Akshay Chudasama flew to Hannover to negotiate a severance deal with Continental. The separation looked fraught with legal difficulties and could involve a heavy compensation bill for Apollo. The Apollo team had spent the previous evening running through the briefing notes. Kanwar is blessed with a very sharp memory and does not like to refer to notes in meetings. He watches and weighs up before speaking.

Manfred Wennemer arrived with his lawyer in tow. Suddenly Kanwar announced that he wanted to talk to Wennemer one-to-one. 'You have your lawyer, I have my lawyer, but we do not need them.' Wennemer, ascetic and frugal and noted for his consistency, and a certain intransigence, looked slightly puzzled but agreed and excluded his own team from the meeting.

'I don't need to take the briefing notes, leave it to me,' Kanwar told Neeraj, Sunam Sarkar and Akshay Chudasama and asked them to wait outside. The three of them shrugged as the two men disappeared.

'I knew that if there were seven people in a room it was not going to happen and everybody would take up positions,' Kanwar says. 'Once we were alone I reminded Manfred that Apollo and Continental had had a great relationship from which we had both benefited equally. We were now getting technical collaboration from Michelin and Conti was not prepared to change its relationship with Apollo to that of investor. We could both walk away from it with our heads held high and with our good relationship intact. There was no need to go to court.'

When Kanwar re-emerged one hour later he and Manfred Wennemer were smiling. They had arrived at an amicable parting of ways.

'This is where you need to give Mr Kanwar a lot of credit,' says Akshay Chudasama. 'He is an absolute natural when it comes to pull and push. He knows when he needs to apply pressure and he knows when to let go and let professionals come into the picture. He has a great ability and a great knack of being able to understand the pressure points of deals and transactions. These are qualities you would expect to see in any entrepreneur and promoter but I have never seen anybody perfect it in the manner that Mr Kanwar does. His instincts are really good, he has a good gut feel. So he knew what he had to discuss with Wennemer; he knew how he had to do it and he just wanted to cut straight to the chase.'

◆

Apollo's senior project team, headed by KP went to Ranjangaon some 70 kilometres from Pune to supervise the civil and electrical engineering involved in setting up the new Michelin Apollo factory on 120 acres of land that Apollo had acquired on a ninety-nine-year lease and where it had already built a small 20-acre factory making tubes, flaps and the bladders used in the tyre curing process. Apollo Tyres had sold the other 100 acres to the joint venture company on which it would build the Michelin Apollo factory. Once it was built Michelin would install the manufacturing and processing equipment.

Early on, KP began to have his doubts that the unlikely marriage would work. 'Michelin seemed in no rush to build the factory. They were now importing their truck radials from their factory in China into India thanks to the joint venture agreement so they were already into the Indian market and taking full advantage of Apollo's dealer network. I don't think they had the same desire and process as us to push this plant. This was their 77th, but only our fourth. There's the difference. They wanted to do it at their pace which is fine from their point of view, but it was not the way Apollo operated.'

Construction tenders were taking an age to process. Prabhakar sensed delays. He had other concerns. 'The agreement stated clearly that my engineers would be trained in Michelin's plant. It had taken me a whole night to get that clause included during our negotiations. Now they were saying that they would not let us in and instead they would send their experts to us.

'I am a project person and not a political person and my priority is to get the plant up, recruit and train my people well and send them to factories to learn new technologies and processes. Michelin did not seem keen for us to learn new technologies. I tried to stand my ground. I had to protect the interests of Apollo at any cost.'

On one of his regular monthly visits to Delhi, Prabhakar voiced his concerns to both Onkar Kanwar and Neeraj. 'The project is not working.'

◆

With no sign of the plant coming up Apollo withdrew its project team as a way of emphasizing its concerns. In early July 2004, Apollo's fears that Michelin was undermining the joint venture agreement came to a head. Apollo had not been given access to information and documents relating to MATL. Revised project costs were showing a substantial overrun and a seventeen-month delay in project implementation would have an impact on the profitability of MATL and cause an adverse cash flow for Apollo. Commercial production, which should have started by September 2005, was now impossible. Even if everything was on schedule there would be a five-year gestation from foundations going in to tyres coming out of a factory. Any delay would have serious consequences for the project's economic viability.

Onkar Singh Kanwar was still determined that the joint venture would succeed and requested a meeting with Édouard Michelin. 'I asked him why Michelin was still importing Michelin/Apollo-branded truck radials made in China when we should be building the factory to make them in India. He told me that Michelin would do that when the market was ready. I insisted that we start manufacturing in India as soon as possible. We had done the research and the market would gradually increase. It was clear that they had their own philosophy which was different from ours.'

Every time Apollo asked for its staff to visit Michelin's factories for technology training, the request was politely declined. 'I sent a series of emails asking Édouard to honour that aspect of our deal,' says Kanwar, 'but they only ever sent their people to us. As a transparent company we had opened our door to them but they kept theirs closed to us.'

Kanwar told Michelin, 'Collaboration is two-way but unless our people can walk into your factories it cannot happen.' He still hoped against hope that the joint venture could be made to work, but Neeraj could see the writing on the wall.

'If the deal had gone the way it was written, it would have been a wonderful joint venture,' says Neeraj. 'But after sixteen to eighteen months I said to my father, "This is not going anywhere. We have given them full access to our dealer network, which they are using to import tyres into our market and we are getting nothing back from them. We are giving our future to them and one day they will eat us alive.'"

Michelin's previous joint venture in India with Chennai-based MRF to produce aeronautic tyres had fallen apart in 1995 when the two firms failed to agree on Michelin increasing its equity from 5 to 26 per cent.

Kanwar voiced his fears to close and trusted friends like Dr Amit Mitra, the Minister for Finance and Excise, Commerce and Industries of West Bengal. 'Onkar spoke to me often about how much he wanted the venture with Michelin to work and how disappointed he was that it was beginning to unravel,' Dr Mitra says. 'I think it was something to do with Michelin also being a family business that Onkar wanted it to work and he had genuine regard for Édouard Michelin. However, Onkar is a realist and as soon as he knew it would not work he realized he would have to bring it to an end. Sometimes these things work and sometimes they don't. Onkar is not afraid to move on. He is not a sentimentalist.'

Onkar heeded his son's warning. In July 2005, Édouard Michelin came to India because he was on the board of Nokia, which had just set up its mobile phone business in the country and they were having a global board meeting in Delhi. Kanwar went to meet him at the Imperial Hotel. They talked for a couple of hours and Kanwar went through all the issues that he had raised in previous correspondence with Michelin. 'It is not working the way we had hoped,' he said. 'We should have a proper divorce otherwise you will hurt and I will hurt. It can work both ways. You are bigger than me globally, but I am king in India so let's have a truce.'

Édouard Michelin tried to persuade Onkar to stay in the joint venture. He was happy seeing the two companies' names on the same tyre sidewall. Kanwar though is first and last a realist. He had decided that he alone would be the Michelin of India. 'It might have taken many years, but I had decided that I did not want to be guided by anybody else.' Michelin agreed reluctantly to a separation.

The two men shook hands, parted as friends and Neeraj was back into a series of meetings with Hervé Richert in the airless office of Michelin's

Delhi lawyers. This time it only took two days to reach a deal. The main issue was shares. Apollo agreed that Michelin could sell off its 14.9 per cent share in Apollo Tyres in small amounts over a period of six months to a year. A bulk sale could have alerted competitors.

On 1 October 2005, Apollo exited from its joint venture with Michelin. Apollo would get back almost everything it had invested in Michelin Apollo, selling its 49 per cent stake to the French company for $10 million. A joint press release said that the Pune project had been put on hold because the radialization of trucks and buses in India was not happening as fast as had been anticipated.

'The separation was actually far smoother than the marriage!' says Akshay Chudasama. 'And surprisingly so; it is usually and inevitably the other way around.'

'Joint ventures and partnerships with strong personalities and groups can be uneasy,' he says. 'I would put this failure down to a cultural difference. There are basic issues of control and in this case maybe there was not enough preparation in understanding what both parties would get out of the deal. The rationality and the logic of the joint venture did not really hold out. I think neither of them got out of it what they hoped to get out of it.'

Sunam Sarkar agrees. 'While Michelin got access to the Indian market, which was their primary requirement, we kept waiting for the technology which we thought we would get.'

'It was not so much to do with operational issues, although there were some of course,' says Jean-Marc François, who left Michelin in 2006 and is now director for external fulfilment, Amazon Europe, in Luxembourg. 'When you are a half-billion-dollar company making a deal with a fifteen-billion-dollar company you may have fears that you are losing your autonomy. On the other hand Michelin had its corporate restraints in terms of the way it shared its technology.

'I think this venture would have worked and we could have found a way around the problems but Onkar decided to go his own way. I can understand his reasons and at no time did it ever become confrontational or aggressive. I think it was a very elegant divorce not just legally but in terms of all those involved because the respect between Michelin and Apollo was always there. After the divorce, I kept in touch with Onkar. I was still based in Asia and would see him quite often in Delhi or Singapore. When I moved back to Europe we continued to see each other in London or Paris and we have gone from being business partners, and competitors, to something that is very close to friendship.'

In May 2006, Michelin ruled out manufacturing in India, citing once again the slow process of radialization in the Indian truck market. That same month Édouard Michelin tragically drowned while on a sea fishing trip. The wreckage of his line-fishing boat, Liberté, was found by a minesweeper about 10 miles off the coast of western Brittany. He was just forty-two years old. He was survived by his father, his wife and six children. It was another tragedy for an illustrious family company. Édouard's grandfather had died in a plane crash and his great-uncle perished in a car accident in the 1930s.

'It was a tragic loss,' says Onkar who had visited Michelin at his home in France and genuinely enjoyed his company. 'It is sad that we will never know what Édouard would have gone on to achieve. Although our joint venture did not succeed we did take positives from it.'

'It made us focus on how to sell and monitor the service of truck radials on the road,' says Neeraj Kanwar. 'Truck radial selling is concept selling and because you are selling at much higher prices you have to get the fuel consumption out and the benefits of greater mileage and if you do not service the tyre properly you will not get those benefits. However, those eighteen months were a wake-up call for me personally. I decided we did not need to be with Continental or Michelin for technological support. We would stand on our own two feet.'

fifteen

Passion in motion

Neeraj had already taken the first steps towards Apollo standing on its own two feet in March 2005, when he invited a senior team of fifteen, including Sunam Sarkar, P.K. Mohamed, Kannan Prabhakar and Satish Sharma, to a three-day meeting at the Wildflower Hall Hotel, near Shimla in Himachal Pradesh. The Swiss chateau-style seven-star, the former home of Lord Kitchener, sits atop a hill surrounded by dense forests with breathtaking views of the Greater Himalayas.

Neeraj chose Wildflower Hall because away from the hubbub of Delhi and the daily demands of business it was the ideal peaceful place to take stock of where Apollo had got to and to recognize its achievements, but most importantly to draw up a route map for the company's future.

'I took a team to whom I could relate and who I felt had good chemistry with me. I hoped that the environment would help us to think differently, totally differently.'

To bring some external wisdom and perspective, Neeraj had also invited a friend of his father's, Arun Maira. Maira is a renowned management consultant, a former member of the Planning Commission of India and had also been the India Chairman of the Boston Consulting Group (BCG). He had also been on the boards of several leading Indian companies including Tata Chemicals as well as written several books on organization and leadership.

Raunaq Singh, the father who inspired Onkar Kanwar to create a world-class organization

Raunaq Singh and his wife Satwant Kaur

The visionary Onkar Kanwar who was to take Apollo
Tyres to unimaginable heights

Onkar Kanwar at the Delhi airport as he moves to the United States of America for
higher studies

All set for the big occasion: Former President of India, Zakir Husain putting the traditional *sehra* on Onkar Kanwar for his wedding

The journey begins: Onkar Kanwar tying the knot with Taru Kapoor

APOLLO

CURES THE FIRST TYRE

ON 15ᵀᴴ NOV 1976

The wheel starts rolling with the first Apollo branded tyre

Raunaq Singh and Onkar Kanwar with the employees of Apollo's Perambra plant

M.R.B. Punja, former Chairman of IDBI, a long-
time advisor and friend to Onkar Kanwar

The perfect picture: Onkar and Taru Kanwar with their children (left to right)
Raaja, Shalini and Neeraj

Taru Kanwar with the former Prime Minister of India, Indira Gandhi

Onkar and Taru Kanwar with Mother Teresa

Onkar Kanwar with the former Prime Minister of India, Dr Manmohan Singh

Onkar Kanwar speaking at the BRICS event in October 2016 in Goa, India

Onkar Kanwar with the President of France, François Hollande

Onkar Kanwar with the former Secretary General of United Nations, Ban Ki-moon

Onkar Kanwar with the former President of Brazil, Dilma Rousseff

Onkar Kanwar with the President of People's Republic of China, Xi Jinping

Onkar Kanwar with the former Prime Minister of United Kingdom, Tony Blair

Onkar Kanwar with the former President of Pakistan, General (retd) Pervez Musharraf

Onkar Kanwar with the former Prime Minister of Japan, Junichiro Koizumi

A happy occasion: The joint family during the marriage of Onkar Kanwar's eldest child Shalini

Onkar Kanwar with father Raunaq Singh and brothers S.P. Kanwar, A.P. Kanwar and N.J. Kanwar

Onkar and Taru Kanwar with Onkar's sister Rani Kapur and brother-in-law Surinder Kapur

Shalini and Vikram Chand with their sons Zubin (right) and Aditya (left)

Raunaq Singh with Onkar Kanwar

Onkar and Taru Kanwar with Raaja Kanwar and his sons Aryaan (left) and Zefaan (middle)

Onkar and Taru with Raaja and his sons Aryaan (left) and Zefaan (right)

A happy grandfather: Raunaq Singh with his grandson, Neeraj Kanwar

The father-son duo of Onkar and Neeraj Kanwar who have taken Apollo Tyres to such great heights that it can now boast of manufacturing presence in Asia and Europe and product availability in over 100 countries

Onkar and Neeraj Kanwar with Édouard Michelin, CEO of Michelin (2nd from left) and the legendary François Michelin (extreme right) and other members of the Michelin senior management on their visit to Clermont-Ferrand, the Michelin HQ

The Limda radial plant being inaugurated by Narendra Modi, the then Chief Minister of Gujarat and now the Prime Minister of India

Apollo Tyres' fourth plant in India near Chennai was built in a record fourteen months

Onkar with Neeraj and his son Jaikaran Kanwar at Apollo Tyres' first European plant at Enschede in Holland

Apollo Tyres Global R&D Centres in Asia (top) and Europe (bottom), are the hubs for designing and creating world class products

Neeraj and Simran Kanwar with Syra and Jaikaran

Syra Kanwar, granddaughter of Onkar Kanwar

Onkar and Taru Kanwar with Neeraj and Simran Kanwar and their children Syra and Jaikaran

The annual Apollo One Family day celebration across all companies on the eve of Onkar Kanwar's birthday

The Kanwar family with India's President, Shri Pranab Mukherjee

Onkar Kanwar being conferred an Honorary Doctorate Degree by Amity University

Apollo's Board of Directors (diagonally from left to right):

Sunam Sarkar, President and Chief Business Officer, Apollo Tyres Holdings (Singapore) Pte Ltd;
Vikram S. Mehta, former Chairman, Shell Group of Companies;
Neeraj Kanwar, Vice Chairman and Managing Director, Apollo Tyres Ltd;
Nimesh N. Kampani, Chairman, JM Financial Group;
Pallavi Shroff, Regional Managing Partner, Shardul Amarchand Mangaldas & Co;
Onkar S Kanwar, Chairman and Managing Director, Apollo Tyres Ltd;
A.K. Purwar, former Chairman, State Bank of India;
Vinod Rai, former Comptroller and Auditor General of India;
General Bikram Singh (Retd), former Chief of Indian Army;
Akshay Chudasama, Regional Managing Partner, Shardul Amarchand Mangaldas & Co;
Francesco Gori, former CEO, Pirelli Tyre
Robert Steinmetz, former Chief of International Business, Continental AG
Dr S. Narayan, former Principal Secretary to the Prime Minister of India

Apollo Management Board members:
Sitting (left to right):
Francesco Gori, Advisor for Strategy;
Martha Desmond, Chief Human Resources Officer;
Onkar S Kanwar, Chairman and Managing Director;
Robert Steinmetz, Director;
Neeraj Kanwar, Vice Chairman and Managing Director;

Standing (left to right)
Daniele Lorenzetti, Chief Technology Officer;
Pedro Matos, Chief Quality Officer;
P.K. Mohamed, Chief Advisor, R&D;
Markus J Korsten, Chief Manufacturing Officer;
Satish Sharma, President, Asia Pacific, Middle East, Africa;
K. Prabhakar, Chief Projects;
Gaurav Kumar, Chief Financial Officer;
Mathias Heimann, President, Europe & Americas;
Marco Paracciani, Chief Marketing Officer;
Sunam Sarkar, President and Chief Business Officer

Onkar Kanwar with the Prime Minister of India, Shri Narendra Modi

Early Seventies: The then Apollo Chairman Raunaq Singh with its VC & MD Onkar Kanwar and its future VC & MD Neeraj Kanwar

The happy couple: Onkar and Taru Kanwar at their silver wedding anniversary

If dramatic portents were needed they arrived soon after the party did in the shape of a massive hailstorm. It was raining ice. 'We went out and stood there watching,' Neeraj says. 'It was just so beautiful.'

The mood to begin with was gloomy. People were disillusioned. The Michelin joint venture was unravelling but nobody seemed to have the energy to talk about it until Prabhakar, whose project team was the most directly affected by the failure to build the Pune plant, bowled a googly ball, something for which he is renowned. 'We have been opening up our networks to Michelin and have been asking for access to their plants but on some pretext or another we have been denied. Instead they come and see our plant and are supposed to give us technological assistance but all they give us is a report which contains everything they have observed about us but without comment and then concluding with homilies like making one good tyre is easy, making a million good tyres is the challenge.'

And with that the dam of resentment and frustration burst.

Everybody was in agreement that Apollo was standing at a crossroads, a pivotal moment in its history, but Neeraj did not wish the Shimla workshop to get bogged down in criticism. Even then he was pretty sure of where the Apollo Michelin narrative was headed. Rather, he wanted the team to focus on the future and wider horizons, which is where Arun Maira came in.

Maira's introductory session focused on 'Why do we need what we need to do?'

Apollo had achieved a lot. It was India's largest tyre maker with 27 per cent of the truck and bus tyre market and 24 per cent of the light truck market. It had invested $60 million in high-tech equipment at its Limda plant to make passenger car radials. PCRs accounted for close to 100 per cent of the automobile market in India and Apollo had a 15 per cent share of that. Apollo was financially robust. Its market capitalization had grown more than six times. It had achieved stable and peaceful industrial relations, improved quality and capacity and had a strong after-sales service.

It was also mature enough to be aware of its weaknesses and address them. On the downside, there had been too much emphasis on fire-fighting crises and on the short term. 'We had become very good at it,' says Neeraj. 'We needed to embark on a new long-term journey.'

During a series of strategy sessions key signposts to that future began to emerge. Apollo should turn its back on any more technical collaboration with foreign companies. Experience had proved beyond doubt that this was not the path to technical excellence and that Apollo would continue to be palmed off with second-tier technology if it continued down that route. It would have to grow its own technological excellence and R&D. This would involve a big training effort as India was still weak in technical and scientific courses related to tyre manufacture. The other option, which could go hand in hand, was to acquire that expertise.

The group agreed that in a fast-changing world, Apollo had to change faster but without losing its values. It was too India-centric in a rapidly growing global economy and too vulnerable to an Indian economy that was volatile. It needed greater exposure to Western ways of doing things to achieve better quality and business excellence if it was ever going to compete effectively in a world market.

At the end of the three days, Arun Maira said to Neeraj: 'You are the general, take some time. Go up the mountain and come down with a plan for your army.'

Neeraj found a secluded terrace where, freed from his mobile phone, he began to think. And then he started to write down his thoughts.

Leaving Shimla, Neeraj, Sunam Sarkar, Satish Sharma and Arun Maira were travelling together in one car back to the airport as everything began to crystallize further into four big strategies: self-reliance; investment in quality, technology and people; specific achievement targets brought in for every aspect of the company; and a business footprint on a global scale.

Neeraj had devised the banner headline that summed it all up: 'Passion in Motion'.

'It was a turning point,' says KP. 'It was a great few days. It integrated all of us tremendously. Going global from an India-centric point of view is very complex and perhaps when we arrived at Shimla not all of us thought it could be done. But Neeraj believed it could be and all credit must go to him. By the end of it we all believed it could be done.'

Returning to Gurgaon, the Shimla workshop team then got down to work on a major presentation that would spell out the next stage of Apollo's journey to the rest of the organization; mapping out the small steps which would together lead to major strides forward.

Onkar Singh Kanwar was excited by the buzz. He had been hinting for a while that Apollo's record was stuck in the same old groove. Impatience is in his DNA, as it is in his son's. 'I can happily confirm that!' Neeraj grins.

In early April, Apollo's senior management group, its Gurgaon staff and those from the Delhi sales offices met at the Taj Palace Hotel in New Delhi.

Sunam Sarkar was the MC for the day. When people walked in he had playing in the background the song from the Live Aid concert of 1985, 'We Are the World' and kicked things off by saying, 'Let's make a better world for ourselves.'

The presentation they sat down to watch was called 'Planning for Our Future'. Early slides were headlined 'The power to accelerate and overtake', 'Transforming for achievement', and 'Expanding our field of vision'. Neeraj Kanwar presented the bulk of the blueprint aided by Sunam, P.K. Mohamed and Satish Sharma. They focused on a future based on self-reliance and self-created technological excellence. They homed in on one message repeatedly: Apollo's journey was a people journey. 'Everyone contributes to the journey. We cannot do it without you.'

'It was hugely energizing for the organization,' says Sunam Sarkar. 'It was the first time we had done a structured strategic planning exercise.' Unlike the early days of clarion calls to short-term action, 'Planning for Our Future' was measured and methodical but also incredibly exciting and achievable. Suddenly, everyone in the room felt that Apollo was putting the pedal to the metal.

Neeraj Kanwar had one very big and breathtaking surprise though. 'We aim to be a $2 billion turnover company by 2010.'

Apollo then had sales of $600 million. When Neeraj had told his father of the $2 billion by 2010, Onkar Kanwar had said; 'Are you crazy?'

But he was smiling when he said it. It was just the kind of audacious goal that Apollo should be known for. 'Go for it,' he told his son. 'I'll back you all the way.'

Once Onkar Singh Kanwar says 'Yes' to something, there is no going back.

sixteen

Buying an icon

After Shimla, Apollo hit the ground running. Of course, $2 billion by 2010 was not going to be achieved solely by organic growth. Building plants from scratch and then getting them up to full production capacity took a long time. It would require inorganic growth as well—the acquisition of other companies; and one of the leading markets of interest was Europe. In terms of technology and profitability Europe has always been one of the most desirable markets in the tyre industry. So after the Shimla workshop when Sunam Sarkar did a study of all the tyre manufacturing companies in Europe, he discovered that the last surviving independent tyre manufacturer in Europe was located in a town called Enschede with a population of 150,000 in the far east of Holland. A few miles from the German border, its name was Vredestein Banden.

'None of us in Apollo had ever heard of it,' says Onkar Kanwar. 'It was time to reach out to them and ask for a meeting.'

Vredestein produced more than 17,000 tyres a day and was decidedly high end with higher prices and higher margins. From the late Nineties, it had teamed up with Italian car designer Giorgetto Giugiaro to produce high performance tyres for Ferrari, Audi and Porsche. The Giugiaro Group had been responsible for designing the Volkswagen Golf 1, BMW M1, Maserati 3200 GT and the Alfa Romeo Brera.

The Enschede plant, which employed 1,800 people, also produced cold-weather alpine tyres. The company had an R&D centre in Enschede employing sixty-five scientists and engineers and crucially it had eleven offices in Europe, one in America, and distribution in seventeen European countries. It was exactly the sort of company that could take Apollo to Neeraj's $2 billion target by 2010 and into Europe and the United States.

Within weeks of the Shimla workshop Neeraj Kanwar and Sunam Sarkar arrived at Vredestein's plant in Enschede. With them was Robert Steinmetz, the former chief of the international business unit of Continental AG, who had joined the Apollo Board after retirement from Conti in 2003.

There they met Vredestein's silver-haired, bespectacled CEO Rob Oudshoorn. In his eighteen years at the company, Oudshoorn—who had previously worked for Michelin in South Africa, Japan and Switzerland—had modernized and turned Vredestein around, investing some 100 million euros in the very best equipment for car and agricultural radial tyres, including automatic tyre building machines of its own invention which could produce one green tyre every thirty seconds, X-ray scanners to search for flaws, and robotic forklifts ferrying finished tyres to the storage sheds.

As they toured the plant the Apollo visitors could tell Vredestein was a well-managed, forward-looking company with great technical know-how but also proud of its past. A plaque inside the plant marks its opening in 1946 by Queen Juliana of the Netherlands. American company B.F. Goodrich had owned just over 20 per cent of the shares. In 1976, the Dutch state took 49 per cent of the company's shares and in the early Nineties, three Dutch investors acquired it back from the government. By 2004, Vredestein reported sales of $286 million.

Oudshoorn was typically polite and hospitable but he and Managing Director Kees Hettema were not oozing enthusiasm towards Apollo.

'Vredestein were a little cagey towards us,' Neeraj Kanwar admits. 'Apollo was still in its relationship with Michelin and Vredestein viewed us doubly suspiciously. They thought we were either leading a Michelin approach into them, or a Conti approach because we had Robert Steinmetz with us. Even though he had left Continental, Robert was still known as a Conti man, having spent close on forty years there.'

Neeraj Kanwar emphasized that companies like Vredestein and Apollo needed to find ways to cooperate and work together being smaller entities and on which the big global entities like Bridgestone and Pirelli could apply pressure, affecting their market share and profitability. He reassured Oudshoorn and Hettema that their visit had nothing to do with attempts at back-door takeovers by Conti or Michelin and that they were purely in Enschede in their own right.

After their visit Kanwar, Sarkar and Steinmetz were standing in the car park waiting to get into their car when Neeraj looked around and said, 'I want to buy this company. Should I tell Rob?'

Sarkar counselled against saying anything there and then. Back in Gurgaon, he started exchanging emails with Rob Oudshoorn and a meeting was set up for March 2005 in Delhi when the Kanwars planned to discuss with him an Apollo offer for Vredestein.

A week before he was due to arrive in India Oudshoorn called Sarkar. 'Sunam, we have to call our trip off because my majority shareholder has just told me he has exclusivity agreements with a company that is looking to buy us out.'

'We would very much like to participate in that,' Sarkar replied. 'How do we get in?'

'I am sorry,' Oudshoorn said. 'I cannot do anything because the exclusivity agreement has already been signed.'

A month later, on 25 April 2005, it was announced that a leading Russian tyre company called Amtel had bought Vredestein Banden for $265 million. 'The transaction will allow Amtel to boost its operations in Europe, Asia, North America and the former Soviet Union,' an Amtel statement said. The new company would be called Amtel-Vredestein.

'It was very serious money from a company that wanted to expand into Europe,' Oudshoorn says. As far as the Kanwars were concerned, Amtel's purchase price hugely overvalued Vredestein.

Thwarted, the Kanwars' attention now turned elsewhere.

◆

Right on cue, Robert Steinmetz tipped them off that the CEO of Dunlop South Africa had told him that the company might be up for sale. Steinmetz had been based in South Africa for some years and so he knew the business well.

The Kanwars realized immediately that although Apollo had lost out on Vredestein, it could add one of the most iconic tyre brands in the world to its stable. This, not Vredestein, would be a major first step in addressing two major building blocks of Passion in Motion: access to a new international market, where Apollo did not have any presence at all, and new truck radial technology. The way things were going with Michelin, he knew they were not going to get access to it from them.

Although one of the world's most recognizable brands from tennis shoes to tyres, Dunlop had long ceased to be a British multinational company. Post World War II it lost market share, particularly to Michelin, and had endured a chequered history of takeovers, break-ups and a disastrous merger with Pirelli in the Seventies, which was dissolved. In the early Eighties, Dunlop worldwide had been acquired by British Tyre and Rubber (BTR), which was then acquired by Invensys which was more into engineering goods. It did not see much future for the tyre business.

Typically, tyre companies have been sold as global international entities but Invensys chose to sell off Dunlop in bits and pieces to different companies around the world. Most of the Asian operations were sold to Sumitomo Rubber, which way back in the 1920s was the original joint venture partner of BTR to take the Dunlop brand into Japan. The first overseas Dunlop factory had been set up in Kobe in 1909.

In the great Invensys sell-off Goodyear acquired some of Dunlop's US operations. A Goodyear–Sumitomo joint venture was subsequently formed, which had the brand rights for Dunlop in Europe and Sumitomo even got a portion of the US venture—which would eventually be dissolved at the beginning of 2016. In India, Dunlop's operations were bought by Manu Chhabria, who featured in another famous Indian family business feud that lasted for nearly a decade. In Malaysia and Singapore the Dunlop brand rights were with Continental.

No companies wanted to acquire Dunlop South Africa. Hived off from the rest of the Dunlop world, it had to merge with somebody to survive. In 1997, CEO Mike Hankinson, who had just joined the company, having been President of the Textile Federation, feared losing his job before he had even had a chance to begin it. He organized a management buyout supported by private equity money and bought the operations from Invensys: two manufacturing facilities in South Africa and two businesses in Zimbabwe.

In April 2005, the Kanwars, Sunam Sarkar and Robert Steinmetz arrived at Dunlop's headquarters on Sydney Road in the heart of Durban, very close to the harbour. Dunlop in South Africa had a very rich legacy. The Durban plant was one of the oldest Dunlop plants outside the United Kingdom. It was set up in 1935 and produced the first car tyre in South Africa that year.

Its grand old British company office building was very similar to Dunlop House in Kolkata and all the other Dunlop Houses around the globe—rattan chairs, ceiling fans and wide floorboards that only needed polishing once a year. A glass case about two feet across displayed the evolution of the Dunlop golf ball from the feather-filled ball wrapped in canvas, progressing to what was known as 'India Rubber', the first dimple ball and through to the latest in the evolution.

In the wood-panelled boardroom, dominated by a large watercolour painting of the construction of the Durban plant, the Apollo visitors were welcomed by Mike Hankinson and Pierre Dreyer, who was the Managing Director and running operations. Dreyer was a tyre industry veteran and icon, a larger-than-life rugby-playing personality who went surfing every morning and was on first-name terms with all the dealers. Before joining Dunlop, he had founded Trentyre, Africa's biggest retreading company that he then sold to Goodyear.

Hankinson and Dreyer gave the Kanwars an overview presentation of the company and showed them around the Durban plant, which was manufacturing truck tyres and giant mining vehicle tyres, some of them twelve feet high. The plant was connected to the harbour by a canal from which it could take water for the manufacturing process and which was also once used to ferry tyres out to the harbour for shipping.

Interestingly, Dunlop also had the licence to market tyres in South Africa for an American tyre manufacturer, Cooper Tire & Rubber Company. It was the first time that Cooper nudged its way on to Neeraj Kanwar's radar. Onkar Singh Kanwar, however, remembered being unceremoniously shown out of the office of Cooper's then Chairman in Ohio, many years ago. 'Apollo? Never heard of it!' He smiled at the irony of Apollo potentially becoming Cooper's South Africa distributor.

The next day, Hankinson and Dreyer took the Kanwars, Sarkar and Steinmetz to Dunlop's Ladysmith plant, about 200 kilometres north, equidistant between Durban and Johannesburg. It had been built in the 1990s and made car tyres. Ladysmith was at the heart of the Boer War; when it was famously besieged and then relieved after 118 days. Dreyer and Hankinson took their visitors to the spot between Frere and Chieveley in what was then British Natal Colony, where a young twenty-five-year-old reporter named Winston Churchill had been captured after his train was derailed by a Boer Kommando force in 1899.

After three days, the Kanwars returned to India having agreed to put together a preliminary offer and valuation for Dunlop. They worked on it with advisors from Nimesh Kampani's firm. In May, the valuation offer was ready and Neeraj Kanwar, Steinmetz and Sarkar flew to Amsterdam and met Mike Hankinson at the Hilton at Schiphol airport.

Apollo put their preliminary valuation offer for Dunlop South Africa of $27 million to $35 million on the table, although they had agreed beforehand to go to $50 million, if necessary. Recalls Neeraj Kanwar, 'Mike stared straight back, grim-faced and said, "Well, gentlemen, let's have a good lunch and I'll take the next flight back."'

'Mike was a wonderful poker player, absolutely deadpan,' says Neeraj. Hankinson said that Apollo had grossly undervalued Dunlop. He argued that one of the attractions of the company was its large pension surplus, which many South African companies had at that time because all workers had been moved from a defined benefit plan to a defined contribution plan. The way the two were valued created a surplus and there was a process to be followed in terms of how that surplus could be liquidated.

Robert Steinmetz said that Apollo could go to $50 million.

Hankinson did not bite on that either. The next plane still beckoned.

Neeraj Kanwar explained to him that Apollo was only after the tyre plants in Durban and Ladysmith and their related sales and marketing outlets. 'That is what our valuation is based on. We are not interested in acquiring the company's pension surplus or its stakes in Dunlop Nigeria or Dunlop Rubber.'

He conceded that Apollo would also take on Dunlop's interest in Dunlop Zimbabwe and a retreading business, National Tyre Service, which it had there. Zimbabwe was not a healthy place to do business in at that time thanks to the basket case economic policies of President Robert Mugabe and his purges of foreign companies. However, the Kanwars reasoned, the ageing dictator could not live forever and with his passing, things could only improve. What attracted them long term was the fact that Dunlop Zimbabwe had excellent trade agreements across much of English-speaking Africa—Dunlop branding rights in Francophone Africa were owned by Sumitomo—while South Africa, as a consequence of Apartheid, did not. It would be a great base for selling to a huge swathe of the continent.

When Hankinson understood what Apollo was basing its valuation on, he stopped talking about taking the next plane home.

Now, the serious talking began, back in Durban. It did not start auspiciously. Apollo's South African lawyer was Carl Stein, an M&A star and senior partner of Werksmans Attorneys, a leading South African corporate and commercial law firm serving multinationals and listed companies as well as financial institutions and government. Stein—whose father had also been a senior partner at Werksmans—had advised on a number of notable deals including acting as lead counsel to Telkom SA Ltd when it listed on the New York Stock Exchange, which at the time was the largest initial public offering (IPO) by a South African company on a foreign exchange.

Stein's talent was not in doubt—he would go on to become the Chairman of Werksmans—but it was not always matched by his punctuality as Neeraj Kanwar was about to discover when he, Sarkar and Akshay Chudasama arrived at the sellers' lawyers' offices ready to start discussions on the agreement.

The meeting was supposed to start at ten but there was no sign of Carl Stein. Frantic calls were made. His secretary was trying to reach him but he was not answering his phone. And then, he walked in at noon, a huge ruddy-faced Afrikaner, calm as anything.

'We've been waiting for you,' Neeraj said impatiently.

Stein shrugged and mumbled something about having his son come over to stay, but not a word of apology. Then he spotted the finger-food buffet. He walked over, picked up a burger and popped the whole thing into his mouth.

Neeraj could not believe what he was seeing.

Over the next few months, Apollo embarked on its due diligence. Working with the lawyers it found a way in which all the assets it did not want to acquire, such as Dunlop Nigeria, could be taken out and sold separately. Apollo also agreed that even after it took control the company's pension surplus process could continue until it was complete and all dividends paid out to shareholders.

Apollo called a meeting of its board in Mumbai, which endorsed the deal, which excluded Dunlop Nigeria, Dunlop Zambia, as well as Dunlop International Limited. On 23 April 2006, the Kanwars took a direct overnight flight to Johannesburg arriving next morning, by which time Dunlop's board had approved the deal. It was then signed in time to send it in to the Indian stock exchange as the markets opened.

Apollo had acquired Dunlop South Africa for $52 million in an all-cash deal.

The acquisition of Dunlop South Africa marked Apollo's arrival in the global manufacturing arena with the combined entity ranking fourteenth in the world in terms of size.

Tire Review magazine reported: 'The acquisition is expected to springboard the combined entity into position as a significant global player and is likely to form the base for future growth initiatives. For Dunlop [it] further enhances its already considerable technology. Its current radial technology will be boosted by Apollo's in-house technology coupled with support from European and North American arrangements.'

'We see tremendous synergy in the operations of the two companies,' said Onkar Singh Kanwar. 'They can leverage each other's strengths to be a global force.'

The stock market reacted positively to what was seen as a good move by Apollo into a global market with new technology and the Dunlop brand resonated strongly in India as it did around the world. At that time Dunlop had better average operating margins than Apollo had in India, which was a reflection of the product mix because South Africa was much more radialized than India.

Onkar Kanwar's approach to takeovers was not the norm. 'Around 75 per cent of takeovers fail because acquiring companies go in and do not listen, do not bother to understand the culture they are coming into and are just looking to sell assets and recoup costs,' he says. 'Our approach was entirely different. I did not want to rock the boat at Dunlop. Yes, Apartheid-era attitudes still hung on. It was only a dozen years since Mandela had become the President and some of the white management at Dunlop clearly felt uncomfortable with an Indian coming in as their boss. But we spent time listening and learning. We invited their people to our Vadodara plant and our office in Gurgaon and laid on social events so they could have a relaxed interaction with us and get some value from us. It was important to me, to all of us, that they knew we felt that they were good people and that we had come to support them.'

To maintain continuity Mike Hankinson and Pierre Dreyer would continue running Apollo Dunlop South Africa. However, 'Apollo put together an integration team,' Neeraj explains. 'KP was asked to go out to South Africa because the most benefit we thought we would get was from improving their manufacturing systems and processes. They really weren't as productive as we were.' There were a number of contributing reasons for that. During Apartheid, South Africa had been cut off from the rest of the world so they lagged behind in technology improvements and enhancements and post-Apartheid it had become a stand-alone company owned by a private equity company whose focus was to maximize profitability so they could sell it on to the next buyer rather than invest long term.

'When we went into Dunlop, South African society was still very stratified,' says Neeraj Kanwar. 'Whites were in management, people of Indian descent were the middle management and supervisors and the shop floor workers were all Africans. And there was no interaction at all which was very unusual for people like us coming from a company which is all one family. So P.K. Mohamed, who was charged with learning about Dunlop's radial technology, would work there just as he worked in India and went on to the shop floor, talked with the workers and asked them questions. Those guys were amazed that the chief of technology was coming to talk to them like this and working with his hands on the machines. But that did something for our reputation as an organization because we built credibility with them.'

It also put P.K. Mohamed on a steep learning curve, building a knowledge that he would bring to bear with stunning success in other arenas.

Kannan Prabhakar and his integration team of seven also started their work on the shop floor. KP was to spend two years in South Africa as Chief Operating Officer. 'It was a good learning—how to work with new people and new cultures was to stand us in good stead. Demographically it was a very complex place,' he says. 'I learned that a lot of patience is needed because the working practices are completely different. For example, at three o'clock on Friday afternoons workers would just stop and go off for the weekend, something I had never encountered before. You had to be very careful about body language and what you said. In India you can always apologize for saying the wrong thing. In South Africa you could never take it back. So we had to build proper relationships by spending a lot of time on the shop floor. Language was another challenge. English was only spoken in the offices. In the factory it was Afrikaans and local languages, none of which we could understand. It was very important that we were good ambassadors. We had to show goodness without it being seen as a weakness. It can be a clever balancing act!'

After the Dunlop deal was done, and approved by the South African Competition Commission and other regulators, it was time to take a look at Apollo's other acquisition, Dunlop Zimbabwe. Neeraj Kanwar, Sunam Sarkar, Satish Sharma and KP, along with Hankinson and Dreyer, chartered a plane from Durban to Bulawayo, Zimbabwe's second largest city. When they landed at Bulawayo International they could not see a terminal building. The plane went straight into a hangar. Stepping out, they realized that the hangar was serving as the terminal. The pilot pointed to a large pile of rubble and explained that that was what used to be the terminal building. President Mugabe had felt that it was not suitable or impressive enough for a city like Bulawayo so he had commanded it to be demolished. However, at a time of rampant inflation when it took a suitcase of cash to buy a packet of biscuits—if you could find a packet of biscuits on the supermarket shelves—there was then no money to build a new terminal, so the hangar was now it.

Even though they had notified immigration they would be arriving there was nobody there to check passports and process them into the country. As Sarkar joked: 'We could be a bunch of mercenaries allowed to just walk in and take over the country, like a Frederick Forsyth novel.'

After waiting an hour they saw a woman cycling determinedly towards them. She was the immigration officer. The pilot said, 'We filed the flight plan, you knew what time we were coming.' Gasping for breath, she replied, 'Well, along with the flight plan you should have sent me some petrol for my car because there has not been any in Bulawayo for the last two weeks so I had to cycle all the way from town.'

Returning to South Africa, Prabhakar was involved in a bad car accident when a truck ran a light and smashed into him. He called Neeraj Kanwar from the hospital and told him what had happened. Neeraj took immediate action. 'Within days, Mr Oberoi arrived at my house with airline tickets and travel money for my wife so she could fly out to see me,' Prabhakar says. 'He had arranged the visa for her personally. That kindness and consideration is typical of the Kanwars.'

Luckily Prabhakar's injuries were minor—a broken bone in his arm—although he had suffered a considerable shock and was in severe pain. Even so, he returned to work as soon as he could. 'A month later when Mr Kanwar and Neeraj came out to South Africa for a review of the company they took one look at me and insisted that I should go home to Delhi and rest for three weeks.'

◆

In 2006, Apollo passed the $1 billion sales mark. By 2007, Apollo Dunlop was producing good results with margins in the mid-teens while the Indian operations were lower than that. In large part, this was down to what Michael Ward, Managing Director, Corporate Advisory at the Royal Bank of Scotland in London and a leading authority on the tyre industry, calls Apollo's 'unique feature'. It remains true to its family ethos. When the Kanwars welcome newcomers to what they call the Apollo Family, these are not just words. This has been a critical feature of that most difficult of tasks, the integration of acquisitions. Few companies in my experience do this so well and its value should not be underestimated. It should remain at the heart of enabling you to remain nimble.'

That nimbleness had not gone unnoticed when on a Saturday in January 2007, Roy Armes, recently appointed CEO of Cooper Tire, arrived in Delhi for a meeting with Apollo. Armes who had a BSc in Mechanical Engineering from the University of Toledo had held various senior positions with the Whirlpool Corporation, a multinational manufacturer of home appliances. Armes was a typically bluff out-there American businessman. A big man who tended to shoot from the hip, he was also very astute. Now he was on a familiarization tour of tyre companies, assessing the competition in a market he had no previous experience of.

Sunam Sarkar gave him a presentation about Apollo in the Gurgaon office and then that evening Armes had dinner at Onkar Singh Kanwar's house, along with Neeraj and the Apollo senior management, where Armes talked about his experiences in India and especially a deal Whirlpool had done back in 1995 to acquire Kelvinator India Limited.

'That was a lousy deal that Whirlpool did,' Kanwar told him with typical frankness.

'Well, actually, I did that deal,' Armes said.

'A strained silence followed,' Sarkar says.

But it did not stop Cooper wanting to talk further with Apollo. Apollo Dunlop CEO Mike Hankinson invited Neeraj Kanwar, who was now Vice Chairman and Managing Director of Apollo, and his wife Simran for dinner at the Cipriani, a renowned and fashionable classical Italian restaurant in London's Mayfair. Also invited was Stephen W. Switzer who as Vice President, global business development for Cooper Tire, was responsible for South Africa where Apollo was now distributing Cooper's tyres through Dunlop. Switzer was keen to discuss what else Cooper and Apollo might do outside South Africa.

With Apollo showing that it could improve the performance and profitability of an overseas acquisition with an international market, the conversation turned to other things, says Neeraj. 'We started talking about the viability of working together, especially gaining access to the European market by building a plant on a greenfield site.'

The previous year, Apollo and Cooper had put a couple of teams together to explore possibilities of cooperation and these met on the sidelines of the annual Speciality Equipment Market Association (SEMA) Show in Las Vegas in November. SEMA is the world's premier show for automotive products and attracts 100,000 industry leaders from a hundred countries. The Apollo and Cooper teams identified four or five areas of work where the companies might cooperate.

In April 2007, Apollo was having its annual sales conference in Dubai. Neeraj Kanwar and Sunam Sarkar left it early to go to Frankfurt for a further meeting with Steve Switzer and Hal Miller, who was President of Cooper's international business. Of all the cooperation options available it was the possibility of Apollo and Cooper working together to build a greenfield manufacturing site in Eastern Europe that appealed the most. For Apollo this was the best route into the lucrative European market.

KP was sent to investigate possible locations. 'My team looked at Hungary, Poland and Slovakia and we zeroed in on Hungary,' he says. 'It had better skilled people, sites very near Budapest airport and we could gain maximum incentives there. In Slovakia and Hungary we were offered good deals on land; there was not much to choose from there. But Hungary edged it because there was better schooling in Budapest than in Bratislava and a better life for expats. The site chosen was on an industrial park near Gyöngyöshalász, a community of about 2,500 some 80 kilometres east of Budapest.'

Through much of 2007 and early 2008, Apollo and Cooper continued discussing how they would work together on setting up this facility. Now they had narrowed it down to Hungary, and the shareholding had more or less been agreed, as had the product mix. They were even negotiating the joint venture agreement. However, the discussions lost their initial impetus and were starting to drag out as more and more technicalities crept in. Both sides were losing patience.

Then everything was stalled abruptly by dramatic events happening more than four thousand miles away. In July 2007, two hedge funds operated by Bear Stearns, the New York-based global investment bank, collapsed. Few outside the hedge fund world took much notice but the following year, Bear Stearns, which was heavily involved in subprime mortgages, collapsed. The world economic recession fuelled by toxic mortgage debt had arrived and in September 2008, Lehman Brothers, which had $600 billion in assets, went into Chapter 11 bankruptcy. It was the largest bankruptcy filing ever in US corporate history. The contagion spread to all corners of the globe.

All talk of greenfield sites in Eastern Europe was now off the agenda.

seventeen

Going Dutch

With the onset of the global recession the Kanwars' focus returned to India and on to 125 acres of land Apollo had bought from the Tamil Nadu government at Oragadam, 47 kilometres from Chennai. 'Mr Kanwar had bought it in 2006. He always likes to buy land so he has it there for the future,' says KP. 'And land prices were only going to go up.'

Neeraj convinced his father and the board that now that Hungary was not happening, it was here that Apollo should build a state-of-the-art tyre factory, highly automated with few layers of management, a highly qualified and motivated staff, who would be stakeholders and where there would be no need for unions.

The Indian economy was beginning to take off and while the US and Europe floundered, Tamil Nadu was fast becoming the Detroit of Asia. The state was already home to BMW, Daimler, Ford, Nissan and Hyundai. Now the State Industries Promotion Corporation of Tamil Nadu (SIPCOT) gave its backing and tax incentives for Apollo to build a new ₹20 billion factory capable of producing 440 tonnes of tyres per day and to be the pioneer developer of a new industrial automotive hub at Oragadam.

'There was nothing there but a new road and an old temple,' Neeraj says. 'Because we were the first company to go into that particular area we had got the land cheaper.' A world in economic turmoil also kept prices down.

Onkar Singh Kanwar laid the foundation stone on 2 May 2008. Neeraj was crystal clear on how the new factory would look and be organized. 'It would be my baby.' KP would build it, equip it and recruit for it while P.K. Mohamed and his team would set up Apollo's first dedicated R&D centre there.

◆

While construction drawings for the Chennai plant were being completed Neeraj Kanwar could not help but notice in the first quarter of 2008 that Amtel-Vredestein was in financial trouble.

The Amtel Group did not have a long history of tyre making. Fifteen years before it had begun as a small trading company buying and selling soft drinks, juices and seating. It then bought a carbon-black producer, a manufacturer of synthetic rubber and three formerly state-owned tyre plants. The creation of Amtel-Vredestein made it the largest tyre company in Russia and it had plans to put up a new plant at Voronezh, 800 kilometres south of Moscow.

However, six months after the deal with Amtel had been signed, Vredestein CEO Rob Oudshoorn, always guided by the need to invest in the future, began to have concerns about the Russians' real motives. Within three months of the merger on 30 June 2005, Amtel-Vredestein closed a round of private equity capital totalling $70 million. In November, it launched an IPO in London and sold just over 27 per cent of its shares for $201 million, valuing the company at $742 million. It was one of the first Russian companies to be listed on the London Stock Exchange. 'A lot of that money went to shareholders and not into expanding the tyre business,' Oudshoorn says.

To mark the sixtieth anniversary of Vredestein Banden, the company launched a tyre called the Ultrac Sessanta. Designed by Giugiaro Design, it had a unique asymmetrical non-directional tread pattern and could support speeds of up to 300 kph. But while Vredestein Banden was still performing well and breaking new ground technologically, overall Amtel-

Vredestein, the parent company created by the merger, was beginning to show cracks. The company had relatively stable revenue of $886 million in 2007 and $881 million in 2008 but losses were in free fall, doubling to $446 million in 2008. For Oudshoorn the alarm bells really began to ring when the Dutch Chief Financial Officer (CFO) based in Moscow was locked out of his office.

For Amtel-Vredestein things were going downhill rapidly. By April 2008, it had been granted provisional suspension of payments.

Amtel-Vredestein had used Vredestein's name and reputation to raise money in the markets and CEO Rob Oudshoorn knew it was his responsibility to try and stop the Russians using Vredestein's cash to pay off its debts. Desperate at the prospect of Vredestein being dragged into the mire, Oudshoorn went to two Dutch banks, ING and ABN Amro, and asked if it was possible to ring-fence Vredestein BV's finances to ensure that no debt repayments could come from there. Sharing Oudshoorn's concerns, the two banks obliged. They were able to do this because the Amtel Group had registered Amtel-Vredestein in the Netherlands.

Neeraj Kanwar spotted a chink of light that might let Apollo back in with a chance of acquiring Vredestein. On an evening in August 2008, Sunam Sarkar was in his room at the Ritz Carlton in Singapore where he was having meetings. He checked time differences on his watch and put a call through to Rob Oudshoorn. Oudshoorn confirmed that the Russian parent company was definitely in distress. Sarkar reaffirmed Apollo's interest in acquiring Vredestein. 'Rob said there were a lot of moving parts and he did not know how things were going to pan out so he did not want to make any kind of commitment.'

On 13 November 2008, there was a public holiday in India to mark the birth of the first Sikh Guru, Guru Nanak, who was born in Punjab in 1469, and Sarkar was on the second hole at the DLF golf course in Gurgaon when his phone rang. It was Michael Ward, who then worked for Nomura. 'Michael told me that he had got to hear that Rothschild was going to run a process out of Russia for the sale of the entire Amtel business.'

Sarkar left the golf course immediately, cursing the fact that he had only played two holes, but knowing that Apollo had little time to get an official letter in to register its participation in the sale process.

'Sunam contacted me and we started moving on the process,' Neeraj explains.

Sarkar again spoke to Rob Oudshoorn. 'Rob, we would dearly love to be involved in this.'

'Sunam, things are unravelling very, very quickly,' Oudshoorn explained. 'There is not going to be enough time to submit an offer because there are only two weeks available to complete due diligence and you have not even started. What I am planning to do is put together a management buyout supported by private equity. Once we have secured the company I will come to you and we can discuss how we can cooperate with Apollo.'

'Let's not rule out the other option of us coming in,' Sarkar said. 'We can and we will do a due diligence in two weeks, but before that Neeraj and I would like to meet with you.'

It was due to Onkar Kanwar's empowering style that Sarkar was able to commit Apollo so confidently to what would be a difficult process.

While Neeraj Kanwar over several phone calls tried to persuade Oudshoorn to consider Apollo, Head of Corporate Strategy Gaurav Kumar was putting together the business case and an entire business plan for merging Apollo with Vredestein. On 2 December, Neeraj Kanwar and Sunam Sarkar flew to Amsterdam where they joined up with Gaurav Kumar, who was already working there on a possible deal, and they met Rob Oudshoorn at the Hotel De L'Europe, a prestigious red-brick five-star hotel, often referred to as 'the other Palace of Amsterdam', overlooking the Amstel River.

'Rob was very passionate about Vredestein and had done very well to protect the company from the Russians,' Neeraj says. 'And while he was keen to see new owners he was also adamant that only the best promoters should come in. I realized that I had to sell myself and Apollo to him and make him understand where I was coming from; why Vredestein, why Europe?'

Oudshoorn though was still favouring a management buyout. He could not believe that Apollo could do a deal in time. At subsequent meetings Neeraj managed to convince Oudshoorn that Apollo had the wherewithal to get the due diligence and an offer done on time. When required, Apollo has a history of moving at great speed. Oudshoorn set up a series of further meetings including one with the head of ING Private Equity, which was supporting the management buyout. Neeraj Kanwar discussed Apollo's plans with him and all agreed that the best option would be for Apollo to go ahead and make the bid and the private equity financed management buyout would recede into the background.

The fact that ING and ABN Amro had ring-fenced Vredestein's finances and that the Amtel Group had registered Amtel-Vredestein in the Netherlands was also a significant factor in helping Apollo in its bid to buy Vredestein. If the joint venture had been registered in Russia Apollo would have had no chance.

Things moved rapidly and on 19 December 2008, Apollo submitted its binding offer from the offices of its London legal advisers, CMS. The offer price was left blank although it did have details of how much loan was involved. Bankers with their love of secrecy like to put in the offer number at the last minute on the final draft and press 'send'.

Neeraj and the Apollo management team then headed for Enschede. 'Having convinced Rob Oudshoorn to go with our bid I would have to do the same with his top team,' says Neeraj. That meeting happened over lunch near the Enschede plant. 'I emphasized to them that a guiding principle of Mr Kanwar's is that we don't want to take dividends out; whatever profits we make we want to plough back either into the prosperity of the workforce or the growth of the factories and the company.'

There was no better evidence of that than South Africa where Apollo had invested close to $100 million in equipment, people and upgrading facilities. 'We are tyre people,' Neeraj told the Dutch. 'We are not here just to make a quick buck by selling off Vredestein. We are here long term. Our objective is to get into the top ten tyre makers and we will do this with Vredestein.'

As the meetings continued Neeraj was keen to emphasize Apollo's family values. 'We invited Rob to India. We showed him our factories, our R&D labs and he spent time with my father. I think that really convinced him.'

'I had visited most of the tyre makers in India,' says Oudshoorn, 'and Onkar was different from all the others. It is the way he looks you in the eye and tells you exactly what he is thinking. The decision to dissolve the agreement with Michelin and to go it alone was very courageous.'

And there was something else that made Kanwar stand out from the crowd and which impressed Oudshoorn. 'Onkar uses the word "family" frequently. He really does want all employees to feel that they are part of the family. It is not PR; it really is genuine. Onkar is the *pater familias* (the Latin term for 'Father of the Family'). Onkar has been very successful, he has made a lot of money and he lives very well, but he is also very modest. He and Neeraj also have a sense of humour and that is important in building trust.'

Getting the Vredestein deal done was to prove far from easy but the Christmas/New Year holiday shutdown in Europe gave Apollo a breathing space to do more groundwork.

The parent company Amtel-Vredestein had two divisions. In one was Vredestein BV, the Dutch tyre making operation. The other included a host of other activities in Russia, including a tyre factory and a distribution network, which was of no interest to Apollo. With bankruptcy looming, an administrator by the notable name of Jacques Daniëls, an insolvency specialist and corporate lawyer, was appointed by the Almelo Court in the Netherlands to sort out the affairs of the ailing parent company.

Apollo fixed a meeting with Daniëls in early April to present its case for taking over the Vredestein asset of Amtel-Vredestein. It was not a one-horse race. Apollo was up against at least two others that they knew of but suspected others in the background. One was Sber Bank, which held most of Amtel-Vredestein's mounting credit. The other was Sibur Tyres, a subsidiary of Gazprom.

A day before Sarkar was due to go to meet Jacques Daniëls, he was diagnosed with kidney stones in Delhi. At the time Neeraj Kanwar was on a holiday with his parents and family at Sun City in South Africa. Onkar told his son, 'I will look after the family. You must go.'

'I only had lightweight summer clothes so I flew to London where I changed into winter clothes at my mother-in-law's house, then on 7 April, I flew to Amsterdam. The weather was freezing.' Neeraj spent a day with Daniëls, outlining Apollo's plans for Vredestein, implications for jobs, the company's history in India and its investment in South Africa. Neeraj was winning Daniëls over to Apollo as the company most likely to secure Vredestein's long-term future after months of uncertainty.

The two men began exploring the contours of a possible deal. Of course the lawyers still had to go to work before any deal could be signed and Daniëls also had to talk to the Amtel Group about their intentions for Amtel-Vredestein and establish if they had a viable recovery plan either for the whole business or sections of it. He also had to talk to creditors, the works council and other stakeholders. But as far as Neeraj Kanwar was concerned he had put Apollo in pole position.

Neeraj then flew back to London, reverted into summer clothes at his mother-in-law's house, took the first flight he could back to South Africa and met his wife and children and his father and mother in Cape Town. He had been gone forty-eight hours. He arrived back in South Africa exhausted.

'Dad was thrilled with the news. While everyone was running away from doing business in Europe, Dad had arrived in Europe.' It was a major consolation for Onkar Kanwar who still regretted that the Michelin deal had broken down.

◆

Not everybody had been optimistic about Apollo landing Vredestein. In an article on *Mergermarket*, the web-based M&A intelligence service, dated 16 February, an anonymous banker, 'working with a number of Indian and European car component companies', was quoted. 'Apollo would not likely be in a position to make any significant acquisition within Europe, and was best suited looking at niche markets. Indian companies have been talked up to such an extent that they are inevitably being re-evaluated and just don't have the financial backing any longer. But many still have an unrealistic perspective on their own size.'

Whether or not Indian companies had been talked up by analysts the previous year, as was now being suggested, it did not deter Apollo in its quest for Vredestein.

On 27 April 2009, Neeraj Kanwar was back in Amsterdam for a second meeting with Jacques Daniëls. With him at the lawyer's office were Sunam Sarkar, Gaurav Kumar, Michael Ward of Nomura which was advising Apollo, Apollo's lawyers, and Rob Oudshoorn. The Apollo team led by Gaurav Kumar had been camped in Amsterdam since the middle of April involved in daily meetings with Daniëls and Oudshoorn.

Neeraj and Daniëls went into the Dutch lawyer's office alone to finalize terms. 'It took us just half an hour to agree. The price was $145 million, a mixture of cash and debt. It was a good price,' Neeraj says. 'The gloomy economic climate in Europe certainly worked in our favour.

'Then we went to the other room and told the lawyers and the deal teams, "Congratulations, the deal is done; thank you." There was a signing ceremony and we opened champagne.'

On 29 April 2009, at its quarterly meeting, the Apollo board approved the acquisition of Vredestein Banden. In an internal email Onkar Singh Kanwar addressed his staff.

> Dear Apolloites, Given our plans for Europe, Vredestein is a perfect strategic fit. The board has constituted a committee of directors and authorized them to finalize and execute all terms of this acquisition, approve investment, raise funds and take any other actions required to close the transaction, on completion of certain regulatory approvals.

The same day Amtel-Vredestein was declared bankrupt in a Dutch court. A brief statement said, 'Given the deteriorating position of the company and the increasing number of creditors' claims to repay debt or foreclose on the company's mortgaged assets, these actions are necessary and unavoidable.'

That evening Onkar Singh Kanwar arrived in Amsterdam at the Hotel De L'Europe where Rob Oudshoorn invited his top fifty people and their spouses to a party so they could get to know the Kanwars.

The day after the closing of the merger deal Onkar and Neeraj Kanwar and Apollo's top team of fifteen managers visited Vredestein's Enschede plant. Their visit coincided with Vredestein's Family Day. The plant had been shut down and all the workers and their families had been invited to tour the facility and enjoy a spread of food and drinks. Games for the kids were organized outside in the car park, which had been cleared of vehicles. Mr Kanwar and Neeraj walked around the plant and met the families. Onkar made a speech, welcoming Vredestein to Apollo.

'I felt that we were in exactly the right space,' Onkar says. 'It was good to be in Europe. It was a great beginning.'

The acquisition of Vredestein was completed on 15 May 2009, after all budgetary and regulatory approvals had been granted. 'Some established players in the tyre industry had pretty much laughed out of court the possibility of an Indian firm buying a company like Vredestein,' says Michael Ward. 'They weren't laughing any more. Their attitude had changed from "Who are these guys?" to "We need to be a bit more concerned about them." A new Asian tiger had arrived. Vredestein was a really good asset which came with an incredible financial structure and a highly motivated management team.'

The Vredestein acquisition pushed Apollo's annual revenue to ₹72 billion with global production capacity of 16.8 million tyres. As the world recession bit ever more deeply the Vredestein deal went against a trend of business retrenchment. At the time it was done it was one of 37 transactions that had been completed so far in 2009 worth a combined total of $693 million. Completed transactions for the same period in 2008 amounted to $7.9 billion.

'This strategic acquisition will bolster Apollo's plans for its European customers,' Onkar Singh Kanwar announced. 'We have acquired one of the most profitable tyre makers in Europe and will get direct access to Vredestein's large market in Europe.' Apollo's share price jumped more than 9 per cent to ₹29 on the Mumbai Stock Exchange at the news.

Kanwar also announced that Apollo had deferred its plan to build a greenfield site in Hungary due in part to the recession and opposition from local winegrowers—who were objecting to a tyre company acquiring land—and a coalition government that was less than enthusiastic.

Apollo had found another door into Europe and Kanwar said Apollo would consolidate its operations in Holland. However, it would also press on with its greenfield site in Chennai where construction had got under way in November 2008.

'We are relieved and happy,' Rob Oudshoorn said in a Dutch newspaper interview with something of an understatement after the completion of the merger with Apollo. He knew that the company he had turned around and the company he cared so passionately about had escaped the clutches of bankruptcy and was now in safe hands.

He was also pleased that while in India during the later negotiations he had persuaded Onkar Singh Kanwar and Neeraj to agree to keep Vredestein's senior management in place for at least three years. 'I told them I wanted to personally make sure that the integration would be smooth and effective. Vredestein desperately needed stability after our experiences with the Russians. Too often in deals like this the senior managers are fired instantly but Onkar said, "That is absolutely understood; there will not be wholesale changes like that. You tell me how fast you think we can go in merging our two companies."'

In early June 2009, the hundred-day integration programme began at Enschede with both sides going after the low-hanging fruits of synergy. Neeraj Kanwar was focusing on bringing down the costs of raw materials. 'I asked the raw materials guys to go away and then tell me how and where we could save money whether in Europe or in India. From there we set targets, either by going to a vendor who was cheaper or going to a new material which was cheaper. There were other teams doing exactly the same for marketing, manufacturing and HR. One of the reasons we had done the deal was that we both believed we could save money through synergy brought about by the merger and the resulting economies of scale. In those hundred days, we came up with plans for all those things we were going to try and attack to get the revenues and profits.'

◆

To bond the two companies together faster Onkar Singh Kanwar now invited Rob Oudshoorn and forty-nine of his Enschede colleagues and their partners to visit India so they could all get to know Apollo better and put faces to those names they had been receiving emails from during the integration phase.

'We had done that with the South Africans too and it was a big success,' Neeraj says. 'It was a big investment but long term it would pay dividends in the shape of a cohesive profitable company where everybody felt they were part of the Apollo family.'

The Vredestein party flew in to Mumbai on 21 November and was taken to Apollo's Limda plant near Vadodara. Their visit coincided with a Sikh religious service that Apollo holds every year. The plant was shut for the day and all the workers and their families, about 8,000 people, came for a prayer service after which they sat in rows and then Onkar Singh Kanwar, Neeraj and their families and senior management went among them serving food on banana leaves just like a *langar* service in a gurudwara.

That day Onkar Singh Kanwar had also invited Gujarat's Chief Minister Narendra Modi to inaugurate the new passenger radial plant. It took investment in the Limda plant beyond ₹20 billion. Limda was now Apollo's largest tyre factory where it had increased passenger radial production from 90,000 tyres a month to 450,000.

For Modi's visit Apollo had to build a landing pad for his helicopter and security was at Z level, India's second highest. For two days before his arrival the plant was crawling with security teams. Nobody else was allowed in.

Modi arrived wearing a multicoloured turban. Welcoming him to the plant, Onkar Singh Kanwar draped a saffron silk scarf around his neck and presented him with a ceremonial sword and scabbard, which had been brought on stage by U.S. Oberoi. Kanwar then asked Modi to speak.

'We were concerned that Mr Modi might not be able to speak Punjabi,' says Neeraj, 'but he had studied in Amritsar and he spoke so well and he said to my son Jai, who was about nine at the time, "look at me because one day you are going to be my voter". The man then spoke for an hour and he was mesmerizing.

'All the Europeans from Vredestein were sitting on the floor and sweating because it was a hot day. I am not sure they knew what on earth was going on!'

For his part Onkar Kanwar said: 'We are very optimistic for the coming year and with road infrastructure the tyre industry is expected to grow at more than double the GDP of the country.' He also announced that Apollo was donating ₹1 million to the Gujarat State Girl Child Education Fund, a Modi initiative providing financial assistance to girls studying in medical and engineering colleges or for civil service exams.

The Vredestein visitors were impressed with the Vadodara plant. 'It was unlike any other I had seen in India, and I had seen most,' says Rob Oudshoorn. 'It was well managed, efficient, a pleasant working environment and very clean, a bit like Vredestein.'

◆

From Vadodara the Vredestein visitors moved on next day to Delhi and had a tour of Apollo's head office at Gurgaon where they had lunch and then broke into small workshop sessions so counterparts from each company, such as the procurement teams, could meet each other while the wives were taken off to see the sights of Delhi.

That evening Apollo had organized what Neeraj Kanwar called 'dine-arounds'. Neeraj and five senior colleagues all hosted a dinner in their houses for ten of the Vredestein guests each so they could get a flavour of Indian home cooking and Indian life and then they stayed the night. 'Some dinners did not finish until three in the morning so some people were pretty groggy the next day!'

The bonding continued the next evening with a Rajasthani Night at Kanwar's farmhouse. Set on four superbly tended acres on the outskirts of Delhi with large lawns fringed with palms and fruit trees decked in lemons, guavas, jackfruit and figs, the farmhouse is a farmhouse in name only; although it stands on what was once farmland and does feature a large organic vegetable garden—Mrs Kanwar's pride and joy. Built seven years ago, Onkar Singh Kanwar's farmhouse is a large square modern building of 2,400 square metres sitting in well-secluded grounds. It is timber-clad on the first floor and built around a light and spacious two-storey atrium. Modern Indian paintings hang on white walls, including a large portrait of Kanwar. Next door there is a similar-sized building which houses the swimming pool, an additional separate swimming lane for lengths and a steam room.

The farmhouse is where every December, around his birthday, Kanwar hosts the Apollo family day with around 2,000 guests, mostly staff and their families, some close friends and his own family. One lawn is set up for the children and the other for the adults. There are presentations and speeches and his ten-year-old granddaughter, Syra, sings a song and performs a dance in his honour. Onkar says it is one of the highlights of his year.

Rob Oudshoorn had visited the farmhouse before with the Vredestein management board while negotiations between the two companies were continuing. He had said to Kanwar: 'Onkar this is a really beautiful farm, but where are the elephants?' The only livestock normally kept there are Kanwar's German Shepherds—Mustard and Ketchup.'

When Oudshoorn arrived this time with the hundred-strong Vredestein party, 'Onkar greeted me with two elephants; and some camels! He also remembered that I had a liking for good wine so he had arranged for some very special vintages to be available.'

'As our guests arrived we put Rajasthani turbans on them and gave them Indian clothes to wear,' Neeraj explains. 'The farmhouse had been turned into a Rajasthani palace. There was a lot of colour with small stalls offering bangles and henna for the ladies. There was food from Rajasthan and a lot of song and dance and drinking, and these guys could drink!'

There were speeches; there were photographs. Followed by more singing and yet more dancing. 'Everybody had a ball,' says Neeraj. 'It was like a big family party. My mother came to join my father; my wife and my son were there. It was a huge success. I finally closed the bar at 1 a.m.'

Then it was off to see the Taj Mahal and Agra. The journey took around four to five hours by road because the Yamuna Expressway had not yet been built. 'They came back exhausted,' says Neeraj, 'but that's the way to see India—on the highway. And they fell in love with the Taj.'

The Vredestein visit ended with a Sunday lunch at Neeraj's house where Simran put saris on the ladies. 'It was a lovely lunch, beautiful weather and a good time,' says Neeraj. 'And then they all went back to Europe as brand ambassadors. They knew that this was the company they had been looking to be part of. Part of the Apollo family.'

'I have seen a lot of India but this visit was very well done,' says Rob Oudshoorn. 'It was thoughtful, welcoming and interesting. Most in our group were seeing things for the first time in their lives; the places they went, the people they met, and the parties!'

Onkar Singh Kanwar of course always remembers the sales numbers. 'In the first three years we had Vredestein, and Rob guiding us into Europe. There were successive cold winters in countries like Germany and across Scandinavia so we sold a lot of snow tyres. In many of those countries you do not get insurance cover if you do not put on a set of studded winter tyres. It was very good for business.'

Rob Oudshoorn now runs his own consulting business in Holland and is an ambassador and agent for Giugiaro Design. 'I still have the utmost respect for Apollo and the Kanwars and what they have achieved,' he says. 'Although Neeraj Kanwar put together so effectively the deal that saved Vredestein, it was the trust I had in Onkar that made the difference in the relationship between our two companies. He asked me what I thought, I told him, he listened.'

'Close relationships are a key USP for Apollo and that comes directly from Mr Kanwar,' Neeraj says. He acknowledges that as Apollo expands internationally and absorbs more cultures, languages and business attitudes and practices, maintaining that key USP is an increasing but essential challenge.

eighteen

The Detroit of India

I n 2009, Neeraj Kanwar had become Managing Director of Apollo to go with his Vice Chairmanship. It was not a sign that Onkar Singh Kanwar was losing his drive or his energy or heading for gentle retirement on the golf course. 'He did try to take up golf,' Raaja Kanwar says. 'I bought him a set of clubs, hired a coach and he began hitting some balls at the Delhi Golf Course, but he did not have the patience for it.'

'I took so much time and energy trying to hit that damn ball,' says Onkar. 'The coach told me to swing like the pendulum of a grandfather clock. I didn't know what he was talking about. I gave it up.'

Aside from family, work remained Onkar Singh Kanwar's first love. Every day senior Apollo staff would get a catch-up call from OSK seeking feedback, following up on issues. Typically, the conversation would start with 'Is there anything I should know?'

Here was a man who enjoyed his work as much as he had ever done, perhaps even more so now that the business and personal trials of the past had receded into history.

He and Neeraj were a double act. Not just father and son. Not just business partners sharing the same mission values, zest and energy. Most importantly they were very good friends.

Neeraj's promotion was simply a logical extension of his appointment seven years earlier to Chief Operating Officer. Neeraj was running the day-to-day operations of the company, but his father remained Apollo's guiding light. Onkar Singh Kanwar was still well on top of where his company was going, with the uncanny ability to ask a very necessary question which people did not always want to answer, especially when it came to productivity, costs and profits. Just as when he started out he was guided by the same mantra: 'I am interested in the top line and I am interested in the bottom line. Everything in between is irrelevant if they are not performing.'

◆

Apollo also had a new brand identity, which made its appearance during 2009. In 2008, the Kanwars felt that Apollo's logo and brand image could do with a major overhaul. It had not been changed from day one. Three major agencies were asked to pitch but it was a doyen of corporate branding, and award-winning Englishman Wally Olins, co-founder of Saffron Brand Consultants with offices in London, Madrid and New York, who won out. Famous for his round glasses and bow ties Olins had worked with topflight clients including Orange, Renault, Tata, Lloyd's of London and McKinsey. He came to Gurgaon in person to do the pitch, something that greatly impressed Neeraj Kanwar.

Olins instinctively understood Apollo, where it had come from and where it planned to go. He felt that in creating a niche Apollo could claim as its own, it was important to create a brand that was distinctive and reflected the characteristics and qualities that made the company special. He would come up with a completely new and relevant identity that would strengthen Apollo's credibility by ensuring that every aspect of the way in which it presented itself was at least as good as the best of the competition.

Out of Saffron's rebranding came the new Apollo legend 'Go the Distance' that would appear on reports, documents and letterheads. Next to it would appear four circles, each one in a different colour with a slightly different inner radius representing the kinds of tyres that Apollo produces. The same motif would be applied physically to Apollo's Gurgaon building and its tyre plants.

The new Apollo logo also came out of these tyre shapes. The old chunky black-and-white logo all in capital letters was replaced by a very contemporary 'apollo' all in lower case—the 'Os' inspired by the tyre circle motifs—and in the company's new colour: purple.

When Olins had made his pitch to Apollo, he produced a map of where all the global tyre companies were located and the colours they used to represent themselves—Michelin in blue, Bridgestone in red and so on. He then showed all the colours on a spectrum and there was a significant gap at purple. He said when it came to fashioning a new identity there was no point in tackling the major brands head on and anyway the competition had become boring, staid and entirely lacking in imagination. Purple was fresh, distinctive and different just as Apollo was distinctive and different. It would make for a clutter-breaking use of colour.

In coming up with a radical rebranding, Olins had also sought the views of dealers, customers and other stakeholders to gain their impressions of Apollo the brand. Reflecting the fact that Apollo was an Indian company striding on to the world map, Olins company website put its branding strategy this way: 'Indian companies had traditionally shied away from talking about where they came from, the result both of a lack of self-confidence and antiquated perceptions about India. We saw an opportunity to break this mould. Apollo's long-term strategy was to target the European market; with this in mind, a compelling proposition began to emerge—tyres made for some of the worst roads in the world would be very much at home on some of the best. And so we developed a brand strategy that underlined Apollo's Indian roots and emphasized quality along with value for money. The IKEA of the tyre world, in a sense. There is nothing else like it in the industry.'

The team loved it, but would the boss? Onkar Singh Kanwar had grown up with the old logo from the earliest days of Apollo. Would he embrace the change? He took one look at the new concept and said, 'That's great, I love it too. Let's go ahead.'

The Wally Olins rebranding of Apollo was met with positive reviews in the trade press and went on to win awards, which was good for Olins and good for Apollo. Olins soon opened a branch of Saffron Brand Consultants in India as more Indian clients beat a path to his door.

◆

Neeraj Kanwar says that his best ideas either come to him in the shower or in the middle of the night. His boldest idea yet was Apollo's ground-breaking Chennai plant, which began commercial production of passenger car radials on 13 March 2010. The first truck and bus radials came out of Chennai on 11 May and in July Apollo shipped its first consignment of passenger car radial (PCR) tyres to an original equipment (OE) customer, Hyundai Motor India, from the new plant.

Construction had begun in November 2008 and the factory, Apollo's ninth in total and fourth in India, had been built in a cracking fourteen months by a team headed by KP.

'The Tamil Nadu government had given permission to JK, MRF, Michelin and Apollo to put up tyre factories in various parts of the state at the same time,' Prabhakar explains. 'Ours was not only the biggest, it was finished the quickest and I believe it is the best.

'Not only that, Chennai is my home town! I have a house there and my parents live there. It was good to come home having travelled the Apollo world. Within a week of being asked to set up the factory I moved with a small team to the site. All that was there was a small shed.'

When it came to buying the equipment the global recession worked in Apollo's favour in terms of currency exchange rates. The euro was worth ₹57 (today it is ₹73) and the dollar stood at ₹47, twenty below what it is today. 'European and US manufacturers had nowhere to sell their equipment,' Prabhakar explains. 'I could get my specification modified to our needs and delivered in six months. Sometimes equipment would arrive in Chennai port before the part of the building where it was to be installed was fully complete. It was coming from America, Germany and the UK.'

The Chennai plant covers 125 acres and employs 1,760 people working in three shifts twenty-four hours a day. The major differences between it and Apollo's other plants, and Indian tyre plants in general, are twofold: its layout and the level of automation, and the lack of hierarchy in the workforce.

'My concept was to break with the old on both fronts,' Neeraj explains. At Chennai the PCR and truck and bus radial (TBR) production line buildings run parallel down the site but between them is an equally long building, a central spine, which houses all the support functions from labs to engineering to quality control that are used by both production lines. This innovative layout avoids duplication and all support facilities are close to where they are most needed.

Inside the production line buildings handling operations are automated at every stage from tyre building, through to curing and finishing. It is the same story with testing, storage and dispatch. Linear transfer robots, overhead gantry robots, automated storage and retrieval systems—where a machine can optimize the process it does so. Everything is clean, cool and compared to Perambra, and even Vadodara, very quiet.

Every process is monitored from the 'nerve centre' in the plant's central spine support building. A wall of computer screens provides to-the-second data and live video feed of every stage of the tyre making process on both production lines. It is modelled on a similar information and management system used at the Vredestein plant in Enschede. Soon after integration Apollo and Vredestein were also sharing technologies in areas such as compound recipes and silica mixing and sidewall design.

The Chennai Unit Head John Devadason looks more like the captain of a large ship or submarine as he and his colleagues monitor all aspects in the nerve centre. 'It means I can see what is going on all around the plant at any time,' he says. 'If there is a problem I can go straight to it. Of course, I still walk around the plant regularly because face-to-face human contact is just as important but in terms of troubleshooting this mission control nips problems in the bud and saves time and money.'

Much of the robotic and automated manufacturing technology that made Neeraj's vision a reality comes from Finnish company Cimcorp. It was founded over thirty years ago and describes itself as building 'dream factories' with its 'architects of intralogistics'. Cimcorp's other tyre company projects include Continental's plant at Aachen in Germany and Sentury Tire's Qingdao plant in China. Cimcorp has also designed dream factories in the food and beverage industries, car manufacturing, retail and e-commerce.

'Internally there was a lot of discussion about how much I was spending on Chennai,' Neeraj admits. 'At first my father and others argued, "Why are you spending so much money? Surely we can do it cheaper. Why are you putting in so much automation?" But I argued that we had to have the best. We had to build a plant to world standards, not just the best Indian plant. While there would be a short-term impact on capital expenditure we would ultimately save on labour costs because the tolerances of machines are much less and the fewer hands you physically put on a tyre before it is cured the better quality and consistency you achieve. By streamlining our material and data flows, the logistics automation systems would allow process machines to be utilized at 100 per cent capacity, thereby increasing the output of the manufacturing lines. It would have a positive effect on the bottom line of our business. I think it is at times like this that my father's real greatness is revealed—he's willing to forgo his past experiences and back us for the future.'

The cost of building the Chennai plant might have been ₹24.5 billion but it is not just machinery and money that has made it capable of producing 18,000 tyres a day and which is now ramping up production to hit 24,000. The second strand to Neeraj Kanwar's vision has been a new way of working and a clue to that is the fact that John Devadason, who is ultimately responsible for running the plant, is known as Unit Head and not plant manager or plant director.

Instead of seven hierarchical layers of management, typical in many Indian companies, the organizational structure at Chennai Apollo is flat with few distinctions. There are just four levels: team member, team leader, group leader and unit head. First and foremost the staff are all engineers—not workers or managers, blue collar or white collar.

The cost of automation is high and the expertise required to make it work smoothly is also high which is why those working at the Chennai plant are all diploma graduates from technical institutes. They are trained for about seven hundred man-days originally at the Vadodara plant but now at the Chennai plant. The plant has close links with local universities and technical colleges and those from farther afield from which it recruits. Apart from technical skills a major qualification for getting a job at Apollo Chennai is the desire and the need to work.

Throughout the PCR and TBR lines there are information boards covering everything from production levels to latest in-house sports results. And, of course, there are no trade unions. 'It is a better way of working,' says Anand Satyamoorthy who is Group Leader-Manufacturing. 'The fact that every unit wants to try and be the best means we end up with wastage of just 0.5 per cent. I would like it to be 0.2.'

Strangely, one of the more controversial issues Neeraj Kanwar had to face early on was catering at the plant. There is not one canteen for the whole factory as would normally be the case. Instead there are nine separate cafeterias, served by a central kitchen. These are located by each section so nobody needs to be away from their area. Time is saved; units bond and they can see their machines at all times through the glass cafeteria walls while they eat.

'At first people would not budge,' says Neeraj. 'They wanted one canteen like other factories. They told me that Chennai food has a lot of gravy and it would spill on its way to the cafeterias and get cold on the way. Suddenly I seemed to be surrounded not by tyre makers and engineers but by catering experts! I told them, "They serve gravy on aeroplanes; let the catering guys work it out."' Nine cafeterias it was. 'Now everybody accepts it as normal.' It is the staff that decides the menus.

Apollo Chennai is now at the heart of a new mini motor city. Renault Nissan has built a plant right opposite. A Mercedes truck plant and Ashok Leyland are nearby. Neeraj Kanwar may refer to the Chennai plant as 'my baby', which is true, but it has taken many fathers and mothers to make his vision happen and Neeraj's father to back a vision when weaker men would have faltered.

◆

In 2010, Apollo bought a 3-acre parcel of land next to the plant and there it built an R&D centre. Costing €25 million, it is headed by P.K. Mohamed, one of Onkar Singh Kanwar's most constant and trusted companions on the Apollo journey going right back to the Perambra days. PK is now Chief Adviser, R&D, and displays the same enthusiasm and energy for his work as the day he set out on the quest that led to Hercules. With forty-six years' experience in tyre technology and manufacturing, PK travels the world lecturing, presenting research papers and attending conferences. He is a past Chairman of the India Tyre Technical Advisory Committee (ITTAC) and the India Rubber Institute, and is a fellow of the Rubber and Plastic Institute London.

However, PK is happiest being responsible for all R&D activities in an industry where science and engineering meet. While KP was responsible for constructing and equipping the Chennai plant, P.K. Mohamed was in charge of process and product development. 'Tyre technology is dominated by physics, chemistry, mechanical and chemical engineering,' he explains. 'A tyre is a unique combination of steel and rubber. The steel withstands the stresses placed on a tyre and the rubber takes care of the strain. In our labs we are always working to increase the efficiency and durability of those two components. Such an intelligent sharing of stresses and strain is rarely seen in any other product.'

Tyre technology is about resolving that conflict between stress and strain. In truck tyres Mohamed and his team have developed products that maximize a complex mix of load carrying, mileage, fuel efficiency, durability, and retreadability, achieving up to 15 per cent better performance than standard tyres and sometimes more. PK talks of them like favourite sons, from Hercules, Mohamed's first Apollo tyre, to Loadstar, Amar—a front tyre, the name of which in Hindi means undying or everlasting—to the XT-7 family.

'In the Eighties, Goodyear introduced a tyre called CT-169 and claimed it was the market leader in terms of the mileage it could achieve,' Mohamed explains. 'U.S. Oberoi, who was Head of Technical Services at that point, asked me to develop a tyre to compete.' U.S. Oberoi and P.K. Mohamed are the closest of friends having met when they worked for Premier Tyres in Kerala. 'He is a man of great integrity, who Mr Kanwar trusted completely to get things done and who believed that the market, the customer, was always the most important element of our industry.'

Mohamed and his team came up with the Apollo XT-7 in 1986 with innovative tread and compounding technology, which achieved 20 per cent better mileage than the Goodyear and became a barometer for price and quality in the Indian market.

Soft-spoken and modest, P.K. Mohamed gives credit to the Kanwars for their vision and leadership. 'I have always received full support from Onkar Kanwar and Neeraj Kanwar. They played a vital role in developing me as one of the well-recognized tyre technologists. I am greatly indebted to them.'

Onkar Singh Kanwar is always keen to bat the compliment back. He knows that without P.K. Mohamed the Apollo story might have been very different.

There was a time in the late Nineties, however, when that story did take a different turn. Kanwar wanted PK to move from Kerala to the head office in Delhi. PK's wife did not want to move, leaving behind her job, home and friends, but eventually he did go north. But corporate life was not for him. PK is not a meetings man. He missed the smell of rubber. He felt he was not keeping up with the latest technological developments.

'One of my friends at the India Rubber Association was the Managing Director of CEAT Tyres and he told me that technology was a major setback for CEAT. He came to Delhi and invited me for dinner and told me there was an opportunity to work in their technology department. With my daughter's marriage and a loan that I had to pay on a house I had built, the salary was attractive so I went to CEAT in Mumbai on a five-year contract in 1996. Mr Kanwar was not happy about my leaving. I was fifty-five years old and CEAT was going to give me time out of the office every month to go home to Kerala and spend time with my family.'

He realized he had made a mistake. In 2001, he got a call from Kanwar, who was staying at The Oberoi hotel in Mumbai. 'I went to meet him. We talked about what was happening at Apollo and then he told me, '"You have to come back."'

Why did Kanwar want him back? Mohamed pauses and then his engaging trademark smile lights up his face. 'That I don't know!'

'I felt that as he was the best he ought to be working with the best,' says Kanwar. It is clear that both men missed working with one another. Apollo was as much in P.K. Mohamed's veins as it was in Onkar Kanwar's.

Mohamed put aside worries that he might be out of step with Apollo's new guard of tyre technologists and returned as Vice President-technology, based in Kerala but travelling to Vadodara where R&D had moved. Following the Shimla workshop and Passion in Motion Kanwar put P.K. Mohamed in charge of developing Apollo's self-reliance in technology. 'At that time we did not have off the road (OTR) or TBR technology or scooter and motorcycle technology. That was one of the major objectives given to me by Mr Kanwar, to develop all of these and self-reliance.'

With Apollo and Vredestein locked in an increasingly fond technological embrace it was announced that the Chennai plant would have a production target of 6,000 truck and bus radial tyres a day. Initially the target had been set at 1,500. The 300 per cent increase came about as a result of a car journey in late 2009, as Neeraj Kanwar explains. 'My father and I visited the plant with Satish Sharma. On the way back to the car we started deliberating and discussing the economy and the market and decided the plant should produce 3,000 a day. In the car I was sitting in the back seat next to my father and Satish was in the front and he and I kept debating. Construction and raw material costs were going up but we could see that future demand was coming into the tyre market. Maybe we should go for 6,000? My father was quietly listening and then suddenly he said, "Why are you debating so much? If you believe the plant can achieve six, go for six. The amount of analysis you are doing will paralyse the whole thing!" By the time we reached the airport three had become six.'

'To set up the Chennai plant with a capacity target of 6,000 without process technology, product technology and marketing was a very bold decision,' says P.K. Mohamed. 'Once the chance was given to me to achieve it, I could not sleep for several days! No other Indian company had managed to do this independently. It was a tough challenge but acquiring Dunlop's TBR technology gave us great insight and knowledge that we could tweak to our needs in India. The tie-up with Michelin also had its plus points even if the joint venture never really happened. The design approach at Dunlop was good but its process approach was not. The Michelin process approach was exceptional. I had the opportunity to interact with a lot of senior people in both companies and the best principles I learned from them I merged and I applied here. Fortunately Mr Prabhakar and I did fairly well!'

An initial production of 250 TBRs a day grew to 4,000 TBRs a day by 2012 and in February of that year, Apollo's Chennai plant produced its millionth truck-bus radial. TBRs accounted for 19 per cent of the total commercial vehicle tyres produced by Apollo and Chennai was an OEM supplier to some of the most established commercial vehicle manufacturers, such as Tata Motors, Ashok Leyland and Eicher.

'In 2015, five years after the plant opened, we were at 100 per cent production and selling it, with a good name in truck and bus radial technology,' says P.K. Mohamed. 'I am really thankful to the management for giving us such challenges. It has been a great learning.'

In May 2015, Apollo would announce that it was doubling Chennai's TBR capacity over the following year to 12,000 a day in an expansion costing ₹25 billion. Production of passenger car tyres would remain at 12,000. Overall Apollo was exporting 100,000 car tyres and 15,000 TBR tyres a month while Vadodara and Chennai between them had a total car tyre capacity of 32,000 units a day.

Now in his seventies, P.K. Mohamed, one of the founding members of Apollo's technology journey and credited with some of the most successful tyres manufactured, shows no signs of retiring. 'There's too much to do,' he says with a grin. The majority of those working in Apollo's Chennai R&D centre are in their twenties and thirties. He finds working with younger people stimulating and they clearly rely on his wisdom and considerable wit and enthusiasm to solve problems and make the technological strides to keep Apollo ahead of the chasing pack. He is still aiming for the ultimate in increased tyre life, safety features and lower fuel consumption.

◆

Apollo Tyres was now regarded as a force to be reckoned with, not just in India, but also in Europe and Africa via its acquisition of Vredestein and Dunlop South Africa. In March 2011, it hit its $2 billion sales objective.

True to form, the Kanwars celebrated hitting a major target by setting an even bigger one. Passion in Motion had to maintain its momentum. On 11 March 2012, Onkar Singh Kanwar told the *Economic Times* 'Apollo is targeting $6 billion in the next five years'.

Onkar Kanwar wanted Apollo to break into the top ten global tyre makers. It would be a tough ask. The face of the global tyre industry had changed dramatically in terms of technological advances and new players but it was a highly consolidated industry and the global top ten revenue earners in 2010 as in 1998 featured most of the same names with Michelin, Bridgestone and Goodyear occupying the top three slots followed by Continental at four and Pirelli and Sumitomo fighting over places five and six.

'But this could not continue forever,' says Michael Ward, Managing Director, Corporate Advisory for Royal Bank of Scotland, formerly of Nomura, and a veteran traveller through the international tyre world. Ward points out that the global vehicle market had grown from 60 million in 1980 to 102 million by 2009 and is heading for a predicted 205 million by 2020 with most of the growth in Asia. The centre of the tyre world was following the vehicle market eastward with Asia set to become as large as the global market.

'One hundred per cent of the new entrants in the global top twenty were Asian and many had designs on top ten positions,' Ward says. 'We had entered a new and challenging paradigm, which presented a substantial opportunity. It also presented risk. The long-established names would not give up their leadership easily.'

Apollo currently was then sixteenth. The Kanwars realized that hitting $6 billion in sales, which would take Apollo comfortably into the top ten, would not happen by expanding existing product lines and revenue sources alone. The gulf was too wide. It would have to be done via another M&A. In tenth place was Cheng Shin Rubber of Taiwan. Founded in 1967, its 2009 global sales stood at $2 billon. However, in ninth place was an American company, which ended 2012 with sales of $4.2 billion, a record operating profit of $397 million and a strong balance sheet with $352 million in cash. It was also a known quantity to the Kanwars and there was no market overlap with Apollo.

Its name was the Cooper Tire & Rubber Company.

nineteen

The Cooper transaction

With its 'Go the Distance' branding and revitalized logo Apollo was increasingly a player on the world stage. It became India's biggest tyre maker in 2011, with revenues of $2.5 billion, a market presence in seventy countries and factories in India, the Netherlands and South Africa. In 2013, Onkar Singh Kanwar was inducted into the Tire Industry Association's (TIA) Hall of Fame at a special ceremony held in Las Vegas. The TIA has 6,000 members. 'For me this honour is vindication of what Apollo Tyres has tried to achieve within and for the Indian tyre industry,' Kanwar said in his acceptance speech. 'It is a recognition of the untiring efforts of every individual in the 16,000-strong Apollo Tyres family who have powered our growth and of our customers and business partners across the globe, for their trust in us and their feedback at all times.'

Apollo opened Apollo Super Zones in Mumbai and Kolkata where tyre models were displayed individually, to be browsed in 'an enhanced retail experience'. With clean lines and gallery lighting, play facilities for children and free Wi-Fi, they were more like boutiques than old-style tyre stores and reflected that the shopping experience in India, with air-conditioned malls springing up in all major cities, was rapidly aping the West.

Overseas Apollo had entered the Sri Lanka market in 2011, through a tie-up with Ideal Motors, the automobile distribution and marketing arm of the Ideal Group of Companies, to distribute passenger vehicle and cross-ply and light truck tyres. In April 2012, Apollo opened one of its concept retail outlets in Dubai. It was the first of its kind in the region. 'It underlines the importance of Dubai as a regional commercial hub and as a focus of our Middle East operations,' Satish Sharma said. Dubai is the world's largest free trade zone. The Dubai Super Zone, inaugurated by Onkar Singh Kanwar, was part of Apollo's $2 billion expansion strategy for the Middle East, which provided about 30 per cent of its export earnings out of India. It came on the back of Apollo establishing a regional headquarters in the country the previous year, along with 10,000 square feet of warehouse space, which reflected the company's significant presence in the region where it had distributors and business partners in fourteen countries.

As part of its international profiling effort Apollo appointed the London office of The Brooklyn Brothers—a creative agency with offices also in New York, Los Angeles, Shanghai and Sao Paulo and clientele including Apple, Jaguar, BBC Worldwide and Virgin—to help build the global Apollo brand in print, electronic and digital mediums.

In 2013, Neeraj Kanwar, Simran and their children, moved to London where he opened an Apollo Tyres office on two floors just off Regent Street where he also set up a Global Marketing Office, responsible for product strategy, marketing communications and product mix management.

Being in London meant he was geographically closer to Vredestein and the European market but the big reason for moving there was that it was in the ideal time zone between Asia and the US. Cooper was still very much on the Kanwars' minds. Senior management of the two companies met informally and talked glowingly about what a perfect fit Apollo and Cooper would be. With no geographic overlap, different product ranges and distinct markets, together they could really challenge the big global players.

In 2013, Apollo also hitched its colours to those of Manchester United. The Kanwars lined up at Old Trafford alongside Ryan Giggs and Rio Ferdinand to announce Apollo as United's Official Tyre Partner in the UK and India. A key element of the partnership would be a joint community commitment to encourage healthy lifestyles and develop sporting skills in young people. Apollo would build 'Go the Distance' football pitches made from recycled tyres in local communities across various markets, with the first being at Old Trafford as part of a fan zone/play zone.

It was an important tie-up for both parties in terms of branding and providing sports facilities to many young people. As Manchester United Group Managing Director Richard Arnold explained, 'Apollo Tyres is a leading player in the tyre industry and its rate of growth and development into new territories made it an attractive partner for the Club. We are confident in providing Apollo with a highly engaged audience, not only to promote its brand, but also to engage and communicate with our fans.'

◆

The Apollo network was now established across three continents but North America remained a big gap on its world map. Neeraj Kanwar had been working on that. In April 2012, he had walked into a Midtown Manhattan restaurant to have dinner with Cooper Tire's Vice President, Hal Miller.

Apollo and Cooper had been in regular contact ever since they had discussed doing a joint greenfield venture in Hungary, which was derailed by the global recession.

'After we did the Vredestein acquisition my father and I met [Cooper CEO, Chairman and President] Roy Armes for a drink at Claridges in London and he seemed very put out that we had not joined hands with Cooper to buy Vredestein,' Neeraj says. 'Mr Kanwar was not impressed by his tone!'

'It was important we kept in touch with Cooper,' says Onkar, always playing the long game. 'I would meet Roy Armes in London or New York and we would have dinner. Neeraj was close to Hal Miller. We kept the relationship going.'

As Neeraj sat down to dine with Hal Miller, 'my purpose was to see if he would be open to Apollo acquiring Cooper. I had to be very strategic. We had already done all the paperwork; we had the financing in place.'

He had been talking for some months to leading American M&A lawyer Scott D. Miller, a partner in Sullivan & Cromwell—considered to be one of the 'magic circle' firms of US lawyers. Miller had been with the company since 1986 and his clients had included Ferrari, AT&T and Fiat Chrysler Automobiles. An early version of a financing structure had been sketched out by Neeraj and Salman Mahdi, Managing Director of Deutsche Asset and Wealth Management, over a drink on a piece of headed notepaper from Harry's Bar on South Audley Street in London. 'That was just an initial thought process,' Neeraj explains. 'The structure went through a hundred changes and a lot of spins but that sketch, which I still have, is the germ of it.'

At a suitable pause in the conversation Neeraj broached the subject of a takeover with Miller and waited.

Prior to this Cooper had asked the Kanwars if they were open to Apollo being taken over. 'We told them we did not want to sell our shares, we were not interested and we finished that off,' Neeraj says. But he and his father kept on building bridges with Hal Miller. 'Slowly, slowly, slowly we waited until we had a window of opportunity to stick a bid in.' It would come to nothing if Miller was lukewarm.

But he wasn't. 'Hal was far from negative,' Neeraj says. 'He said that Apollo acquiring Cooper would take us to different heights. It would be a game changer for the entire industry.' There was no market overlap between the two companies. There were good synergies wherever you looked. Putting Apollo and Cooper together would parachute Apollo into the top ten tyre producers at around number seven.

Discussions began in earnest. Apollo kicked off with a preliminary offer of $22 a share, valuing Cooper at $1.44 billion.

Over several more meetings and dinners in New York and London with Roy Armes, the Kanwars discovered that they were not going to bag Cooper for $22 a share. Those discussions went on for fourteen months. It seemed to Neeraj Kanwar that he spent as much time in the air flying to meetings as he did on the ground attending them.

As the two sides moved closer Onkar took Roy Armes out for dinner at The Post House, 'an old-guard steakhouse' on Manhattan's Upper East Side. 'I knew Roy liked steaks and over drinks and dinner we talked again about putting our companies together. He said there were two conditions. One was an assurance that if we took over Cooper, we would not immediately start selling parts of it off. I assured him that it was not Apollo's style to do that. Secondly he told me that for the deal to work for him he would need a break fee. It was a new concept to me. I asked him what a break fee was. He said it was necessary in case I backed out. I told him I had never backed out of a deal once it had been agreed. He insisted that his board would not accept an offer from Apollo unless there was a break fee.'

Kanwar was slightly affronted. 'I had the best of relationships with the best of companies, all built on mutual trust, but I am pragmatic so we agreed that if Apollo pulled out of the deal we would pay Cooper $112 million and if they pulled out he would pay us $53 million.'

A similarly pragmatic approach was now required in South Africa.

◆

By the end of May 2013, Apollo sold the Ladysmith plant and the sales and marketing operation to Sumitomo for $60 million. Apollo closed down the Durban factory and sold it to a real estate developer. The Zimbabwe operations were sold to local investors.

However, the exit from South Africa was driven by internal problems rather than the need to monetize the asset to fund a bid for Cooper Tire.

Between 2006 and 2010, Apollo had improved Dunlop's operating margins even further in spite of the 2008 financial crisis causing a big dip in the South African economy as demand for oil and minerals slumped. That was counterbalanced to a certain extent by the 2010 World Cup coming to South Africa, which led to a construction boom and massive infrastructure projects.

However, the World Cup revealed the endemic level of corruption involved in awarding those contracts and the mood in South Africa changed dramatically. Unions became extremely aggressive. They saw the extent of corruption and people making a lot of money while they had not seen their wages rise. The government was losing control of the economy and prices began to rise. Suddenly there were year-on-year electricity price rises of 35 per cent, which were particularly injurious to Apollo Dunlop and all tyre companies, which are power-intensive and regard electricity as a raw material.

In 2010, the port workers had gone on strike so no raw materials, such as rubber, could come into a country that is heavily dependent on imports. When that strike was lifted the tyre industry went on strike for three months. In South Africa, the unions are industry-wide so if the tyre union calls a strike over any issue all tyre companies are shut down.

'The union said that wages would have to be renegotiated so all companies would shut until they were revised, even though we had a four-year agreement,' says Sunam Sarkar. When the tyre dispute got fixed the transport unions went on strike. For Apollo Dunlop, like many companies, it was a three-ringed cash flow nightmare. First it could not bring in rubber, then when it could import, it was unable to manufacture. When eventually the production lines got rolling again it could not transport tyres and therefore could not sell to customers.

'In the first four years things had gone well,' says KP, 'but the culture of industrialization was in decline across the country. Suddenly Apollo's operations were not as good.'

Apollo needed to find a way to reduce its risk. It looked to bring in a co-investor. The South African government had passed an act to ensure Broad-Based Black Economic Empowerment, known as B-BBEE, to encourage companies to give share ownership to disadvantaged communities. Apollo agreed to take part even though it felt that B-BBEE was not being implemented as originally envisioned and did not necessarily benefit those it was designed to help.

Manufacturing costs were also very high in South Africa. Employee cost to sales was 26 per cent when Apollo went in. They managed to bring it down to 22 per cent but not through reducing employee costs but by improving sales. At Vredestein's plant employee to sales costs are closer to 15 per cent.

The huge increase in imported tyres also had a major impact. 'When we moved into South Africa imports were about 19 per cent of total domestic tyre sales,' Onkar Kanwar says. 'When we left it was 55 per cent because the South African market was being flooded with cheap Chinese tyres.'

But there were significant pluses for Apollo such as operating in a multicultural environment, gaining experience of international business practices and it provided a huge shortcut in its journey for truck radials because Dunlop had a radial product at a time in India when Apollo had nothing whatsoever and so cut short its learning curve by three years at least.

Meanwhile, in Gurgaon, on 12 June 2013, the Apollo board assembled for a landmark meeting that would last all day. Bankers and financial advisers lined up to give presentations and Scott D. Miller leading a legal team from Sullivan & Cromwell ran the directors through takeover law in the United States.

◆

It was a red-letter day, 13 June 2013, for Onkar Singh Kanwar. 'At age 70, Onkar Kanwar has sealed the biggest deal of his business career,' *Forbes* magazine wrote in a feature entitled 'The Quiet Rise of Onkar Kanwar—The New Owner of Cooper Tire'.

Apollo had indeed signed the biggest acquisition in its history. The marriage with Cooper would cost Apollo $2.5 billion, making the deal even bigger than Tata's $2.3 billion takeover of Jaguar and Land Rover in 2008 and the largest overseas automotive acquisition by an Indian company. The vision had been Onkar's. His admiration for Cooper went way back to when he had first asked it for technological support. 'They were making a lot of money. I told my people to study this company.' However, it was Neeraj who had put in the hard negotiating yards.

'Neeraj Kanwar announces his arrival', *Business Standard* reported. 'Neeraj Kanwar can take credit for pulling off one of the largest overseas acquisitions by Indian companies in recent times.'

'The Cooper deal was Neeraj's coming of age moment', *Forbes India* commented. 'The senior Kanwar said of his son, "Watch out for him. He has the fire in his belly like I had in my younger days."'

The fanfare had hardly died away when it became clear that the Indian stock markets were not dancing for joy. Investors and analysts did not like the smaller Apollo taking over the much bigger Cooper in what is known as a leveraged takeover. A day after the deal was announced the price of Apollo stock was taking a beating. On the National Stock Exchange of India and the Mumbai Stock Exchange it plummeted from the previous day's close of ₹92 to ₹68.60. A day later it hit a 52-week low as concerns mounted that Apollo had taken on too much debt to buy Cooper. Was the deal sustainable?

'We had expected this reaction', Neeraj says. 'In fact we had anticipated it would fall to ₹50.'

'Some of the financial advisers were surprised it went down as much as it did', says Scott Miller, 'but buyers' shares usually take a hit when a transaction is announced and recover. I don't think it troubled the Kanwars in any meaningful way.'

However, reassurance was needed and on 14 June, Apollo called a press conference at the Leela Palace Hotel in Chanakyapuri, Diplomatic Enclave, New Delhi, one of a group of eight luxury hotels and resorts founded in 1987 by the late Captain C.P. Krishnan Nair, known as 'Captain Courage' due to his military exploits.

'Neeraj Kanwar took centre stage, making a presentation, answering questions and as always looking confident', *Forbes India* reported. 'Neeraj was convinced that the Apollo–Cooper merger would result in the perfect global tyre company. From a geographical perspective, Apollo was already big in India, Europe and Africa. Cooper was established in North America and China. In terms of products, Apollo had made inroads into getting contracts with car companies like Volkswagen and General Motors.

Cooper had a significant presence and experience in the replacement tyre market. Compared to their individual insignificant market position (Cooper at No. 11 and Apollo at No. 17), after the merger, the combined entity would become the seventh largest tyre company in the world.'

Neeraj told the analysts and journalists that only $450 million of the total $2.5 billion debt would be serviced by Apollo's business in India. 'I explained that the remaining debt was a non-recourse debt, taken on the cash flows of Cooper and Vredestein.'

The financial community was not won over. The same day Apollo's share price dipped another 5.6 per cent. Even so, the Kanwars were convinced that in the end the market would realize the value in the deal. They had booked their flights to Ohio to complete what they thought would be the final formalities with Cooper. So sure were both parties that the deal was in the bag they had inserted a six-month closure cause. Everything would have to be finalized by 31 December 2013.

Far from dotting the 'i's' and crossing the 't's', the Kanwars' problems were only just beginning.

◆

A month before the Cooper deal was announced Neeraj Kanwar had flown to Beijing on 15 May to meet a fifty-seven-year-old Chinese businessman called Che Hongzhi. Known to all as 'Chairman Che', he was Chairman of the Chengshan Group, which employed 7,000 people in the city of Ronghcheng overlooking the Yellow Sea. Hongzhi was also a former local government official made good, Communist Party apparatchik and politically well connected. His Chengshan Group was in the businesses of tyre and steel cord manufacturing and rubber processing alongside a scattergun mix of real estate development, ocean biology engineering, loans to small- and medium-sized businesses and pawnbroking. Tyres though were its biggest earner.

The Chengshan Group also had a joint venture with Cooper Tire called Cooper Chengshan Tire Company (CCT). Cooper had a 65 per cent shareholding in the joint venture, which contributed about 25 per cent annually to its global sales turnover. Cooper was strong in the replacement tyre market but saw China as part of its strategy to increase sales to car manufacturers, a strategy that appealed also to Apollo.

Sitting on his 35 per cent, Chairman Che may have been a passive minority investor with no rights to participate in discussions about the sale of Cooper, but it turned out that Che posed a problem. He was not by nature a passive man.

Neeraj's Beijing meeting with Chairman Che, which had been organized by Cooper, did not go smoothly. Neeraj did not speak Chinese and Che did not understand English and although they both had interpreters, discussions were understandably stilted and at arm's length. 'He listened patiently but he seemed distant,' Neeraj says. 'I told him that I would confirm in writing that the 5,000 jobs in CCT's tyre factory were guaranteed and that we had plans to expand and upgrade the plant to produce truck radials.'

Che told Kanwar, 'I have been a good son and the father is good. Now the father is divorcing me and the stepfather is coming in.'

Neeraj was slightly nonplussed by the riddle but 'after lunch and a toast to the future, Che said, "I don't care who my stepfather is; someone needs to tell me who is looking after me."' Neeraj Kanwar had been around the block enough times to know that this was code for some form of compensation should the deal with Apollo go through.

◆

Back in the United States, Apollo's due diligence carried on apace. What Neeraj did not discover until much later was that on 15 June, three days after Apollo had announced the Cooper acquisition, Chairman Che had flown to the United States and had himself bid $38 a share to buy Cooper, an offer that was $3 better than Apollo's. Cooper had turned him down.

Che Hongzhi returned to China empty-handed. According to *Forbes* magazine, 'he was seething with anger'.

'I did not discover this until it was too late,' Neeraj says. 'If he had come to me I would have treated him entirely differently. From what he told me he was not even offered a cup of tea! I would have looked after him and tried to make him feel part of the family. Instead he had lost face and I think he was determined to show the Americans what he was made of.'

Sure enough, within days of the deal being announced, CCT's workers went on strike in an attempt to derail the merger of Cooper and Apollo. In a statement Yue Chunxue, director of the Cooper Chengshan union branch, said, 'we oppose this purchase because Apollo does not have sufficient [financial] strength'. Workers' wages and benefits could not be guaranteed. He was concerned about 'cultural problems with future Indian bosses'.

In a paid advertisement in the *Wall Street Journal* the union alleged that the deal did not comply with Chinese law, involved excessive debt and asked, 'Who can guarantee the success of integration between Chinese culture and Indian culture?'

The debt level in the deal was not out of step with previous leveraged buyouts in the industry. As the *Financial Times* pointed out, 'the lenders involved, Standard Chartered, Deutsche Bank, Goldman Sachs and Morgan Stanley, have no recourse against Apollo or Cooper for five years, even if they do struggle to repay their debts, giving the two parties time to marry Apollo's presence in India, Africa and Europe with Cooper's well-established manufacturing and distribution operations in the US and China.'

Nobody in China was listening where events were moving at an alarming speed. The Chengshan Group now filed a complaint in the local Intermediate People's Court, claiming that the proposed merger had caused CCT's unions to stop work and that if it went ahead it would result in further operational risks. It sought to dissolve its joint venture with Cooper Tire.

CCT was the most profitable factory of Cooper's eight global plants, producing 35,000 tyres a day, and the Chinese market was the world's largest. If it lost CCT the sale value of the entire Cooper Tire business would decrease markedly.

The workers grudgingly returned to the factory. Negotiations between Cooper and CCT to try and solve the problem began on 26 June and continued into July.

To try and find out what was really happening in China Apollo hired US corporate investigators Kroll. It produced a report that suggested Che Hongzhi himself had orchestrated the strike.

At Apollo's behest, Roy Armes flew to China in early July to meet Chairman Che to try and reinforce in his mind that if the merger went ahead, Apollo would safeguard jobs, increase capital expenditure and invest in technology at CCT. It had no effect.

Chengshan's workers staged a second strike on 13 July. This one lasted eighteen days. 'Cooper insisted we sell to Apollo, but we will not agree,' Dong Zhaoqing, deputy director at the Chengshan Group office the told reporters. 'We do not want to be acquired.'

Some said Apollo was sitting on the sidelines and ought to be more actively involved in solving the dispute. 'Our argument was that this was an internal matter between Cooper and CCT,' says Neeraj Kanwar. 'Once Cooper had fixed the issue we could and would complete the acquisition.'

◆

On 1 August 2013, a second obstacle flared up on the road to union in the shape of the powerful United Steel Workers (USW) union. It represented the employees at Cooper's plants in Texarkana, Arkansas and Findlay, Ohio. It announced it was commencing arbitration alleging that under Cooper's collective bargaining agreement, the USW had a right to require Apollo to negotiate a new contract with the union before the merger could be completed. Cooper had advised Apollo that no such right existed under the union contract and that Cooper would prevail in the arbitration so the parties resolved to fight the action. In the same month CCT workers went on an indefinite strike. Not only that, CCT management barred any

Cooper staff from entering the plant or having access to financial figures. 'CCT literally threw them out, as well as denying them access to the computers,' says Neeraj Kanwar. 'But I still believed we could complete the Cooper transaction.'

In spite of his optimism, the clock towards a 31 December completion deadline was ticking ever faster while final agreement was heading just as quickly in the opposite direction. On 13 September, the arbitrator ruled that Apollo could not acquire Cooper until Apollo struck a new deal with the USW. Three days later Onkar Singh Kanwar, Neeraj and Sunam Sarkar boarded a 2 a.m. flight from New Delhi to New York to meet Cooper's executives and discuss the negotiating strategy they should adopt with the USW. Those negotiations opened in Nashville, Tennessee, where the union presented Apollo and Cooper with ten demands covering bonuses, bargaining rights and other issues. The meeting ran for two tortuous days.

It was clear to Apollo that the cost of a new labour agreement proposed by the USW would be much higher than envisaged and would have a major impact on Cooper's valuation. 'We reckoned that it would cost in the region of $125 million,' Neeraj says. Cooper disagreed, putting the figure at nearer $10 million. Says Sunam Sarkar, 'Cooper and its lawyers first said that Apollo should stand firm and reject the union demands until it dawned on them that Apollo would bear the entire costs of any new USW deal and that their shareholders would get the same amount of cash whether Apollo spent $10 million settling with the steel workers or $200 million. Their lawyer then aggressively started pushing us to agree to whatever the USW was asking for.'

The Kanwars do not respond well to being pushed around but they continued to talk to the USW, this time without Cooper. Cooper was not happy. 'The arbitrator had placed responsibility on Apollo and the USW to find a solution,' Sarkar says.

'There was also the fact that the USW leaders in their first meeting with us, in the presence of the Cooper management, told us in as many words that their recent experiences with Cooper management had been very disappointing and that they were looking forward to the Apollo takeover, as they had done their own due diligence on Apollo's labour practices in India, Europe and South Africa and were more than satisfied. It was felt that Apollo and the USW together would be able to move faster and more constructively towards an agreement without the Cooper presence.'

'Cooper and the USW were like an old married couple who were divorcing and couldn't help sniping at each other,' Scott Miller says. 'They could not be in a room together without bringing up old slights and fights. There had been a three-month lockout at Cooper's Findlay, Ohio, plant in 2012 and the USW still had some pretty hard feelings towards Cooper as a result.'

◆

Onkar Kanwar needed somebody to help him build bridges directly with the USW and Ohio politicians. Who better than a former governor of Ohio, Richard 'Dick' Celeste? In 1985, when he was governor, Dick Celeste, who was born in Cleveland, had brought a trade mission to India, the first American state to do so. Celeste had also put together the most ethnically diverse cabinet in Ohio's history with six women, four African Americans and at an average age of thirty-five. Celeste had great affection for India having worked there for four years in the 1960s as staff liaison officer in the Peace Corps. Two of his children had been born in India.

'On the trade mission we met a group of prominent business leaders from the Delhi region and one of those was Onkar. What struck me about him was how he was so open to the world and wanted to compete globally. He also had great affection for Ohio where he had lived and worked as a young man. I should have made him an honorary citizen!'

In 1997, Celeste returned to India when President Bill Clinton appointed him as America's ambassador. 'My wife and I saw Onkar and his family quite a bit during that period of time.' The energetic and likeable Celeste arrived to a controversial in-tray. The newly elected Vajpayee government had embarked on nuclear weapons testing which immediately put a strain on India–US relations. It would take all Celeste's diplomatic skills to foster relationships and understanding in Delhi. Onkar Singh Kanwar played his part. 'Very early on Onkar and Taru had a dinner party at their house to introduce us to his business colleagues, friends and neighbours. Those connections and others were to be hugely important in my role as Ambassador.'

Dick Celeste agreed to help the Kanwars who went to Ohio where he introduced them to USW officials. 'Onkar did most of the talking and he was good at sharing his vision of what Cooper's role in Apollo would be. He also talked about his time in Ohio and about his life since. I think the steel workers would love to have seen a new ownership at Cooper. There were obviously challenges and the USW wanted to safeguard its members and to know that Apollo would honour their contracts, but I don't think they had a high level of respect for the Cooper leadership.'

Rodney Nelson, head of USW Local 207 branch, told the *Financial Times*: 'He (Kanwar) seemed very sincere and confident in what they wanted to do. He told us they planned on keeping the Cooper plants operating as they are today. They showed up with Dick Celeste. That impressed me since he was a trusted government official.'

Onkar Singh Kanwar also had meetings with Ohio's two senators while Dick Celeste 'discussed the merger with the current Governor of Ohio, John Kasich, and some of his people who were all very positive'.

As Apollo and the USW edged closer it was clear to Neeraj Kanwar that it would cost $150 million to settle. 'I told Cooper we needed to revise the offer price, suggesting around a $2.50 a share reduction on our $35 per share offer.'

According to *Forbes India*, Roy Armes was furious. 'I am being asked to pay for something, which I can't even negotiate. I can go back to my board for a buck but two bucks fifty is a lot.'

It was another impasse. It was not the last. Because Chairman Che was refusing to let Cooper staff into the CCT plant to inspect the books and financial records, it was questionable whether the assurances required for the marketing phase of the Apollo–Cooper deal financing to begin would be forthcoming.

Although Cooper staff were barred—as one worker put it, 'we have changed the locks at the family home and we are not letting them back in'— Che Hongzhi was happy to give the *Financial Times* a tour of the plant. The *Financial Times* reported that he 'was in a fiery mood and remained extremely bitter about the Apollo–Cooper transaction which [he] had been briefed on just a few weeks before it was formally announced'.

A week after that announcement Roy Armes had visited CCT and was surprised by the hostile reception he received. Apollo cancelled a planned follow-up visit to the plant by Onkar Singh Kanwar. The time was not right.

It was only later, in November 2013, that Apollo finally discovered that Chairman Che had himself been a bidder for Cooper. The Kanwars finally understood his hardline attitude. 'Part of his anger was monetary and part of it was loss of face,' says Sarkar, who was involved in the deal from the start. 'He was asked to bid and he bid higher, but then Cooper didn't even consider it.' Che Hongzhi thought that his money was as good as anyone else's. Cooper obviously felt otherwise.

As the weeks rolled on Apollo was becoming concerned that Cooper had repeatedly revised down its consolidated revenues and operating profit forecasts for the 2013 fiscal year. It had done so five times since 21 July. Then Cooper had predicted $4.3 billion sales and $380 million operating profits. In any takeover this information is an essential part of a deal's financing for the acquiring company.

By the first week of October, Cooper was forecasting revenues of £3.4 billion and operating profits of $257 million, 25 per cent and 48 per cent lower respectively. To put that further into a gloomy context, in 2012, Cooper had reported EBITDA (earnings before interest, taxes, depreciation and amortization), a key indicator of a company's financial performance, of $526 million.

The alarm bells were ringing all over Apollo Tyres. In a five-page, single-line-spaced letter to Cooper, Apollo accused Cooper of 'reckless hopefulness, bad faith or worse' in its financial forecasting. The repeated revisions were seriously impeding Apollo's efforts to raise money to finance the takeover, Apollo argued. 'These revisions will necessitate that a revised business plan be presented to the ratings agencies and our financing sources, notwithstanding the embarrassment from having already [adjusted] the forecast multiple times over the past six weeks alone to account for the accelerating negative trajectory. These persistently missed forecasts have eroded any shred of credibility you had with us.'

Then on Friday, 4 October 2013, Cooper filed litigation in the Delaware Chancery Court in the United States asking that Apollo 'be required to expeditiously close the pending merger between the two tire companies in accordance with the terms of the definitive merger agreement'.

Cooper alleged that Apollo was dragging its feet by deliberately not concluding a deal with the USW, thereby breaching the merger agreement. 'Cooper has an obligation to protect the rights of our stockholders who voted overwhelmingly in favour of the merger,' said Roy Armes. 'With their approval, we have met our conditions for closing.'

In short, Cooper was accusing Apollo of buyer's remorse and doing anything it could to wriggle free of the merger. Understandably the Kanwars were not at all happy with Cooper's decision to go to court. In their view the litigation had no basis and the deal could still be done.

'The entire Apollo team was surprised that Cooper took this action when they did,' says Scott Miller. 'After all, there were still two months to go before the deadline of 31 December. Normally you would keep working.'

As with all legal cases it would come down to an interpretation of the wording. In its agreement with Cooper, Apollo had promised to use its 'best reasonable efforts' to negotiate a deal with the USW. Discussions between Apollo and the union had only been going on for two weeks when Cooper filed the lawsuit but it would try to argue in court that Apollo was not making best reasonable efforts and that the opposite was the case. If Apollo succeeded in proving that it was indeed doing its reasonable best to strike a deal with the USW then it would gain a significant advantage in potentially negotiating a revised purchase price to reflect the costs of the USW agreement and the other problems Cooper was facing, which would mean Cooper's shareholders taking a big financial hit.

There was a pressing reason why Cooper wanted to force Apollo to conclude the merger quickly. It was still barred from its plant in China and if it could not provide updated financial information by 10 November, the deadline by which it had to file its third-quarter earnings with the US regulators, then Apollo could walk away from the deal without paying the $112 million break fee. 'Cooper therefore, asks the Court to schedule this action for an expedited trial and resolution by 7 November 2013.'

Certain things now made sense, says Scott Miller. 'Around the end of September, we had started to get a little nervous that Cooper could be planning something precipitous because the language they were using to communicate with us changed. It became a lot more formal. It seemed that they were trying to set up a record that would make them look better if we ever ended up in litigation. We were to learn later than Cooper had been preparing for a lawsuit from August, six weeks before they filed.'

On 14 October 2013, Apollo filed a counterclaim detailing what it believed to be Cooper's failure to provide financial and other information under the merger agreement which was in no small way due to its apparent inability to exercise control over its Chinese subsidiary, Cooper Chengshan Tire. Cooper, it said, 'had failed to meet its contractual obligations under the merger agreement', and called for a 'declaratory judgement that the conditions precedent to the closing of the merger have not been satisfied'.

◆

By the end of October, Neeraj and his father, Sunam Sarkar and Gaurav Kumar travelled to London to give witness depositions in the Delaware court proceedings at the London offices of Sullivan & Cromwell in New Fetter Lane. Sullivan & Cromwell had advised Apollo from the start of negotiations with Cooper and would represent Apollo throughout the legal proceedings.

There they were cross-examined by Cooper's lawyers from Jones Day, an international corporate law firm, which operates in forty-one countries. The depositions were taken in separate rooms, each of them set up like mini courtrooms complete with a court reporter, a videographer and video screens. Jeffrey D. Ubersax, a Jones Day partner based in Cleveland, took Neeraj's deposition, which ran for over four hours of forensic questioning. The transcript was close to 200 pages.

Onkar Kanwar spent two hours giving his evidence. Neeraj had decided that he did not want his father to give evidence in the trial at the Delaware court. 'Dad knew all the facts and handled his deposition in London very well, but he had not been involved in the day-to-day detail of the agreement as I, Sunam and Gaurav had. And out of respect for him I did not want to see him put in a position on the witness stand where he would be aggressively grilled by Cooper's legal team.'

Neeraj had then flown to New York to be briefed by litigating attorney John L. Hardiman, a partner of Sullivan & Cromwell who would be representing him in court. Hardiman had been rated on several occasions as a leading lawyer in commercial litigation by *The Best Lawyers in America*. He had also spent nearly five years in London, where he headed Sullivan & Cromwell's European Litigation Group, which has about 800 lawyers working across four continents. Hardiman was hugely experienced and Neeraj could not have been in better hands. Another Sullivan & Cromwell attorney briefed Sunam Sarkar and Gaurav Kumar on courtroom procedure and how to handle examination and cross-examination.

'The Sullivan & Cromwell office was just like a scene in a John Grisham movie,' Neeraj recalls. 'John Hardiman had his whole team there, all running around, poring over stacks of documents. They had only been given three weeks to prepare and they were going crazy reading transcripts, trawling through hundreds of emails and reams of notes of all the meetings we had had with Cooper and the USW. We had to go back through two years of history.'

twenty

'I make tyres'

Hotel du Pont, 11th and Market Streets,
Wilmington, Delaware, 4 November 2013

After long flights from India, Singapore and London Neeraj Kanwar, Sunam Sarkar and Gaurav Kumar checked into the Hotel du Pont, which without a second of self-doubt describes itself as 'one of the grandest hotels in the world'. When it opened in 1913, about 25,000 visitors rushed to tour its 'elegant rooms, mosaic and terrazzo floors, [and] handcrafted chandeliers which had been created by a host of French and Italian craftsmen'.

The paintings, the $40-million facelift and the gilded hallways welcome them by as they were shown to their rooms. They were tired, apprehensive and a little homesick. They had left home on Sunday, 3 November, on the Hindu festival of Diwali when traditionally Indian families the world over come together to celebrate. Suddenly their families seemed a very long way away.

As they walked into the bar on the first evening, Roy Armes and his Cooper colleagues, who were also staying at the Dupont, were just leaving. The two sides shook hands politely but that was about it. This was no time for small talk.

The same evening Apollo's lead litigator John Hardiman came to the hotel and walked them the short distance to North King Street and the offices of Richards, Layton and Finger, the firm of local lawyers that he and his Sullivan & Cromwell team, including Scott Miller, were working with, to present the case. It was there that Hardiman had a preparatory session with Kanwar, Sarkar and Kumar that lasted until around 10 p.m.

There were new developments to consider. On 1 November, Cooper had announced that it had independently reached a settlement with the USW union, which Cooper said ensured that the merger could go ahead. Apollo dismissed this as a twelfth-hour stunt. In a letter filed by Sullivan & Cromwell with the Delaware court dated 4 November, Apollo accused Cooper of taking extraordinary steps to force the USW union into agreement ahead of the trial.

Apollo would stick to its guns. 'Cooper's decision to file a complaint is inexplicable and can only be seen as diversionary smokescreen or an unfortunate acknowledgement that it will be unable to meet its obligations necessary to complete the transaction.'

On the morning of Tuesday, 5 November, Neeraj Kanwar walked into the Court of Chancery Courthouse in Wilmington. The case was being heard there because Wilmington is where Cooper has its registered office.

He felt more tense than he ever had in his life. It was not a grasp of detail that he was worried about. He knew the Cooper transaction inside out, back to front. But he was acutely aware that what was about to happen to him would not be like going into a bankers and analysts conference, which was comfortable, well-known territory and where he excelled. He was stepping into a completely alien arena.

Thoughts flooded through his head. He tried to stay focused on the advice of how to conduct himself in court that he had been given by John Hardiman and his team back in New York, and which they had gone through again the previous evening. Answer the questions calmly and simply. Do not digress or head down cul-de-sacs. Video deposition evidence under oath and coaching in a Lower Manhattan lawyers' office could not completely prepare the Apollo three for what they were about to experience in a live courtroom.

The Wilmington courthouse, used to more esoteric corporate cases, was buzzing with hordes of newspaper journalists and TV reporters. There was such media interest in case 8980, *Cooper Tire & Rubber Company* vs. *Apollo (Mauritius) Holdings Pvt. Ltd, Apollo Tyres B.V. and Apollo Acquisition Corp*, that the courtroom was not big enough to hold them all. For those who could not be accommodated, the proceedings would be beamed by live video link into the adjacent court. Niche publications, including *The Findlay Courier*, *Modern Tire Dealer* and *Leveraged Finance News*, jostled for the best seats with heavyweights from Reuters, the *Wall Street Journal*, Bloomberg News and the *Financial Times* from London.

The world's media had been following the Cooper transaction story closely for months. This was a saga that strayed exotically beyond their normal business beats. For a start, it involved the biggest overseas automotive takeover by an India company, even bigger than Tata's takeover of Jaguar Land Rover. Then there was the controversy and friction the proposed merger had caused in China, and the intriguing 'Chairman Che'. If that was not enough grist, there was the might and muscle of the USW winning its legal battle against Cooper for new negotiating and other rights.

◆

All rose as the Chancery Court's Vice Chancellor, the Honourable Sam Glasscock III walked in to hear the non-jury case, which was expected to last four days. Glasscock, who is also a Professor of Law and teaches corporate litigation, had resolved a wide range of corporate disputes. Glasscock's court also had a reputation for settling disputes quickly. On 23 October, he had ruled out Apollo's request to dismiss Cooper's lawsuit, filed just four days previously. Instead he had fast-tracked the trial.

'We had gone from a lawsuit being filed to a full trial in four weeks, which is unheard of,' says Scott Miller, who was working on trial strategy. 'To some extent it was unfair to Apollo, although we were confident in our case.'

Several observers took this fast-tracking as a sign that Glasscock was favouring Cooper, but there were legal reasons for Cooper wanting a quick decision. As Scott Miller explains, 'If the deal with Apollo was not completed by the middle of November, then Cooper would have problems preparing financial statements for the third quarter of 2013, something that was required by the acquisition agreement for the lenders to provide the finance necessary to complete the deal.'

'For Cooper to win, it will have to score at least two victories,' wrote Steven Davidoff Solomon in *The New York Times*. Davidoff Solomon is professor of law at the University of California, Berkeley, and author of *Gods at War: Shotgun Takeovers*. The judge would have to assess whether Apollo was not negotiating in good faith with the USW. 'Even if the judge does rule in Cooper's favour, it is hard to see what he can do in terms of pushing Apollo to negotiate,' Davidoff Solomon wrote. 'He can certainly order Apollo to negotiate in good faith, but how can that be measured?'

The bigger issue was whether Cooper's loss of control over CCT was a breach of the acquisition agreement.

'If Apollo wins on this second issue, it can walk away from the deal without paying Cooper the $112 million reverse termination fee,' said Davidoff Solomon who writes a weekly column as 'The Deal Professor'. 'Similarly if the November date passes, [and] Apollo isn't found to be in breach of the agreement and Cooper can't provide its lenders with what they need, Apollo will also be able to walk away without paying anything to Cooper.'

Legal arguments would revolve around three major issues. Did Apollo purposely slow down negotiations with the USW in order to walk away from the merger? Did it use the cost of settling with the USW to leverage a reduction in its share offer price for Cooper and did it realize in advance, as Cooper was suggesting, that its Chinese partner could pose a problem?

Apollo would counter all of these allegations. It would also argue that Cooper's inability to provide detailed financial statements had meant that the marketing period—the twenty-day business window for Apollo's banks, Morgan Stanley, Deutsche Bank, Goldman Sachs and Standard

Chartered Bank to find buyers for the deal's bonds, which would be required to replace the bank debt—had never been able to start. This made a merger impossible.

The courtroom had barely settled down when Cooper's attorney Robert S. Faxon, a partner from the Cleveland office of Jones Day, leapt to his feet. Faxon had appeared in courts throughout the United States on commercial litigation cases involving corporate control, corporate governance and M&As. He moved a motion that all the witnesses should be sequestered, meaning that none of them should be in court to hear the evidence given by the others or talk to each other about the case. This is designed to prevent collusion and more commonly employed in criminal trials.

John Hardiman objected. He saw no reason why this was necessary.

Vice Chancellor Glasscock ruled: 'I grant the motion. Please have the witnesses sequestered.'

One of those sequestered witnesses was Scott Miller who now found himself in the strange position of not being able to speak to his Apollo clients or support them in court.

John Hardiman responded by asking that Neeraj Kanwar, who had been involved in the whole process, be allowed to remain.

Glasscock agreed to this, but warned Neeraj that he, Sarkar and Kumar were not allowed to discuss the case with each other outside the court. The three of them assured him that they would respect his instruction. Then Sarkar, Kumar, Scott Miller and all the Cooper witnesses left the court and went to the witness room.

'There were four walls, a table, some chairs, tea and coffee and big boxes full of legal papers from which paralegals would keep coming to retrieve bundles of documents,' says Sarkar. 'We had no mobile connection and no idea of what was going on.'

Roy Armes was the first to take the stand. He was typically bullish. As he gave his version of events Neeraj Kanwar's blood began to boil. Armes's account was at complete variance to the facts, as he knew them. Armes told the court that Apollo should have understood that a lockout at Cooper Chengshan Tire was a known risk and factored it into its acquisition price offer. He reiterated his surprise at Neeraj Kanwar's request to reduce Apollo's share price offer on account of the costs of resolving the dispute with the USW, costs that Cooper disputed. 'I was offended, frankly,' he said. He could and would not ask his shareholders to pay such a steep price. The risk of labour problems should have been part of the price that Apollo negotiated, he insisted. Armes described some of Neeraj Kanwar's statements during negotiations as confusing and contradictory.

Neeraj resisted a natural instinct to stand his ground. He relaxed slightly when John Hardiman began his cross-examination of Armes. Hardiman suggested that Armes' recall was faulty and selective and he began to take apart his evidence forensically. In court Hardiman had an aura about him. Flamboyant but not flashy, he was in total command of his brief. He reminded Sunam Sarkar of TV's Perry Mason. Neeraj clung to the advice that Hardiman had given him many times for when it was his turn to give evidence. A witness getting riled and combative in court was completely counterproductive. Leave the combat to the lawyers!

Under cross-examination by John Hardiman, Roy Armes admitted that the breakdown with CCT was 'a big problem', Bloomberg Business reported. 'This disruption has caused problems in getting financial information. But it's all been brought on by this acquisition.'

It continued, 'James P. Dougherty [an M&A lawyer for Jones Day] told the court the Cooper buyout agreement was structured in such a way that required Apollo to go through with the deal despite the Chinese labour problems. The agreement was written to ensure that Cooper would not bear the risk of adverse reaction to the deal "by either the USW unions or the Chinese venture partners," Dougherty said'.

And so it went on. 'I think there's some buyers' remorse there,' Armes said. After two hours, he went back to his chair and there was a break. Neeraj walked out of the courtroom and straight into Armes. Neeraj admits that he still felt aggrieved by what he had heard inside the court. 'Roy was all smiles, hail fellow well met, and just doing his job I guess. He told me this was all part of the American drama and not to worry. We would get there with the deal.' Before he could respond, John Hardiman stepped in. 'No talking. Roy, please leave.'

Cooper's CFO Bradley Hughes told the court that Cooper's multiple revisions of financial forecasts were due to short-term issues such as pricing, the tyre industry's competitive environment and costs associated with the merger. According to a court report in *Tire Business,* Hughes quoted one of his former supervisors at Ford, 'The one thing you know is that the forecast is going to be wrong.'

Hardiman reminded him that Apollo's concerns about Cooper's financial revisions undermined confidence in its ability to provide credible statements that were necessary to make the merger a reality.

'I'm surprised that they were surprised,' Hughes said.

◆

The first to take the witness stand for Apollo on the first day was Neeraj Kanwar. Sunam Sarkar and Gaurav Kumar would follow him. John Hardiman asked him, 'What do you do for a living?'

'I make tyres,' Neeraj said simply. A murmur of laughter went around the court, which relaxed him. Hardiman raised an eyebrow. He hoped that Neeraj was not going to go off script. He was to spend the next four hours giving evidence.

Hardiman's next question was, 'Why did you want to buy Cooper?'

Kanwar answered at some length, describing Apollo's history from his grandfather's day, his father's role in transforming the company from a local player to a global corporation and the rationale and logic for wanting to come to America.

'I probably went on too long but the lady stenographer asked me to speak slowly because she was having trouble understanding my accent!'

Already the intriguing but distant figure of Chairman Che Hongzhi was hanging precipitously over the proceedings. In cross-examination Kanwar was asked about Apollo's offer to buy out Chairman Che's stake in CCT.

'$150 million to $200 million was offered,' he confirmed, but it had not been accepted and there were no current negotiations. 'It's in the interests of all parties to work together,' he insisted, to resolve the disputes in China and with the USW.

Neeraj was finding the cross-examination tiring. It was about to get a lot more taxing. 'It was done by Jeffrey D. Ubersax, who did my deposition in London, so I was used to him and his style of attack.' In more than twenty-five years at Jones Day the square-jawed, Harvard-educated Jeff Ubersax had won some big cases ranging across antitrust, fraud, securities claims, and commercial disputes involving contracts. He was persistent and methodical. He suggested that Apollo had known of the problems Cooper was having getting its books out of CCT, back in August 2013. Neeraj insisted it was 2 October. And so it went on, question upon question. He felt like he was facing serve from Novak Djokovic.

'Ubersax kept trying to make me lose my cool and irritate me, going through endless emails, questioning my memory of every line, and insisting that we were actively delaying the merger beyond the deadline so we could walk away without paying the break fee,' Neeraj says.

Neeraj Kanwar has many strengths and talents, but being obliged to sit in one place for hours on end and being quizzed by people who are needling to get under his skin is not one of them. Now he smiles about it. 'John Hardiman had prepared me beautifully!'

At the end of the afternoon the court adjourned. Neeraj Kanwar would have to continue with his evidence the following morning. Vice Chancellor Glasscock reminded him of his undertaking not to discuss anything to do with the case with Sunam Sarkar or Gaurav Kumar.

◆

Over in Delhi, where he was nine hours thirty minutes ahead of Delaware, Onkar Singh Kanwar had never felt so out of the loop, so out of control. He hated not knowing what was going on as it happened. He had had some contact from Sunam Sarkar who had moved out of the witness room and to the offices of Richards, Layton & Finger where he could use his phone but he had no idea how Neeraj was faring.

Onkar knew that when he went to bed that evening Neeraj would still be giving evidence and when he woke up in the morning Neeraj and others would be asleep. He now regretted not being in court to give evidence, although he accepted that Neeraj's decision for him not to attend had been the right one. Onkar had every confidence that his son would win the day, but even so he wanted to be there to fight for the reputation of his company.

After the court adjourned on day one of the trial Neeraj did call his father. It was evening in Delaware but it would be early morning of the next day in Delhi. Onkar Singh Kanwar is an early riser. Every day he is up by 6 a.m. and spends an hour or more working out on the running machine, cross-trainer and other apparatus in his large basement gym—something of which he is very proud. He follows exercise with prayer, reflection and tea.

Neeraj could hear the concern in his father's voice. 'I think my mother was crying.' He did his best to reassure his father that everything was going well, but even so Neeraj Kanwar did not sleep well that night.

◆

After breakfast alone Neeraj was back on the witness stand next morning, 6 November, for another three hours. Cooper's legal team obviously regarded him as the big fish and they were determined to land themselves a catch. The questioning was relentless and forensic. They wanted to know more about Chairman Che and the USW. What were Apollo's real intentions?

All the legal tricks and trips were employed against him but somehow with the interventions and support from John Hardiman and his legal team and expert witnesses Neeraj Kanwar walked out of court unscathed.

Sunam Sarkar was next to take the stand. He acknowledged that Neeraj Kanwar and Che Hongzhi had met in Beijing in May, where Chairman Che had expressed unhappiness at the deal. Sarkar agreed that the merger agreement had not included a specific payment for Che. However, at the time of that meeting Apollo had not been aware that Hongzhi's superior bid for Cooper had been turned down flat and that he was aggrieved.

Sarkar confirmed that Apollo had since made Cooper Chengshan Tire a buyout offer, code-named 'Project Charlie', as a way of removing a key obstacle to closing the deal. It had not been accepted by Chairman Che.

During the hour that Sunam Sarkar was giving evidence Cooper's attorney became very excited about an email sent by Sumit Dayal, Global Head-Corporate Finance at Standard Chartered Bank, to Neeraj Kanwar which referred to a phone conversation between himself, Kanwar and Sarkar. It was put to Sarkar that the conversation suggested the victory of the USW would give Apollo the chance to renegotiate the deal price.

Cooper's lawyer leapt on this as evidence that Apollo had mala fide intentions. It was trying to wriggle out of its agreed deal and was guilty of bad faith.

Scott Miller, who would also be questioned about similar emails from Apollo's bankers, admits that they 'were unfortunate. But the simple fact was that since the arbitrator had ruled in favour of the USW, Neeraj, Sunam, Gaurav and other Apollo executives had flown thousands of miles in two weeks to Ohio, Nashville and Pittsburgh [the headquarter of the USW] to try and seal a deal with the union, which was evidence enough that Neeraj Kanwar was completely focused on getting it done whatever a banker might say.'

The Cooper attorney persisted. 'Mr Sarkar, what are your recollections of that telephone conversation?'

Sarkar replied that at the time of the conversation he was with his eldest son Sanjit at a Premier League football match at Manchester United's stadium Old Trafford. On Monday Sarkar would see Sanjit enrol at university.

'I took the call during the match,' he told the court, 'but the noise in the corridor outside the hospitality suite was so bad I could not hear what anybody was saying, so I was not able to participate.'

The questioning went on. Finally Sarkar was told he could step down. At this point Vice Chancellor Glasscock intervened for the first time.

'May I ask a question?'

Sunam Sarkar braced himself.

'Which university were you taking your son to?' the judge asked.

'Lancaster University, Sir.' Sunam's alma mater.

'You must be a very proud father,' Glasscock said.

This very personal intervention made the Apollo team think that maybe Vice Chancellor Glasscock was feeling some empathy for Apollo.

◆

Neeraj Kanwar, Sarkar and Kumar agreed that after two days in court there was no point in hanging around in Wilmington waiting for the verdict. After hearing all the witness evidence, Vice Chancellor Glasscock would take final legal arguments at his home court in Georgetown, Delaware.

'We were all mentally and physically exhausted,' Sunam Sarkar says. 'We all just wanted to get home.' He flew to Singapore for pre-scheduled meetings while Neeraj and Gaurav took flights to London, from where Gaurav would go on to Delhi.

◆

Neeraj arrived home on Friday, 8 November, off a flight from Philadelphia and went straight to bed. He eventually woke up that evening. At around 9.30 p.m., he was in his sitting room enjoying a drink with his wife Simran when 'suddenly I just burst out crying; all my emotions came out.'

Then his phone rang. It was Scott Miller of Sullivan & Cromwell. 'Congratulations! You won the case!'

Just after landing at Singapore airport Sunam Sarkar switched on his phone and received the same message. A relieved smile came on his face, the first in a while. He could just imagine how the Kanwars must be feeling now!

In his summing-up Vice Chancellor Sam Glasscock dismissed Cooper's claims. Apollo had made every effort to achieve the merger but had been prevented from doing so, he ruled. He rejected Cooper's argument that Apollo had been stringing out negotiations with the USW. 'Apollo has in fact used reasonable best effort to reach an agreement,' he wrote. He said he was convinced by Neeraj Kanwar's evidence that he wanted the merger to be completed successfully, albeit at a lower price. Apollo was not in breach of the merger terms. Cooper on the other hand had not satisfied all of the conditions to close the merger.

As far as the Kanwars were concerned this was about more than an important legal victory or that the news of it caused Apollo's shares to rise by as much as 6 per cent. 'The integrity and values of Apollo were being questioned,' says Onkar Singh Kanwar. 'The court ruled that we had acted in accordance with those values. We had acted in good faith from the start.'

Glasscock had also rejected Cooper's attempts to win a court order 'that would relieve it of the obligation to disclose third-quarter financials to Apollo and its lenders, as would otherwise be required by financing agreements in support of the merger'.

Cooper announced that it would appeal the verdict to the Delaware Supreme Court. But who said the merger was dead? As Glasscock said in his ruling, 'Ample time remains since the Merger Agreement does not terminate until 31 December 2013. The parties should confer and notify me how they intend to proceed on the issues remaining.'

While negotiations with the USW might be solvable, John Hardiman, speaking post-trial, said the real roadblock to the Cooper deal was elsewhere. 'Let's face it, when 25 per cent of your business goes into a black hole after you've signed up to a deal which is going to be financed, it's an issue.

'The way to resolve this matter and go forward is to resolve the issues in China.'

twenty-one

A date with Chairman Che

Ronghcheng, Northeast China, 13 November 2013

Ronghcheng is an unremarkable city of 700,000 souls in the far east of Shandong province overlooking the Yellow Sea. Onkar Singh Kanwar, Neeraj Kanwar and Sunam Sarkar had arrived in Beijing the previous day and chartered a private jet to fly on to Ronghcheng, convinced that they could do a deal with Chairman Che Hongzhi for his share of Cooper Chengshan Tire which would help them complete the Cooper merger by the 31 December deadline. China was the world's largest market for commercial vehicles and the Kanwars were still keen to secure an Apollo presence there.

The Kanwars usually fly scheduled airlines but the high-ranking political intermediaries who had secured them a meeting with Chairman Che had advised them that arriving in Ronghcheng in a private jet would create the right impression and make a statement of intent, and anyway there was only one scheduled flight a day from the capital.

On arrival they were driven out along the coast until the road appeared to end at a gate. The gate opened remotely and they drove on along a private road built on stilts out over the ocean. Around the headland they climbed up a small hill and perched right on top of it in a secluded wooded area was a government guest house.

It had at least ten bedrooms and the kind of lavishly over-the-top showers featured in luxury interiors magazines and found in villas of rock stars.

Soon after the Kanwars and Sarkar had freshened up, two black SUVs pulled up and out stepped first the bodyguards and then Chairman Che Hongzhi.

He walked into the room where they were to meet. 'He immediately sat down at the big round table facing the door, which symbolically in China is supposed to be the position to influence the room,' Neeraj explains. 'This forced Mr Kanwar to sit opposite him, with his back to the door, which is considered to be a weaker position.'

Neeraj, Sarkar, the intermediaries and a translator all sat down. 'Almost immediately Che started shouting at my father,' Neeraj says. 'He was ranting, "I have been told you have come here to apologize, so apologize!" Dad looked at me as if to say, "What on earth do I need to apologize for?"'

Nobody has ever seen Onkar Singh Kanwar lose his temper. 'I decided it would cost me nothing to apologize, however,' he says. He told Hongzhi, 'If there has been a misunderstanding then I do apologize. I want to allay this fear that Apollo will come in and change your working relationships with Cooper. The company will stay Cooper Chengshan Tire. It will remain a subsidiary of an American company. It is only the shareholders who will change.'

Kanwar emphasized again that Apollo would invest more in technology at CCT than Cooper had and safeguard jobs. 'Che was not really listening. He kept saying, "I don't like the stepfather."'

'Why don't you give me your proposal, tell me what you want to do,' Kanwar asked. 'I just want to understand whether there is a way forward for us together, rather than looking back or blaming people. We are also prepared to buy your share of the business at what we think is a fair market valuation.'

Once the translator had finished, Chairman Che stood up, turned on his heel and stormed out, leaving the senior intermediary to apologize to the Kanwars for his rudeness. The meeting had lasted just thirty minutes.

It had been a long journey to get nowhere.

'The next morning Che turned up at the guest house with a minibus and his mood had completely changed,' says Neeraj Kanwar. 'He told us he had come to show us the tyre plant.'

Whatever the intermediary had said to Che overnight had obviously worked. A deal with Chairman Che now looked more positive. 'It was a very big factory, and he took us around personally on a golf cart,' says Onkar Singh Kanwar. The reception area had a wall of screens showing live video of different areas of the factory. There were photographs of visiting VIPs such as former Chinese Premier Li Peng. The CCT plant could make around five million tyres a year, mainly under the Cooper brand, but there was a surprise for the visitors. Says Onkar Kanwar, 'We spent about half an hour on the shop floor, seeing everything, but the strangest thing was that there was no physical evidence of Cooper having ever been there.'

'We were shocked,' Onkar Kanwar adds. 'There was not a photograph, a Cooper banner, not a single Cooper tyre in the display centre, only Chengshan Group tyres. Cooper had been written out of the story.'

After the tour they moved to the Chairman's office where the conversation turned to money. 'He looked us straight in the eye and said, "I want you to buy me out for $550 million,"' Onkar Kanwar says.

Onkar Kanwar took this to be an audacious opening gambit. He assumed that they would bat figures back and forth until an acceptable compromise was reached and then the rest could be left to the lawyers.

'Our valuation of your 35 per cent share of the business is in the range of $150 to $180 million,' Kanwar replied. He waited for the translator to finish and then added, 'But we are prepared to go to $230 or $240 million.'

Che listened then paused. 'No! 550, please.'

He repeated his demand over lunch in the directors' cafeteria where he opened beers and proposed a toast.

'I was not sure why we were toasting as we had not agreed on anything,' Neeraj says. Later that day the two sides had a meeting at the guest house. It lasted seven minutes. It was $550 million or nothing, Hongzhi insisted.

'The guy was not going to budge,' Neeraj Kanwar says.

Back in Beijing the Kanwars went to see Chairman Che's lawyer. 'Is there any point in discussing this further,' Onkar Kanwar asked him.

'He has given you his value expectation,' the lawyer said. 'This is what he expects to get.'

And that was that. Apollo and Cooper would not happen. Cooper withdrew its appeal to the Delaware Supreme Court and on 30 December 2013, announced that it was calling off the merger deal with Apollo. There was some further sabre-rattling by both sides regarding damages and counter-damages but these came to naught and Apollo did not have to pay the $112 million reverse termination fee.

Apollo said it was disappointed that Cooper had terminated the deal and issued a statement. 'While Cooper's lack of control over its largest subsidiary and its inability to meet its legal and contractual financial reporting obligations has considerably complicated the situation, Apollo has made exhaustive efforts to find a sensible way forward; however, Cooper has been unwilling to work constructively to complete a transaction that would have created value for both companies and their shareholders.'

'The merger would have been wonderful for Apollo and a very positive step forward for Cooper,' says Dick Celeste. 'The USW did not take sides in this but I sense there was a quiet regret in Pittsburgh [the USW's headquarters]. The roadblock to this deal was never the union; the roadblock was in Shandong province.'

In October 2014, Cooper Tire sold its 65 per cent stake in CCT to Chairman Che for $284.5 million. Roy Armes told the *Wall Street Journal* that China remained a 'core growth market' and would focus its future investment on a second plant, which it wholly owned in the city of Kunshan in Jiangsu province, where the Apollo takeover had caused no unrest whatsoever. 'China is extremely important,' Armes said. 'We can succeed with or without CCT.'

'There is no doubt that Chairman Che was the big winner,' Scott Miller says. 'He got the business at a relatively reasonable price.'

The Kanwars had been completely exonerated in the court proceedings but after the thousands of extra miles they had travelled to make the Cooper merger work they must have had regrets that in not securing it Apollo had failed to make it to the top ten tyre manufacturers.

'I did not take it as a personal defeat,' says Neeraj Kanwar, 'but it was a major setback; the biggest setback [of my career].' Has the experience put him off acquisitions? 'Not at all... If an acquisition comes up which is affordable and makes sense in terms of synergies, I will do it. I don't want to stop. Even if it is Cooper back on the table!'

'We had got very close and we had done a lot of the integration work with Cooper,' Onkar Singh Kanwar accepts, 'but you cannot regret, because everything happens for the best. Equally you cannot go forward if you are looking backwards. We didn't look back. We said, "Let's move on."'

twenty-two

Fast forward

A year after the end of the misfiring Cooper saga and told-you-so investors and pundits had been panning Apollo for its abortive $2.5 billion bid, its stock price had almost tripled. The tide had turned for the Kanwars. In July 2015, Apollo announced another ₹20 billion investment in its factories in Chennai and Kerala on the back of a ₹10 billion profit for the 2015 financial year. In the second quarter of 2015, profits were up 44 per cent and Apollo was about to launch the Vredestein brand in India.

On 10 April 2015, Onkar Singh Kanwar and Neeraj Kanwar joined Hungary's Prime Minister, Viktor Orbán, at the industrial park near Gyöngyöshalász to lay the ceremonial cornerstone of Apollo's latest venture, its first greenfield tyre plant outside India where it would invest €475 million over the next five years The government was now favourably disposed to Apollo and saw the plant as an important step in the industrialization of the country. Opposition from local winegrowers had disappeared.

Due for completion by early 2017, when the first tyre will roll out, the Hungary plant will have the capacity to produce 5.5 million passenger and light truck tyres and 675,000 heavy commercial vehicle tyres a year under both the Apollo and Vredestein brands.

Kannan Prabhakar is in charge of delivering the plant, which will be modelled on the Chennai plant but be even more modern and automated. With construction started in 2015, the plant will provide jobs for 975, the majority hired locally. Newly appointed Apollo staff from Hungary were soon arriving in Apollo's Enschede and Chennai plants for training.

'The challenge of putting up a greenfield plant is huge,' Onkar Kanwar admits. 'It takes a lot of resources, both capital and human, but it is also a significant milestone in Apollo's international growth journey which will increase our competitive strength in the European market.'

It was in Italy that the next seismic shock in the tyre industry occurred in March 2015. China National Chemical (ChemChina) announced that it was buying Pirelli, the world's fifth biggest tyre manufacturer. The state-owned conglomerate paid in the region of $7.7 billion for one of Italy's iconic companies, which supplies tyres to Formula 1 teams. Not everybody in Italy saw the industrial logic but there is little room for sentiment in the global tyre industry. The deal gave Pirelli greater access to Asia's fast-growing tyre markets.

Onkar Singh Kanwar though was to benefit from Pirelli's input. In October 2015, Apollo announced that it had hired Francesco Gori, former CEO of Pirelli Tyre, as an adviser. Gori would help Apollo identify and develop new opportunities aimed at international growth. For both Kanwars having Gori, who had spent thirty-three years with Pirelli, on board was both a privilege and something of a coup. 'He is widely accepted as the architect of the successful premium strategy of his former company,' Neeraj Kanwar said in the press release. 'We look forward to his insight and guidance to sharpen Apollo's focus and implementation in the brand and technology areas.' Gori also brought to Apollo a vast knowledge of the tyre industry.

Going right back to the days of M.R.B. Punja urging Onkar Singh Kanwar to professionalize his board, Kanwar has just done that. Today the board that Francesco Gori joined is an impressive group. The tyre industry is further represented by Robert Steinmetz, once of Continental AG, but the other independent board members bring the kind of extensive experience of other fields that is necessary for a company of Apollo's stature and ambition. General Bikram Singh is the former Chief of the Indian Army. Arun Kumar Purwar was Chairman of the State Bank of India, Dr S. Narayan was Finance Secretary and Economic Advisor to former Prime Minister Atal Bihari Vajpayee and Vikram S. Mehta is a former Chairman of the Shell Group of Companies. From the legal world come Pallavi Shroff and Akshay Chudasama, both partners from one of India's leading law firms, Shardal Amarchand Mangaldas & Co.

'Onkar is not interested in people who just sit there and say yes,' says long-serving fellow director Nimesh Kampani. 'He has taken good people on the board from all over the world who are knowledgeable and bring a good perspective.'

'Everything that the company does is laid bare for the board members,' says Vinod Rai, a former Comptroller and Auditor General of India, and a scourge of opaque and wasteful government departments. Appointed recently as the first Chairman of the Banks Board Bureau, Rai is one of Apollo's newest independent directors, although he did serve on the board back in the 1990s as the civil servant nominated by the Government of Kerala. 'What attracted me to come back in a private capacity is that Apollo is such a transparently run company. I feel that everything I need to know is freely available to me.

'Because the Apollo board is so varied in its experience of different industries, it has many ears to the ground so when, for example, we discuss how the Indian road network is going to grow in the next three to five years, one of our members has seen the kilometre projections and how many more cars and commercial vehicles will be on those roads and that means more tyres. Those projections are very important to a tyre company planning for the future.'

Onkar Kanwar handles meetings efficiently. Business is brisk but not rushed. Discussion is extensive and to the point. The Chairman is known to chip in with significant and direct questions. 'May I ask,' he said at a recent sales presentation, 'why when you gave us a budget just two months ago that forecast a profit are you already forecasting a loss?'

As former director Raaja Kanwar says, 'At the end of the day my father is a numbers man.'

◆

Onkar Singh Kanwar is also a highly networked man. As a member of many Indian overseas trade missions, Kanwar has dined at the Kremlin, met several British Prime Ministers, Chinese President Xi Jinping, the Emperor of Japan, President Hollande of France and UN Secretary General Ban Ki-moon, among many others.

Kanwar is also Chairman of the Indian Chapter of the BRICS Business Council, set up in 2013 to promote economic cooperation between the BRICS countries (Brazil, Russia, India, China and South Africa). Following some powerhouse economic performances, all the BRICS now face economic challenges and in 2014, they set up the New Development Bank (NDB) headquartered in Shanghai with $100 billion to support private sector and public infrastructure, energy and other projects with loans, equity participation and guarantees.

Onkar Singh Kanwar was Chairperson of the eighth BRICS Summit hosted by India in Panaji, Goa, in October 2016. He sees that it is synergy and cooperation not discord that will propel this group of countries, which account for about 20 per cent of the global GDP, to greater economic prominence.

'We are all strong in some fields and so we are working together to learn and share and combine those strengths to the benefit of all. The New Development Bank has been set up and a number of projects have been identified. For example, Indian companies are working in Russia in the energy sector.'

Kanwar is, however, an industrialist and entrepreneur and a realist first and last so while politicians are wedded to their slogans he recognizes that there are tensions between BRICS countries that can lead to discord, whether it is the falling oil price or sanctions against Russia. One major issue is the dumping of cheap Chinese tyres in India and across the world, which threatens to take away the lucrative replacement tyre market where the margins are higher. In the 2016 financial year, the import of truck and bus radials into India rocketed by 64 per cent, mostly from China. Every chance he gets, Kanwar lobbies the government to level the taxation playing field so Indian companies can compete. 'If we import raw materials into India to make tyres we pay customs duty, countervailing duty, anti-dumping duty, protection duty for Indian industry, all of which amount to an average of 26 per cent tax. If I import finished tyres, I only pay 8 per cent tax. Tell me how that encourages manufacture in India where we and other companies have made major investments.

'On top of that the cheaper imported tyres are lower grade, do not last as long and there is no service backup. That is not a reason to be complacent, however. Chinese tyres will improve. If you think back to when the Japanese started exporting, their electronic and other products were considered lousy. Look at them today.'

Bridgestone, located in Kyobashi, Tokyo, produced its first tyre in 1930 and today is the world's largest tyre and rubber company, swallowing up Firestone in the 1980s. It has 180 manufacturing plants in twenty-six countries and selling to more than 150.

In Onkar Singh Kanwar's mind there can be no deviation from Apollo's trajectory of becoming a $6 billion company and overcoming any obstacles that changing markets and raw material fluctuations throw in its path. 'We are looking for greenfield opportunities in Thailand, where we have a good distribution set-up catering to Southeast Asia and the United States or the chance to buy factories in those countries. Expansion is becoming very challenging because the industry has consolidated.'

If anyone can do it, the Kanwars can, according to Michael Ward. '[Their] ability to think and act quickly, decisively and sometimes unconventionally in an industry that is not perhaps well known for that has helped them. Add to that a large helping of dogged persistence.'

There is little talk of succession at Apollo, not in public at least. 'There is always a generation gap and a father should understand that and make sure that the son is a friend first before there is a succession plan,' says Nimesh Kampani, who on reaching his seventieth birthday, in 2016, handed over control of JM Financial after forty-three years at the helm to his thirty-nine-year-old son, Vishal, although he remains its Non-Executive Chairman. 'At the same time the father must make sure that the son goes through solid training within the firm,' Kampani adds.

'You cannot just make him sit on a chair and say run the business. Neeraj has gone through the training. That's what I have done with my son over sixteen years, starting at lower level and slowly, slowly coming up and then you know they are grown. And then your son should be bright and well educated because if he is good, people will respect him for being dedicated and professional. Neeraj Kanwar scores highly there too.'

There is no sign of Onkar Kanwar heading for an honorary role. 'I keep telling him he should follow my example and spend more time enjoying himself,' says Dr A.C. Muthiah, who likes nothing better than following his racehorses around India's tracks and going to England every year for the Royal Ascot and the Test match at Lord's. 'But Onkar will not hear of it.' Dr Muthiah laughs. 'Perhaps I will give Onkar a racehorse for his birthday!'

'I believe that I will die in my shoes, sitting in my chair or walking on the factory floor,' Onkar says. 'I don't know anything else. I have this burning desire. I need to move fast. I am still young mentally and I am healthy and I love to work. I have made sure that I changed with the times but the basics don't change.'

Time's passing, however, is inevitably marked by the loss of good friends. In 2015, his brother-in-law Dr Surinder Kapur, Founder-Chairman of Sona Koyo, died in Munich after a short illness aged seventy-one, survived by his wife Rani and their three children—Sunjay Kapur, Suparna Motwane and Mandira Koirala.

'Surinder was a very good man, a warm man, like a brother,' Onkar says. 'I was very fond of him.'

'I think my brother misses him almost as much as I do,' says his widow Rani. 'He was the most marvellous husband—Onkar chose very well for me. I was so lucky to go with Surinder everywhere he went on business.'

Onkar lost his other great friend and ally, Gyan Chand Burman, who died in 2001, aged just fifty-eight. As Onkar says, nobody chooses the moment when they die and until that point life has to go on. Now he is older he says he does not feel the pressure. 'When I had the problems with my father I hardly slept at all. Now I go to bed at 12 a.m. and wake up by 6 a.m. Ninety minutes in the gym and a good walk every day, especially in London's parks.'

'He loves his walks,' Raaja Kanwar says. 'When I was a teenager, like all teenagers I liked to get up late and suddenly Dad would be standing at the end of the bed saying, "Come on, we are going for a walk." I might have protested but it was on those walks that I learned so much about his life, his attitude to business and the values which have always guided him.'

'Go for a walk with Dad, and he will tell you everything,' Neeraj echoes.

Tyre industry leader Bridgestone has a mission statement that says 'Serving society with superior quality'. It is based on the words of its Founder Shōjirō Ishibashi, who as a seventeen-year-old began a remarkable business life making rubber-soled socks. It is a mission statement with which Onkar Singh Kanwar would agree completely. But as a man and as a devout Sikh he also believes something else just as strongly: However big Apollo becomes, it must serve society but not just with tyres.

twenty-three

The Apollo family

Onkar Singh Kanwar has often said that he wanted to create not only a successful company but also an institution. 'We are moving in the right direction but there is still work to be done,' he says. 'I want to create a greater feeling of ownership in every single person who works for Apollo so they feel that it is their company. They are my first customers so we have to develop the family values and leadership. We are sending more and more people for training. It is also important to remember that staff have families and we have to listen for any issues they have at home, such as a health problem, so we can see how we can help out. The basic principles do not change when you become big but I remind the HR people that they must listen to staff. As I keep saying, listening is learning.'

A company built on personal relationships where everybody feels part of the family is a key Apollo USP. 'I think we lost a little bit of that as the company became international and I moved to London', says Neeraj Kanwar. The Cooper transaction had also taken up much of Neeraj's time, distancing him from the day-to-day. 'So in 2014, we said there is a void in this sense of belonging; people back in India don't see as much of me any more and they feel they are not interacting with Dad and me enough.'

It was time to put that right. Under the 'Apollo One Family' umbrella the company brought 150 Apollo employee families, including children, from its operations around the world to London, on 7 November 2014, for a five-days-and-four-nights' stay hosted by Onkar Kanwar and Neeraj. Some of them had never been outside their home country before.

One of the invitees was M.R.B. Punja, by now in his eighties and living in Bangalore. 'Onkar called me and asked me to come. I told him I was much too old to travel to London but he said he really wanted me to be there and so he arranged for a senior person to travel with me all the way from my home and to look after me while I was there. That consideration and attention to detail is very typical of him and Neeraj too. It was a wonderful experience. Although I had not been a director for some years, I still felt very much a part of the family.'

On the first night after the guests arrived in London and checked into their hotels, there was an 'Apollo One Family Welcome Dinner' at Madame Tussauds—London's world-famous collection of waxworks—which Apollo had taken over for the evening. The guests took pictures of themselves next to the stunningly lifelike wax models of David Beckham, Barack Obama, Usain Bolt, the British Royal Family and figures from history. They also climbed aboard the Spirits of London simulated taxi ride through four hundred years of London life.

Over the next four days there was a huge variety of events and visits from which to choose. On 8 November, Neeraj Kanwar took a party of 280 up to Manchester to watch Manchester United play a Premier League match against Crystal Palace, preceded by a tour of Old Trafford and lunch. Those who stayed in London took a trip on the London Eye, the giant Ferris wheel on the south bank of the Thames River and then on to a performance of *The Lion King*. On other days there was a trip to Windsor Castle, Thorpe Park with its thirty rides, London sightseeing tours, a visit to a traditional pub and a shopping trip to Bicester village just north of Oxford where designer fashion brands are available at discount prices. There was a Medieval Banquet next to the Tower of London. Everywhere they went they travelled in buses bearing Apollo 'Go the Distance' and Manchester United logos.

The visit culminated in a gala dinner for four hundred people at the Grand Connaught Rooms in Covent Garden, one of London's most opulent and stylish event venues with acres of marble and chandeliers. Neeraj Kanwar had asked the Connaught Rooms Grand Hall to be decked out in the Apollo colours of purple and white. There were bars and banquettes and vast vases of flowers, giving the Hall the feel of a maharaja's palace. Shankar Mahadevan and his band were flown in especially from India to provide the music and there was a stunning light show.

Throughout, the wine flowed and the food kept coming, as did the shopping and the culture. Every detail was taken care of for all ages. From start to finish the trip was done with style. Equally importantly it was a chance for the Kanwars in their speeches and presentations to remind and reinforce the Apollo core values and to talk about the future. It also gave the board the opportunity to meet at Apollo's new London offices for the first time.

At the end of the trip and before they headed home, each of the 150 families was presented with an iPad mini engraved with the words: 'Apollo: Go the Distance'.

These international trips now happen every three years. There are also national 'Apollo One Family' days. 'The sense of belonging was driven by my father from the earliest days,' Neeraj says. 'He really enjoys meeting employees and having a good time with them and their families, whether it is his birthday party at the farmhouse or at smaller events. Then I decided to take it to the next level, with more bonding and bringing in the families.'

◆

The Apollo family ideal extends beyond employees to the wider community where Onkar Singh Kanwar is committed to make a difference.

'I believe that India has a great future but first more of its infrastructure has to be rebuilt. We need more roads and bridges and to improve our railway system and less speculative, unplanned housing and office development. I sometimes find it frustrating that India with all its skills and talents does not fulfil its potential. We still have 650,000 villages without basic water, power, education and health facilities.'

To tackle some of these problems the Apollo Tyres Foundation was set up to provide both environmental and social programmes in the communities where the company operates. Under its Environment Initiative it has inaugurated a purified drinking water project for 5,000 residents in three villages near its Chennai plant. A ten-stage filtration and treatment process, run by Waterlife India, can produce 1,000 litres an hour at nominal cost and reduce the incidence of waterborne diseases. Wetland parks, butterfly gardens, ponds, apiculture and helping farmers plant 100,000 teak trees are among a host of other projects. Discarded tyres are turned into play structures at 'Go the Distance' playgrounds and women in villages are being taught skills such as tailoring to boost family incomes.

A key social initiative is the HIV-AIDS Awareness and Prevention Programme. India is suffering an AIDS epidemic and truckers are a high-risk group with an estimated 500,000 people living with HIV/AIDS. In 2001 Apollo opened its first Health Care Clinic at Sanjay Gandhi Transport Nagar in Delhi which daily sees around 5,000 trucks coming and going. The clinic offers truckers medical testing and diagnosis with a specialist doctor, education and counselling and free condoms. The Health Care Clinic staff, many of them volunteers, also do outreach work, distribute healthcare pamphlets and stage street plays to spread the message.

Today there are twenty-five Apollo Health Care Clinics for truckers at major transport hubs in sixteen states across India. They also conduct awareness programmes on other sexually transmitted illnesses (STIs) and substance abuse. To date 400,000 truckers have used the clinics' services. Some 82,400 have been tested for HIV with 830 registering positive. Over 6,500 truck drivers have been treated for STIs. Over 230,000 people have received counselling.

It was Onkar Kanwar's grandson, Jaikaran Kanwar—Neeraj's eldest child—who was working at Sanjay Gandhi Transport Nagar during his school vacation, who first suggested that Apollo could also offer truckers eye tests. It is an undeniable fact that vision problems cause accidents on India's congested roads. A pilot survey conducted at Sanjay Gandhi

Transport Nagar revealed that 60 per cent of truckers needed eyeglasses. More than one hundred and twenty eye check-up camps for drivers have been rolled out to other transport hubs, offering tests and dispensing close to 2,500 pairs of glasses. For just ₹15 a month truckers can use any of the healthcare centres whenever they want.

'The truckers and their families are major stakeholders in Apollo,' Onkar Kanwar explains. 'It is this kind of targeted intervention that raises awareness and helps change behaviour. I believe that preventive healthcare not only improves health and well-being but also the productivity and quality of the community and the whole population.'

Education is also close to Onkar Kanwar's heart as it was to his father's. Raunaq Public School (RPS), founded by Raunaq Singh in 1971 a hundred metres or so from the BST factory in Ganaur, is still going strong with a large new teaching building, its foundation stone laid by Taru Kanwar, and the latest in computers, science laboratories, a busy programme of arts, languages, music and sports. The school's coat of arms bears the words 'Integrity, Discipline, Courage'. RPS is rated one of the best and most popular schools in the area. Students are brought in on the school's distinctive yellow buses from up to twenty miles away. In all the Kanwars have four schools in the state of Haryana responsible for educating 3,000 children.

'We believe that the purpose of education is to replace an empty mind with an open one,' says Onkar Singh Kanwar, 'but we also encourage active parental involvement with our teachers because school is an extension of home. We all have a part to play in helping our children to grow academically, physiologically and socially.'

◆

In 2007, Onkar Kanwar decided to open a hospital, the Artemis Health Institute in Gurgaon. In Greek mythology the goddess Artemis is the twin sister of Apollo and protector of women in childbirth. Today the 418-bed hospital is on a 9-acre campus and employs three hundred full-time doctors with forty different specialities. Its eleven centres of excellence include woman and childcare, heart, cancer, neurosciences, joint replacement and orthopaedics, infertility, plastic surgery and liver, kidney, cornea and bone marrow transplant. A new building will add another 200 beds when completed. The Artemis brand also has a fifty-bed super-speciality hospital in New Delhi and clinics in Gurgaon, New Delhi and Rewari in Haryana. It is one of a handful of Indian hospitals to have the world's highest hospital accreditation awarded by America's Joint Commission International (JCI). JCI inspectors who come in from Chicago every three years have 1,650 inspection standards and hospitals are only allowed to fail four.

That puts Artemis on a par with American hospitals but five years ago, it was a very different story. By the end of 2010, the future of Mr Kanwar's hospital, which then had 200 beds, looked bleak. Patients were not coming and it was losing a lot of money. Onkar Kanwar was visiting the hospital most days trying to figure out what was going so wrong. He even set up an office there. He contemplated closing Artemis down. Then one day he arrived as a patient and went for some routine tests in the radiology and imaging department which runs MRI, CTC scans, ultrasound and X-rays. Those tests were conducted by the department's head, Dr Devlina Chakravarty, who had worked at Artemis for four years.

'We interacted well,' Dr Chakravarty recalls. 'I had always found the Chairman to be incredibly approachable. I reassured him everything was fine with his scans and did not think much more about it.'

Kanwar then started performing some major surgery of his own. As he is fond of saying, 'you don't nurse gangrene, you cut it'.

'One evening he called everyone into the hospital's auditorium to tell us that virtually the entire senior management was leaving,' Devlina Chakravarty explains. 'There was at that point no medical director and no CEO. Mr Kanwar then went back to his office and called my department, asking to see me.' Dr Chakravarty feared that she was the next for the exit.

'I sat down in his office and he said, "I want you to be the medical director because you are a medical professional and I want you to hold the post until at least one of the top two posts is occupied and we decide what more we want to do."

'To say I was surprised and shocked is an understatement. I asked him if I could get back to him in a day's time. I needed the chance to decide if I could deliver what he wanted me to do.'

Kanwar replied, 'There is no time. You will have to tell me now. I want the answer.' Then he smiled and added, 'I want the answer to be a yes, but no pressure. Trust me; I can see beyond what you can see and you will not regret it.'

Dr Chakravarty accepted. 'If you have that confidence in me, Sir, I shall definitely take it up. I shall try my best not to let you down, but you will have to guide me until you get the right medical director and CEO to join the team.'

Dr Chakravarty had experience of working in other private hospitals in India and instinctively understood the nuances of what to do and how to run a place. Onkar Kanwar's role was that of a sounding board and to continue with his young medical director to put the right people into key posts.

The results were almost instant. Artemis in no time became the preferred hospital in Gurgaon where there are thirty-nine private hospitals, which range from 75 beds to 2,500. Six months later Onkar Kanwar promoted Devlina Chakravarty to Chief Operating Officer. After a year, she became CEO and today, as the CEO and Executive Director, she is on the Artemis board.

So what had Onkar Kanwar seen in Devlina Chakravarty? 'I liked her personality very much and the way she worked and when Artemis was in crisis the radiology department was the one department that was running effectively.'

Onkar Kanwar's daughter Shalini Chand, who works as a psychotherapist in Singapore, is on the board of Artemis. 'I love that hospital. Devlina has done a fantastic job. I had open heart surgery when I was twenty-four and so I saw a lot of hospitals and unlike most of them, Artemis has a soul. All the patients are looked after as people.'

Of Gurgaon's thirty-nine private hospitals, 60 per cent are either shut or up for sale. Artemis is bucking the trend. Losses have become profits. 'Many who went into private hospitals thinking it would be a sunrise business were proved wrong,' Dr Chakravarty says. 'To get it right requires a complex mix of committed staff, the best technology and of course the best outcomes.'

◆

At the centre of Onkar Singh Kanwar's Apollo family is his own family and particularly his six grandchildren. As a devoted grandfather he is always willing to give advice and encouragement when they ask. 'I have always been an optimist and I tell them that if they have a day-dream, then follow it through but not a night-dream because night dreams come and go. Every day follow your dream and be consistent. You are going to have ups and downs so you have to be adaptable, but if you are passionate you will get there.'

His eldest grandchild, twenty-five-year-old Zubin Chand, completed his master's in Public Health at Imperial College in London in 2016. His first degree was in Mathematics at Carnegie Mellon University in Pittsburgh and he went into private banking in Lugarno, Switzerland, but he hated it. 'I realized that my passion was healthcare, especially in India. I stayed in my grandfather's house in Delhi for a year, which was a great experience because he is so open-minded with so much energy. He said that if I was interested in healthcare I should come to work in his hospital and go out to the villages. After three months of doing that he suggested I try healthcare consulting so I went to work with Ernst & Young in Mumbai. Those two experiences motivated me to do my master's. He has always been a great supporter and believer. I think he has been a parent to everyone, not just his own children and grandchildren, but also to his brothers and sister, nephews and nieces. He, along with my grandmother, is the centre point of the entire family.'

Zubin's brother, Aditya Chand, is twenty-three. When he was nineteen, he started his own film production in New York where he still lives and works closely with Warner Brothers and Paramount. Raaja Kanwar's youngest son, Zefaan, aged sixteen, was designing apps at the age of ten, and armed with a business plan was marketing them two years later. 'He wants to be a movie director and tells me that he has already written his Oscar acceptance speech even though he has yet to make a movie,' Raaja says. Zefaan obviously has his grandfather's follow-your-dream philosophy. Raaja's eldest son, Aryaan, is eighteen and wants to study engineering and come into the family business. 'I think it is important that he goes and works somewhere else first,' Raaja says. 'My father has often said to me that perhaps he made a mistake in bringing Neeraj and me into the business too early.'

Neeraj's son Jai, also eighteen, is a student at Charterhouse, one of the UK's leading public schools set in magnificent grounds south of London. The school with its motto *Deo Dante Dedi* ('God having given, I gave') was founded in 1611 on the site of a Carthusian Order monastery in Charterhouse Square in the City of London, hence its name. Today it is co-educational with 800 students aged 13–18.

It was Jai's grandfather who came across the school. 'I was impressed by its history and ethos and its facilities and I thought it would be character building for him to go there.' Standing on one's own two feet has been something of a creed for Onkar Singh Kanwar ever since he went to the United States as a young man.

Jai's mother Simran was not at all sure, especially when two days after enrolling Jai broke his ankle playing soccer.

'I have spent a lot of time with my grandfather, visiting most of the tyre plants and working in the Health Care Clinic in Delhi,' Jai says, 'and he has told me a lot of stories about the things he has experienced and I have learned from that. In spite of all his success he is very down to earth and maintains all the values of a traditional Indian family, no matter how modern and international we become in other ways.'

Jai is aiming for a degree at university 'and then one day maybe, the tyre business.'

Onkar Singh Kanwar definitely dotes on his youngest grandchild and only granddaughter, Jai's sister Syra who is ten and a student at Hill House, a preparatory school in London once attended by Prince Charles and singer-songwriter Lily Allen. 'I love drama and singing,' says Syra, 'but my grandfather says that he would like me to become a doctor or a lawyer. I do want to become a lawyer but I would also like to be an actress and a singer.' It was no surprise that on the 'Apollo One Family' visit to London, Syra opted to join the party that went to see *The Lion King*.

Wherever he is in her part of the world, Onkar turns up for Syra's birthday without fail. 'He has never missed a single one since I have been born,' Syra says. They cook and bake together and he calls her 'Princess Cupcake', a nickname now used by all the family. When he is in London Onkar also takes Syra out for lunch or dinner at a restaurant of her choice. 'Last time she asked to go to Yo Sushi,' he says. 'I didn't know that Yo Sushi was a fast-food Japanese restaurant. We were in and out in fifteen minutes. It's the shortest lunch date I have ever had!'

'My grandfather loves telling me stories,' says Syra. 'This is one of his favourites. Guru Nanak was trying to save a scorpion from drowning, but when he put his hand in the water the scorpion bit him. Guru Nanak tried again and the scorpion bit him once more. Every time he tried to save the scorpion it bit Guru Nanak's hand. Then somebody asked, "Guru Nanak, why do you keep trying to save the scorpion when all it does is bite you and give you pain?" And Guru Nanak replied, "He is doing his job and I am doing mine."'

The story fits Onkar Singh Kanwar's philosophy perfectly: if you mean to do good, you must try to do good in any case, whatever obstacles are thrown in your path.

In 2016, as he approached his final academic year at Charterhouse, Jai Kanwar was made Head of House, the first Indian ever to have been accorded the honour. It was an incredibly proud moment for his parents and grandparents, particularly his grandfather. The house, one of twelve Charterhouse houses, is called Girdlestoneites, after Frederick Girdlestone who founded the house in 1874. Quaintly, as only the English can, the house is known to one and all as 'Duckites'. Frederick Girdlestone was always referred to as 'The Duck' because of his idiosyncratic way of walking.

To fulfil his extra duties as Head of House, Jai was given a bicycle to help him get around the school's extensive grounds. Onkar Singh Kanwar is justifiably proud of his grandson but as he thinks of him cycling around the grounds of one of England's finest schools, and which charges fees of £12,000 a term, his thoughts cannot also fail to turn to that other teenage boy, who seventy years ago was cycling around the dusty streets of Lahore selling irrigation pipes and who would one day build an empire.

Postscript: A celebrated life

Mr Onkar Kanwar is a true-blue Indian entrepreneur who poured his heart and soul into a single idea to create what has now become the prestigious Apollo Group. At a time when most businesses barely looked beyond their operating geography, the visionary Mr Kanwar dreamed of going global with high-value speciality products. It is with pride that I have witnessed Apollo's phenomenal rise from a domestic to a globally admired and respected multinational corporation.

My father Mr Dhirubhai Ambani and Mr Kanwar's father Mr Raunaq Singh shared a special friendship. India needs more Dhirubhais and Onkars who will chase their dreams and achieve excellence. I wish him continuing good health and happiness to take Apollo to even greater heights!

Mukesh D. Ambani, Chairman and Managing Director of
Reliance Industries Limited

Apollo Tyres has been a tremendous Indian success story. This could not have been achieved without the vision and immense business acumen of my good friend Onkar Kanwar. Now, under the leadership of Neeraj, the company will continue to prosper and grow and I will be closely following the next part of this exciting story.

Lakshmi Mittal, Chairman and CEO of ArcelorMittal

The publication of Onkar Kanwar's biography has come at a very opportune time, telling a wonderful story of a visionary and astute entrepreneur whom I have had the honour of knowing for more years than I can remember. I have known him as one of India's leading industrialists and as a dynamic businessman who has expanded the family business internationally. His success has come through astute investments and acquisitions. Onkar has also been a leading and influential member of the wider Asian business community and his business acumen and experience, as well as his understanding of the economic landscape of India, is valued by the Government of India.

It is heartening to see that alongside his thriving business career, Onkar is a true philanthropist in education and healthcare: his Apollo Group established Artemis Health Sciences, a modern multispeciality medical facility offering highly advanced medical services and holistic treatment.

Decades ago I had the pleasure of meeting Onkar's dear father, Raunaq Singh, on his frequent visits to Tehran, and ever since we have witnessed how the close friendship between both families has flourished. Onkar is fortunate to have the undivided love and support of his dear wife Taru and his three children Shalini, Raaja and Neeraj along with his son-in-law, daughters-in-laws and grandchildren. It is a real pleasure to see that our own children Sanjay and Dheeraj and their wives Anu and Shalini are also close friends to Onkar's family.

I wish him continued good health, prosperity and love of his family and friends for the many years that lie ahead of him.

Gopichand P. Hinduja, Co-Chairman of the Hinduja Group, and Chairman of Hinduja Automotive Limited, UK

Onkar has completely modernized Apollo, bringing in new technology ten years ahead of most companies. He has recognized the opportunities of globalization in a changing world to put himself in a different league to his father, who was himself a highly significant figure. But overall it is Onkar's simplicity that endears him to all, every strata in the company.

He is someone they can talk to and relate to because they respond to his openness. It has always impressed me because it is so unusual compared to most companies.

Dr Amit Mitra, Minister for Finance and Excise, Commerce and
Industries, Government of West Bengal

It has not always been easy for Indian companies to be taken seriously on the world stage so the fact that Onkar has created a global brand in the automobile and tyre industry speaks volumes about his ambitions and abilities. It has been a major contribution to Indian manufactured products and Indian-sponsored products manufactured overseas now being seen as cutting edge and among the best in the world.

Sunil Mittal, Founder and Chairman of
Bharti Enterprises

I am sure there will be many stories told and virtues extolled, of Onkar, given his successful stewardship of Apollo over many decades. I would like to point out two that have always stood out for me. Onkar's curiosity has always struck me as one his great strengths. A conversation with him almost always features a number of deep, insightful questions and careful attention to the answers. This trait will keep him constantly in learning mode, which in turn might be the secret of his ever youthful attitude to life. The second very endearing attribute is his great personal warmth. Onkar is interested in others, takes great interest in them and has the ability to build long-lasting ties very rapidly. He is a special man.

Anshu Jain, former Co-CEO of Deutsche Bank

Onkar is a great listener. I have talked to him many times over the years, four to five times a year, and we would have whole-day meetings where he wanted advice on financial strategy. He always wanted to initiate things to a degree that I did not see in other promoter groups. I am not saying he always took my advice but he would seek it as he would from those who knew about production, design or engineering. By listening to all he has been able take really good decisions.

Nimesh Kampani, Founder and Chairman of the
JM Financial Group

For many, Onkar S. Kanwar is the man who turned a family enterprise into a global conglomerate spanning countries and continents. For me, he is much more. When I moved to Delhi from Kolkata, he and his family were my family. His elegance, grace and above all, compassion have to this day remained unchanged. As did his ability to see what most people can't—both in business, and in terms of where humanity is headed.

A devout Sikh, an extraordinary family man and a doting husband, he epitomizes what most people aspire to be. He has been the bulwark of Indian industry for as long as one can remember, but, more importantly, he is a brilliant ambassador for 'Brand India'.

As he turns seventy-five, he brings with himself a level of sagacity and wisdom that is worthy of emulation and admiration. Just like the tyres he produces, he has many miles to go. Seventy-five is like one of those milestones that his tyres see. But what he sees is not just one destination but multiple destinations: for his family, his country and his company.

Suhel Seth, author and marketing maven

OSK maintains his friendships. He is not an opportunist. If you become his friend you remain his friend whether you are in power or not in power. This was a quality lacking in Raunaq Singh to a certain extent.

R.K. Dhawan, former personal secretary to the
late Prime Minister Indira Gandhi

Mr Kanwar is a very perceptive person in the sense that he has the remarkable distinction of having done it all by himself. He literally started from the shop floor so that has given him the kind of confidence not only in his own ideas but to glean the experience of others. He is a good team leader because he is always setting challenging targets. The bar keeps going up. Today competition is cut-throat. If you do not increase your share of the market somebody else will eat into your share. It really is survival of the fittest. Thanks to him Apollo is a very fit company.

Vinod Rai, Chairman of the Banks Board Bureau, and former Comptroller and Auditor General of India

Onkar and I have been working together as businessmen for many years, defending ourselves from and working with governments that had many controls and regulations so we needed each other's support. We were distinctly different in terms of our industrial programmes but we were Apollo customers and we regarded them very well because my father, H.P. Nanda, was a contemporary of Raunaq Singh's. They too were very good friends socially and commercially. They were people who participated and led the business community at home and abroad and Onkar has followed that tradition most notably. He has faced many challenges in his life, both business and personal, but he has remained steadfast and displayed great courage where others might have buckled or given up. Onkar has always moved with the times but he has remained true to his values.

Rajan Nanda, Chairman and Managing Director of the Escorts Group

What I like and admire about this company is that the father and son have decided that their sole focus is tyres. Unlike Indian conglomerates they are not interested in also being in hotels, textiles, chemicals, entertainment and resorts. It's just going to be tyres. When Mr Kanwar asked me to join the Apollo board he did not come across as an owner doing favours to a retired bureaucrat but much more as somebody wanting to integrate me into the family that he has developed around Apollo and that touched me a lot and continues to do so. Yes, he wants and values the expertise I can bring after many years in government service at a high level—although Apollo appealed because it is in an industry where I had never had a policy role—but he also takes care of my well-being and he is that way with everyone. It is very, very special.

Dr S. Narayan, former Finance Secretary, Government of India, and advisor to former Prime Minister Atal Bihari Vajpayee

Onkar Kanwar is a young man. He never looks 'tyred', he never gives up. His determination is a great drive for all his team members, and translates in a behavioural leadership that goes beyond the respect due to his top position in the company and to his, well, apparent age! He's a man of inspiration. He's also pretty smart, and knows how to get things made the way he wants, without imposing his will. I share with him the same passion for our old, low-profile, black and round business: tyres.

Francesco Gori, former CEO of Pirelli Tyres

During my time as Ambassador in Delhi and in getting to know Onkar, I saw that Apollo was a very well-run and outward-looking company. In those days Indian companies tended to fall into one of two categories. Some wanted to protect the Indian market and not compete globally. Then there were those who wanted to open up the Indian market and compete globally. Apollo was very much in the latter category with Onkar playing a leading role in many FICCI missions overseas. He was one of those who realized that you had to be world-class in order to compete. Onkar has always reached out to people. He is one of the most dedicated men I know.

Richard F. Celeste, former Ambassador of the United States of America to India

I first met Onkar as a business acquaintance, when I was responsible for the International Division in Continental AG and we were providing technical collaboration to Apollo Tyres. I was especially honoured when he sought permission from my management to take me on to his board of directors, something which not many people would have done in the relationship we were in. Once I retired from Continental, he asked me to continue, and it has been a greater honour for me to serve there for the last fourteen years. Over the course of time Onkar and Taru have moved to the status of dear personal friends of my wife and me, in large part due to the warmth and openness with which they welcome people into their extended family. He is an astute and visionary entrepreneur, with the ability to surprise competitors with his moves and does not hesitate to back his own instincts. I believe he has built a wonderful institution in Apollo Tyres which has already achieved much, and has the foundations to achieve much more. I wish him all the very best personally, and for his company as well.

Robert Steinmetz, former chief of the international business unit of Continental A.G.

To take over Apollo was an extremely courageous decision in its time and he fought every inch of the way. It was a huge basket of trouble. That first six-month lockout must have really tested Onkar but he didn't show it. He had a steely resolve, loads of patience, a hell of a lot of business courage to go through what he has been through and like all successful people he has that sixth sense, an intuition that somewhere in life he would pull this through. Back in 1982 I was just his twenty-two-year-old bag carrier/executive assistant and travelled a lot with him. When I became an entrepreneur he gave me great support and encouragement. I have a very big soft spot for him.

Vinayak Chatterjee, Founder and Chairman of Feedback Infra Pvt. Ltd

The one big difference between the Kanwars and other old-style Indian family companies is that the Kanwar family is still very, very entrepreneurial and hands-on. Just as Raunaq Singh led from the front, Onkar leads from the front and Neeraj leads from the front, while the other families tended to become much more ensconced in a sprawling bureaucratic organization and you can see the results. Onkar and Neeraj have built a phenomenal senior management team, which knows exactly what it is doing, but they don't have a bureaucratic organization; although I am sure Onkar and Neeraj know exactly what is going on every single day.

Salman Mahdi, Managing Director of
Deutsche Asset and Wealth Management

I first met Onkar at the International Chamber of Commerce meeting in Paris, few years back. I can never forget how he introduced himself as 'on car'; that was a very easy way to remember him and his name. My wife Olfat and I are so privileged to have made his acquaintance, which has led to a solid relationship on a personal and family basis. Onkar is a person we look up to and respect highly. We wish him all the best of health and happiness always.

Khaled Juffali, Managing Partner and
Vice Chairman of E.A. Juffali and Brothers

Acknowledgements

When somebody puts their life in the hands of a writer, it is a huge leap of faith for both the author and his subject. It was also a huge leap of faith for this subject's wife, his children, grandchildren, his friends and colleagues.

That this has been such a rewarding project for me is due to Onkar Singh Kanwar and his openness in sharing a life for which the words fascinating and eventful are an understatement. Throughout many interviews Mr Kanwar has been candid, considerate, hospitable (and very patient). This book is not just the history of Apollo Tyres and how Mr Kanwar created a global company from virtual bankruptcy. It is also the history of India as seen through Onkar Kanwar's eyes as the nation approaches its seventieth anniversary in 2017.

The old saying that behind every great man there is an equally great woman is not applicable in the Kanwars' case because Taru Kanwar has been alongside her husband throughout this journey. I thank her equally for her contributions to this book and for talking about her family and a marriage that celebrates its fiftieth year in 2017.

The other great contributor and facilitator for this book is Neeraj Kanwar, Vice Chairman and Managing Director of Apollo Tyres. From growing up in India to creating and managing a global $2 billion company (and rising!), Neeraj has shared the many ups and the several downs of his life candidly over many hours in London and in Delhi. I greatly appreciate his time, his enthusiasm and humour and for showing me the heartbeat of Apollo, not just as a company but as a family of people.

Equally, I would like to thank Neeraj's wife Simran and their children Syra Taru Kanwar and Jaikaran Kanwar for agreeing to meet me and share their experiences. Particular thanks go to Jai, who devoted much of his summer vacation to researching family dates and history and to sourcing the photographs that appear in this book.

Other members of the family who have been most helpful and generous with their time are Onkar Singh Kanwar's other children, Raaja Kanwar, Shalini Chand and her son Zubin Chand, his sister Rani Kapur and Taru Kanwar's brother Jot Kapoor and his wife Pamela.

I am also very grateful to the following people for their help: Ashi Burman, Richard F. Celeste, Dr Devlina Chakravarty, Vinayak Chatterjee, Akshay Chudasama, Mahendra Chowdhari, Y.C. Deveshwar, R.K. Dhawan, Jean-Marc François, Gopichand P. Hinduja, Nimesh Kampani, Salman Mahdi, Scott D. Miller, Sunil Mittal, Dr A.C. Muthiah, Dr Amit Mitra, Rajan Nanda, Dr S. Narayan, Fali S. Nariman, Rob Oudshoorn, M.R.B. Punja, Vinod Rai, Indranath Sinha, and Michael Ward.

If you have enjoyed this book and learned something from it that is due in very large part to Sunam Sarkar, Apollo's President and Chief Business Officer. Sunam has been there every step of the way as sounding board, fixer of interviews, and to somebody who initially knew nothing of the world of radials, bias and cross-ply, he has been an astute and nuanced guide to the tyre industry in general and Apollo Tyres in particular. Above all he has been a delightful companion and a wise friend.

I would like to thank all those others at Apollo Tyres who have been unfailingly helpful and generous with their time and sharing their knowledge of the company and the tyre industry, notably, P.K. Mohamed, Chief Advisor R&D, Chennai, Kannan Prabhakar, Managing Director, Apollo Tyres (Hungary), and Satish Sharma, President-Asia-Pacific, Middle East and Africa (APMEA). In addition, P.N. Wahal, Company Secretary and Head of Legal, has not only been tireless in finding historic documents, dates and minutes but also shared his experiences and insights gained over forty years of working with Raunaq Singh and Onkar Singh Kanwar.

For his knowledge of the earliest days of Apollo, I thank Harish Bahadur, the company's 'Employee No. 2' (Raunaq Singh was 'Employee Number 1'), who is now the Head of Corporate Investments. I am also most grateful to Baljeet Ravinder Singh, Head of Corporate Affairs and Administration at Gurgaon, not only for logistical support and his insight into the tyre industry over many years but for also taking me on a fascinating and memorable tour of Gurudwara Bangla Sahib in Delhi. Yograj Varma, Head of Communications, also provided great backup and was unflinching in his battle to retrieve material from the *Times of India* archive, while Gaurav Kumar, Group Head, Corporate Strategy and Finance, has kept me straight on all financial matters—and cricket! Rajesh Dahiya, Group Head-Sales Asia-Pacific, Middle East and Africa, provided clarification and guidance on Apollo's relations with tyre dealers.

In touring Apollo plants, I am indebted to my hosts and guides: George Oommen, Unit Head, Perambra, Thomas Mathew, Unit Head, Kalamassery, John Devadason, Unit Head, and Anand Satyamoorthy, Group Leader-Manufacturing at Chennai and Henri De Leeuw, Manager, Tyre Information Centre, Apollo Vredestein, Enschede. Also at Perambra, I thank T.V. Poly and E.C. Warrier and representatives of the trade unions, C. Rajeev, K.A. Joy, T.C. Sethumadhavan and Baby Varghese.

On my visits to Perambra and Chennai A.S. Girish, Head of HR, smoothed my path, setting up interviews and following up on research and photographs with unfailing enthusiasm and good humour.

At Apollo's London office many thanks are due to Kicky Rottink, executive assistant to Neeraj Kanwar, for her endless help and cheerfulness and also to her colleague Leanne Varney.

Nothing can happen without agents and publishers, so I thank Julian Alexander and Ben Clark at LAW agency in London and Dibakar Ghosh, Editorial Director of Rupa Publications India, and editor Ananya Sharma. For his insights and guidance into Sikh history and Sikhism early on in the research process I am eternally grateful to my good friend C.S. Chadha.

I would never have made the deadline if it was not for my faithful interview transcriber, Marian Stapley-Jones, and I would never have got to the Delhi and Gurgaon interviews on time if it had not been for my Apollo driver Raj Singh, who negotiated notorious jams with remarkable dexterity.

I have read many books about India for the historical background against which the Kanwars have lived their lives, notably: *India* by Patrick French; *Business Maharajas* by Gita Piramal; *The Portfolio Book of Great Indian Business Stories* (anthology); *Before Memory Fades: An Autobiography* and *The State of the Nation* by Fali S. Nariman; *The Days of My Years* by H.P. Nanda; *The Sanjay Story* by Vinod Mehta; *Amritsar: Mrs Gandhi's Last Battle* by Mark Tully and Satish Jacob; *Kerala—An Economic Dilemma* and *A Journey Through Time 1857-2007* (Kochi Chamber of Commerce and Industry).

Finally, but far from least, I thank my wife Sarah for her great love and patience, especially during my frequent absences from home in India and Holland researching this book and then, when I returned during the hours and days when I was wedded to a keyboard and screen.